WHAT YOU MADE ME DO

WHAT YOU MADE ME DO

A NOVEL

BARBARA G. AUSTIN

NEW YORK

This is a work of fiction. All of the names, characters, organizations, places and events portrayed in this novel are either products of the author's imagination or are used fictitiously. Any resemblance to real or actual events, locales, or persons, living or dead, is entirely coincidental.

Published in the United States by Crooked Lane Books, an imprint of The Quick Brown Fox & Company LLC.

Crooked Lane Books and its logo are trademarks of The Quick Brown Fox & Company LLC.

Library of Congress Catalog-in-Publication data available upon request.

ISBN (hardcover): 978-1-63910-839-8
ISBN (ebook): 978-1-63910-840-4

Cover design by Nebojsa Zoric

Printed in the United States.

www.crookedlanebooks.com

Crooked Lane Books
34 West 27th St., 10th Floor
New York, NY 10001

First Edition: August 2024

10 9 8 7 6 5 4 3 2 1

For my parents and Aunt Dot

PROLOGUE, AUGUST 2004

Wexalia, an island in the Wadden Sea, Netherlands

THE ROTTEN-EGG SMELL of the mudflats was stronger at night. Or maybe it just seemed that way because his senses were on red alert.

He didn't dare turn on the car's headlights. Hunched over the steering wheel, he concentrated on the feel of the old dike road beneath his tires. When the car veered too far to the left, the tires sank into soft, spongy weeds. Too far the other way, and the wheels scraped the basalt boulders lining the dike down to the mudflats.

Once past the gate to Doeksen's dairy farm, he slowed the car and parked alongside the barbed wire fence. He groped for the trunk release switch below the radio, pressed it, and heard a muted thud. Then he stepped into the weeds and for a moment let the damp wind whip across his face. He tasted salt on his lips.

His eyes shifted around warily.

The nearest village was miles away, on the other side of the polder. Behind the fence was a pasture, dotted with dark mounds that he took to be sleeping cows. The windows in the farmhouse were dark. The barn was dark except for a security light over the door. In the other direction, beyond the dike, a motley collection of fishing boats was moored to the pier.

He started around to the back of the car. His insides turned suddenly wobbly, and his legs gave way. He grabbed the fender to keep from collapsing into a quivering heap, a moan swelling up inside him. He squeezed his eyes shut. Gave himself a moment. He was all right; he could do this—he could do whatever it took.

He opened his eyes, heaved a deep sigh, steadied himself. He raised the trunk lid, stupidly hoping that the body had magically vanished, that he would wake up and find today hadn't happened yet. But she was still there. Wrapped in a tarp and bound with rope. He lifted the head end of the bundle and pulled, his back straining. The feet flopped to the ground, and he lugged her by the shoulders, picking his way backward over the dike.

Doeksen's dinghy was tied up halfway along the pier. He nearly lost the bundle overboard before finally wrestling it into the boat, sweat running down his back. He returned to the car for the flashlight and shovel, tossed them into the dinghy, and sat down on the rear seat. His hands shook violently, and he lost precious minutes untying the dock lines.

He had to get the job done before the first gray light of morning, before the early risers—fishermen, farmers, runners. All potential witnesses. He didn't turn on the motor, afraid of attracting attention and being remembered. The tide was coming in. Perfect. Safer to row against the current than to risk being caught in the outgoing tide, which might sweep the dinghy through the channel and into the raw North Sea. He wiped his sweaty palms on his trousers and gripped the oars.

As he rowed, the dinghy bounced on the swells, and the dark sandbank grew larger. Clouds masked the stars, but the moon was huge and low on the horizon, casting a ghostly path on the sea.

Twenty minutes later, the bow scraped sand. He laid down the oars and stepped into the muck, which rose to the top of his boots. Cold water sloshed inside, soaking his socks. Glancing back at Wexalia, he made out the black silhouette of the island, shaped like the whale carcass he had once seen floating in the sea. A once magnificent animal, rendered grotesque by death.

Shoving the dinghy up the slope was like budging a piano up a ramp. He heaved and got it out of the water, but no further, so he tipped it on its side and dumped the bundle onto the sand. The little craft was still heavy, but light enough to push past the tidemark. He went back, seized the rope that bound the tarp, and tugged, burning his palms. He should have worn gloves. What else had he forgotten?

He dropped the bundle next to the dinghy, picked up the shovel, and trudged across the sandbank. He leaned into the wind, the roar all but drowning out the hiss and gurgle of the tide. The flashlight illuminated ghostly clumps of marram grass and flowering searockets, colorless in the night. His foot struck something solid: a small sign warning that trespassers would be prosecuted. Trespassing! He gave a short, hysterical snort.

Halfway across, he stopped. It was the highest point and escaped flooding at high tide or even during a severe storm—the reason the sandbank was a resting place for birds and seals.

He had worried the sand would be packed too hard to shovel, but the top layer was loose, mixed with broken seashells. He set about digging a trench six feet long and two feet wide. The deeper he dug, the firmer the sand, until it was impossible to dig further. Three feet down would have to do.

He followed his footprints back to the dinghy and pulled the bundle up the rise. The tarp kept catching on clumps of grass, and he had to yank it along. He stopped at the edge of the trench.

As he stooped to untie the rope, an urge came over him to see her face one more time. He peeled back the tarp and, with shaking hands, aimed the beam.

The pale blue eyes staring back at him blinked.

JULY 2000

CHAPTER

1

Willem

"*Jeetje*, Dad. Do I have to go? I'm still coughing."

Willem gave a little cough to demonstrate. He was perched on the edge of his bed in a pair of smelly pajamas. His sheets hadn't been changed in a week, all through his sweating and shivering. The bottom sheet was stained yellow. Jurriaan said it looked as if he had wet the bed, but it was sweat, not pee.

Hendrik stood in the doorway, wearing the suit that made him look like a sleek black crow. His black hair was slicked straight back and his head moved in little jerks as he eyed the room before his gaze landed on Willem.

"Take a shower and be downstairs in ten minutes. Don't forget to bring your cough drops," he said, and flapped away.

Willem bunched his fists. His temperature was back to normal, which meant he could play in the field hockey match tomorrow. He had already telephoned his best friend, Bas, with the good news. But it also meant he had to attend his mother's concert tonight. An hour in the car. Two boring hours in the music hall, without an intermission. How many of the stupid concerts had he attended? A million?

He was still perched on the bed when Jurriaan came in a few minutes later, rocking from one foot to the other, his arms dangling by his sides.

"Hey, twinnie. Dad's waiting in the car."

Willem heaved a sigh but didn't move.

Jurriaan limped to the wardrobe, his right foot turned in—the only outward sign he was different from other twelve-year-old boys. Willem felt a twinge of guilt as he always did when he contemplated his twin's disabilities.

Jurriaan handed him a pair of dark blue trousers and a white shirt. "Put this on. Hurry."

Their mother was in Rotterdam, rehearsing, dressing, ticking off boxes. She expected them to be sufficiently early for the preconcert backstage ritual—and Willem knew better than to keep Louisa Veldkamp waiting.

He pushed himself up and swayed for a moment before the room righted itself. His fever might be gone, but he was still weak, and the hockey game tomorrow was the most important one of the season. He couldn't miss it. Attending the concert was the price he had to pay.

"Your hair." Jurriaan pointed and giggled, jabbing at his glasses, which had slipped down his nose.

Willem stumbled into the bathroom and looked in the mirror. His hair stood up in spikes. There was no time for a shower. He stuck his head under the faucet, and when his hair was thoroughly wet, he ran a comb through it. Taking a washcloth, he wiped his armpits, conscious that good old Jurriaan waited for him just outside the door, like some kind of watchman. They had each other's backs. Always.

* * *

Hendrik's big Mercedes idled in the driveway.

"Dibs on the front seat," Jurriaan shouted as he hobbled quickly to the car.

Willem shrugged and climbed into the back. The car smelled of leather and air freshener and something foul. He sniffed. *Jeetje*, it was himself.

Soon, they were speeding on the highway, the darkness broken only by headlights and streetlamps whizzing by. The air blasting from the car's vents tickled Willem's throat. He started coughing and couldn't stop. Shit. He had left the cough drops on the night table.

Hendrik glanced over his shoulder. "Take a cough drop."

Willem swallowed hard. "I forgot them."

"Godverdomme," Hendrik cursed and fell silent for a moment. "Jurriaan, look in the glove compartment. Maybe there's a stick of gum."

Jurriaan rummaged through the papers. "Sorry, Dad," he said.

"You shouldn't have made me come," Willem grumbled.

"Your mother said you had to unless you had a fever."

Willem rolled his eyes.

Hendrik pulled off the highway at the next exit and stopped at a bright, sprawling service station with four empty bays. He handed Willem his wallet.

"Get yourself a pack of cough drops. No dawdling."

Willem coughed all the way across the tarmac to the little shop with glaring lights and a security mirror mounted on the wall. He paced the aisles, checking out the shelves. Weird brands of junk food. Stupid plastic toys. Half-dead flowers in buckets. Through the window, he saw the Mercedes creep toward the entrance, engine running like a getaway car. Willem walked slower. Suddenly, he wanted to be late for the concert.

He felt the eyes of the cashier watching him. As if he would steal any of the crap. The shop didn't sell cough drops except the kind that tasted like cow dung, so Willem bought a bag of hard candy for himself and a package of licorice allsorts for Jurriaan.

In the car, Willem unwrapped a cherry-flavored candy. The cellophane crinkled. He tensed. Louisa had a built-in sensor, attuned to any sound he made. Would she be able to hear the crinkling from the stage? He unwrapped all the candies and wiped his sticky fingers on his socks.

They arrived too late for the ritual backstage kiss on Louisa's cheek—Willem's fault. Everything that went wrong was his fault even when it wasn't. But this time the blame was fair. If he hadn't forgotten to bring the cough drops, they wouldn't have stopped at the service station. There would have been time. Sweat pooled under his arms.

Most of the audience was seated when the three of them sat down in the front row next to Miss Klunder, his mother's new secretary. Most of the time Hendrik lived in a world inside his head, so Louisa tasked her secretary with spying on Willem and Jurriaan during her concerts. Willem gave Miss Klunder what he hoped was a cherubic smile. The lights in the concert hall blinked twice and went out except for pinpricks along the carpeted aisle, and the audience fell silent. The curtain swept open. A spotlight illuminated a grand piano in the center of the stage.

Louisa emerged from the wings, to thunderous applause. Her blonde hair fell halfway down the back of her glittering gown. She laid a hand on the piano and bowed to the audience. Her eyes homed in on Willem like a heat-seeking missile. He squirmed. She arranged her skirt, sat down, and moved the bench an inch closer to the keyboard. The first piece was Piazzolla's spicy *Libertango*, one of Willem's favorites, but tonight he couldn't settle back and listen.

Smells prickled his nose. Flowery perfume. Woodsy aftershave. Stale cigarettes. Old shoes. His own armpits.

He tried his best not to cough. His eyes watered. His nose ran. It was no good. He sounded like a two-pack-a-day smoker.

Miss Klunder leaned forward, her head swiveling toward him. Willem reached for a candy, and the bag crinkled. He froze for a moment and withdrew his hand as silently as possible. When the Piazzolla piece ended, Miss Klunder nudged Hendrik and whispered something into his ear.

Then Hendrik nudged Willem. "Wait in the lobby."

Willem slid past Jurriaan and scurried up the aisle without looking back. Halfway up, he missed a step and fell, candy scattering across the carpet and under the seats. He felt around. Found a piece. It felt gritty. He left it there. He heard Louisa's voice in his head: *"Klutz. Watch where you're going."* He scrambled to his feet, clutching the bag in his hand.

Jeetje. What if he coughed for months—like the soldiers with tuberculosis during World War II? His legs felt heavy when he descended the spiral staircase to the lobby and sank onto a plush sofa. The room was empty except for the guy washing glasses behind the bar. Willem's eyelids drooped.

He woke up to find people streaming into the lobby. People in fancy clothes, suits, dresses, shiny earrings. Chatting. Laughing. Fussing.

"I would kill for a cigarette."

"Where did you park the car?"

"The performance was below par, don't you think?"

"Did you see the boy trip and fall?"

Willem's face burned with embarrassment.

Hendrik and Jurriaan were among the last to appear. His father sat down on one side of Willem, Jurriaan on the other.

"How do you feel?" Hendrik asked.

"Like crap."

"Watch your language."

"Sorry."

"I should've let you stay home."

Willem almost smiled but caught himself. He glowered at his father instead, not ready to let him off the hook.

"A hot drink might help," Hendrik said. "Let's get you a cup of tea. Louisa won't want to hear you cough all the way home."

* * *

Louisa sat in the front seat, Willem and Jurriaan in the back. Miss Klunder wisely took the train. Louisa had changed into a white trouser suit with wide legs and had screwed her hair into a tight bun, but she hadn't scrubbed off her makeup. Her face made Willem think of a clown with shiny red lips. She rested her hands in her lap, as if they were precious belongings separate from her body. Then she wrinkled her nose and lowered her window halfway.

"You were magnificent tonight," Hendrik said.

"No, I wasn't. The performance was a disaster."

"Now, Louisa. Don't be so hard on yourself."

She was superstitious about her preconcert rituals, and Willem braced himself for a rant. Her silence was ominous. He prayed he wouldn't cough. He felt inside the bag. Three pieces left. He popped one into his mouth and sucked, but not too hard, desperate to make his supply last the trip home.

Jurriaan dozed in the opposite corner of the backseat, his glasses slipping down his nose. Willem wished Louisa would yell and get it over with. She would blame him for screwing up the performance. She would blame him for their tardy arrival at the concert hall, for coughing, for sitting out the concert in the lobby. For stinking.

It was nearly midnight when the Mercedes turned into the Apollolaan, a wide boulevard lined with mansions, and glided onto the brick-paved driveway. The three-story mansion—five if you counted the attic and the basement—resembled a fortress with loopholes for windows. Bas called it "the fort."

Hendrik let them out at the front door before opening the garage with the remote control.

Inside, the house was dark and hollow, as though unoccupied for years.

"Go up to bed, Jurriaan. I want to talk to Willem," Louisa said softly, her voice as treacherous as ice on a canal. Jurriaan gripped the handrail and began pulling himself up the stairs, dragging his lame foot.

Willem's eyes met hers. She smiled—a smile making the back of his neck prickle. She opened the door to the basement stairs.

"Mom, I'm sorry about tonight . . . about the coughing. I didn't do it on purpose.

"I'll only take a minute," she said.

"Can't it wait?" Willem asked, his panic rising. "I'm tired."

"If you're that tired, you're too sick to play hockey. I'll keep you home tomorrow. Your choice."

"One minute," she had said.

He heard the garage door grind shut. Hendrik would come inside at any moment.

What could she do to him in one minute?

He trudged down the stairs, Louisa on his heels. She unlocked the crypt—Bas's nickname for the piano studio. In the middle of the room stood two baby grands: Louisa's pristine Steinway and Willem's good old Yamaha. The studio was soundproof. She could practice whenever she wanted, without disturbing the household. Sometimes she practiced all night and slept all day. To keep from waking her, Willem and Jurriaan tiptoed around the house and watched television with headphones on.

Louisa glided to the sofa and patted a cushion. "Sit down."

He obeyed and closed his eyes for a moment. His body ached with weariness. He wanted to go to bed. He didn't care if the sheets were smelly and stiff.

She towered over him, her shiny red mouth twitching.

"Go ahead. Cough your lungs out. No one will hear," she said, smiling.

He didn't know what she meant until she glided from the room and he heard the lock click.

CHAPTER

2

July 2000

Louisa

Louisa rose early the next morning, careful not to wake Hendrik, and padded downstairs to the basement. But she stopped at the bottom of the stairs when she saw what looked like a pile of clothes in front of the locked door.

On closer inspection, she saw that the pile was Jurriaan, curled up asleep, his head on a cushion from the living room sofa, his body wrapped in a throw. Her heart softened, as it always did when she found him sleeping, when he was at his most vulnerable. Long lashes; plump pink cheeks; thick, dark blond hair. Innocence written all over him. Damaged goods. Some might say he was her cross to bear, but they would be wrong.

She bent over Jurriaan. "Sweetheart."

His eyes opened and blinked. He groped around the floor with his hand.

She spotted his glasses a few feet away and set them on his face.

"Did you sleep here all night?"

He nodded and adjusted the glasses on his nose. "Are you going to let Willem out?"

The twins had a bond, no denying that.

She said, "You'll catch the flu next if you're not careful. Go to your room, and don't tell your father that I locked Willem downstairs."

He nodded and she watched him mount the steps in that awkward way he had, dragging the throw behind him. The footsteps stopped when he was just out of sight, and she knew he had sat down on a step.

"Jurriaan," she said, her voice harsher than she had intended.

The footsteps resumed, and she unlocked the door.

Willem was awake and lying listlessly on the sofa, his eyes glazed, his cheeks flushed. She laid her hand on his forehead.

"You have fever. Go upstairs to bed."

He sat up, his hair askew.

"What about hockey?"

"You'll have to miss the match."

"That's not fair. I did what you wanted." His voice was a croak.

"But now you're sick."

"I feel fine."

He coughed, a deep, wet sound from his chest.

She stepped back to avoid the spray and lifted her eyebrows. He looked mutinous and balled his fists, but the bravado was only for show. Defeat settled in his eyes. He staggered to his feet. She followed him upstairs, watching him enter his room and slam the door.

In the master bathroom, she washed her hands with antibacterial soap and lavished them with lotion. The doctor had assured her Willem wouldn't be contagious after a week, but he'd felt hot. No harm in taking precautions.

After applying makeup, she dressed in an expensively tailored skirt suit and high heels, and drove the Mercedes toward Amsterdam Noord, on the other side of the IJ River. She took the route through the IJ tunnel because it was shortest. The concrete walls closed in on her. For a moment, she imagined the big car scraping the concrete and spinning out of control. So she straddled both lanes and pressed hard on the gas pedal, sighing with relief when she emerged into daylight.

The Van der Pek neighborhood was still sleeping, except for dog walkers and nearly empty buses. It had been built early in the century to house dock workers, but now all kinds of working-class people lived there. She passed the Jasmijnstraat and turned onto the Oleanderstraat—the streets were named after flowers, although there weren't any in sight. Battered old cars and vans lined the curbs. She found a parking space at the end of the street near the canal and walked back along uniform terraced houses with somber brown-brick facades and gable roofs. Rentals, owned by the housing associations. The click, click of her heels on the pavement echoed in the crisp morning air.

It was early for a Saturday morning—only eight o'clock. The perfect time to catch Katja at home.

Louisa used her spare key to let herself into the ground-floor apartment. Katja's cat, curled up in the armchair, raised its head. The place reeked of a neglected litter tray.

A stack of clean laundry teetered on the sofa. She walked around the apartment, assessing the damage inflicted by her stepsister. Spilled candle wax on the rickety table. Dirty pans in the kitchen sink. Empty wine bottles next to the overflowing garbage can. But no lasting damage to the apartment itself. Nothing to prevent Louisa from getting back her security deposit.

The bed was unmade, and her stepsister wasn't in it. Louisa shuddered to think when Katja had last washed the sheets and who had slept in them. Then she thought of Willem's sheets. They must be rancid by now. She made a mental note to ask the cleaner to change them.

Where was Katja?

The only tidy spot in the apartment was in the corner of the bedroom where an old desk stood. On it was the electric typewriter Louisa had paid for and next to it, a stack of typed pages.

She picked up the top sheet and frowned at the words "Chapter One."

After dumping the laundry on the floor, she sat on the sofa and started reading the manuscript. It was a story about two girls, best friends, who lived at opposite ends of the Magere Brug, a narrow bridge over the Amstel River. One was a dancer, the other an ordinary girl with no special talents of her own, who worshipped her friend. It was obvious the dancer was based on herself and the friend on Katja. The first page pulled her in, and the story kept her turning the pages, but she wouldn't tell Katja that.

A key rattled in the lock.

A few moments later Katja wheeled her bicycle into the living room. Her wavy copper hair was windblown, her cheeks flushed. She wore a tight dress, hem halfway up her bare thigh. She couldn't have ridden her bicycle without revealing her panties. The unmistakable smell of sex wafted off her.

"Good morning," Louisa said.

Katja stopped in her tracks. The surprise on her pale, freckled face would have been comical under different circumstances.

"Where have you been?" Louisa asked.

"At a friend's house."

"A boy's?"

Rhetorical question. She had once caught Katja—then fourteen to Louisa's thirty—making out with a boy, his hand up her skirt. Louisa had lost no time in putting her on the pill.

"You should have called first," Katja said, her eyes darting to the manuscript on Louisa's lap.

"I left two messages on your answering machine."

"Sorry, I've been busy." Katja propped her bicycle on the kickstand.

"But not with schoolwork."

"What do you mean?"

Louisa set the manuscript on the floor and dug an envelope from her shoulder bag.

"This letter came for you from the university. Based on your progress to date, you won't earn enough credits to continue. It also says they warned you."

"You opened my mail?"

"I'm paying your tuition."

Katja snatched the letter.

"Didn't we thrash this out before you enrolled? You can write a novel after you get your degree."

"I can do both."

"That hasn't worked out, has it?"

Katja took a deep breath. "I told you I didn't want to study accounting."

"It's a practical degree. You can't expect me to support you forever."

"But accounting? That's not who I am."

"You're only nineteen. You don't know who you are. Trust me."

"I'll bring up my grades. I promise."

"Too late. I canceled the lease on the apartment."

"Without talking to me first?"

"There's nothing to talk about."

"Where will I live?" Katja's mouth quivered.

Louisa softened her tone. "Darling Katja. I won't turn you out on the street. You can live with us and help Hendrik keep an eye on the boys."

"You want me to be your nanny?"

"That's one way of looking at it."

"What happened to the au pair?"

"She quit without giving notice. Those foreign girls are so unreliable." Louisa had docked the au pair's pay for breaking two crystal wineglasses by stupidly putting them in the dishwasher instead of washing them by hand. She had left in a huff the same day, leaving Louisa in the lurch.

She glanced around at the shabby furniture. "Think of it as a chance to get yourself sorted. I'll send Hendrik with the car tomorrow to pick up your suitcase."

"What about my stuff?"

Louisa was tempted to give her opinion on the sagging sofa and the table with a coaster wedged under one leg. But then she saw the rebellious expression on Katja's face. A small compromise was in order.

"If there's anything you're particularly attached to, we can store it in our basement. I'll arrange for a thrift shop to pick up the rest on Monday morning. They'll find a new home for it." *Or, more likely, incinerate it.*

Katja picked up the cat and sank into the armchair. "Did you read any of my novel?"

"A few pages."

"What did you think?"

"You're wasting your time."

Katja's shoulders drooped.

Louisa leaned forward. "Let me tell you what it takes to be a great artist. I started playing the piano when I was three years old. I gave my debut concert at eight. I practiced six hours a day. I won my first international competition at sixteen." Louisa paused, not sure if Katja was listening. "Katja?"

The girl's chin jerked up, a spot of pink on each cheek.

"My point is, I didn't wake up when I was your age and decide I wanted to be a concert pianist."

"But—" Katja said.

Louisa stood up. "I'm going on tour next week. I'll expect you to move in before then. School's out for the summer, and I don't want to leave the boys alone all day with Hendrik. You know how obsessed he gets when he's working on one of his projects. The house could be burning down." Her voice trailed off. "Find a home for the cat, or take it to the animal shelter." She nudged the manuscript with the pointed toe of her shoe, and the pile toppled. Katja knelt and gathered up the pages, putting them back in order.

I should have torn it up, Louisa thought.

She drew herself up to her full height and strode out the door. She was halfway to the car before she realized Katja hadn't said yes.

CHAPTER

3

July 2000

Willem

THE ONLY GOOD part about being sick was that he got to skip piano lessons, which almost made up for missing the hockey match. But it was Monday morning, his temperature was normal, and he'd stopped coughing. So the lessons resumed.

Willem sat at the good old Yamaha. Its walnut finish was chipped in places, but all the keys worked, and it was in tune. Louisa sat at the Steinway, its ebony finish gleaming. They were practicing a duet.

Willem didn't dare take his eyes off the sheet music, but his brain reeled with plans for the summer vacation. Bas was coming over later. They were going to mess around on their guitars, maybe compose a new song. And because he wasn't concentrating, he lost track. His hands froze above the keyboard. What came next? The Steinway fell silent. The metronome ticked, and the ventilating system hummed.

"Concentrate," Louisa snapped. "Let's start again from the beginning."

Patience wasn't one of her virtues, but relentless determination was, and right now she focused on him like a magnifying glass directing a hot beam of sun. Sweat broke out on his forehead.

He turned back to the first page.

"One, two, three . . ." she said.

After only a few measures, she screeched, "Stop!"

He nearly jumped off the bench in alarm. "What?"

"Are you deaf as well as stupid?"

Willem didn't answer.

She rose and switched off the metronome. Arranged her long skirt over the back of her bench and sank down again.

"Listen to me play. Keep the tempo. And don't bang on the keys. Strike from the surface. You'll get a more fluid, relaxed sound."

He tensed up. Listening hard, he kept the tempo and didn't bang on the keys. But achieving a fluid, relaxed sound proved impossible because he was stiff, like a guitar string wound too tight. Playing well enough to please her just wasn't going to happen.

His fingers stumbled, and he lost his place.

The Steinway fell silent again, but before that alarming fact penetrated his brain, he caught movement from the corner of his eye. Not in time to duck. Something walloped the side of his head. He saw sparks, then red pain. His hair felt sticky next to his temple, a knot forming. Dazed, he glanced around for the offending missile and spotted the edge of the bench was gouged. On the floor next to the pedals lay the metronome, the pendulum and the sliding weight separated from the cracked casing.

His head swam, and the ground beneath him seemed to shift. His heart raced, jumping hurdles in his chest, booming in his ears. His skin buzzed.. He knew what was coming, but knowing didn't help. He couldn't stop himself. He never could. Sweat poured down his sides, and all rational thought deserted him.

He kicked the metronome as hard as he could with the toe of his trainers. He grabbed the sheet music and ripped it to shreds, hurling the pieces into the air. Then he swung around with his fists balled and glared at his mother, standing frozen next to the Yamaha. She held her hands out in front of her, big as a man's, fingers splayed. She was staring at her hands, the color drained from her face. She had gone too far, but she wouldn't apologize. Not now or ever. *Sorry* wasn't in her vocabulary.

He seized the keyboard cover with both hands and slammed it down hard, his chest heaving. He lifted it and slammed it again. And again.

"Stop!" she shouted. "Show respect for the instrument. And put an icepack on your head."

* * *

After lunch, Louisa locked herself in the piano studio to practice.

Willem holed up in his bedroom with Jurriaan and Bas. He sat in the desk chair, pressing an icepack against his temple. Bas lay on the bed with his hands behind his head, ankles crossed, and Jurriaan slouched in the beanbag chair.

"So, why the icepack?" Bas asked.

Jurriaan fiddled with his glasses, frowning.

Willem reluctantly told them. Maybe because he was still weak from the flu, he couldn't think of a plausible explanation for the welt on his head, except for the truth. Maybe he was tired of making up excuses and lying to his best friend.

From the desk, he had a view out the window of the three bronze figures erected on the grassy median. The spot where the Germans shot twenty-nine prisoners in October 1944. Executed without trial, in reprisal for actions taken by the Resistance. Willem doubted he would have had the courage to join the Resistance—the smuggling, the killing, the fear of betrayal. Jeetje. He couldn't even stand up to his own mother.

"I swear. That was my last piano lesson."

"I've heard that before," Bas said, running his hand through his dark hair. He was a year older and bossy.

"I mean it," Willem said.

After a silence Bas said, "You should tell your dad what happened."

"Dad won't believe me."

"Then tell the coach. Or the police."

"If Dad won't believe me, why will they? Besides, she's my mother."

"My mom wouldn't do something like that. Not in a million years."

Mrs. Debose wouldn't hurt a spider. Willem had seen her coax one into a paper towel and shake it off in the garden.

"She shouldn't hurt you," Jurriaan said.

"That's right," Bas said. "Has she done something like this before?"

Willem and Jurriaan answered at the same time. Willem said no and Jurriaan yes.

"She's never thrown the metronome at me before," Willem clarified. Once, a lamp. Another time, a book. But she threw like a girl and usually missed.

"She could have killed you," Bas said.

"Don't exaggerate."

Bas jumped up and started pacing. "Does she hit you?"

"Not with her hands."

"What does that mean?"

"She hit me with a belt."

"And she pinches him," Jurriaan said, bouncing nervously on the beanbag chair.

"How often?"

"Not often," Willem lied. If he told the truth, Bas would think he was a wuss, even if he pretended otherwise.

Bas turned to Jurriaan. "Does she hit you too?"

"No . . . never. It's not fair."

It wasn't fair, Willem thought, but if their mother started picking on Jurriaan, war would break out. He would make her sorry. Sometimes he fantasized about attacking her precious piano with a hammer.

Bas fixed his eyes on Willem's. "Do you want me to ask my parents to talk to yours?"

"Mom would kill me."

"Don't be a wimp."

Willem felt his face burn. No one could know. This was between him and his mother. The last thing he wanted was to become a story in one of those magazines for sale at the grocery checkout. He imagined a headline: *"Concert Pianist Charged with Child Abuse."* Or worse: *"The Secret Agony of Louisa's Son."* He didn't want people thinking of him as a victim. He would be thirteen soon. He could take care of himself.

"Bas, promise you won't tell anyone."

Bas dove onto the bed and rolled over onto his back. "If you promise to tell your dad."

"I will."

"Today?"

Willem felt a fluttery feeling inside his chest. "Yes, this afternoon."

Bas rolled onto his side and arched an eyebrow. "I didn't see Marina when I arrived."

"She quit," Willem said, grateful for the change of subject.

"Another au pair quit? I liked her. She was hot."

Willem rolled his eyes.

"Does your mom have another one lined up?"

"No. Katja is coming to stay with us."

"Katja?"

"Mom's stepsister. You must have met her at a birthday party or something."

"Oh yeah."

"She's nice," Jurriaan said.

Willem placed the icepack on the desk and reached for his guitar. "I've been working on a new song. Want to hear it?"

* * *

After Bas left, Willem found Hendrik in his ground-floor workshop. The only answer to his knock was the scream of an electric drill. He opened the door and slipped inside. Hendrik, in coveralls and safety goggles, was bent over a worktable, drilling holes in a strip of metal. Willem caught a whiff of sulfur.

"Dad."

No response. Willem tapped him on the shoulder. Hendrik jumped, then switched off the drill and pulled out his earplugs.

He was a mechanical engineer turned inventor, inventing component parts the average person had never heard of. Like the cog he'd invented that was used in the manufacture of drums. Not the kind of thing Willem could brag about to his classmates. He imagined their eyes glazing over and the conversation shifting to his famous mother. Although most of the kids didn't have a clue about classical music, Louisa had also written the score for the hit movie *SS Athenia*, and the theme song had played on the radio for months. Even Lex Dickhoff, the most feared bully in the school, had asked Willem for her autograph. Willem saw it as protection money, and for a few months Lex left Jurriaan alone.

"What brings you down here?" Hendrik asked, raising the goggles.

Willem showed him the knot on his head and the cut, which was an angry red.

Hendrik probed the spot with his finger. "You don't need stitches. What happened?"

"I was playing a duet with Mom, and I lost my place. She threw the metronome at me."

"Your mother wouldn't do that."

"She did."

"She pushes you because she wants you to reach your potential. But she would never hurt you. She loves you."

Willem wanted to puke. "Are you saying I'm lying?"

"I think you want to get out of taking piano lessons."

"Is that a *yes*?"

Hendrik didn't reply.

"How do you explain this?" Willem said, jabbing at his temple.

Hendrik shrugged. "Does it hurt much?"

"What do you think?"

"Take an aspirin. And watch your attitude."

Willem balled his fists, digging his nails into his palms. Louisa never hit him when Hendrik was present, and if he suspected she caused the bruises and bumps, he turned a blind eye. Why had he listened to Bas? It had been pointless to tell Hendrik and would piss off Louisa if she found out.

"Don't tell her what I said."

"Sure, son." Hendrik looked relieved that the issue was solved, or at least closed. He shoved the plugs into his ears and lowered the goggles. The scream of the drill filled the workshop.

Willem consoled himself with the knowledge that he'd kept his promise to Bas, and in his book that counted for something.

CHAPTER

4

July 24, 2000

Diary entry

TODAY I MOVED into the Veldkamp mansion.

I felt like a beggar as I stood on the doorstep, clutching my tattered overnight bag in one arm and Smokey my cat in the other. Sometimes I hate my dear stepsister, but she's the only family I have, and she's always been there when I've needed her.

After Louisa turned me out of the apartment, I stayed away for five days. I spent the first night on the sofa at Marieke's converted loft, but Smokey triggered her asthma, so I moved on to Joop's moldy apartment, a dump rented cheap to keep out squatters. Joop is an ex-boyfriend, and he knows I'm involved with a man who is in no position to help me. He threw a lumpy, stained mattress onto the floor in the living room, where I spent four nights trying to sleep while he and his friends came and went at all hours. Even as a temporary solution, the arrangement sucked. But I'm penniless. My job at the university library ended when I withdrew from school. I can't even afford a night in a youth hostel.

I swallowed my pride and rang the doorbell. A rotund boy wearing glasses with thick lenses answered the door. I knew it was Jurriaan because of the glasses, but he'd gained weight since I saw him last.

"Jurriaan. It's nice to see you."

He nodded and we exchanged the traditional three kisses on alternating cheeks.

"May I hold the cat?" he asked.

"Her name's Smokey." I shifted the cat into his arms. "Is Louisa home?" I asked, hoping she had gone out, giving me time to settle in before the inevitable confrontation.

"She's downstairs practicing. I'm supposed to take you to your room."

"And Willem?"

"In his room with Bas. He's our best friend."

Jurriaan led the way, gripping the rail with his free hand. He didn't trot up the stairs the way Willem would have. Each step was labored.

The attic room had been cleared out and converted to a bedroom with a small desk, a wardrobe, and a single bed.

"I arranged your books," Jurriaan said, pointing to the bookshelf above the desk.

He had ordered them by color. "Thank you."

He smiled and stroked the cat.

The room was bigger than I remembered from my visits on school holidays. Sometimes I had hidden in the attic to be alone and read a book.

My typewriter took up most of the space on the desk. I opened the wardrobe and found my clothes folded inside, even my panties and bras. At least they weren't sorted by color! Louisa had known I would come. She knew she had me cornered, that I had no choice but to do her bidding.

Then I heard birdsong. I climbed onto the bed and peered out the casement window. The garden below was a palette of green, violet, and blue. A gravel path wound from the terrace to the end of the garden, where the canal flowed by, a glimmering silver ribbon framed by rich green foliage. For the moment I felt lighter. If only it were anyone else's house.

Slow, deliberate footsteps sounded on the stairs.

Louisa ducked when she came through the doorway. She was wearing a long gold and white kaftan and metallic leather sandals. "Welcome, Katja."

The top of her blonde head brushed the low-beamed ceiling. The atmosphere in the room darkened, and I felt a sudden chill. But Louisa smiled as if no ill will had ever passed between us, as if we were on the best of sisterly terms.

"Jurriaan, go downstairs," Louisa said with a smile that bordered on genuine.

"Yes, Mom." He set Smokey on the floor and tripped on the edge of the rug in his haste to leave.

Louisa turned the desk chair around and sat down majestically. I perched on the edge of the bed, and Smokey sprang onto my lap.

"I'm glad you accepted my proposal," Louisa said.

"Proposal? You gave me no choice," I snapped.

Louisa tutted. "What is the cat doing here?"

I hugged Smokey closer and swallowed hard. "Sorry. No one could take her. Besides, Jurriaan will love having a pet. And it's a big house. You won't know Smokey is here."

"Is the animal house-trained?"

"Yes, I have a litter box."

"We'll call it a trial run."

"Thank you, Louisa," I said, relieved. But I couldn't help wondering what was in it for her.

She continued. "These are my ground rules. The boys can entertain themselves. But you need to keep tabs on them. Know where they are at all times. A cleaner comes once a week. A woman normally comes at four o'clock to cook the evening meal, but she's away nursing a sick relative. You'll have to do the cooking until she returns."

My eyes darted to Louisa's smooth hands. She didn't do any cooking or cleaning herself. She spent most of her life in five-star hotels with maid service, crisp white sheets, fresh towels, a rose on the pillow. And when she was home, she avoided any activity that might wrinkle, redden, or roughen her hands. Or injure them. Her hands were the tools of her trade. She would be lost without them.

"I don't know how to cook," I said.

"Didn't the boarding school I sent you to teach the girls how to cook?"

"The school had a modern curriculum. It wasn't the 1950s."

"There's no call to be sarcastic."

I tried for a neutral expression.

"Cooking isn't rocket science, Katja. You'll find cookbooks in the kitchen."

"Anything else?"

"No boyfriends in the house. Is that clear?"

"I'm nineteen."

"I expect you to spend the nights alone in your own bed."

"Am I allowed to go out with my friends?" If Louisa said no, I was going to pack my bag and walk out. Even if it meant sleeping under a bridge and slinging coffee in a café.

"Of course. As long as Hendrik and the boys get their dinner. Any more questions?"

"What would you have done if I hadn't come?"

"You're here, aren't you? And your timing is perfect. I leave tomorrow." Louisa rose from the chair and glided to the door.

After she was gone, I unpacked my suitcase. At the bottom was the draft of my novel. Leaving it on the desk was risky. I didn't put it past her to confiscate the manuscript or even destroy it. The desk had a single drawer underneath, with a key dangling in the lock. Was it a trap? Louisa might have a spare. But she was leaving tomorrow, so I locked the manuscript in the desk and looked for a place to hide the key. I considered hiding it under the mattress, but that was too predictable. Or inside the boots that I wouldn't wear again until winter. I decided on the tight gap between the back of the wardrobe and the wall. I worked the key along the floor until it was out of sight.

After living like a nomad for nearly a week, my hair was limp and greasy, and my clothes grubby. The guest bathroom was on the floor below. I grabbed clean clothes and went down the attic stairs. As I turned into the hall, I heard a shout of laughter from behind a door. On impulse, I knocked.

A beautiful boy opened the door. Willem? He and Jurriaan no longer looked like twins: Jurriaan's weight gain, glasses, and timidity had seen to that. Willem's honey-blond hair was shaggy and combed straight back. He regarded me with frank, golden-hazel eyes, fringed with thick blond lashes. I couldn't help wishing I had washed my hair and changed into clean clothes first. Ridiculous to let a boy that age make me self-conscious.

"Hi, Willem." Curious, I peered around him at the other boy, who was sitting cross-legged on the floor. Chestnut brown hair, turquoise eyes, and a prominent cleft chin.

"You must be Bas."

"You're Katja, right? We met at one of Willem's birthday parties."

I recalled a young boy with the same coloring, pretty enough to be a girl. He was growing up to be a heartbreaker.

Willem opened the door wider, and Jurriaan waved from the beanbag chair.

"Am I interrupting?"

"It's okay," Willem said.

"The bunk beds are gone," I said, looking around. The Legos and the stuffed animals were gone too, replaced by an acoustic guitar lying on the desk and an electric one leaning against the bed. On the wall was a black and white poster of Kurt Cobain holding a guitar in his lap.

"We have our own rooms now," Jurriaan said.

"That's nice. What are you guys up to?"

"We're writing a song," Willem said.

"May I hear it?"

"Maybe, when we're finished."

He pushed back a lock of hair that had fallen forward, drawing my attention to a goose egg on his temple, the cut in the center scabbing over.

"What happened to your head?"

Bas opened his mouth, but Willem shot him a warning glance.

"Bumped it on the corner of a cabinet," Willem said.

"Did you tell your mother?"

"It's nothing."

I recalled he was accident-prone. Once when I visited, his arm was in a cast—broken in a tumble down the stairs. Another time, he was missing a front tooth—knocked out in a soccer match. Or was it a hockey match? At his tenth birthday party, I glimpsed a bruise on his back when his T-shirt rose. Happened in a fall from a tree, he'd said, and showed me the tree next to the canal.

Jurriaan fiddled with his glasses, Bas gazed at my chest, and Willem avoided looking me in the eye. The welcoming sunshine was spent. Shadows cloaked the house. I left the boys to their songwriting.

Thank God, Louisa is leaving tomorrow.

DECEMBER 2004

C H A P T E R

5

Anneliese

ANNELIESE AND HER big brother, Daan, were turned around on the sofa, their elbows propped on the back. They were watching the excitement at the house next door through the big picture window. Mr. Grootheest tied blue balloons to the bench in his front garden. Visitors bearing gifts swooped on the house like a flock of cawing rooks.

Mrs. Grootheest had gone to the hospital for two days and come home with a baby.

"Where did the baby come from?" Anneliese asked.

"It grew in her belly," Daan said.

He was nearly seven and knew almost as much as Papa. Maybe she would get smart too, once she was old enough for school.

Anneliese hiked up her T-shirt and looked at her own round tummy, running her finger over her bellybutton.

"How did the baby get out?"

"The doctor took it out."

She nodded, imagining Mrs. Grootheest's ponderous belly opening like the trunk of Papa's car.

"I grew inside Mama," Daan said, "but you didn't."

Daan was always telling stories, and she never knew when to believe him.

"Where did I come from?"

"From another mama's belly. She didn't want you."

Anneliese frowned.

"I have the same blood as Mama and Papa. But you don't," Daan said.

Daan had taught her what blood was. It oozed bright red from her skin when he sliced it gently with a knife. She wondered how her blood differed from his. Didn't she belong to Mama and Papa? Would they decide not to keep her? Her insides twisted into a knot.

Daan smiled and patted her on the head.

She batted his hand away, and he shrieked with laughter. Tears stung her eyes as she clambered up the stairs to their parents' room, where Mama was smoking in bed, still in her nightgown, and listening to the radio. She spent most of her mornings in bed, coming downstairs in the afternoon to throw out yesterday's empty wine bottles and fix dinner before Papa got home from work.

"Do you like the music?" Mama asked.

Anneliese nodded and climbed onto the bed.

"That's Louisa Veldkamp playing the piano. The song is from a movie . . . one about a ship that sank."

Anneliese laid her head against her mother's bony shoulder and listened for a minute to the song. "It's pretty."

She gave a sob.

"Something wrong, Liese?" Mama tapped her cigarette into the overflowing ashtray.

"Daan says I didn't grow in your belly."

Mama drew deep on the cigarette, then balanced the butt on the rim of the ashtray and watched, as if her answer depended on which way it fell. After a moment, the butt landed on the nightstand.

"It's true."

"So . . . we don't have the same blood?"

"Me and Papa don't either."

Anneliese pondered for a minute.

"Why didn't my mommy want me?" she asked with a loud sniff.

"She wanted you, but she went to heaven when you were born. So we adopted you."

"What was my mommy's name?"

Mama reached for a tissue and swiped at Anneliese's nose. "I forget. The name isn't important. I'm your mama now."

"Ap . . . dotted," Anneliese said, testing the strange new word as she snuggled against Mama's thin chest just as the pretty song ended.

MAY 2024

CHAPTER

6

Anneliese

ANNELIESE WAS CURLED up on the sofa in her third-floor walk-up on the Vechtstraat. She was streaming *SS Athenia* on her laptop—a movie she never tired of because of the popular film score by Louisa Veldkamp. At the same time, she scrolled through her phone, checking emails and messages and downloading the dismal balance in her bank account. She was connected to the world in every way except in the way it mattered. So when her phone vibrated, she paused the movie without thinking twice.

But she hadn't realized what today's date was until she saw the caller ID. Her mother. A shivery sensation passed through her.

"Hi Tineke," she said warily.

"Anneliese? Is this a good time to talk?"

"It's fine."

A silence fell.

Then Tineke gave a theatrical sob. "It was eight years ago today."

"I know."

"Can you come home on Saturday? Catch up?"

"Sorry, I have plans."

"For once, couldn't you take the time to remember your brother?"

My adoptive *brother,* Anneliese silently corrected; they didn't have the same blood.

"Dr. Hummel will be there," Tineke said, as if the doctor were a carrot and Anneliese a donkey.

She usually tuned out during Tineke's gossipy phone calls, but she recalled news about Dr. Hummel. He had been Daan's therapist and afterward Anneliese's. During his career he had lost several patients to suicide. Retired now, maybe bored, he had started visiting the bereaved families on the anniversaries of their loved ones' deaths, like a murderer returning to the scene of the crime.

"Hang on a sec while I light a cigarette," Tineke said.

Anneliese heard a clunk, then Tineke's footstep, and the pop of a cork. A minute passed, then another. If Tineke had forgotten her, it wouldn't be the first time.

She ended the call. Eight years was a third of her life, though sometimes it seemed as if it had happened yesterday. She had been sixteen, Daan nineteen. When she had left home for university a few years later, she'd resolved never to return to Noorddorp, even for a brief visit. But staying away hadn't worked. Just last week she had dreamed about him and woken up with a lurch. Her skin prickled whenever she saw a slim figure with curly black hair in a crowd on Dam Square, or buying a salted herring at the Albert Cuyp Market, or sitting alone at the back of a tram. She needed closure by whatever means she could get it.

She picked up the phone and called Tineke back.

* * *

On Saturday morning Anneliese took the Intercity from Amsterdam Central Station to Utrecht, where she transferred to the train that would take her as far as Assen. She kept picking up her book and putting it down, unable to concentrate for more than a few lines.

She gazed out the window. Flat green polder crisscrossed by drainage ditches; sheep grazing on top of a dike; poplars lined up along a road running parallel with the railroad track. So different from Noorddorp, perched on the edge of a dying forest that was succumbing to disease and pollution. Would her childhood have ended differently if she had grown up far from a forest? If she had grown up in one of Amsterdam's crooked houses, the wooden pile foundations rotting in the swampy ground? Or would Daan's evil have manifested itself anyway, in a dark, moldy basement or in a secret attic room?

From the station in Assen, she boarded a bus, and a half hour later, a second one. She trudged the last half mile to her childhood home on the outskirts of Noorddorp, where the forest began.

Tineke and Ray had tried to sell the house after Daan's death. While there had been no shortage of people interested in viewing, most weren't interested in buying, and the serious buyers didn't want a home where someone had died violently. They just wanted to look. The house became a tourist attraction for the locals, some never going past the entrance hall where the tragedy had played out.

The "For Sale" sign was stolen twice, spray-painted with obscenities, and finally decapitated. After years of suffering Daan's abuse, his schoolmates felt sufficiently safe to take their revenge, even if it was on the innocent bereaved.

The neighborhood had prayed for years for the Bakkers to move and rid the village of its most hated bully, but once he was dead, they overflowed with sympathy. They brought casseroles and cakes and baskets of fruit. *"It's such a terrible thing to lose a child,"* they said. Overnight they forgot the mutilated cats and the excrement smeared on their front doors—wicked deeds attributed to Daan. But he was sly, and nothing could be proven.

They had taken the house off the market after a year. Anneliese helped Tineke scrub the nicotine stains off the walls with ammonia. Ray bought a new living room set in a horrid blue, laid a new tile floor over the old, and recarpeted the stairs.

Anneliese rang the bell; using the key might have sent the wrong message. The tiny front garden was paved, weeds poking through the cracks along the foundation. Tineke opened the door and waved her inside with a cigarette.

Anneliese stepped gingerly over the spot where Daan's urine had pooled and followed Tineke into the living room.

Her heart jumped into her throat when she saw the framed photo of Daan propped up on the coffee table. She took in his mocking eyes, his dark curls, his smirk. Beautiful, but dangerous.

Ray staggered to his feet like a sleepy bear and drew her into a sweaty embrace. She extricated herself and glanced around, ignoring Dr. Hummel, who was smiling smugly in a chair. The room was sliding back into its former state. The walls and net curtains had yellowed, the cheap sofa sagged in the middle, and the new floor tiles wobbled under her feet.

Something was missing.

"Where's my piano?"

A look passed between Tineke and Ray.

"We gave it away," Ray said.

"Why?"

"It wasn't worth anything."

"It was just taking up space," Tineke added.

"Why didn't you give it to me?"

"When was the last time you played the piano? Or visited? It's been five years, Anneliese," Ray said.

Dr. Hummel saved her from replying. He sprang from the chair and pumped her hand. He looked younger than when he had treated her, his eyes clear, his cheeks full. He seemed to burst with energy, as if retirement had lifted a weight from his shoulders. So why did he want to revisit his worst failures? Did he have unfinished business? She felt a twinge of alarm.

Anneliese plopped into a chair, and Tineke poured her a glass of port. Ray crossed his arms over his chest.

A silence settled.

"Now that everyone's here, we can begin," Dr. Hummel said.

"Begin what?" Anneliese asked.

"Tineke and Ray are ready to talk about Daan. They feel that if they'd been better parents, he wouldn't have taken his own life."

"I didn't come here to—" she said, and stopped. Because it was precisely the reason she had come.

"If you'll let me finish, Anneliese." He harrumphed, a nervous habit she remembered from before, and said, "We were working through Daan's problems in therapy. I didn't consider him a suicide risk. If the signs were there, I missed them."

Their faces turned toward Anneliese—Dr. Hummel's glowing pink, Ray's a deep magenta, and Tineke's sallow.

Anneliese gulped the port. "What do you want from me?"

"Teenagers might not turn to their parents when they're depressed. More often to friends."

"Daan didn't have any friends," she said.

Dr. Hummel flashed a professional smile. "Or they confide in a sibling. Is there anything you haven't told us? Anything at all?"

Ambushed.

She set her glass on the table with a clink. "He was disturbed."

"If only I'd known how unhappy he was," Tineke wailed.

The doctor was right; Anneliese was holding back. They hadn't listened to her when he was alive. Why would they now when they'd placed him on a pedestal? When they had made *him* the victim? She wondered how soon she could leave.

Ray said, "I worked too much. I should have taken him camping."

Dr. Hummel harrumphed, a sign he was about to throw his opinion into the pot.

Before he could, Anneliese jumped to her feet and excused herself. She felt three sets of eyes drilling into her back as she stumbled from the room, the sickly-sweet port souring in her mouth. After visiting the toilet, she took a deep breath and climbed the stairs, trailing her hand along the rail. She paused on the landing, her legs shaking, and forced herself to peer over the balustrade at the floor below. But there was only empty space between.

CHAPTER

7

May 2024

Anneliese

IT DIDN'T SURPRISE Anneliese to find Daan's old room just as he'd left it: the bed made with sharp corners, empty food jars lining the bookshelves, an anatomy book open on the desk. But his sour smell had gone, replaced by the stink of Tineke's cigarettes.

His pocketknife lay next to the anatomy book. She walked over to the desk and stared down at the knife: dark red handle, three and a half inches long. She forced herself to pick it up, and using her thumbnail, she opened a blade, but when she saw the brown stains, she let the knife fall with a clunk. She turned and strode toward the door, which she felt like slamming behind her—slamming the door on the bedroom, on Daan, on the past. If only it were that simple to consign memories to oblivion.

Her old bedroom was next to Daan's. Tineke had converted it to a sewing room—sewing was her mother's one redeeming talent. She had made all of Anneliese's clothes and made them well. Still, Anneliese had longed for dresses like those of the other girls who shopped at Zara and H&M on the village high street. Tineke was a binge seamstress, disappearing in a flurry of paper patterns and bolts of fabric each July, sewing Anneliese's wardrobe for the coming school term. It looked as if she hadn't binged in years. A thick layer of dust covered the fancy sewing machine that stood in the spot once occupied by Blueboy's birdcage. She ran a finger through the dust and drew the letter *B*.

Moving to the window, Anneliese looked down at the garden shed, a squat brick building with a flat bitumen roof. She could almost smell the dank inside, reeking of gasoline and pesticide. She fought back a shiver, remembering.

* * *

Tineke and Ray gave Anneliese a parakeet for her eighth birthday. Blueboy had blue and white feathers and bright eyes. His feet tickled when he hopped around on her forearm or ate birdseed from her palm. She kept his cage in her bedroom and guarded Blueboy closely whenever Daan was home.

One afternoon she found Daan standing in front of the cage.

"Get out," she said.

His eyes took on a familiar intensity.

"You know, Liese, parakeets die. Eventually."

Goose bumps shot up her arms. "What do you mean?"

"There's a box of rat poison in the shed. Bottom shelf."

He drew his thumb across his throat, snickered, and walked away.

She told Tineke she was sick and took up vigil in her room. The smell of braised beef and cabbage wafted upstairs. Cutlery clattered. Dusk deepened into night. Blueboy went to sleep on his perch, feathers fluffed up, eyes closed. She covered the cage, climbed into bed, and listened to the familiar household sounds signaling the end of the day: doors closing, Tineke and Ray brushing their teeth, water rushing in the pipes, Daan pacing in his bedroom. Finally silence.

At midnight she crept barefooted down the staircase, eased open the back door, and paused on the patio under an overcast sky. The chilly wind whipped at the hem of her nightgown. Traffic rumbled from the far side of the forest. The hair on the back of her neck bristled as if someone were watching, and her eyes darted to Daan's window. But the curtains were drawn and the room was dark.

She tiptoed across the gritty concrete to the shed and switched on the dim overhead light. A spider dropped onto her arm. She yelped and brushed it off in a panic. After taking a calming breath, she peered into the shadows, her eyes searching. The box was right where Daan had said it would be.

If she was to get any peace, she had to stay a step ahead of Daan.

Back in bed she turned toward the wall and squeezed shut her eyes. It took her forever to fall asleep. The room was growing light when a noise woke her—a soft crunching coming from Blueboy's cage. Her heart raced. She clasped her hands over her ears and hummed, blocking out the sound.

She didn't check on Blueboy until it was time to get ready for school. She steeled herself before removing the cover from his cage. He lay on the soiled newspapers, his stick legs pointing at the ceiling.

She had beaten Daan.

Reaching into the cage, she gently stroked the parakeet's little head and told him how sorry she was, but she kept her sorrow locked up inside her all day.

She broke the news during supper.

"Didn't you give him water?" Tineke asked.

"Don't think I'm going to buy you another parakeet, young lady," Ray said.

Anneliese lifted her chin. "I never want another pet as long as I live."

Daan laughed, which earned him a smack on the ear from Ray.

When Daan biked to the woods that afternoon, Anneliese followed. She couldn't keep up, and he disappeared around a bend, but she knew where he was headed. It would be stupid to let down her guard, but she felt bolder, and she wanted to test an idea. The spruce forest merged into a graveyard of beeches, some felled by a storm. Others, bare of foliage, were standing like crucifixes. Rumor had it the beech forest was haunted.

She laid her bicycle on the ground and crawled through the brambles.

Daan squatted next to a log that was clustered with what looked at first glance like severed human ears, but they were only jelly ear mushrooms. Catching sight of her, he nodded.

"Liese, you're just in time."

Her eyes darted around.

He pulled a jar from his backpack and reached inside for the fat frog trembling on the bottom. In his other hand was a lighter.

He grinned. "I know what you did last night."

She heard a snap and a tiny flame flickered.

She squeezed her eyes shut and hummed. Daan's smirk, the doomed frog, the rotten log—all disappeared. She had felt nothing except for the relief of cold emptiness.

* * *

Anneliese turned away from the window and hummed to herself as she went down the stairs. She rejoined the others in the living room, where Ray and Tineke were competing for the worst parent trophy. She poured herself a glass of port and endured the contest for as long as she could. After a half hour, she picked up her backpack.

Dr. Hummel scrambled to his feet, jangling the keys in his pocket. "I have to go too. Do you want a lift to the bus stop?"

On the way, neither of them spoke, the silence reminding her of the hours she had spent in his therapy room. Some shrink he was. The bus stop was in sight when Dr. Hummel said, "I'm curious. If you don't mind me asking. Did you stop wetting the bed?"

Betsy Wetsy.

"Yes, when I left home."

The car slowed to a stop.

"You should consider seeing a therapist in Amsterdam," he said in his best therapist voice.

She had no words.

"Try visiting your parents more often."

"They aren't my parents. Not my real ones."

"You need to talk to someone."

"How do you know what I need?"

She stepped onto the curb, slammed the door, and didn't look back.

CHAPTER

8

May 2024

Anneliese

Anneliese took a mid-morning train to Den Bosch. She had called in sick to work, which wasn't exactly a lie. Her stomach roiled from nerves.

She tried to keep her expectations low. After all, her biological parents were dead. What could she possibly gain? Maybe a little knowledge about her origins. Maybe confirmation that her blood family was better than the Bakkers.

The Foundation for Aiding Unwed Mothers (FAM) took up a floor in a boxy five-story building, the kind furnished with drab metal desks and sagging venetian blinds.

Reception didn't disappoint: orange plastic chairs and a scuffed gray linoleum floor. She had only just sat down when an interior door opened, and a middle-aged woman came through.

"Miss Bakker? I'm Miss Jansen. Please come this way."

Anneliese took the chair indicated in front of a beige metal desk that was littered with stacks of papers.

The social worker smoothed her blonde hair, though it looked as if it hadn't moved a millimeter in decades. "Your adoption was one of my first cases. The circumstances came back to me as I was reading the notes. You were born in a hotel."

"Why didn't my mother go to a hospital?"

"There wasn't time. She experienced an unusually rapid labor and delivery." Miss Jansen cleared her throat. "Your mother named you Mirella. The Bakkers changed it when they adopted you."

"Mirella," Anneliese repeated softly. It was a pretty name, but she didn't feel like a Mirella. "What was my mother's name?"

"As I mentioned on the telephone, your adoption was closed. I can't tell you her name without her express permission."

"How can she give her permission when she's dead?"

Miss Jansen's eyes narrowed. "Why do you think that?"

"Tineke and Ray told me both my parents were dead."

"I'm sorry, Anneliese. We urge adoptive parents to be truthful about their child's origins. Your mother was very much alive when she placed you for adoption. She came here with her sister."

Anneliese's fantasy of star-crossed lovers like Romeo and Juliet was instantly shattered. Why would Tineke and Ray lie? After thinking about it for two seconds, she realized it was typical of their behavior. They had lied to everyone, including themselves, about Daan, their precious biological son.

"What *can* you tell me about her?"

Miss Jansen opened a folder. "Your mother was nineteen years old and in good health. She was a university student and unmarried. That's all I can say. I'm sorry."

"And my father?"

"Your mother said she didn't know who he was."

She must have had some idea. There was only a tiny window each month when the fruit was ripe for plucking, narrowing the field of possibilities.

"Did you believe her?"

"Some clients don't want the father to know about the child, for instance, if the relationship is over, or he's married, or she's afraid of him. There are many reasons, as I'm sure you can imagine. It's not my place to speculate."

Anneliese considered. Maybe her mother had slept around—or worse, been raped.

"Are you all right?" the social worker asked, pity on her face.

Anneliese took a deep breath and squared her shoulders.

"My mother might have changed her mind after twenty-four years. Can you put me in touch with her?"

"I can write her a letter and propose a meeting."

It was possible that Anneliese's mother, father, and aunt were still alive. Maybe she had cousins or even siblings. Blood relatives. The only kind that counted.

* * *

The next day, Anneliese went back to work at the upscale office in the center of Amsterdam. In the seventeenth century, the house had been owned by a rich merchant. Now it housed the private equity firm that managed the inherited wealth of the merchant's undeserving descendants. Blood trumps.

"I'm glad you're feeling better today," her boss said while peering down the deep V of her blouse. Her wardrobe was her means to keeping the job for which she was unqualified, but he had taken one look at her and offered her the position. A very capable man in the office took up the slack. Her biggest challenge was managing her boss's sexual expectations. If things got sticky, she would quit and request a new assignment from the temp agency.

* * *

Two weeks later Anneliese had had enough of Mr. Private Equity. She sat in her tiny apartment waiting for a call from the temp agency about a new *opportunity*, as if a menial administrative job could be more than a means to pay the rent and put food on the table. When her phone rang, she snatched it up.

"Miss Bakker, this is Irene Jansen."

It took her a moment to remember that Miss Jansen was the social worker at FAM.

Her heart took off at a gallop. "Yes?"

"I received a reply from your mother in the post today. Do you want me to mail it to you, or do you want to pick it up?"

"I have the day off," Anneliese said, which was true in a way. "I'll pick it up."

A few hours later, she was sitting in front of Miss Jansen's messy desk. The social worker smiled stiffly and handed Anneliese a cream-colored envelope. She could tell at a glance that it was expensive stationery. Anneliese turned over the envelope. "Why is it blank on both sides?"

"The envelope was inside one addressed to me."

Her hands trembled as she picked the seal loose. She read the letter slowly, weighed each word. Her mother didn't want to meet her. She didn't even want to know Anneliese's name. Certain phrases in the letter stung her heart like nettle.

Dear Mirella, Your adoptive parents are your real parents . . . I think of you every day . . . after everything we did to keep the pregnancy a secret . . . no wish to hurt anyone . . . please don't contact me again . . . I wish you the best.

The letter was unsigned—no *Mom* or *Mother* and no name.

Anneliese swore.

The social worker tutted and held out her hand. "May I?"

Anneliese handed over the letter.

Miss Jansen took her time reading and laid the letter on her desk. She stroked her helmet of blonde hair, probably deciding which of several stock responses to make. "Perhaps your mother isn't ready. We might try to contact her again in a few years."

"In a few years? She's had twenty-four years already."

"I'm sorry—"

"Give me the letter," Anneliese said.

"Of course, after I make a copy for our file."

"I want a copy of my adoption papers too."

"It's your right, but first I need to mark through text that might reveal your mother's identity. Do you want to wait or—?"

"I'll wait."

Anneliese returned to reception, picked up a magazine from a side table, and squirmed in a plastic chair with all the contours in the wrong places. Disappointment milked her heart.

An hour later the redacted version of her adoption papers was ready, tucked into a transparent plastic file.

* * *

Lost in thought, Anneliese retraced her footsteps along the Visstraat, toward the train station. She was barely conscious of the bustling shops she passed. She planned to read the file at her leisure on the train, but she couldn't wait. After crossing the bridge, she sat down on a bench facing the river and opened the file. Swipes of black highlighter hid names and other personal details. She turned the pages, searching for clues the social worker had missed.

Miss Jansen hadn't struck out the name and address of the hotel where Anneliese was born, and it was located right there in Den Bosch. She opened the maps app on her phone and took a moment to get her bearings. The hotel was only a twenty-minute walk away.

CHAPTER

9

May 2024

Anneliese

Anneliese rang the bell in the deserted hotel lobby.

A minute later she rang again, and when the desk clerk failed to appear, she followed the faint clanking of cutlery into the dining room. The furnishings were dark and heavy, and the daylight that filtered through the dirty windows was pale. Strange artifacts that looked like antique tools hung on the walls. Next to a scarred mahogany bar was an old upright piano; and in the corner, a pool table covered with a tarpaulin. The tables and barstools were unoccupied. A shapeless girl in her late teens was emptying the dishwasher.

"Hello," Anneliese said.

The girl's head jerked up. She wiped her hands on her apron. "Can I help you?"

"A white wine." Anneliese set her backpack on the floor and hopped onto a barstool.

The girl reached into a refrigerator and pulled out an almost empty bottle. "Lucky you. This is the last glass." She tipped the remains into a tumbler and slid it across the bar.

Anneliese sniffed the wine. She wasn't picky. She had drunk just about every cheap wine known to humankind. This one smelled like Magic Marker.

"Have you worked here long?" she asked, pretending to take a sip.

The girl's eyes narrowed. "Who wants to know?"

"I don't mean to pry. It's just . . . I was born in this hotel. In the year 2000."

The suspicion on the girl's face lifted.

"I heard the story. Only one baby ever born in the hotel. What are you doing here?"

"I wanted to see my birthplace."

The barmaid dunked glasses in a sink full of soapy water. "The hotel isn't Noordeinde Palace, is it?"

Anneliese's mother must have had no class and no money, or she had chosen the hotel because the staff wouldn't ask questions.

"My mother gave me up for adoption. I don't know her name. I'm trying to trace her."

"I love mysteries," the girl said, inspecting the chip on a glass as if trying to solve how it had happened.

"My name is Anneliese."

The girl set the glass on the bar, and they shook hands. "I'm Sophie."

"Will you help me?"

"How?"

"Does the hotel have records of the guests from 2000?"

Sophie snorted. "I doubt it."

"Can you find out?"

"I would have to ask Rob, the manager, but he's not in today."

"Can you phone him?"

The girl frowned. "We're not allowed to call him on his day off unless it's an emergency."

Anneliese fixed her eyes on Sophie's Delft blue ones. She pictured Sophie coddled by loving parents and surrounded by plump sisters—blood sisters. She pictured jolly birthday parties, lovely presents from her siblings, never a dead mouse wrapped in gift paper and tied with a silver ribbon. Sophie didn't have to sleep at night with a chair wedged under the doorknob. Anneliese cleared the lump in her throat.

"Do you know who your mother and father are?"

"'Course, I do."

"If you didn't know, wouldn't you want to find out?"

Sophie looked down at her hands and picked at a cuticle. "I suppose."

"Help me. Call Rob."

The girl let her hands drop. "I guess he won't fire me. Wait here."

Sophie left her post and disappeared into the lobby. Anneliese hazarded a sip of wine, and as she expected, it tasted sour. She reached over the bar and emptied the glass into the sink. It seemed like an hour but was probably only minutes before the girl returned, her face flushed deep red.

"He swore at me."

"I'm sorry, Sophie. But what about the records?"

Scowling, the girl crossed her arms over her chest.

"It's like I thought. They don't have records from that far back."

Anneliese sagged. A dead end. She might never know who her mother was. She paid for the wine, picked up her backpack, and turned to go.

"Hold on," the girl said. "Old Radboud has worked here forever. He might remember something. He's upstairs fixing a leak. Can you wait until he's done?"

Anneliese sat down at a table and after perusing a grimy laminated menu, she ordered a salad. When she finished eating, she wandered over to the piano, a full-sized upright, taller than modern pianos. She sat down on the bench and played a scale. The keys were sticky, and the piano was out of tune. She flipped through the dusty sheet music piled on top.

A tap on her shoulder made her jump.

A broad, coarse-featured man with a long silver ponytail glared at her. "Sofie says you want to ask me about the baby."

"About me. I was the baby."

"I'll have to take your word for it. I never saw the child, but I heard it wailing. We got complaints from the other guests."

Anneliese smiled. "Sorry about that. Can I buy you a drink, Radboud?"

His expression lightened a little. "I eat and drink here for free, but you're welcome to join me."

"Done."

They sat down at the same table where she had lunched. Sofie brought two steaming coffees and apple pie for Radboud.

"Mind if I join you?" she asked.

"Sit down." Anneliese nodded at a chair.

The old man squinted at Anneliese. "I don't remember what your mother looked like, but I remember thinking she was pretty."

"Tell me about her." Anneliese leaned on her elbows and rested her chin on her hands.

"She and her sister stayed in separate rooms. They checked in a couple of months before you were born. They kept to themselves. It made the staff curious. Gave us something to gossip about. You know." He stopped talking to shovel in two big bites of pie. "They didn't go out. They took their meals in their rooms. We figured they were hiding from the baby's father."

It made sense. The year 2000 wasn't the Victorian Era; a single mom wasn't ostracized, but she might have had good reason to keep the father in the dark.

"Do you remember my mother's name?"

He shook his head. "Sorry. But I don't think she was using her real name anyway."

"Why do you think that?"

"Because I know for a fact her sister wasn't. I recognized her."

Anneliese's heart skipped a beat. "Was she someone local?"

"No. She was a big celebrity." He pondered for a moment. "She wrote the theme song for *SS Athenia*."

"Louisa Veldkamp? The concert pianist?" Anneliese had all her CDs stashed in a box in Noorddorp.

"That's her. She didn't play a note while she was here."

"What else do you remember?"

"The housekeeper was worried about your mother."

"Why?"

He pulled on his earlobe. "I don't recall her exact words. She said something wasn't right."

"What did she mean?"

"Maybe nothing. Bep was high most of the time."

"Are you in touch with her?"

"I've loaned her money a few times since. She still owes me."

"How do I contact her?"

He shrugged. "She finds me."

"Does she live in Den Bosch?"

"No idea."

"Last name?"

He shrugged again.

"If it comes back to you, will you call me?"

Anneliese gave him her number and watched him type it into his phone.

* * *

As the train chugged from the station, Anneliese pulled out her phone. *Yikes.* Her battery charge was down to one percent.

She tapped the words: *Louisa Veldkamp's sister.*

No matches.

She opened the entry for Louisa in Wikipedia. Conscious the battery was close to empty, she skimmed over the section "Accolades and Awards" and lingered a moment over "Mysterious Disappearance," before tearing her eyes away to "Family and Personal Life." The gist of it was she had been an only child and was survived by twin sons and a husband. Then the screen went black.

Who was the pregnant woman in Den Bosch posing as the pianist's sister?

AUGUST 2000

CHAPTER

10

Willem

A LOUD BANG.

Jurriaan's door.

Willem laid his guitar on the bed, crossed the room, and peered down the hall.

This wasn't the first time Jurriaan had slammed the bedroom door when he came home from the pool. He was taking swimming lessons for kids with special needs. Swimming wasn't easy for him. He couldn't make his limbs on one side move differently from the limbs on the other side. Like patting his head and rubbing his stomach at the same time. But he rarely got angry.

Something must have happened.

Willem knocked on Jurriaan's door.

"It's me."

"Go away."

Willem turned the knob anyway, and opened the door a crack.

Jurriaan was sitting cross-legged on the floor. He was wearing shorts and a T-shirt with "Nirvana" printed across the chest. Beside him was his backpack, a wet towel sticking out. His face was red and scrunched up.

Willem sat down next to him, their knees touching. "What's wrong?"

Jurriaan took off his glasses and wiped his eyes with the back of his hand. "I'm not going back."

"You're supposed to get your certificate in two weeks."

"I don't care."

"I thought you liked the lessons."

Jurriaan said nothing.

"Is the teacher nice?" Willem asked.

"Yes."

"Then what's the problem?"

Jurriaan's lower lip jutted out.

Willem dragged over his brother's backpack; pulled out the wet towel and bathing suit, reeking of chlorine; and dropped them on the floor. He inspected Jurriaan's goggles, the lenses still beaded with water. The house key and his swimming pass were tucked in the outside pocket. There was nothing else, nothing missing that he knew of, and nothing broken.

"Do you want me to go with you next time?"

"I told you: I'm not going back."

The doorbell rang. That would be Bas. They were going to the basketball court to shoot baskets, something else Jurriaan wasn't good at. Willem knew Katja would let Bas in, so he stayed put.

A couple of minutes later, someone knocked on the door. "Hey Jurriaan, is Willem in there?"

"Come in," Willem yelled.

Bas strolled in and with him wafted the scent of a spicy cologne. He bopped Jurriaan on the head with his fist. "Hi, dork."

"Hi," Jurriaan said, smiling a little.

Willem sat up straight. "Why did you do that?"

"I always do that when I see Jurriaan."

"Well, don't. And don't call him *dork*."

"Whatever," Bas said, and sat down cross-legged. "What's up?"

"Jurriaan wants to quit swimming lessons. He won't tell me why."

Bas looked Jurriaan over. "What happened to your knee?"

"I tripped."

Bas's forehead furrowed. "Is someone picking on you?"

Jurriaan looked down at his hands. "Two boys knocked me off my bike on my way home."

"Where?" Willem asked.

"In the park by the elephant tree."

Willem caught Bas's eye. Even though Beatrix Park was in an affluent neighborhood, it had earned a reputation, and Bas called it "Beat-Up Park."

"Who were they?" Willem asked.

"I don't know their names."

"What did they look like?"

"Don't remember."

Willem didn't know whether to believe Jurriaan.

Bas leaned forward. "Has this happened before?"

"They said I'd be sorry if I told." Jurriaan nudged his glasses higher on his nose.

"How many times?" Bas asked.

"Once. No, twice."

"Anything else?" Willem asked, his heart racing.

"They poured a can of Coke over my head."

Willem had heard enough and jumped to his feet. "Come on, Bas. Let's go get the assholes."

"Hold on. We don't know if they're still in the park. They could be in Amstelveen by now."

Amstelveen, a suburb on the other side of Ringway 10, was the absolute pits.

"They can't get away with this," Willem said.

Jurriaan reached into the drawer of his nightstand, produced a sack of licorice twists, and passed it around. Willem lowered himself to the floor, chewing thoughtfully on a red twist. Bas held one between his fingers, as if it were a cigarette, and pretended to blow smoke rings.

"I have an idea," Willem said. "When is your next lesson?"

"Thursday."

* * *

On Thursday Jurriaan reluctantly went to the pool for his lesson.

Bas lay supine on Willem's bed, his stockinged feet dangling off the end. He wore his funky blue socks with pink toes.

"Your plan sucks," Bas said. "Someone could get hurt."

"Won't happen."

"You know how you get sometimes."

"I'm cool."

"See that you stay that way."

An hour later Willem and Bas tugged on their hockey backpacks and snuck downstairs to the front door. Willem's hand was on the doorknob when Katja appeared on the stairs, wearing short shorts and eating an apple.

"Where are you going?" she asked, as if she were interested and not just keeping tabs on them.

Bas ran his hand through his hair and grinned, but she ignored him. Jeetje, Bas was girl crazy.

"Hockey training," Willem said.

"I thought training was over until September."

"This is the last time."

"I must have misunderstood." She took a bite of apple. "Dinner's at five thirty. Don't be late."

CHAPTER

11

August 2000

Willem

WILLEM AND BAS cycled down Beethovenstraat and turned onto the Princess Irenestraat that led into the park. They passed the Christus' Geboorte Church on their right and followed the trail over a bridge. The canal beneath was dark and stagnant, topped with little islands of bright green moss. After the bridge, the trail wound through a thicket of trees and bushes. They easily found Jurriaan's elephant tree, a tall beech with wrinkled gray bark. Willem and Bas hid their bicycles behind the trees and took their hockey sticks out of the bags. They crawled into the bushes close to the path. Willem checked his watch.

Something landed on his nose, and he batted it away. Bas lit a cigarette. Bas's parents and grandparents smoked, and as far as Willem could observe, so did all their relatives. Birthday parties at the Debose home were toxic.

"Want one?" Bas asked.

"No. Can you blow the smoke in another direction? It stinks."

"Not as much as your armpits."

Ten minutes dragged by. The only sound was the drone of traffic on the nearby highway.

"Where the hell is he?" Bas whispered.

Willem shrugged.

A minute later, Jurriaan appeared on the path. He rode slowly, his bicycle wobbling, while he peered into the bushes on either side.

"He's going to fall," Bas said.

"Nah. He's all right."

Willem heard the whir of spinning wheels seconds before he saw the two boys with fiendish grins on their faces. One blond and well built, the other redheaded and skinny. Both wore gleaming white trainers. Blondie kicked Jurriaan's bike, spilling him into the bushes like a sack of potting soil. The two bullies laid down their bikes in the middle of the path.

"Now!" Willem shouted.

He burst from the bushes, yelling and brandishing his hockey stick, Bas on his heels. The two bullies had such astonished faces, Willem almost laughed.

"Leave my brother alone or else."

"Or else what?" Blondie sneered.

"We'll beat your ass."

Willem and Bas brandished their sticks.

"I'm out of here," the skinny boy said, jumping on his bicycle and speeding off.

But Blondie held his ground. "Go ahead and try."

This wasn't part of the plan. Both boys were supposed to hightail it, but Blondie was spoiling for a fight, and Willem was happy to oblige.

"Your brother's a retard," Blondie said in a singsong voice. He took a few dragging steps, arms dangling by his sides, his hands flapping. Mimicking Jurriaan.

Willem tossed his stick onto the ground and punched the boy in the face. The boy yelped and stumbled back. From the corner of his eye, Willem saw Bas drop his stick and help Jurriaan up. Blondie lunged forward, grabbed Willem's waist, and knocked him off his feet. They rolled over the ground, arms flailing. When they stopped, Blondie was on top. His fist smashed into Willem's nose. Red lights flashed before Willem's eyes, and warm blood gushed over his mouth and chin. He spat into the boy's face.

Bas yanked Blondie off Willem.

Willem scrambled to his feet. His stick was too far away, and he grabbed Bas's.

"What are you doing?" Bas said.

Willem's blood pounded in his ears, and his vision narrowed. Every nerve buzzed. He couldn't stop himself, like careening downhill on a bike without brakes. He brought the stick down hard on the boy's thigh.

The boy grunted in pain and grabbed for the hockey stick. Missed by a mile.

Willem swung again, this time hitting Blondie's arm.

"Klootzak!" the boy swore, and glanced at his bicycle a few yards away. Willem raised the stick over his shoulder, both hands gripping the smooth wood, and took aim. The boy covered his head with his arms.

"Enough!" Bas yelled, grabbing the end of the stick. Willem yanked, but Bas held on tight. Willem yanked harder. They struggled, and the stick suddenly snapped in two. Willem was panting, his heart going berserk. Jurriaan tugged on Willem's elbow.

Willem jerked his arm free.

Blondie jumped on his bicycle.

"Your friend's crazy!" he shouted at Bas as he sped away, throwing a look over his shoulder before disappearing around the bend.

"For Christ's sake," Bas said, pacing in a tight circle. "You could have broken his arm. Or his head."

"Jurriaan's my brother," Willem said, his chest heaving—and he owed him.

"Idiot. No one was supposed to get hurt!"

"Do you know what's wrong with you?" Willem shouted.

"Why don't you tell me?"

"You're chicken. That's what."

Bas glared, his blue eyes turning gray, the way they did when he was really pissed off. Willem had gone too far, but he wasn't going to say *sorry*.

He clenched his jaw and crawled under the bushes to retrieve his backpack. His nose throbbed, and a red glob of blood landed on a leaf. He stuck the tip of his finger in it. The blood was cool and slimy. *Yuk.* He wiped his finger on his jeans. Louisa was away on tour, but if she somehow found out that he'd been fighting again, he was screwed. She might ground him for the rest of the summer. He seized the strap of his backpack—and Bas's too—and dragged them toward the path, the branches clawing at his hair. He stood up and brushed the dirt and twigs from his knees.

"Don't tell my mom," he said, handing Bas his backpack.

"What do you take me for? Christ!"

"Stop it! Stop!" Jurriaan screamed, clapping his hands over his ears.

Willem slung his arm around Jurriaan's shaking shoulders. "It's okay. We're just having a little argument."

"What about my hockey stick?" Bas snatched up the remains of his stick and hurled the pieces one at a time into the bushes.

"That crappy old thing?"

Bas grabbed Willem's new top-of-the-line stick and inserted it into the sleeve of his own backpack. He swung his leg over the crossbar of his bicycle. "Goodbye, Jurriaan," he said, without even a glance at Willem.

Willem watched his best friend cycle down the path and wondered how they could patch things up.

He squeezed Jurriaan's shoulder. "Those boys won't bother you again. Let's go home."

* * *

Willem hesitated before unlocking the front door. His shirt was dirty and torn, his nose caked with dried blood, and his hair tangled with twigs. After one look at him, Katja or Hendrik would know he'd been fighting.

"Jurriaan, you go inside first. Let me know where Katja and Dad are."

It seemed like forever before Jurriaan returned. "The coast is clear," he whispered. "Katja's in the kitchen, and Dad's in the workshop."

Willem closed the door softly and tiptoed upstairs. He undressed in the bathroom and took a shower, careful not to let the water hit squarely on his nose. Even a drizzle hurt. Afterward, he wiped the condensation from the mirror with his hand. His nose resembled a potato. Hendrik wouldn't notice—he never noticed anything. But Katja would. If she found out about the fight, she might tell Hendrik or even telephone Louisa. He couldn't risk it, so he had his story ready.

He slunk downstairs to the kitchen. Katja stood in front of the stove, holding the lid to a pan in one hand and a ladle in the other.

"Katja," he said, his voice nasal, as if he had a cold. He couldn't smell a thing.

The ladle clattered to the floor. "You startled me," she said, and her eyes widened. "What happened to your nose?"

"I got hit with a hockey stick."

She strolled over and peered at his nose, her green eyes squinting. She was so close his eyes crossed when he focused on her face. He had never noticed before she had freckles—on her forehead, her nose, her cheeks. Loads of them. She wore a T-shirt with a low neckline. He followed the freckles to the tops of her breasts and wondered if she had freckles everywhere. Heat rushed through his groin. He swallowed hard. This was good old Katja. Confused, he took a step backward.

"It doesn't look broken," she said.

"I don't think so either."

"The swelling isn't bad."

"No."

Her head tilted to one side. "I looked at the hockey club calendar. The season finished last week."

"Uh . . ."

"I know there wasn't a practice game either, because I phoned the hockey club."

Her steady gaze broke him.

Staring at the floor, he poured out the story—about the bullying and the ambush. He told her everything except the part about hitting Blondie with Bas's hockey stick. As the reasonable adult, Katja couldn't condone his fighting, even if she wanted to.

"The bastards," she said when he had finished.

"Am I in trouble?" he asked.

"Look at me, Willem."

He raised his eyes.

"You're a hero in my book."

He felt a grin spread across his face.

"But don't lie to me again. Deal?"

"Deal."

CHAPTER

12

August 15, 2000

Diary entry

LOUISA FLEW HOME from Madrid this morning.

We lined up in the arrivals hall at Schiphol, and she kissed each of us on the cheek. Hendrik and the boys carried her luggage while she linked her arm in mine. She told me I was glowing and asked me if I was in love. I felt my face flush. She laughed and wanted to know who the man was. Although she pressed, I repeatedly denied the existence of a lover, and she soon let the matter drop.

Louisa reeked of perfume, making me wonder if she had spilled a bottle. She combed her long blonde hair with her fingers and put on her sunglasses. In her ears were gold bangles; and around her neck, strings of colored beads. She wore a loose-fitting gypsy blouse, a maxi skirt, and black ballerinas on her feet. Heads turned as we crossed the terminal. Even if they didn't recognize Louisa, they sensed she was a star.

When we got home, she went upstairs to shower and asked me to draw the blackout curtains in her bedroom. She intended to sleep until six o'clock, at which time I should bring her dinner on a tray. Willem and Jurriaan listened to music with their headphones on, and Hendrik worked in his workshop without turning on his electric saw or drill.

As I've chronicled in this diary elsewhere, my cooking has improved with practice. I prepared a dish with chicken in almond sauce, one I had made several times for Hendrik and the boys. At six o'clock I took up her dinner with a glass of her favorite white wine. She was smiling, propped up on pillows, and motioned for me to set the tray on her bedside table.

The suffocating scent of perfume wafted up from the discarded clothes on the chair.

"Shall I open a window?" I asked.

To my amazement, her demeanor darkened. Her eyes narrowed.

"Why?"

"The room needs airing."

"Are you saying I stink?"

I was taken aback.

"No. Of course not. But the room was closed up while you were away."

"What do you smell?"

"What do I smell? The dinner," I said, sensing I shouldn't mention the perfume.

"Nothing else?"

"No, nothing," I said as convincingly as I could. "You should eat before your dinner gets cold."

She studied the tray.

"What is it?" she asked.

I described each dish.

She picked up a fork, inspected the tines, and took a bite of chicken.

"It's tough and dried out." She laid her fork on the tray.

"Is it?" I asked in surprise.

"Take the chicken away, and bring me something else."

Did she think I was room service? That I wanted to go downstairs and cook her another meal? Was she crazy? I considered telling her off, but it occurred to me she might be ill, not just exhausted. The concerns about her odor were peculiar. My intuition told me she would reject any dish I prepared. I was the nanny, the poor relative, her drudge. And I needed her more than she needed me.

"What would you like?" I asked, my voice strained.

"Something vegetarian. Soup, I think."

I had picked up the tray and turned to go when she said something I didn't catch.

"Sorry, what did you say?" I asked.

"I said . . . the cook's sister-in-law finally died. Isn't that lovely?"

"How is that lovely?"

"She's coming back to work starting tomorrow. We won't have to eat overcooked chicken with almond sauce."

I clenched my jaw but said nothing.

"Katja, darling, I have exciting news for you."

"What?" The tray was growing heavier by the second.

"My secretary quit without giving notice."

Imagine that, *I thought, but I kept my sarcasm to myself and waited for her to continue.*

"I want you to take her place for the rest of the tour. I'll pay you a salary plus expenses. And next school year, I'll arrange a lovely apartment for you. We fly to Milan in ten days."

The idea repelled me, but even as I made a mental list of my objections, a part of me realized what a fantastic opportunity it was—the chance to meet the greatest living musicians and composers, to visit Europe's top cities, to stay in five-star hotels. I knew Louisa spent most of her day practicing. She had her hair done, her makeup applied, her nails manicured, and sometimes she had a massage. On the evenings that she didn't perform, she retired early. I would have plenty of free time. That's what I told myself, because I knew I was going to accept. I don't have the backbone to stand up to my stepsister.

"Who will look after the boys?" I asked as a matter of form.

"I can't get an au pair on such short notice. Hendrik will have to do."

I pretended to give her proposal some more thought.

"All right," I said gravely.

"Wonderful. Take the tray, but leave the wine," Louisa said, yawning and settling into her pillows.

The cloying scent in the bedroom was too much. Louisa was too much. I felt queasy and hurried out the door, the dishes rattling on the tray.

NOVEMBER 2000

CHAPTER

13

Louisa

LOUISA LOUNGED ON the bed, with a blanket covering her bare feet, and the hotel phone pressed to her ear. She gazed out the window at yet another bleak day in Den Bosch. A thick fog that shifted like smoke obscured the view, but she could faintly discern a pigeon perched on the gutter across the street. The only month more depressing than November was December, when the hours of daylight shrank even more.

"I miss you too, Hendrik," Louisa purred into the phone while she fingered the necklace around her neck, a present from her lover—a gold chain with a pendant in the shape of a piano. It was a decent piece of jewelry, but not expensive enough to raise Hendrik's suspicion should he someday notice it.

"I ate my breakfast on the terrace," she said. "Can you believe it? Sunshine! I saw a patch of turquoise on the horizon. The nurse said it was the Ionian Sea. Why don't you come for the weekend? Take a break from dreary old Holland?"

She was counting on him to decline. If he said yes, she would be obliged to change his mind because she wasn't in Italy. She was nowhere near the Ionian Sea. The hotel where she was hiding was only fifty miles from Amsterdam.

"Sorry, Louisa, but it's a long drive to stay for a weekend."

He was afraid of flying. She smiled, her spirits lifting at the game she played with Hendrik.

"In that case, come for a week or two, and bring the boys." She knew she was pushing her luck, but she couldn't seem to let well enough alone. Boredom was the worst part of this elaborate charade.

"I can't take them out of school," he said. "I have an idea. Send Katja to Amsterdam to look after Willem and Jurriaan. I could come for a long stay."

Oops. Time to backpedal.

"Dear, I can't spare Katja. She's rescheduling my tour, taking phone calls, answering mail."

"Can't she work from here?"

"Not really. You know how slow the mail is. And the phone bill would go through the roof."

"Don't worry about the expense," he interrupted.

"To be honest, Hendrik, I don't know what Katja would get up to in Amsterdam if neither one of us were there to supervise."

"I think she deserves more credit than that."

"She's only nineteen. Don't you remember what that was like?"

Hendrik grunted.

He had probably been as serious and boring at Katja's age as he was at forty-two. And as boring as she herself had been, when all she had dreamed of was playing the piano.

"We can talk on the phone every day," Louisa said, to block any more talk of a trip to Catania.

"How did you sleep last night?" Hendrik asked.

"Better than the night before." The noisy Brits had vacated the room above hers, and a quiet Belgian couple had moved in. She could hear their footsteps, but not their TV. Once, she'd heard their soft Flemish accents in the stairwell.

"Did you ask the doctor when you can play the piano again?" Hendrik asked.

"He said I need complete rest for the time being." Sacrifices had to be made to ensure her anonymity. Giovanni was one of them, she thought, as she fingered the gold pendant.

"Be patient. A burnout can last for years if you don't take care of yourself. Maybe I can bring the boys during the Christmas holidays."

"Wonderful idea," she said, and made a mental note. In December she could fake a setback, and the imaginary doctor would forbid all visitors. It wouldn't be the first time she had missed spending Christmas with Hendrik and the boys.

She heard a tap at the door.

"Hendrik, I have to go. I'll call you tomorrow. Same time?"

"Okay, dear."

Louisa folded back the blanket and swung her legs over the side of the bed. Before going to the door, she reached for the bottle of perfume on her nightstand and sprayed herself. No one would ever say that she stank if she could help it.

She crossed the shabby carpet on her bare feet and tried not to think how many bare feet had trod the carpet before hers. *Filthy.* She could afford a better hotel, but this one suited her purpose. It wasn't one of the luxury hotels in the city center, where she might run into someone she knew—as unlikely as that might be in a provincial city like Den Bosch. The hotel was smallish, with five floors, four rooms to a floor. It had a glass elevator that barely fit two people if they weren't carrying any luggage. When the maid came to clean, Louisa went to Katja's room, and vice versa. They took their meals in their rooms. They spoke only to each other unless a word with an outsider was absolutely necessary. They rarely left the hotel. If the desk clerk recognized Louisa, he pretended not to.

She drew back the bolt. Katja stood in the hall, looking miserable, her coppery hair in need of washing, her face puffy and pale. Even her freckles were pale. She was wearing the same shapeless dress for the third day in a row.

"Don't just stand there," Louisa said, stepping aside to let her stepsister pass.

She shut and bolted the door.

JUNE 2024

CHAPTER

14

Anneliese

ANNELIESE TYPED THE temporary password into the library computer. While she waited for access, the memories of her student days rolled over her: the all-night parties, the pills and booze that kept her dancing, the hangovers. Thanks to a horny professor, Britta Haun, she'd earned enough credits to graduate—grades for sex, an age-old bargain, harking back to the days of the Roman Empire. Anneliese, who was straight as a pin, had looked upon the experience as a rite of passage.

Now she was free, but free to do what? Because of her pathetic GPA, her degree was worthless, and she resigned herself to scratching out a living as an office temp. Most of her earnings went toward rent and utilities. She didn't have a special boyfriend or close girlfriends. She had nothing, she had nobody, and her life was going nowhere. But she clung to the belief that if she could reunite with her biological mother and become a part of her real family, the pieces of her life would fall into place.

The library's database program was user-friendly. A few clicks located the digital archive for Dutch newspapers. She selected *De Telegraaf*, known for having more sensational reportage than the other broadsheets. She typed *Louisa Veldkamp disappearance 2004* into the search field. Dozens of articles popped up.

Anneliese started with one published the day after Louisa went missing on Wexalia. Her husband had raised the alarm when she didn't return from her morning run. A search was launched; the island scoured; her shoes found on the dunes, with her socks tucked inside. A local resident speculated that

Louisa had waded into the water and drowned. The undertow was powerful that day because of a storm in the North Sea.

An article published a week later stated that the search operation had changed from rescue to recovery, and the police were treating Louisa's disappearance as suspicious. A beachcomber was questioned. The police said he was a person of interest, which Anneliese assumed meant they didn't have enough evidence to arrest him.

The obituary didn't mention a sister.

In the local Amsterdam paper, *Het Parool*, Anneliese learned that Louisa's parents had divorced when she was three. Her mother, Gerda Martensen, was credited with shaping her daughter's career. According to *De Volkskrant*, Gerda married Leo Hart when Louisa was eighteen.

Anneliese tried American newspapers and found an obituary in the *New York Times* archives, accompanied by a photo of Louisa performing in the Lincoln Center's Alice Tully Hall. The last paragraph made her sit up.

Veldkamp is survived by husband, Hendrik Veldkamp; sons, Willem and Jurriaan; and stepsister, Katja Hart. Arrangements for a memorial service have not yet been announced.

She pushed back the chair, her heart pounding. *Not a sister*—a stepsister.

Was it possible? There could be more than one person named Katja Hart. But *the* Katja Hart was a Dutch writer who was best known for her debut novel, *The Blue Bridge*, required reading in literature classes.

She went to the ladies' room and splashed water on her face. Dazed eyes in the mirror stared back at her.

She returned to her seat and willed her trembling fingers to type *Katja Hart* in the search window.

Click, click, click.

One by one, she clicked on the links and scanned for a writer's bio. She opened a book review with a photo of Katja Hart and, underneath, her date of birth and birthplace. Anneliese did the math in her head—not her strong point. Hart's age matched that of her biological mother, but Anneliese found nothing linking her to Louisa Veldkamp until a line jumped out at her.

Hart married Hendrik Veldkamp, her stepsister's widower, in 2009, the year the pianist was declared dead.

Katja Hart was her mother.

CHAPTER

15

June 5, 2024

Diary entry

I DIDN'T THINK I would write to you again after August 2004, but something happened, and I have no one in whom I can confide.

The social worker who arranged baby Mirella's adoption wrote me a letter. Mirella wants to reunite with her biological mother. The question is: Am I willing to meet? My heart nearly stopped, and I pressed the letter to my cheek. Then I closed my eyes and inhaled, imagining the scent of a baby's talcumed skin.

Louisa always got what she wanted. It's something I both admired and hated about her. I'm still ashamed I couldn't stand up to her. She might still be alive if I had.

A hundred questions raced through my mind as I read the letter. Questions that will forever remain unanswered if I have any say in the matter. There is nothing to be gained by a reunion and everything to lose.

I must protect the others.

AUGUST 2024

CHAPTER

16

Anneliese

ANNELIESE LOCKED HER bicycle to the rack outside the building that was the former commodity exchange.

"Hey," said a girl with bottle-blonde hair and thick eyeliner. Her bubbly cheerfulness set Anneliese's teeth on edge.

"Hey. Carola, isn't it?"

"Right." Carola locked her bicycle. "Isn't Katja an amazing teacher? I've learned so much in the workshop. Are you nervous about your story?"

"No." Anneliese had never written a short story before, but she was Katja Hart's daughter, and writing must be in her genes.

"I'm afraid my story sucks. No one's read it except for my mom. She loved it, but you know how moms are."

Not all moms are created equal, Anneliese thought.

They walked together up the steps to the entrance and pushed open the heavy door. The enormous central hall was impressive with its columns and soaring ceiling. Small offices on the upper two floors opened onto a balcony that surrounded the central hall. The interior smelled musty, like old books. The geriatric elevator jerked them up to the second floor.

The others were seated at a long table: Pim, Diederik, and Saskia. A collection of manual typewriters was displayed on shelves at the back. Overflowing bookshelves lined the left wall; photos of famous writers, the right.

Katja Hart stood at the head of the table, impeccably dressed in a cream skirt suit and matching pumps. She came from a different planet than Tineke Bakker.

Anneliese had spent yesterday, the first day of the workshop, studying Katja instead of listening. They were about the same height and both petite, though Katja was curvier. Her coppery hair was pulled on top of her head, a few loose strands softly framing her face. Annelise's was black and cut in a short, blunt bob. They both had fair complexions that burned and freckled, though Katja had masses of them, and Anneliese only a scattering.

"Welcome to day two of the workshop," Katja said, nervously winding a tendril of hair around her finger. "We have a lot to do today, so let's get started." She moved around the table in a cloud of jasmine perfume and collected the stories.

"After I read a story out loud, we'll spend thirty minutes discussing it. Keep your comments constructive and specific. Remember what we discussed in the session yesterday. Don't just say you like or dislike something. Tell us why."

The room darkened and rain slashed the window as Katja read the stories and then critiqued them. Anneliese felt sick. The others were accomplished writers, not beginners like her. She wanted her turn to be over—to end her agony. She almost wept when the second-to-last piece was Carola's and not hers. Worse, Katja's voice took on an excited buzz as she read.

When she was finished, she laid the pages on the table. "Comments?"

"Wow," said Saskia, wiping away a tear.

"The death scene resonated with me," Pim said.

"The imagery helped create the mood," Diederik agreed.

All faces turned toward Anneliese. They were looking down their nose at her. Gloating. She was an imposter and didn't belong there among the real writers. Panicking, Anneliese thought back on the workshop yesterday and mumbled that the pacing was good.

When the timer went off. Katja said, "Now for our last piece."

Anneliese's face burned as soon as Katja read the opening line, which had sounded literary and profound when she wrote it, but now sounded dumb. The sentences were choppy, the dialogue stilted, and the transitions abrupt. Anneliese hummed to herself, an old trick from her childhood when she felt stressed.

Finally, Katja came to the end. "Who wants to start?"

"I don't know what the story's about," Pim said, chewing on his pencil.

In a just world, he would get lead poisoning.

"I don't think Rose would say that." Saskia pointed to dialogue on page two.

"I agree," Katja said. "An example of dialogue that's working is on page seven."

Pages rustled.

"The story doesn't get interesting until page nine," Diederik said.

"Why is that?" Katja asked.

He shrugged.

"There's too much backstory," Carola offered.

Katja pondered a moment. "If the writer starts with the action, the story would be more compelling."

Anneliese scribbled notes she didn't plan to look at again and stared at a cookie crumb on the table in front of her. She had failed. Instead of impressing Katja, she had humiliated herself.

"Thank you for attending the workshop," Katja said. "I hope to see all of you at my party next week."

Anneliese slipped away to the ladies' room to kill some time, hoping to corner Katja alone when she returned. She had expected an instant connection, a warm, cuddly mother–daughter feeling, but she had felt nothing. Katja could have been a perfect stranger. Maybe it was Katja's workshop persona getting in the way. Maybe if it were just the two of them . . . But when she came back, Katja and Carola were talking, heads together like Siamese twins.

"I know an editor at a literary magazine who might be interested in publishing your story," Katja said.

"Seriously?" Carola gushed.

"It needs editing. I can—" Katja fell silent. "Anneliese, can I help you with something?"

"No. Uh, I'll see you at the party."

She jerked on her windbreaker and crammed the copies of her story into her backpack. She dropped her pencil into the plastic container in the center of the table that held pencils, a stapler, an eraser, a pair of sharp scissors. She glanced at Katja and Carola, who looked as if they had forgotten her existence, and slipped the scissors into her pocket.

The sky was overcast, the sun only a silvery glow. Puddles stood on the pavement, though the rain had thinned to a drizzle. Two trams, packed full, trailed by.

She pulled up her hood and stomped through the puddles, the scissors banging against her side. The oncoming pedestrians gazed over her head or off to the side or at the ground. She was just a small, faceless figure. Invisible. She squatted next to Carola's bike, angling her body to shield the scissors from view, and tried to push the blades into the tire. Her hands shook. The scissors slipped. She tried again, but the blades were dull or the rubber too tough. Suddenly she heard a footstep behind her and the sound of a throat clearing. She expected a hand to grip her shoulder.

Without turning around, she put away the scissors and unlocked her own bicycle. She pedaled furiously toward home, stopping once to throw the scissors into the Herengracht and watch them vanish into the murky water.

CHAPTER

17

August 2024

Willem

WILLEM WAS WRITING the progress notes from his one o'clock session when the buzzer sounded. Frans Ringnalda's little round eyes appeared on the video screen, too close to the camera—as if he were trying to see Willem. He was always ten minutes early.

Frans suffered from general anxiety, a disorder treatable with medication, but Willem had wanted to try therapy first.

Willem pressed the button to unlatch the front door and went through the waiting room, to the hall. He allowed thirty minutes between sessions, time he used to update his notes and mentally reboot. Thirty minutes prevented patients from running into one another.

"Your office is an oasis of peace," Frans said, as he always did when he arrived for a session. He flopped into the plump Italian leather armchair facing Willem's desk.

"How have you been?" Willem asked.

"I didn't sleep much last night."

"Tell me about it."

Frans scratched at his wrists as his eyes scanned the room: the blank walls, Willem's empty desktop, the two ficus trees in bronze pots flanking the windows, and finally the ceiling. He looked everywhere but at Willem. Frans seldom made eye contact, a habit that made Willem feel invisible and unable to connect with his patient in the way he should.

"I had the dream again," Frans said, addressing one of the ficus plants. "I was driving, and the brakes failed, but I woke up before I crashed."

The dream symbolized Frans's lack of control over his life. At least he was dreaming it less often.

"How did the dream make you feel?"

"Panicky at first, but then I was okay with it."

"Why were you okay with it?"

"Suddenly I knew it was only a dream."

"How did you know?"

"It wasn't my car."

Frans explained that the car in his dream was a sporty convertible with a powerful engine, not his sort of car. In his waking life, he drove a hatchback, a hybrid. Willem turned the conversation to problems Frans was experiencing at work.

They were twenty minutes into the session when the door flew open. Willem gave a start. Frans clutched the armrests so hard his knuckles turned white.

Hendrik was standing in the doorway, dressed in baggy pajama bottoms, his skinny chest bare. The hair on his head stuck up in woolly tufts.

Willem rose. "It's okay. This is my father, Hendrik Veldkamp," he said, omitting his patient's name out of respect for his privacy.

"Pleased to meet you," Frans said, his voice warbling.

Hendrik's eyes narrowed with suspicion at the peculiar little man in the chair. Then he twirled, taking in the room. "What have you done with my workshop?" He peered closer at Willem. "Who are you?"

"Your son Willem."

"No, you're not."

Willem's hands briefly clenched. "Why did you come downstairs?"

"I'm looking for Louisa."

On most days, Hendrik was lucid. He read and comprehended scientific journals, followed the global news, and enjoyed his hobbies. He took strolls alone in Beatrix Park and found his way home. On good days, the family's secrets were safe, but his condition would worsen in time. A danger lurked in the shadowy past, drawing nearer, the risk on a bad day Hendrik might say the wrong thing to the wrong pair of ears.

"She's not here, Dad." Telling Hendrik that Louisa was dead would lead to an emotional scene he didn't want to play out in front of Frans.

Hendrik said, "I'll look in the basement."

Willem watched him shuffle from the room. When the door closed, he turned. "I apologize for the interruption."

Frans scratched his forearms.

"How do you feel about what just happened?" Willem asked.

"I think I'll go, Dr. Veldkamp." Frans rolled up his left sleeve, exposing white skin streaked with red. He was going to scratch the skin raw.

"Shall we reschedule? Same time tomorrow?"

"I'll check my agenda when I get to the office," Frans said, avoiding eye contact.

After escorting his patient to the front door, Willem walked back to his office, his fists buried in his pockets. He had probably seen the last of Frans, unless his patient complained about Willem to the Healthcare Disciplinary Board. Frans had an aversion to confrontation, but he had a history of lodging frivolous complaints about products and services. Online, of course.

Hendrik's deteriorating health was a bigger concern. They couldn't risk putting him in a care home until he could no longer communicate—a state Willem wouldn't wish on anyone.

A familiar but nearly forgotten sensation washed over him. His thoughts blanked, his skin tingled, and his chest tightened. He struggled to breathe. By the time he identified the feeling for what it was, it was too late. His foot shot out. Made contact. The wastebasket skimmed the carpet, bounced against the far wall, and rolled back a few feet.

Relief was instant. He inhaled, pulling air deep into his lungs, and exhaled slowly, the tightness letting go. He wiped sweat from his forehead with the back of his hand. But relief was short-lived, and he started shaking. He swore. He hadn't experienced a loss of control in years. *Why now, for God's sake?* Gradually the shaking subsided and his heartbeat slowed.

He retrieved the wastebasket and rotated it, looking for damage. There was only a small dent no one would notice if it faced the wall.

He collapsed in his chair and rested his head on the desk. Two years ago, the biggest hurdle to starting a private practice had been money. Around the same time, Hendrik had been diagnosed with a degenerative nerve disease. He wanted Willem close by in case Katja needed help caring for him, so he'd proposed that Willem move into the family mansion and set up his office on the ground floor.

It had seemed like a win–win situation, especially since Jurriaan lived in the neighborhood too. Hendrik paid the cost of converting the former workshop into office space and a small apartment for Willem. Hendrik and Katja had the top two floors to themselves; and Willem, the ground floor. The piano studio in the basement belonged to Louisa, as much a shrine as her empty grave in Zorgvlied cemetery. Willem had convinced himself he could handle the emotions living in the house might trigger, but now he wasn't sure.

His desk phone rang, jarring him back to the present.

"Good afternoon. Dr. Veldkamp speaking." He noticed too late that the caller was phoning from London, and he braced himself.

"Willem? This is Jeanette Bruin. Have I caught you at a bad time?"

"It's fine. A patient just left."

Dr. Bruin was Dutch. She had earned a doctorate in clinical psychology in the UK and now worked for the National Health Service. They had met at a psychiatric conference in Amsterdam a few months before. On impulse he'd invited her to dinner, drunk too much, and spent part of the night in her hotel room before he came to his senses and left. Not his finest hour.

"You sound stressed," she said in her warm, caring voice, reminding him why he had found her attractive in the first place.

"It's been one of those days. What can I do for you?" He hoped he had been clear at the hotel.

"I want to apologize about the way we parted. What I said."

Willem thought for a moment. "Do you mean about my *expletive deleted* briefcase?"

She laughed.

He hadn't blamed her for swearing; he'd deserved it and worse, but in that brief moment she had given him a peek behind the facade. He saw a side of her that made him run out of the hotel and not look back.

"Apology accepted."

A silence fell.

"You're not making this easy," she said.

"Sorry, what am I doing?" But he knew what he was doing, or rather, what he was not doing. He was not encouraging her.

"Remember the family reunion I mentioned? It's next week in Amsterdam. Will you have dinner with me on the sixteenth? Then I can apologize in person. I won't be back in town for a while."

Why couldn't she leave things the way they were? Now he had to disappoint her a second time, and he'd had his fill of disappointing people a long time ago.

"I'm sorry, Jeanette, I'm busy the whole week."

She was intelligent enough to read the subtext.

After a silence, she said, "I was afraid you might be, but you can't blame a girl for trying. Goodbye, Willem."

He heard a click.

The day could only get better, he thought, before remembering tonight was Katja's annual bash. In a moment of weakness, he had promised to attend.

CHAPTER

18

August 2024

Willem

It was five pm, and Willem's last patient for the day had left. Katja fidgeted in the chair on the other side of his desk. He had noticed a stain on her sand-colored chinos when she came into the office, and the sleeves of her knit pullover were rolled up. A band of sweat around her hairline darkened her coppery hair.

She heard him out. When he was finished, she said, "I'm sorry Hendrik barged in like that, but I can't watch him every second."

"I probably lost a patient."

Willem was angry with Katja. He was angry with her nearly all the time, though he tried not to show it because he knew he was being unfair. She was his father's wife, but she wasn't his keeper. On most days, writing demanded her total focus. And today she had been occupied with the caterers and the cleaners to prepare for the party. It had been bad luck that Hendrik was having a bad day.

"Maybe your patient won't file a complaint. Maybe he'll call to make a new appointment," she said.

"Wishful thinking."

"What do you want me to do about it?" she said testily.

"It's too late for you to do anything."

"Then you're wasting my time."

She rose to her feet. He expected her to sweep out of his office without another word, but she didn't. She stood there gazing at him, as if waiting for him to do or say something to smooth things over.

He felt ashamed of the way he had spoken to her.

He went around the desk and lightly touched her wrist, as though testing the temperature of a hot griddle. He wanted to take her hand and hold on tight. Moving into the house with her and Hendrik had been a mistake. The sexual tension between him and Katja simmered under the surface. At least, that's how he felt. Maybe it wasn't the same for her at all.

"I'm sorry I took out my frustrations on you. I've arranged for a locksmith to install a lock on the door to my office."

"Where's this hostility coming from, Willem?" She seemed genuinely puzzled.

"I've got a few things on my mind."

"Anything you want to talk about?"

"Thanks, but I have to work this out for myself." He gave her a reassuring grin.

She glanced at her watch and sighed. "I still have a ton to do before the party. You will come tonight, won't you?"

"I said I would."

CHAPTER

19

August 2024

Willem

WILLEM WAITED TO join the party until after it was in full swing. He wanted to circulate without drawing attention. He was too drained to make polite conversation with strangers, people with whom he had nothing in common: publishers, editors, novelists, poets. Bas had promised to come at ten, but there was no sign of him.

It was a balmy night, and the party was outside on the terrace. Willem drifted, a glass of jenever in his hand. He caught snatches of conversation about the demise of brick-and-mortar bookstores, the rise of self-publishing, and the popularity of eBooks.

Someone tugged at his sleeve. "Willem. How are you?"

He recognized her: a poet. She had cornered him at the party last year. He hid his irritation and pasted a smile on his face. The poet grinned wolfishly and raised her glass. After some excruciating banter, he made his excuses and joined a short line at the bar set up under a white party tent.

The woman ahead of him handed an empty wineglass to the bartender. While he uncorked a new bottle, she turned, her head swiveling on a long, delicate neck. Willem gave a small gasp. She was exquisite—small and fragile-looking, maybe twenty-five years old. She had chin-length black hair; thick bangs; and dark, almond-shaped eyes. Her lips were curved oddly, but prettily, turned up at the corners. He wanted to run his finger over those lips and feel their softness. She was dressed all in red, the color of arterial blood.

He stepped up to the bar and ordered a shot of jenever, but his eyes remained fixed on the woman, who was now on the move. He grabbed his drink and followed her into the crowd.

She stopped a few feet away from where Katja was talking to a tall man with rounded shoulders and thick white hair. The woman took a deep breath, as though gathering her courage, and joined them. Katja introduced her to the man. Willem didn't catch his name, but hers was Anneliese.

One of the caterers appeared and whispered something into Katja's ear, and she accompanied him into the house, leaving Anneliese and the white-haired man to their own devices. Willem moved closer so he could eavesdrop, but he made out only snatches of the conversation.

"Are you her husband?" she asked.

The man laughed and shook his head. "I'm an old friend."

"How long have you known her?"

"A long time," he said.

"How did you meet?"

The man clasped his hands behind his back and gave her a hard look. When he spoke, his voice was louder than before. "Are you a journalist?"

"No. I promise."

"I met Katja when she was at university."

Willem didn't know Katja was in touch with anyone from her youth, but that shouldn't surprise him. Their conversations revolved almost exclusively around Hendrik.

The old friend pointed to Anneliese's glass.

"No, thanks. I'm good," she said.

The man vanished into the crowd. Anneliese waited for five minutes, a long time to stand alone at a party, and her right leg started to jiggle. Willem figured the man wasn't coming back.

Anneliese must have drawn the same conclusion, because she marched to the bar, ordered another drink, and picked her way along the gravel path away from the house. Willem followed. She looked as attractive from behind as from the front. He liked her girlish shape, her petiteness, and her catlike grace when her heels weren't sinking and twisting in the gravel.

Halfway to the canal, the light from the hanging lanterns dissolved into darkness. Anneliese halted at the pond, which straddled the light and the dark. Willem stepped into the shadow of a tree and watched her place her glass on the low wall bordering the pond. She sat down and kicked off her shoes, twirled around on her butt, and dangled her feet in the water.

After several moments, she turned her head and stared straight at the spot where he was standing. "Is someone there?"

Willem felt like a stalker.

"Hello?" she said.

He stepped onto the path and strolled toward her. "Did I frighten you?"

"Of course not. There are fifty people only a few yards away."

She suddenly shrieked and jerked her feet from the water, wobbled precariously on her perch, and started to topple backward. He darted forward and grabbed her shoulders just in time.

"Something bit me," she said as he pulled her to her feet.

"Nibbled, you mean. I keep koi. One of them is a foot long." He dipped his hand in the pond and spread his fingers. A torpedo-shaped fish appeared and wriggled over his palm like a dog wagging its tail.

"This is Doc."

Anneliese crept closer. "Hello, Doc."

Her closeness and her husky voice made Willem's heart race. "Let me help you with your shoes." He dried off his hands on his trousers and held her elbow while she squirmed her feet into her high heels. He felt her sharp elbow joint move under velvet-smooth skin.

"Why were you lurking in the shadows?" she asked.

"Escaping, not lurking. I live here, but it's Katja's party. Her guests. My name's Willem."

She looked at him doubtfully, as if undecided whether to trust anything he said. "I'm Anneliese."

"Are you a writer?"

"A beginner. Did Katja mention me?"

"I don't remember."

Her shoulders dropped in disappointment. "And you, Willem? Are you in the writing business too?"

"No, I'm a psychiatrist."

She took a step back. "You don't look like a shrink."

"What does one look like?"

"Short, skinny, wire-rimmed glasses, a pinched face."

"That's pretty specific."

She crossed her arms across her chest. "Do you have a couch in your office?"

"No couch."

"Do you just write prescriptions?"

"I give therapy in addition to—"

She interrupted. "I don't believe in fortune tellers, escape artists, or shrinks."

"Did you have a bad experience?"

"My brother was seeing a shrink before he killed himself."

"I'm sorry for your loss."

"Thank you."

"I hope you won't hold my profession against me."

"I'll try not to." She uncrossed her arms and smiled at him.

"Can I get you another drink?" he asked.

"My glass fell into the pond."

"I'll get it out tomorrow."

"A white wine, please."

* * *

When he returned, Bas was talking to Anneliese, his hand resting on her arm as if he owned her. He was in his trademark colorful attire—opting tonight for a fuchsia shirt over blue patterned trousers. They didn't seem to notice Willem.

"Anneliese is a sweet name. Old-fashioned," Bas said. "But I bet you aren't sweet or old-fashioned. Am I right?"

Her head tilted to the side. "Bas sounds like a portly, bald-headed old man."

"Maybe, in time, I'll grow into it."

She laughed.

"If there were music, I would ask you to dance," Bas said, swaying his hips to an imaginary tune.

"I might say no."

"You would be the first," Willem said, handing Anneliese her wine.

She brushed Bas's hand from her arm and smiled at Willem.

"I could use a refill," Bas said, holding up his glass.

Willem raised his eyebrows.

"Sorry, I didn't say please, did I?"

"You know the way to the bar," Willem said firmly.

"I seem to have worn out my welcome. I'll catch up with you later." Bas winked at Willem and staggered off.

"Is he a writer?" Anneliese asked.

"No, he's an artist and my best friend."

"Then he must have some redeeming qualities."

"He does when he's sober."

She swilled down the wine as if it were water. "I saw someone at the window." She pointed to an upstairs window, the curtains drawn halfway.

"My father. He doesn't like parties."

"Parties are fine, but I prefer one-on-ones. And you, Willem?"

"I'm the same."

"Proost."

They clinked glasses. Hers was empty. He studied her for a moment. The people he met outside his therapy room fell into three categories: those who clammed up, those who at once confided their problems, and those who watched what they said, as though negotiating a mine field. He guessed Anneliese fell into the last category.

"Are you analyzing me?"

He felt his face burn. "What? No. When I'm not working, I try not to think like a psychiatrist."

Her dark, almond-shaped eyes bored into his. He felt a pull between them, a connection he couldn't explain. Then she rose on her toes and kissed him on the mouth. A feeling like an electric shock pulsed through his body.

She broke away.

"What was the kiss for?" he asked.

"I like to get the first kiss out of the way. It breaks the ice."

He liked the sound of that. "Consider the ice broken."

She began massaging her temples, a soft groan escaping her lips. "It's time for me to go."

"Let me call you a taxi. You shouldn't drive."

"No worries. I'm on my bicycle."

He watched her slim figure totter toward the house. She was tipsy, and the kiss meant nothing. She might not even remember him in the morning. *Let her go.* She was too young for him, she had a grudge against psychiatrists, his relationships always ended badly. If he did nothing to stop her, she would walk out of his life. He froze with indecision. Never seeing her again was not an option. He sprinted after her and caught hold of her arm.

"Wait. Will you have dinner with me tomorrow night?"

They agreed on eight o'clock at Antonio's, a small Italian restaurant in the neighborhood. He wanted to grab her waist and kiss her goodbye, but he was afraid of coming on too strong. It was like dancing, only the woman had to lead.

CHAPTER

20

August 2024

Anneliese

AFTER TAKING AN aspirin, Anneliese threw open the bedroom window and sucked in the fresh air.

Below, the street was empty except for a cat slinking into the bushes, probably toying with a mouse, or possibly a rat. She always felt slightly sick when she imagined that the spaces between the walls of the building were overrun by tiny squeaking creatures with quivering whiskers—their bodies full of warm blood like water balloons on legs, ready to pop.

Ignoring her headache, she sat down on the bed and opened her laptop. Katja's party had been a success, if not how she had expected. She was used to men flirting with her, but Willem was special. She had felt an immediate click.

He fit the stereotype she had in her head of a big Swede or a lumberjack. Tall, broad shoulders tapering to narrow hips, honey-blond hair, straight white teeth, but hazel eyes instead of blue. She pictured him wearing a red plaid flannel shirt. Only his profession and his weird hobby of fish-keeping struck a discordant note. His hands fascinated her, large and strong, with long fingers and short-clipped nails. Desire fluttered in her stomach.

With a gigantic effort, she pushed lovely Willem to the back of her mind. It was time to investigate Katja's old friend from her university days.

Nico *something.*

She logged into Facebook. Katja's friends numbered over two thousand. Too many to scroll through. So Anneliese typed the letters *Nic* and found a Nicolaus, a Nicole, a Nicoline, and two Nicks.

Bingo.

Nicolaus Peereboom.

He hadn't bothered to apply any privacy settings. His relationship status was *divorced*, he had two sons, and he was a retired publisher, which might explain why he and Katja had stayed in touch. His hobby was breeding Silkies, an ornamental breed of chicken. Her stomach heaved at the photos—at the dark maroon combs, exaggerated breasts, fleshy wattles.

She snapped away the photos and scrolled through Nico's posts, most posted by his two sons, who appeared to be in their early thirties. They were tall, with light brown hair. One was stocky, the other lanky like his father. Both had their father's long face. There were photos of Nico and his sons skiing and sailing, but no photos of the ex-wife. Either they had divorced in the pre-Facebook era, or Nico had been thorough in deleting her digital existence.

She considered Nicolaus Peereboom's date of birth, relationship status, the photos of his sons, the repulsive chickens. Was he a real possibility? Was she wasting her time? Her biological father might be dead. He might live in another country. If Katja knew who her baby's father was, she would have banished him as she had banished her daughter. They wouldn't be Facebook friends.

She opened a Word document with the innocuous name *Tree,* as in family tree, and started typing.

After a few lines, she stopped, suddenly remembering that Louisa Veldkamp had two sons. She thought back . . . but no . . . Willem hadn't mentioned a brother. Did he live in the mansion too? She finished typing and reread what she had written. It was disappointingly little, but she had a date with Willem tomorrow night, a chance to fill in the gaps—if she could stay on point and not be distracted by the sexy shrink.

JULY 2004

CHAPTER

21

Willem

WILLEM RECEIVED THE ball in midfield and dribbled toward the shooting circle, a Bloemendaal defender sticking to him like a shadow. The score was tied, but there were eleven minutes left in the hockey match. The game could go either way. Bloemendaal had trounced Artemis earlier in the season, the worst defeat Willem's team had experienced in the A pool. He was determined to beat them this time.

Bas, who played a forward position, appeared a few yards ahead. But before Willem could pass the ball, he felt a hard shove in the back. He stumbled wildly and a split second later crashed on his left shoulder, his hockey stick flying. The referee's whistle shrilled.

Willem opened his eyes in time to see the referee wave a yellow card at the Bloemendaal defender. Anxious faces peered down at him. An airplane roared low over the trees toward Schiphol Airport. His left arm was bent at an awkward angle under his body.

"Are you okay?" Bas asked.

Willem sat up and cautiously felt his left arm. He opened and closed his fist and bent the arm at various angles, trying hard not to let on how much it hurt.

"Is it broken?" a teammate asked.

"Come on, Willem. We need you," said the goalie.

Willem knew from experience what a broken bone felt like, and in his opinion the arm was only sprained, which was disastrous enough. He looked up at his team's anxious faces and at the ground next to their feet. Where was his stick?

Wouter, their coach, jogged up, huffing and puffing. "Can you move the arm?"

"It's fine." The last thing Willem wanted was to be benched.

"I'll help you up," Bas said, pulling him to his feet.

"Hold on, Willem. Get your arm looked at," Wouter said. "I'm bringing in Floris."

What was the coach thinking? Floris was a fast runner, but he froze up at crucial moments. Artemis needed Willem if they wanted to score in the remaining time.

"I can play," Willem said, though he wondered if he could. He'd had plenty of practice hiding injuries and pretending they didn't hurt, but how could he swing a hockey stick with only one arm?

"Floris," the coach yelled and motioned for him to enter the field.

"Floris, Floris, Floris" . . . Coach's voice echoed in Willem's head, the words swelling, growing larger until they were too big. An invisible band tightened around his chest, making it difficult to breathe.

The Bloemendaal defender watched from a few feet away, looking stupidly content with his yellow card. A lousy five-minute suspension was a small price to pay for eliminating Willem from the match. The boy looked smug and not at all sorry. Triumphant was more like it. He was tall and wiry. Fit. A fast runner. He should have run.

Willem lunged.

"No," Bas shouted, grabbing at Willem's shirttail.

Too late.

Willem reached the defender in a few strides. He couldn't stop himself. He punched the startled player in the nose. Blood gushed. Tears gushed—even more satisfying than the blood. But not satisfying enough. Willem's heart thundered in his chest, the storm roared inside his head. He barreled into the boy, knocking him backward to the ground. Willem landed on top, felt his opponent's sharp ribs. Whimpering, the boy didn't even try to defend himself. The coach bellowed. Two pairs of hands grabbed Willem before he could slug the boy again, and yanked him to his feet. He flailed and jerked, forgetting his hurt arm.

"Steady," Wouter said, his voice low with a rough edge.

The two referees held Willem fast: a wiry man who was stronger than he looked and a heavy-set woman with a grip like one of Hendrik's vises.

"For Christ's sake, Willem," Bas said, shaking his head.

Willem's arm felt suddenly as if it were on fire, and the fight whooshed out of him. The referees' hold loosened. He looked across the field at the spot where Hendrik and Jurriaan sat with the other parents behind the sideline fence, partly hidden by a banner advertising the Rabobank. Bas's girlfriend, Kara, and her friend, Deborah, stood farther back, drinking from cans. From that distance, Willem couldn't make out the spectators' expressions, but he could imagine his father's: shame.

Hendrik and Jurriaan attended all his matches. If it was a home match, the three of them cycled to the hockey club, which was next to the Amsterdam woods. If it was an away match, they went by car. Jurriaan watched from the sideline, jumping and yelling when he got excited. Hendrik always sat quietly, looking bewildered, even though he knew the rules; he had memorized the rule book. But he was more suited to chess, sometimes mulling over the board for hours before making a move. A hockey match was too fast and confusing, the swinging sticks, the ball racing along the field or bouncing off the goal posts or shooting into the net.

A man in a suit, no tie, probably the defender's father, stormed onto the field. He bellowed at the female referee, jabbing his finger in Willem's direction. Willem caught a few words: *maniac, out of control, dangerous.* She should tell him to take stock of his own kid.

She reached into her pocket and pulled out the dreaded red card, thrusting it angrily in the air. No substitute allowed. Not with a red card. The dad yelled some more, and then the referee suspended Willem from next week's match too. He felt sick when he saw the disgust on his teammates' faces. He had let them down. It wasn't fair since the other player had started it. He trudged off the field.

Play resumed, with Willem slouched on the bench, trying to act as if he didn't care about any of it.

Bloemendaal scored another goal in the last two minutes.

* * *

Willem plodded across the field to where his team huddled, listening to Wouter give the debriefing.

They had not played like a team. They had made mistakes. They had given away the ball time after time. Fighting would not be tolerated.

No one looked at Willem, not even Bas. Probably no one was more pissed off with Willem than Bas, who never got angry enough to throw a punch.

The huddle broke up, and Willem shuffled toward the gate where Hendrik and Jurriaan waited. Bas stopped to talk to Kara and Deborah, his back turned to Willem. Deborah kept peering in Willem's direction. She had red-gold hair and tan freckles like Katja. According to Bas, she had a crush on Willem. She was nice, but she giggled at everything he said, and worse, she smelled faintly of mothballs.

Willem counted himself lucky that Katja had declined his invitation to attend the match, to witness his fall from grace.

"How's the arm?" Hendrik asked.

Willem shrugged.

"You're too old to get in a fight."

Those were harsh words coming from Hendrik, and Willem's face flooded with heat.

"I didn't start it."

"You finished it, though, didn't you?"

Willem looked at Bas's back, still squarely turned toward him. Deborah's green eyes darted away.

Jurriaan slung his arm around Willem's neck. "I'm sorry that Artemis lost. Want to share my soda?"

* * *

That afternoon, Louisa summoned Willem to her piano studio.

She rose from the piano bench, smoothed her skirt, and seemed to float toward him.

Now he was in for it.

For the past six months she had been away more than she'd been home, giving concerts in North and South America, and in a few days, she was leaving to teach summer school in Italy at Lake Como. If only she had left a few days earlier, or the hockey match had been a few days later.

She stood silently before Willem, their eyes almost level with each other's. He was now taller than she was, which made him feel . . . He searched for the word: *empowered*.

"I guess Dad told you what happened." Willem's voice cracked despite his newfound bravado.

"He should have, but the coach called me."

Good old Wouter. He had wasted no time.

"They want you to write a letter to the disciplinary committee, giving your side of the incident. They might expel you from the club."

"They can't do that." *Or could they?* His heart beat wildly.

Louisa shrugged. "Take it up with Hendrik. He knows the rules better than anyone."

Willem tried to imagine life without hockey: the afternoons of practice gone, the Saturday matches gone, his teammates gone. Bas gone.

"Which arm is it?" Louisa asked.

His mouth went dry. "My left."

He tensed as her fingers lightly brushed his forearm. After a few moments, her hand dropped to her side.

"Willem, dear, as I've said countless times, when you misbehave it reflects on the family. What will people think when they read *Louisa Veldkamp* on the posters outside the concert hall? Will they think about the greatest living pianist or about an out-of-control teenager?"

"Mom, no one will—"

"Besides, these phone calls disturb my concentration."

She made it sound as if she got such calls all the time.

"I couldn't help it—"

"Save it, Willem."

"I'm trying to explain. Sometimes I get so angry, it takes over—or wants to." He paused and scanned her face, searching for a gleam of understanding, but her expression was immobile, like wax. Still, he pressed on. He had something to say and was determined to get it off his chest. "When that happens, I do bad stuff. Stuff I can barely remember doing. Like a dream, kind of. Afterward, I feel better. Normal. And I'm sorry afterward, you know, for what I did. Don't you ever feel that way?"

She gave him an icy glare.

"Definitely not, Willem."

His heart sank. He had been stupid to think she would admit to a weakness or help him.

"Take off your shirt," she said.

"What for?"

"I want to take a look at your injuries."

"I'm fine, Mom. Really."

"I'll help you."

She had that I-won't-take-no-for-an-answer tone. He let her pull the T-shirt over his head. Her eyes ran over his shoulder and down his arm. He flinched when she poked at a rib, but there was nothing to see except for a red streak: no bruises or swelling. Not even a scratch.

"This might hurt a little. I'm going to check if your bone is broken." She squeezed his forearm, at first gently—then her grip tightened.

"Jeetje, Mom," he said, dancing away. "May I go now?"

"I'm not done." She grabbed hold of his arm again.

He yanked free and strode to the door, afraid of what he might do if he stayed even a second longer.

CHAPTER 22

July 2004

Willem

WILLEM TOOK THREE plates from the kitchen cabinet while Jurriaan set the paper bags from the snack bar on the table.

Louisa was humming "Für Elise," somehow making Beethoven's famous Bagatelle sound ominous. She grabbed a fistful of cutlery from a drawer and waltzed across the room. *Weird.* The last time he saw her wound up like this was when she was short-listed for the Royal Philharmonic Society's Gold Medal. They had all breathed a little easier when she'd won.

She was flying tomorrow to Lake Como to teach summer school. Tomorrow couldn't come fast enough for Willem, but first he had to survive the evening. His bad news could wait until the others were downstairs; there was safety in numbers.

Willem opened the bags: friet, kroketten, and frikandellen—the deep-fried, skinless sausages that Jurriaan loved. The salty, greasy smell of the fast food filled the kitchen.

Hendrik came in, a piece of tissue stuck to his face where he'd cut himself shaving. He wore the navy blazer that Louisa had given him for his birthday, and beige chinos. He walked over to the wine rack, shaped like a honeycomb, and chose a bottle of red. He found the corkscrew, grabbed two glasses, and sat down at the table.

"Boys, your food's getting cold," Hendrik said, uncorking the bottle. He and Louisa were going to a fancy restaurant, and the cook had the night off.

Louisa picked the piece of tissue off his face. "I told Katja to be downstairs at six thirty. Late as usual. I wish she would show some common courtesy. Not to mention gratitude for the free room and board."

Willem rolled his eyes at the familiar refrain. She had cut off Katja's allowance when she graduated from university a few weeks before, forcing her to give up her apartment.

Katja stormed into the kitchen, her green eyes blazing. "By my watch, I'm two minutes early. And I'll move out as soon as I get a job."

Willem's eyes darted to Katja's breasts, prominently defined under her white knit top, then took in the rest. Her copper hair hung in fluffy waves to her shoulders. She wore a short skirt and white sandals, the platform heels accenting the lovely curves of her calves. Bas would have given a wolf whistle, but Willem just swallowed the sudden lump in his throat.

"Don't expect a job to fall into your lap. You have to put yourself out there," Louisa said.

Hendrik twisted around in his chair. "Katja, you look gorgeous."

"Wow," Jurriaan said, and giggled.

Louisa's face darkened.

Hendrik reached for her hand. "You look beautiful too."

Too little, too late, Willem thought. Maybe it would be better if he told her his news on the telephone, when she was far away in Lake Como.

"Everyone, sit down," Louisa snapped, taking the seat at the head of the table, leaving the chair between her and Hendrik empty. Willem and Jurriaan sat on her left, and Katja took the empty chair.

Willem bit into a kroket and watched his father pour a glass of wine and pass it over Katja's plate to Louisa.

"I want to make a toast. To Lake Como!" Hendrik said, and clicked glasses with Louisa, inches from Katja's nose. Louisa gave a tight smile.

Katja shook some friet onto her plate.

Louisa picked up the squeeze bottle of curry ketchup. "Ketchup?"

Willem's breath caught as she aimed the spout at Katja, like a gun.

"No, just mayonnaise."

Jurriaan handed Katja the jar.

Willem grabbed the ketchup from Louisa, squirted some on his plate, and set the bottle out of her reach, at the other end of the table.

"Where are you and your date going?" Louisa asked, eyeing Katja over the top of her glass.

"To a film."

"Which film?"

"Does it matter?"

Louisa's jaw tightened. "Don't forget I'm leaving early in the morning. Don't stay out late."

A silence fell. Hendrik swirled the wine in his glass. Jurriaan buried his frikandel under a blanket of ketchup. Katja nibbled on a friet.

Willem couldn't help comparing Katja's bare freckled face with Louisa's painted one. Katja had long eyelashes and impossibly green eyes. She wore small gold loops in her ears. Even her ear lobes were freckled.

Louisa's blue eyes were framed by harsh black lines and spiky black lashes. Around her neck was the ugly necklace she never took off, the pendant, shaped like a grand piano, dangling in her cleavage.

"Who's the lucky fellow, Katja?" Hendrik asked.

Katja dipped a friet into mayonnaise. "If you mean my date, he's a friend from university."

"Doesn't he have a name?" Louisa said.

"Of course, but you don't know him."

"Why doesn't he pick you up at the house?"

"It's easier to meet at the venue."

"Call him. Tell him to come to the house so we can meet him," Louisa said.

Willem had to admit he was curious about her date too. He felt something else as well. He was on Katja's side—always on her side against Louisa—but part of him didn't want her to go out with this fellow, whoever he was.

"I'm twenty-three, not sixteen," Katja said.

Willem felt as if she had punched him in the gut. He was sixteen. Seventeen next month. Did Katja think he was a kid?

"I never get to meet any of your friends," Louisa said.

"If you were home more often, you might," Katja said.

Willem choked on a bite of kroket, his mouth gone dry. Jurriaan stared at the pale sausage on his plate. Hendrik topped up his glass.

"May I be excused? I don't want to be late." Katja laid down her fork, most of her friet uneaten, and waited for permission.

Louisa acted as though she hadn't heard. She downed her wine. "Hendrik, more, please."

He took her glass, filled it, and held it out over Katja's plate.

Louisa reached for the wine, her long fingers wrapping around the stem. The glass tilted. In a split second, a full glass of red wine splashed down the front of Katja's white top. She scraped back her chair and jumped up, her face flushed with fury. Willem couldn't be sure that Louisa had spilled the wine on purpose, but he wouldn't put it past her.

"Oh, Katja. I'm sorry," Louisa said, trying to hide a smirk as she sauntered to the kitchen sink. She grabbed a dish cloth and dabbed at the stains on Katja's top.

"Stop it, Louisa. It won't come out." Katja yanked the dish cloth from her stepsister's hand, wadded it into a ball, and hurled it onto the table.

"A shame about the top," Hendrik said, rising to his feet.

"Yes, isn't it?" Katja gave a disgusted snort and went upstairs to change.

Louisa sat down, her mouth twisting at the corners, looking pleased with herself while trying not to. "Jurriaan, give me your plate." She scraped Katja's friet onto his plate and handed it back to him.

"Waste not, want not," Hendrik said as he lowered himself into his chair.

Willem took a bite of his half-eaten kroket, then put it down. It was soggy and cold, but it didn't matter because he had lost his appetite anyway. A silence settled as Louisa and Hendrik drank wine and Jurriaan crammed one friet after another into his mouth.

After a few minutes, the front door slammed.

"How rude," Louisa said. "She didn't say goodbye."

"Jeetje, Mom, what do you expect? You ruined her T-shirt," Willem blurted out.

Louisa ignored Willem and shot Hendrik a look. "She acts like I spilled the wine on purpose."

"Of course not. It was an accident, and entirely my fault," Hendrik said on cue.

Smiling, Louisa leaned back, relaxed and in control again. "Hendrik, we need to leave or we'll be late to the restaurant. Willem, you have cleanup duty tonight."

"I'll help," Jurriaan said in a small voice.

Willem decided that his bad news could wait, having learned from experience that timing was everything.

CHAPTER

23

July 2004

Louisa

Louisa traveled so often that she packed on autopilot, which meant she might forget something important. She ticked off the items on her checklist: sedatives, earplugs, birth control pills.

Her two enormous suitcases lay open on the king-size bed. She was going to teach at a summer school for gifted young pianists. Willem should have been one of them, but after the little incident with the metronome, he had refused to take another lesson. She had tried everything—beaten him, starved him, locked him in the studio. Nothing worked. He was stubborn, and now it was much too late. His talent was dead on the vine.

A faint rustling reminded her that Katja was lounging in the window seat like a sulky teenager. Her face was pale and her eyelids were swollen with sleep.

"Get your feet off the cushion," Louisa snapped.

Katja gave a jolt and took her time unfolding her legs.

Louisa placed her hands on her hips. "If something's the matter, spit it out."

Katja blew out her breath in an exaggerated huff.

Louisa said, "I didn't spill the wine on purpose."

"I don't believe you."

"There's nothing I can do about that."

"My top is ruined."

"Buy a new one." Louisa rummaged in her large designer handbag, pulled out a fistful of bills, and tossed them into Katja's lap.

The bills lay there for a minute. She counted them and shoved them into the pocket of her shorts. "You treat me like a servant."

"I don't."

"You expect me to cook and clean at the summerhouse."

"It's not as if you were otherwise gainfully employed."

"A job will turn up."

"You can always come work for me. You must know, Katja, how fond I am of you."

"I guess."

Louisa slipped a blue silk dress from its hanger and held it against her chest. "Do you think Roberto will like it?"

She knew Katja's answer would be yes. The fabric's rich shade of blue enhanced the color of her eyes. Roberto said that he could swim in her eyes, that they were twin azure seas. She smiled at the memory.

"Who's Roberto?"

"He's the good-looking bass player I met in Madrid."

"What happened to Giovanni?"

"That's finished," Louisa said, turning away because she didn't want Katja's pity. She folded the blue dress and laid it carefully in the suitcase that still had free space.

"Since when?"

"A while ago. He wants to work on his marriage." Louisa didn't know if that was the truth or if he had found someone new, someone younger.

"You're still wearing the necklace he gave you."

Louisa reached up and fingered the gold piano pendant. Giovanni had commissioned a jeweler in Milan to design it especially for her. "I like it. That's all," she said, forcing a light tone.

"Is Roberto going to Lake Como too?" Katja asked, switching subjects.

"For a few days."

Katja frowned her disapproval.

"What?" Louisa demanded.

"Hendrik will be devastated if he finds out."

"He won't find out."

Katja's loyalty to Hendrik was annoying, but it was a loyalty that had limits. Katja would never betray her. They had too much dirt on each other. Even as a child, Katja had been a sneaky little thing. She listened at doors, eavesdropped on conversations, and scribbled away in her notebooks as if she were recording it all for posterity. Louisa had searched countless times for the notebooks, but she'd never discovered their hiding place. She felt queasy whenever she imagined a tabloid reporter getting hold of them.

"Be a doll, Katja, and close the suitcases." Brushing her hair with an ornate silver hairbrush, Louisa glided to the door. "Willem! Jurriaan! Come here."

A minute later, Willem knocked on the doorjamb, Jurriaan close behind, stepping on his brother's heels. Jurriaan eyed the hairbrush warily. She felt a stab in the heart. He had no reason to be afraid of her. She had never hit him or even yelled at him. By the time Jurriaan was nine months old, it was clear something was dreadfully wrong. He didn't turn over or sit up when he should have, whereas Willem met his developmental milestones early.

She had sued the doctor and the hospital for malpractice but lost the case. The judge ruled Jurriaan's disabilities were because of an unpreventable accident at birth. It was a terrible blow. Louisa Veldkamp was a winner, not a loser, and the defeat begged the question: Whose fault was it?

The fact was, she had failed to deliver Jurriaan safely into the world, and he could never reach the promise locked in his genes. But he was sweet and gentle and always did his best, which was more than she could say for Willem. She tucked the hairbrush into her carry-on bag, smiled at Jurriaan, and clapped her hands.

"Okay, boys. Take my suitcases downstairs, and tell your father the taxi will be here in five minutes."

* * *

Downstairs, Hendrik, Katja, and the boys lined up behind the suitcases.

Louisa smoothed her skirt before speaking. "Katja will be in charge of housekeeping. I'll join you at the summerhouse on the fifteenth of August."

Hendrik's mop of thick black hair looked like a wig, but it was all his and firmly rooted to his scalp. He stepped forward and pecked her cheek, his lips cool and dry, reminding her of last night's obligatory lovemaking. For a moment, she indulged in the memory of Roberto's hot, greedy mouth on hers and his strong, youthful body.

"Have a safe trip," he said.

Katja inspected the green polish on her fingernails, her chin tucked into her neck. Jurriaan gave Louisa a fierce hug. Willem kissed her cheek and stepped back in line, like a soldier giving a salute. She studied him and was gratified her gaze could still make him squirm. Was Willem glad she was going away for a month? Maybe *ecstatic* was the right word. Teenagers were programmed to hate their mothers—something to do with DNA, hormones, and undeveloped brains. She was sure that one day he would come to appreciate his strict upbringing. Boys needed a firm hand, and Hendrik wasn't up to it.

CHAPTER

24

July 15, 2004

Diary entry

Who does Louisa think she is? Why do I tolerate her behavior and keep her sleazy secrets?

Get a friend! I want to shout at her. Instead, I sulk. The Veldkamps are the only family I have, and I'm dependent on Louisa until I land a job. She's right about one thing: jobs in journalism are scarce, and the handful of pieces I sell as a freelancer earn only token amounts.

Those were my thoughts tonight while I waited furtively in the darkest corner of the hotel bar.

He had been late once or twice before, held up by traffic, the A2 backed up to Abcoude. He stood me up twice—once because his youngest son fell ill with a high fever, and another time because his wife surprised him with a babysitter and dinner reservations. He swore she gave him no opportunity to pick up a phone and let me know.

I'm sick of the whole thing. I'm no better than Louisa. The sneaking around, the lying, and the secrets, not to mention the lonely times between assignations. He'll never leave his wife—and rightly so. It was time to acknowledge my shame. I ordered another glass of wine and tossed it back in a few big gulps.

I couldn't do this any longer. It was a revelation and a liberation.

After paying the bar bill, I made my way through the dimly lit lobby, dotted with plush chairs and low tables, the scent of potpourri mingling with cigarette smoke. I pushed through the revolving doors and strode down the sidewalk to my bicycle, parked half a block away. I bent down to unlock it, and as I straightened up, I spotted his lanky figure running toward the hotel's entrance. I felt gutted. How could I live without him . . . without the moments of joy? I stood there frozen for what seemed like ages but might have been only a minute.

CHAPTER

25

July 2004

Willem

WILLEM SLID A bottle of beer across the kitchen table to Bas. Jurriaan, who was sipping Coke through a straw, pored over pictures in a book about cats, but Willem could tell by the tilt of his head that he was listening to their conversation. Jurriaan missed little.

"To Wexalia," Bas said, and chugged some beer.

He was going with them to the summerhouse. The holiday promised to be the best ever because they were both old enough to drink beer legally, and they both wanted to see Katja in a bikini.

She had gone out with her secret friend again, someone whose face Willem had never seen and whose name he didn't know. A burning sensation filled his chest. How long had she known this mysterious friend? Were they in love? Maybe they were having sex at this very moment.

"We could kick a ball around at the sports field," Bas said.

Willem grunted.

"I take that for a no. How about a movie? The video shop is still open," Bas said.

"Nah. I'm not in the mood."

"What *are* you in the mood for?"

Good question. Louisa was at Lake Como by now, and Hendrik was in bed. Willem could come and go as he pleased, but to do what? A boring evening stretched out before him. He twirled the lukewarm bottle of beer. An idea struck him, though he doubted Bas would go along with it.

Willem said, "We could go for a drive."
"What are you talking about?" Bas asked, his eyes narrowing.
"We can take Dad's car."
"Sneak out?"
"Yep."
Jurriaan's head jerked up.
"But you don't know how to drive," Bas said.
"I've watched Dad drive plenty of times. There's nothing to it."
"Do you know the traffic rules?"
"Hold that thought."

Willem ran upstairs but stopped when he reached the landing. He peered down the hall. After checking that the light in his parents' bedroom was out, he tiptoed to his own room, reached under the bed, and returned to the kitchen with a well-thumbed book.

"I've memorized everything. Ask me a question," he said, and handed the book to his friend.

Bas flipped through the pages. "What does this mean?" he asked, pointing to a traffic sign.

"No access to vehicles with more than two wheels."
"And this?" Bas pointed to another.
"No passing."

Bas quizzed Willem for a few minutes without catching him in a single mistake.

"What do you think? Are you in?" Willem asked.
Bas tossed the book onto the table. "You've been drinking."
"Only a few sips." Willem held up his bottle as proof.
"We'll be screwed if your father finds out."
"He's asleep. He'll never know we were gone."
"You're already in deep shit with your parents."

By *shit* he meant being expelled from the hockey club. As requested, Willem had written a letter to the disciplinary committee, giving his side of the incident behind the red card. He described the Bloemendaal defender's provocation. He expressed his deep remorse and closed with the heartfelt promise never to hit anyone ever again, on or off the hockey field. But his letter wasn't persuasive enough. The phone call—a heads-up—came two days ago. A formal letter was underway.

"I haven't told Mom."
Bas groaned. "Why not?"
"I haven't found the right time."
"There'll never be a right time."

"I'll call her from the summerhouse."

"What if she reads the letter first?"

"The letter will come here, and she's in Italy." Willem grinned. All his bases were covered. "What about going for a drive?"

"I don't know, Will."

"Nothing will happen."

Bas squeezed his eyebrows together. "I guess so. Just around the block."

Willem beamed and turned to Jurriaan. "Hey, twinnie. Are you in?"

Jurriaan closed the cat book.

"Sure."

* * *

The inside of the garage was thick with the smell of diesel. Willem unlocked the Mercedes with the spare key and pointed the remote control at the overhead door. Bas climbed into the front passenger seat, and Jurriaan into the back.

Reversing down the driveway proved more challenging than Willem had expected.

"You're too far to the right!" Bas screamed.

Willem turned the steering wheel.

"No, turn it the other way."

Jurriaan's scared face appeared in the rearview mirror, and Willem gave him what he hoped was a reassuring smile.

After more zigzagging, they reached the end of the driveway.

"Is anything coming?" Willem asked.

Bas's head swiveled. "All clear."

Willem backed into the street. Twilight had fallen. The evening was soft around the edges, though still muggy. Nervous sweat streamed into his eyes.

"Bas, turn on the air conditioner."

Seconds later, refreshing cold air hit Willem's face.

Driving forward proved easier, and he stopped overcorrecting. He felt indestructible, as if he were driving a tank behind enemy lines and meeting little resistance. It was a Tuesday night, not a weekend, when there would have been more cyclists and cars on the road. They crawled along the Apollolaan, and soon Willem noticed a car tailgating them.

"Is that a cop behind us?" Willem asked.

Bas looked over his shoulder. "No, but speed up. You're driving too slow."

Willem sped up, but he was careful not to exceed the speed limit.

"Turn on the headlamps," Bas said.

"I don't know how."

"Pull over."

Willem pulled over, the wheels scraping the curb, and the other car roared past. Bas took the handbook from the glove compartment, and together they figured out how to turn on the headlamps.

"Maybe we should go home," Jurriaan said, poking his head over the center console.

"I'm just getting the hang of it."

"I thought we were only going to drive around the block," Bas said.

"It's up to you guys. Go home or go to the Amsterdam woods?"

"Is it open at night?" Bas asked.

"There's one way to find out."

"Can we go home after that?" Jurriaan asked.

"Yes. I promise."

"Oh, all right," Bas said.

They passed the Olympic stadium, its tall tower black against the fading sky, and drove under the Ring 10 overpass. Trees lined both sides of the street, deepening the night. There was little traffic, and they reached the turnoff for the park in a few minutes. The park was open in the sense that it wasn't enclosed by a fence or blocked by a barrier, but there wasn't much to see other than shadowy woods and the gleam of the rowing lake.

"Let's not press our luck. We should go back," Bas said.

Willem turned the car around.

* * *

His stomach sank when the mansion came into view. The windows upstairs and downstairs were ablaze with lights. As he drove into the driveway, the front door flew open, and Hendrik stepped outside, the cordless phone pressed against his ear. The door to the garage gaped wide. Willem inched the Mercedes inside, but his leg was shaking so hard his foot slipped off the brake pedal and the bumper hit the back wall. The three of them piled out. There was a sour taste in his mouth.

He could hear Hendrik talking on the phone. "It's okay, Louisa. They're back, the three of them. Yes. Okay, I'll tell him." He ended the call.

"Sorry, Dad," Willem said.

"Have you done this before, son?"

"No, never. I swear."

Bas and Jurriaan shook their heads no in unison.

"You were lucky you didn't have an accident. You could have killed someone." Hendrik turned to Bas. "I'm sorry to have to tell you, but you're no longer welcome to go with us to Wexalia."

Bas's face twisted in panic. "I understand, Mr. Veldkamp. Honestly, I do. We broke your trust. What we did was irresponsible, but I promise not to do something like that again."

"You can't uninvite him," Willem blurted out. "His parents are going on holiday, just the two of them. It's their twenty-year wedding anniversary. They've been planning the trip for months. Ground us at the summerhouse, give us chores, but let Bas come with us."

Hendrik nodded thoughtfully, and Willem's heart soared with hope. He knew it was Louisa's idea to ban Bas; for some reason, she had it in for his best friend. Hendrik redialed. When he had her on the phone, he explained about the Deboses' holiday plans and laid out a convincing argument on Bas's behalf. Then the call went sour.

"But, Louisa . . . Yes, I know. But Bas's parents have been planning . . . No, you're right. It's not our problem."

Hendrik hung up and stared at the phone before turning to Bas.

"We're sorry for the inconvenience to Mr. and Mrs. Debose, but what you boys did was illegal and dangerous. Go home and explain things to your parents. If they have questions, they can call me."

"Yes, sir," Bas said, his feet kicking at the ground.

Willem wondered if Bas would tell his parents that he wasn't going on holiday with the Veldkamps, or if he would let them depart in ignorant bliss while he stayed home alone. The rest of the summer was ruined, and Willem knew it was his own fault.

"Willem?"

"Yes, Dad."

"Your mother will deal with you at the summerhouse."

Shit. A whole month! He should have already told her about being kicked off the hockey team. The list of grievances was growing. No telling how long it would be in a month. He bunched his fists and wanted to hit someone, but the person he wanted to hit was hundreds of miles away.

AUGUST 2024

CHAPTER

26

Willem

WILLEM LAID DOWN the menu and looked at his watch.

"Are you ready to order?" the waitress asked, pushing her flaxen hair behind an ear with creepily long fingers—long fingers like Louisa's. He self-consciously dropped his own hands out of sight under the table.

"Not yet. I'm waiting for someone."

"No problem, sir."

Anneliese might have forgotten their date or changed her mind. Maybe she was simply running late. He took out his phone, stared at it for a few moments, and shoved it back into his pocket. Calling might make him come across as anxious.

Laughter and clapping erupted at a long table in the back. It was a family dinner, judging by the ages, ranging from a baby to an elderly man in a wheelchair.

Five more minutes. If Anneliese didn't show up or phone by eight thirty, he would leave.

Black-and-white photos of Sophia Loren hung on the walls. Candles flickered in glass holders. The decor was romantic without being formal. The restaurant was perfect for a first date—if she showed up.

At one minute past the deadline, Anneliese walked through the door, and their eyes met. He couldn't move, or even breathe. The din of the restaurant died. She drifted toward him in a thin white blouse over black velvet palazzo pants.

He rose to his feet and pulled out a chair.

"Sorry I'm late."

"Apology accepted," he said, willing to forgive her anything now that she was here.

She gave him a shy smile. "I drank too much last night."

"It was a party."

"I insulted your profession."

"No offense taken."

She sat down, and they ordered dinner and a bottle of Italian red.

The conversation wound around safe subjects. She was vegetarian—not on moral or environmental grounds, but because she disliked the taste of meat. He craved a good steak once or twice a week. They both liked art-house films and classic rock. Her dark eyes widened and narrowed as she spoke, like punctuation marks. Her left front tooth had a slightly jagged edge.

Halfway through their second bottle, the infant at the table in the back started screaming. A woman jumped up, clapped the baby over her shoulder, and jogged toward the restroom. A face at the big table caught Willem's eye: Dr. Jeanette Bruin. Willem wanted to sink through his chair, but he gave a polite nod and cursed to himself. This was the family reunion she had mentioned.

"See someone you know?" Anneliese asked.

"An acquaintance."

He recalled their evening together after the conference had ended. If only he had left it at drinks in the hotel bar or dinner at the Indonesian restaurant. He shouldn't have gone back to her room and raised her expectations. She was a sensitive, intelligent woman, and he had wounded her, his honesty too late, the timing brutal. The least he could have done was have dinner with her this week and parted as respected colleagues.

Over tiramisu and coffee, Anneliese giggled and laid down her spoon. "I've drunk too much again."

She must know he was smitten; he felt transparent. "It was excellent wine," he said.

"There's something I want to ask you."

He smiled. "Anything."

"Was Louisa Veldkamp, the pianist, your mother?"

His smile slipped. No one had asked him the question in years. "Yes, she was."

"Did they ever find her?"

"No, her body was swept out to sea."

"I'm sorry." She twisted the corner of her napkin. "My first piano book was *Veldkamp's Piano for Beginners, Level 1.* I completed all the lessons through level twelve."

"Do you still play?"

"No. Not in years."

"And now you're a beginner writer," he said, remembering their conversation at Katja's party.

"Yes, but writing is harder work than I ever imagined. I might give it up."

He laughed.

"Are you and Katja close?" Anneliese asked.

"Not especially."

"But she's married to your father."

"That's true."

She looked at him with dark, unblinking eyes.

"Is there something you want to know about Katja?" he asked.

"She's a wonderful writer. I want to know everything."

He laughed. "I'll answer three questions."

Anneliese chewed on her lip. "In the workshop, she said a writer needs a trusted first reader. Who is hers?"

"Hendrik, I guess. She dedicated *The Blue Bridge* to him, and she always thanks him for his support in the acknowledgments at the back of her novels." Hendrik believed in and encouraged Katja, maybe the reason she married him. Of course, the Veldkamp money may have entered the equation too.

Anneliese pondered for a few moments. "Does she have any children?"

He fell silent, recalling Anneliese's grilling of Katja's old friend from her university days. Privacy was important to the family, not just to Katja. He felt himself close up.

"No," he said at last.

"Why not?"

"I don't know. You'll have to ask her."

"Since you didn't answer my last question, I get another one."

"But I did answer. Now it's my turn."

She grinned. "That's fair."

"Tell me about your childhood."

"There's nothing much to tell. I grew up in a village in Drenthe. Neighbors looked out for one another. Kids walked to school, even the younger ones. There was a forest to explore. Clean air. Plenty of kids to play with. Soccer teams. Horseback riding."

"Sounds idyllic."

Anneliese smiled, the candlelight glinting off the front tooth with the jagged edge.

Just then, Willem saw the diners at the big table stand up and move toward the entrance—except for one. He swore under his breath as Jeanette weaved unsteadily around the tables toward him. In his memory, she was an attractive woman with short blonde hair and a lush figure, but tonight she looked untidy and middle-aged.

She loomed drunkenly over them, her thighs pressing against the edge of the table.

"Hello, Willem. What a coincidence," she said, her voice slurred. Her gold choker fit snugly into the folds of her neck and her dress strained across her breasts and hips.

"Was the family reunion a success?" he asked.

"Yes, thank you for recommending the restaurant."

"I did?"

"Yes, in the hotel bar. That was a lovely night. Too bad about the next morning. No hard feelings. Eh?"

Willem forced a smile.

"Who's your little friend?" Jeanette asked, her condescending tone reminding him of Louisa.

"Anneliese, meet Jeanette Bruin. Jeanette is a psychotherapist in London."

"It's *Dr.* Bruin. And what do you do, honey?" Jeanette asked.

"I'm a novelist."

Willem straightened up.

"You look too young to be a novelist," Jeanette said.

"You sound like my mother. She says anyone under thirty looks like a teenager."

Jeanette's face reddened.

Willem was almost amused—but not quite—by the women's jabs at each other. He glanced toward the entrance, hoping Jeanette's family would come to the rescue, and was relieved to see the woman with the baby, waving.

"Jeanette, a woman's trying to get your attention."

She turned. "My sister. I have to go. Willem, call me."

"I will," he said, so she could save face.

As soon as she departed, the waitress approached and announced the kitchen was closing. Willem paid the bill, and they walked outside into the cool night air.

"Why did you say you were a novelist?" Willem asked.

"She was so full of herself. How do you know her?"

"We met at a mental health care conference."

"Are you two . . . together?"

"No."

"That's my bicycle," Anneliese said, pointing to a rusty heap with a warped basket on the front.

"I'll ride with you."

"You don't have to. My apartment is just on the other side of the Rijnstraat."

"I want to make sure you get home safely."

* * *

Willem wondered if he should kiss her or not, whether she would invite him inside, and what might happen if she did. He thought of Jeanette and their drunken love-making, the tumble of limbs and soft flesh—satisfying a physical need, but little more. He didn't want it to be like that with Anneliese.

Her street was lined with acacia trees. The old apartment buildings had tiny windows, arched doorways, and geometric architectural elements. After she locked her bicycle, he walked her to the front door, where they stood staring at each other for a few moments. The urgency between them was tangible. His heart pounded. Just when he leaned forward to kiss her, she thanked him for dinner, stepped over the threshold, and closed the door.

He gaped at the solid-looking hardwood door a few inches from his face. Six tiny windows at the top and a vent at the bottom. Behind it would be a steep staircase rising to the upper floors. He had seen dozens of apartments in buildings like this one. Was Anneliese jealous of Jeanette? Did she feel insecure because she didn't have letters after her name?

He retreated to the sidewalk, where he peered up at the building and waited. A few seconds later, a window on the third floor lit up.

* * *

He cycled along the Churchilllaan, brooding over Jeanette Bruin. She didn't handle rejection well, and he was partly to blame. He would call her when she was back in London, and apologize.

He cycled past the darkened sports complex and stopped at the traffic light that was blinking yellow.

His thoughts turned to Anneliese's idyllic childhood in a village with ordinary, middle-class parents. The picture she had painted was too rosy, or maybe he was projecting, because his own childhood had ended in a nightmare. Then it came to him. Anneliese hadn't mentioned the brother who had killed himself while under a psychiatrist's care. She had a secret. In his experience, most people did.

His phone vibrated in his pocket. Not a patient at this hour, he hoped, but he couldn't answer fast enough when he saw the caller ID.

"Jurriaan? Are you okay?"

"The window," he sobbed.

"What about it?"

"They broke it."

"I'll be there in ten."

CHAPTER

27

August 2024

Willem

JURRIAAN'S LIVING ROOM window was shattered in a thousand pieces but held together inside the frame. There was an obvious impact point, with circular cracks radiating outward like lines on a weather map.

Praying that the glass wouldn't rain down, Willem squatted on the ground to examine the flower bed: an empty soda can, a few cigarette butts. The shrubbery had been trampled. Someone had spent more than a few minutes under the window, probably spying on Jurriaan. Willem spotted a chunk of concrete the size of a grapefruit, which could have come from any one of the construction sites in the neighborhood. He took it inside to show to Jurriaan.

The living room was decorated in shades of purple, from pale lavender to deep plum. It was tidy, the pillows arranged on the sofa just so and the pictures of cats hung in a straight line. Willem didn't have to do the white-glove test to know the apartment was dust-free.

Jurriaan examined the chunk of concrete. His face was pale, with dark patches under his eyes. He wore green and brown patterned pajamas and sandals with Velcro straps.

"Tell me what happened," Willem said.

Jurriaan set the concrete carefully on the coffee table and drew the curtains. "You can touch the glass."

He was right. The windows were double-glazed, only the outside pane damaged.

"Did you see who did this?"

"No. I was watching television. I heard a big bang. Mr. Verhoeven came downstairs and pounded on my door. He swore at me," Jurriaan said, rocking from side to side.

"Never mind Mr. Verhoeven. He was scared too." Willem silently cursed the old man. Bored teenage boys had tormented Jurriaan for years. There was a new crop every year. It was as if tormenting Jurriaan had become a rite of passage for up-and-coming young thugs. Most of it was low-level stuff: name-calling or ringing the doorbell and running. But it could escalate to violence. Jurriaan had a scar on his forehead to prove it.

"They followed me home from the bakery."

Jurriaan's shift ended a half hour after school was out.

"Go on."

"They called me a *useless freak*."

"You're not useless or a freak."

"I know."

Willem laid his hand on Jurriaan's shoulder. "What else?"

"They threw condoms."

Willem's eyebrows shot up.

"Used ones."

As if on cue, there was a smack against the door to the building, followed by another one.

"Stay here," Willem said,

He ran out the apartment and through the short hall to the entrance. He pulled open the door and jumped back, as raw egg slithered down the wood. Two boys stood on the sidewalk across the street, hooting with laughter.

"Hey," Willem shouted. "Come here."

They froze for an instant and took off, but not before he got a look at them. T-shirts and shorts. Blonds. One slim like a dancer, the other built like a bull. They seemed fit. If they were hockey players, Willem would never catch them, but he could try.

The boys raced toward the Olympiakade and nearly knocked down a couple out for a stroll. They sprinted over the bridge and turned onto the towpath. Tonight, the current in the canal was visible. Several times a week, the city closed most of the locks and pumped in fresh water from the Ijssel Lake. The stagnant water was flushed out to sea. It wasn't the ideal time for a dip, even if swimming had been permitted.

Willem's heart hammered. The distance between him and the boys lengthened. He was ready to call it quits, when Dancer stumbled and fell. Bull slowed, twisted his thick neck around, but seeing Willem still on their tail, sped up and fled around the corner.

Willem reached Dancer in a few seconds and extended a hand. The boy ignored him and scrambled up on his own.

"You're going to come with me and wash the egg off my brother's door."

"You're the freak's brother?"

"He's not a freak."

The boy gave a maddening shrug.

"You and your friend are cowards, you know that? You're picking on someone weaker, someone who can't fight back."

"Maybe somebody like that is better off dead."

Willem bunched his fists, using all his willpower to keep his arms by his sides.

"What's your name?"

The boy hesitated. "Finn."

"Well, Finn—or whatever your real name is—what would you do if he was your brother?"

"Dunno. Put a pillow over his face?"

Willem seized the punk's arm. "You're coming with me if I have to drag you."

"Get your hands off me or I'll sic the cops on you."

Willem dug in harder. "Let's go."

Finn elbowed him hard in the ribs and jerked free, reeling backward toward the canal only a few steps away. Willem tried to grab him but missed, and the boy plunged backward, arms flailing, into the water.

Willem rushed to the edge. The water was black at night and the surface rippled, the current pushing the old water out and fresh water in. There was no sign of Finn. Could he swim? Had he landed on something sharp? On a bicycle? A refrigerator? A car? Amsterdammers had used the canals as a dump for centuries. The current would pull Finn downstream. Willem crept along the bank, peering into the water. He thought his eyeballs would explode.

A few yards farther, Finn's head broke the surface halfway to the other side, arms plowing through the water and legs thrashing. Because the brick sides of the canal were straight up and too high to climb out, ladders were attached at intervals along the wall, but Willem didn't see one nearby. It was up to him to pull Finn out of the water. He took his bearings. He was on the towpath between two bridges, closer to the one he had crossed over a few minutes before. He ran back, legs pumping like pistons, heart working overtime.

Willem flew over the bridge and along the towpath on the other side, peering into the black water, trying to spot Finn. There was no sign of a swimmer: no kicking, no thrashing, only the relentless flow of the current. Cold dread spread over him.

He made out a figure climbing into a small boat tied to a mooring ring. Finn stood up and stretched up his arms, his fingers clawing at the top of the wall. He fell back.

"Hold on!" Willem yelled.

Finn tried again and this time pulled himself over the side. Without pausing to catch his breath, he sprinted away.

Willem slowed to a stop, gasping, heart pounding, and watched the boy disappear into the night.

* * *

"Did you catch them?" Jurriaan asked.

"I caught one of them." Willem collapsed onto the sofa.

"Did you beat him up?"

Willem shot his brother a look. "That's not allowed. We chatted."

"Are you going to call the police?"

Willem looked away. He had grabbed the boy's arm hard enough to bruise. Worse, Finn might say Willem had pushed him into the canal. If the boy brought assault charges, Willem could face removal from the medical register, but he had to protect Jurriaan.

A patrol officer named Meyer, with the rank surveillant, arrived fifteen minutes later. Willem guessed he was only a few years older than Finn. His uniform was a size too big, as if he hoped to grow into it. He blew his nose into a handkerchief.

While Jurriaan served coffee, Willem explained that the bullying had escalated, culminating in the broken window. He admitted chasing the boys, but tweaked the story to put himself in a more favorable light, the way his patients did when confessing to shameful behavior.

The surveillant shook his head. "It's antisocial."

"It's a hate crime," Willem corrected him.

"Maybe."

"What are you going to do about it?"

"I'll patrol the street for a few weeks. If the boys try anything again, I'll nab them."

Willem glanced at Jurriaan, who was sitting on the end of the sofa, his shoulders hunched, trying to make himself smaller.

"Thank you, Surveillant." Willem meant it, despite the risk that Finn might accuse him of assault. Jurriaan needed to be safe.

Meyer set his cup on the coffee table. "Is there somewhere your brother can stay in the meantime?"

"Jurriaan can stay with me, but you should address your question to him."

Meyer flushed. "Sorry. Jurriaan? What do you want to do?"

"I want to stay here," he said, which settled the question.

Jurriaan carried the empty cups to the kitchen. Meyer blew his nose again, shoved the handkerchief back into his pocket, and Willem ushered him to the door.

The surveillant stopped to examine the lock. "I could open the door in seconds with a credit card. Your brother needs a dead bolt."

"I'll see to it tomorrow." He made a mental note to call the locksmith, the glazier, and the insurance company first thing in the morning.

After Meyer left, Willem got a bucket of soapy water from Jurriaan and scrubbed the egg off the front door. He emptied the bucket into the toilet and said goodbye. As he stepped outside, a dried-up old man smoking a cigarette shuffled up the sidewalk. A Jack Russell terrier trotted by his side. The dog's mouth hung open, its pink tongue lolling, giving it a happy, friendly appearance, unlike that of its frowning owner. It was Mr. Verhoeven, Jurriaan's upstairs neighbor.

"Excuse me. Can I talk to you for a minute?" Willem said.

"What is it?"

"Some boys are giving my brother a hard time. Here's my card. Would you call me if—"

"I know," the old man interrupted, raising his hand to ward off the card. "I've seen the little bastards. Thank the lord Jurriaan took the foil off the window,"

"Foil?"

"Last week he covered the window. People will think he's growing weed. Apartment prices are shooting up everywhere. But I've had to reduce my asking price—twice." He pointed to the sign in the first-floor window. "I'll soon have to give the place away. It's time Jurriaan moved back home or to assisted accommodation. No one wants to live above a retard."

"Jurriaan has learning disabilities—"

"Whatever."

Willem punched himself hard in the thigh. *Ignorant pensioner.* "Jurriaan has as much right to live here as you. He's not hurting anyone. He's just different. The problem isn't Jurriaan. It's people like you."

"Is that so? I've lived here twenty-five years. I never had a lick of trouble until your brother moved in."

The old man snatched the card from Willem's hand, strolled inside with the dog, and slammed the door. At least he'd taken the card, a victory in Willem's book.

CHAPTER

28

August 2024

Jurriaan

IT WAS EVENING and already dark. Jurriaan sat at the dining room table, hunched over his notebook, drawing clock faces without hands. When he was done, he dragged the chair to the big window. The friendly glazier had swept away the broken glass and installed a new pane.

Jurriaan turned out the lights so no one could see inside and placed three objects within reach on the lamp table: his phone, the notebook, and a pencil with an eraser. He liked erasers because they rubbed out mistakes as if they had never happened.

Numbers were easier to read than words. There were only ten if he counted zero. They didn't represent ideas or stories or tell him what to do. Numbers told him simply how many, how much, and how big. For example, he had *two* feet. His shoes cost *one hundred and twenty* euros. He was *six* feet tall and weighed *two hundred and seven* pounds.

Numbers were also used to tell time. He preferred clocks with rotating hands pointing to numbers, telling him when, how much longer, or how long ago.

Leaning forward in the chair, he opened the curtains a crack.

After a while Surveillant Meyer drove by in his patrol car, his head swiveling like an electric fan. Jurriaan turned on his phone's flashlight app and filled in the first clock face. Little hand on nine, big hand on twelve.

He waited.

Muffled footsteps sounded in the stairwell and the door to the building banged. Mr. Verhoeven appeared outside on the curb, wearing a bathrobe and house shoes. He was letting the dog out, a little terrier named Tricksy, who didn't know any tricks. She couldn't even shake hands. The dog scampered across the street to a laurel hedge, where she did her business while her owner smoked a cigarette. Mr. Verhoeven didn't bother to pick up after his pet. *He should get a fine!* Jurriaan thought. Then Mr. Verhoeven tossed his cigarette butt on the ground and whistled. Tricksy raced back. A moment later the outside door closed, and footsteps faded up the stairs.

A scooter roared by, and a few minutes later, a car. Afterward the street stayed empty for a long time. Jurriaan squirmed on the hard seat and considered whether to leave his post to grab a cushion from the sofa. If he had, he would have missed Meyer drive past in the same direction as before. The police officer looked straight at him. Jurriaan ducked. When he raised his head, Meyer was gone.

Jurriaan filled in the second clock: little hand between nine and ten, big hand on nine.

Ten minutes later two figures appeared in front of the laurel hedge, their heads together, throwing glances in Jurriaan's direction. His mouth went dry. He needed Meyer to return. *Return now.* The boys crossed the street to the bike rack and bent over Jurriaan's bicycle, first the front wheel, then the back. It was too dark to make out what they were doing. Punching a hole? Removing the valve? Either way, he would have two flat tires by morning.

The next time Meyer drove by, the little hand was on ten and the big hand on six. His last appearance was at a quarter before one. The surveillant's patrolling was as predictable as the clock.

Jurriaan closed the curtains and stood up, stiff after sitting so long. He turned on a lamp. After a bathroom break, he drank a cup of tea. He set his alarm for a half hour earlier than usual because he would have to walk to the bakery instead of cycling.

The nice police officer couldn't help, and Jurriaan was reluctant to bother his twin again. Willem might insist Jurriaan go to live with him. There was plenty of room in the mansion, but Jurriaan loved his purple apartment with pictures of cats on the walls—a place he arranged any way he liked, a place where he stocked his refrigerator with vanilla vla and pastries from the bakery. He loved his job as kitchen help: refilling the ingredient bins, sweeping the floor, scrubbing the display cases and worktops. The baker was training him to bake bread. It was just a matter of reading the numbers: this much flour, that much yeast, the right temperature. Set the timer on the oven and watch the clock.

There was another reason he didn't want to move back to Dad's. *Never!* Mom's presence lingered in the house, making everything sick. Willem didn't understand stuff like that. He wouldn't be living in Dad's house if he did.

But Willem knew what to do about bullies.

CHAPTER

29

August 2024

Jurriaan

THE NEXT NIGHT Jurriaan began his vigil at eight o'clock. His new broom handle lay across his lap. He had bought it that afternoon at the hardware store. It was four feet long and, according to the sales clerk, made from Forest Stewardship Council–certified wood, which Jurriaan hoped also meant sturdy.

He parted the curtains just enough to watch the bike rack. If the bullies came anywhere near his brand-new tires, he would chase them away with the broom handle.

He could set his watch by Surveillant Meyer. Each time he cruised past, Jurriaan penciled in the hands on the clock faces: eight fifteen, nine, nine forty-five.

He had been in a blue funk for weeks, but now he had a plan. He felt stronger—more like Willem. He could do most things for himself: clean his apartment, wash his clothes, shop, cook, get to work on time. But the bullies were a thorn in his side. As soon as one got bored, another took his place. They called him names, broke his window, slashed his tires. Until now, he had cried like a baby instead of acting like a grown man.

He kept asking himself: *What would Willem do?*

By ten thirty it was dark. Yawning, Jurriaan peeped through the gap in the curtains. Right on schedule the patrol car's headlights appeared, but the street was quiet, and Meyer continued on his round.

No sooner had the car disappeared than Jurriaan saw a flicker of movement near the laurel hedge where Tricksy did her business. His heart quickened, and his hand slipped on the broom handle, his palms suddenly slimy with sweat. His body tensed. Timing was tricky. He wanted to catch the bullies red-handed, which meant being quick on his feet. No one had ever accused Jurriaan of being quick—not quick on his feet or quick in any other way. All he could do was be ready and try his best.

Two figures emerged from the shadows and slunk across the street like panthers. When they drew near his bicycle, he tried to stand up, but his legs were shaking too hard.

Footsteps sounded in the stairwell, and the outside door slammed. He saw old Mr. Verhoeven shuffle down the sidewalk in his bathrobe and fuzzy slippers. Next to him trotted Tricksy.

His neighbor was going to spoil the plan; the bullies wouldn't try anything right under Mr. Verhoeven's big nose. Jurriaan wanted to say *shit*, but he had been taught not to swear, so he only thought the word. In spite of his disappointment, he was a bit relieved. Whatever was going to happen, it would not be tonight.

He watched Mr. Verhoeven pull an object from his pocket and shake something into his hand. A match flared. The old man and the boys exchanged words. Jurriaan couldn't make out the conversation, but the tone was clear—Mr. Verhoeven complaining and the boys jeering.

His neighbor turned and pointed toward the repaired window. From reflex Jurriaan ducked, felt at once like a coward, and forced himself upright, telling himself that Willem wouldn't hide.

To his amazement the skinny boy shoved Mr. Verhoeven. The old man stumbled backward, fell, and landed on his butt in the grass. Tricksy began barking and leaping into the air with excitement. Suddenly she lunged at the boy, her teeth latching onto the leg of the boy's pants, or maybe into his flesh. The other boy kicked the little dog. Despite the double glazing, Jurriaan heard her yelp and saw her little body sail through the air and land a few feet away, where she lay still.

His head spun. Tripping over his feet, he rushed from his apartment to the building's entrance. He flung open the door and charged down the sidewalk, yelling and waving the broom handle.

Mr. Verhoeven and the bullies gaped at Jurriaan, who was hurtling toward them with his odd loping gait and the broom handle raised over his head. The boy who had kicked Tricksy fled. The skinny boy laughed out loud.

"Go ahead, retard. Try to hit me." He danced toward Jurriaan, then danced away.

Jurriaan threw worse than a girl. He couldn't hit a ball with a hockey stick to save his life or knock over a bowling pin without kiddie bumpers.

But when he was close enough, he swung down the broom handle. The boy leaped away—a mistake. He should have stayed put because he jumped right into the broom handle's path. There was a crack when the sturdy wooden stick hit his skull.

Jurriaan stared around him in disbelief.

Mr. Verhoeven cowered on the grass, with his arms covering his head, as though afraid Jurriaan was going to attack him next.

Jurriaan let the broom handle drop to the ground. "Are you all right, Mr. Verhoeven?"

The old man nodded and lowered his arms.

Jurriaan knelt beside Tricksy, stroked her warm little body, and rubbed the wiry fur between her ears. After a few moments, she whimpered and got to her feet, tail wagging slowly.

The boy stayed motionless on the pavement. His face was partially concealed by a fan of blond hair soaked with blood. Drool hung from the corner of his mouth. Jurriaan blinked. Tasted bile. Something stirred deep inside his head, crawling out of a dark mire into a shadowy light—a secret hidden for decades. A chill rippled through him, and he started shaking.

"Don't just stand there, Jurriaan, help me up. I'll run inside and call 112," Mr. Verhoeven said, holding out his hand. "The little bastard needs an ambulance."

Jurriaan helped the old man to his feet and watched him scurry into the building. The boy on the ground didn't move. Jurriaan hugged himself tightly, trying to keep his body from fragmenting into a zillion pieces like his front window had done.

CHAPTER

30

August 2024

Willem

PARKING SPACES WERE scarce at night. It would be faster to take his bicycle.

By the time Willem arrived, a small crowd had gathered outside Jurriaan's apartment. A police car was parked at an angle to the curb, and an ambulance with a blue beacon on top blocked the street. Two strapping women in blue and yellow uniforms lifted a boy onto a stretcher.

"I don't need to go to the hospital," the boy protested.

"Hush, Finn. You were knocked unconscious," cooed a squat blonde woman stuffed into capri pants. Gold glinted in her ears and on her wrist.

"Mom, I'm fine."

"It's precautionary," the ambulance nurse said.

Finn lifted his hand, acknowledging a stocky boy who watched from a few feet away. Willem recognized Dancer and Bull, the boys who had egged the door and broken the window.

Where was Jurriaan? Was he hurt too? On the phone, Mr. Verhoeven had told Willem to get over there quickly—and hung up before he had a chance to ask a single question.

The street looked otherworldly in the blue glow from the ambulance. Willem followed the sounds of a commotion. A tall man with a fluff of beard on his chin shouted and gestured at Surveillant Meyer. Mr. Verhoeven shouted back, one arm draped around Jurriaan's shoulders, the other clutching his little terrier.

"Excuse me," Willem said, loud enough to attract attention.

The bearded man fell silent, his eyes flashing.

"Dr. Veldkamp, I'm glad you're here," Meyer said, looking relieved.

Willem scanned Jurriaan. His twin's eyes were overly bright, but he appeared to be unharmed. Willem turned to the surveillant. "What happened?"

"I'm trying to get to the bottom of it," Meyer said, typing something into his handheld device.

"Who are you?" demanded the bearded man.

"I'm Jurriaan's brother."

"I'm Rob Prins, Finn's father." He pointed at Jurriaan, his finger shaking. "Your brother is a danger to the community. Just look at the size of him! They should lock him up. He attacked my son with a wooden pole and with no provocation."

"With no provocation?" Mr. Verhoeven sputtered, spittle flying. "The little bastard pushed me down, and his friend kicked Tricksy."

"My son is the victim here. Don't try to spin this."

Willem said, "The boys have been terrorizing Jurriaan for weeks. They broke his front window."

"They slashed the tires on his bicycle two nights ago," Mr. Verhoeven added.

This was news to Willem.

"Can't the idiot speak for himself?" Prins said.

Jurriaan shrank back, like a rabbit ducking into its burrow.

Willem sized up Prins. Jurriaan had injured the man's son, arousing the basic instinct to protect his offspring. But stressful situations showed a man's character, and Prins was a bully too—like father, like son.

Willem took a deep breath.

"My brother's name is Jurriaan."

"Sorry if I wasn't politically correct," Prins said, his lip curling.

Willem's heart broke for his brother, who expected little from life. He only hoped to be left at peace so he could work at the bakery and cook dinner in his own apartment.

"Surveillant, I demand you arrest Jurriaan," Prins said.

"You'll have to fill out a report, Mr. Prins. Online or in person at the station."

"I'll come to the station."

"Hold on," Willem said. "Don't forget your son committed several crimes."

"Do you have proof?"

"Not for the broken window. But Jurriaan saw Finn shove Mr. Verhoeven and kick the dog. I propose we call it quits. Lesson learned. Is that acceptable to you, Surveillant Meyer?"

The police officer held up a finger and consulted the screen of his handheld device before replying. "Finn Prins has the right to report the assault to the police. Likewise, Mr. Verhoeven has the right to file a complaint against Finn. Jurriaan Veldkamp has the right to report a hate crime and seek compensation for the broken window and the slashed bicycle tires. But none of you is *obligated*. You are only obligated to report very serious crimes like murder or kidnapping."

Prins looked unhappy, but he didn't look stupid.

"I want to talk to my lawyer," Prins said as the doors to the ambulance slammed shut. "First, my wife and I are going to the hospital. I'll be in touch, Suveillant Meyer."

Prins stalked over to his wife and towed her by the arm to their car. They drove behind the ambulance as it trundled off at a normal speed. The crowd disbursed.

"Thank you, Jurriaan, for coming to my rescue." Mr. Verhoeven gave a small bow.

Jurriaan frowned. "I just wanted to scare them."

The little terrier trotted over to Jurriaan, lay down on the grass, and rested her chin on his shoe. He looked down at her and then at his neighbor. "Is Tricksy okay?"

"She's probably bruised, so be careful petting her," Mr. Verhoeven said.

"What about the boy I hit?"

Willem hugged Jurriaan. "Don't worry, twinnie. Leave it to me."

JULY 2004

CHAPTER

31

Willem

WILLEM STARED OUT the ferry's porthole at the flat gray water that resembled a vast lake more than a sea with waves and tides. On the horizon, the island of Wexalia looked like a submarine, its cigar-shaped hull a shade darker than the sky.

He vowed to make the most of the next four weeks because the shit would hit the fan when Louisa arrived. She would punish him for driving the Mercedes—as if banning Bas from the holiday weren't punishment enough. He would have to tell her about getting kicked off the hockey team before she heard it from someone else.

But he couldn't help finding a silver lining in Bas's absence, which must make him the worst friend ever. Willem wouldn't have to compete for Katja's attention, an idea as thrilling as it was frightening. Bas was the expert on getting girls, once comparing it to fishing. If he didn't use the right bait and technique, the fish got away—but Willem had no idea what those were. He had no sexual experience unless he counted kissing Deborah. The arousal he had felt had been quickly extinguished by the odor of mothballs wafting from her clothes.

The ferry docked at noon.

Willem couldn't keep his eyes off Katja's swinging hips as he trailed behind to the parking deck. Her cargo pants were snug enough to show the curve of her rear. Because he wasn't watching where he was going, he smacked hard into Jurriaan, who had stopped to tie a shoelace. Louisa's voice rang in his head: *"Klutz! Watch where you're going."* Heat flooded his face.

After they piled into the car, Hendrik drove down the ramp and turned onto the dike road.

The road ran parallel with a fifteen-mile-long dike protecting the island from the Wadden Sea in the south. Giant basalt boulders lined the dike to the mudflats. In the village of Oerd, they passed a pub and a handful of shops before turning onto a wooded lane. To the North, clouds gathered, but overhead the sky was smoky blue.

The summerhouse was at the end of the lane, screened from view by trees and vines, the property encircled by a narrow ditch like a miniature moat. Willem recalled trying to jump over it when he was a kid. He had plunged into the stagnant water more than once while Jurriaan watched, cheering him or doubling over with laughter.

A bridge spanned the ditch, and on the other side was a gate. The car stopped and Jurriaan jumped out. He knew the combination of the padlock by heart. Beaming, he rode the gate as it swung open, and they drove up the gravel drive to the carport.

They lugged their suitcases to the porch, where they waited while Hendrik fumbled with his key chain until he found the right key. The door swung inward, and they entered a dark, musty hall lined on either side with closed doors. They filed up the stairs to the bedrooms to unpack.

* * *

After unpacking, Hendrik and Jurriaan took the car to the village to buy groceries. Katja sat down at the kitchen table and opened a book. Willem paced. They were alone, but he didn't know what his next move should be. It felt as if a golden opportunity was slipping through his fingers.

Katja laid her book on the table. "You're going to wear out the linoleum. What's up?"

"Do you want to cycle to the beach?" he blurted out.

Her eyes raked over him. "It might rain."

"You won't dissolve."

She laughed. "Okay. I'll leave a note for Hendrik." She found paper and pen in a kitchen drawer, started writing, then stopped. "What time will we be back?"

"Um . . . in time for dinner."

"Won't they mind if we're gone the entire afternoon?"

"Nah. Dad won't care and Jurriaan brought his PlayStation."

"We had better take our raincoats."

While Willem stuffed bottles of water into his backpack, his thoughts turned guiltily to Bas. He wondered if Mr. and Mrs. Debose had arranged for him to stay with a relative or if they'd canceled their holiday. Bas might not have told them he'd been uninvited, and could now be home alone, angry with Willem. Shit. Once they had fallen out over something stupid—not as bad as this—and hadn't spoken to each other the entire summer vacation. It had been the worst summer of his life.

"Ready?" Katja asked.

She had changed into short shorts, and the sight of her legs and the faint scent of her jasmine perfume drove thoughts of Bas from his head.

They left the house through the mudroom and crossed the terrace to the shed. Inside, the bicycles leaned against the wall under a shelf.

"Shit," Willem said. "The tires are flat."

"We can walk," Katja said, as if it was no big deal.

The beach was on the north side of the island, through woods that were crisscrossed at odd angles by hiking trails and cycling paths. The route markers were confusing, but it didn't matter because Willem knew the way. The trail was carpeted with copper-colored pine needles the color of Katja's hair, and under the trees grew bright green ferns the color of her eyes.

"Are you looking forward to university?" she asked.

"I can't wait. I'm going to share an apartment with Bas on the Vrolikstraat."

"That will be fun. What will Jurriaan do in September?"

"His school found him a job at a bakery. He's thrilled."

"I'm glad for him. And you? What do you want to be?"

He tensed, waiting for her to add *when you grow up*, but she didn't.

"Mom wanted me to be a concert pianist, but since that's not happening, she wants me to be a doctor."

Her face grew earnest. "It's your life. Not Louisa's."

"I know that. I'm not a kid." He kicked a pine cone and watched it spin into the bushes.

"I didn't mean to sound condescending. It's just that Louisa forced me to study accounting my freshman year. I flunked out. Because of university policy, I couldn't enroll in the same degree program again, thank goodness. Louisa let me switch to journalism. But I wanted to study literature."

"What are your plans now that you've graduated?"

"I'm writing magazine articles freelance. And I'm writing a novel," she added. "Don't tell Louisa."

"Is it a secret?" he asked, feeling honored.

"She thinks I ought to pound the pavement looking for a job."

"What's the novel about?"

"It's about two girls who live on opposite sides of the Amstel River in the 1950s. One girl is rich, the other poor. They become friends, but it's an unequal relationship, with the rich girl calling the shots."

"Oh . . . interesting." He read little fiction, only the required reading in school, though he had gone through a science fiction phase when he was twelve.

They hiked in silence for a while. Where the path narrowed, Willem dropped back and let Katja take the lead, picking her way nimbly over the tree roots. Her shorts rose up, revealing the edge of her panties. After a half hour, the woods gave way to heather, and a little farther, dune grass and sand replaced the flowers.

"Let's walk to the shipwreck house," Willem said.

"What's that?"

"It's a wooden hut on stilts. In the old days, it was a refuge for shipwreck survivors."

"How far is it?"

"An hour walking."

"That'll work."

The wind was behind them, and Katja's hair blew forward, hiding her face. He measured their progress by the beach markers placed at regular intervals. The shipwreck house was in sight when the sky darkened and cold needles of rain stung their faces. Showers happened nearly every afternoon, lasting from fifteen minutes to an hour. He grabbed Katja's hand, and they raced, laughing and whooping, to the hut.

Katja scrambled up the metal ladder first and waited for Willem on the narrow porch.

"The floor won't collapse, will it?" she asked.

He tested his weight on a board. "It's solid."

The hut was empty except for a wooden bench that ran around three sides. Graffiti covered the walls and the ceiling: initials, dates, times.

Water dripped off the end of Katja's nose. Willem sat on the bench to remove his wet shoes and socks. Katja followed suit. Her slender feet were shapely, the nails polished green, a shade that matched her eyes. She tucked her coppery hair behind her ears.

The rain clattering on the roof was deafening.

Katja hugged herself.

"Are you cold?" he asked.

"Freezing." She huddled against him and her touch was like an electric shock. Did she feel it too? His heart bonked against his ribs.

"A penny for your thoughts," he said.

She raised her eyes, mesmerizing him. Her lips moved, but he couldn't hear over the rain.

"Sorry. What did you say?"

"I wonder how Louisa is getting on at Lake Como."

"I'm sure she's fine. Why do you ask?" he said, trying to hide his disappointment about where her thoughts lay.

"Oh nothing. Forget I said anything."

An image floated into his head of Louisa sipping wine on a terrace, the lake shimmering under a broiling sun. He felt sorry for her students, but he was glad she was there and not here.

He had to know if he could trust Katja.

"Are you and Mom close?"

She shifted away from him. "What do you mean?"

"Do you confide in each other? Are you close like me and Jurriaan?"

"She tells me things. Why?"

"Did she ask you to watch me and report back to her?"

Katja said nothing for several moments, her chest visibly moving up and down.

"Yes, she did. Louisa is a bitch."

Willem blinked in surprise.

"I hate her. She's tried to control me since I was little. After my father and stepmother died, Louisa was the only family I had. I was dependent on her. I had to do what she wanted."

"And now?"

She hesitated, blushing. "Not much has changed."

A silence fell, filled only by the rain and the wind buffeting the shipwreck house.

"Willem . . . I've wondered. Does Louisa hit you?"

"God no. What made you ask a thing like that?"

"I saw bruises. And you broke your arm."

"I fell out of a tree. A hockey stick once hit me right between the eyes. You should have seen the goose egg. I'm not the cautious type." The last thing he wanted was for her to think of him as a boy who needed her protection.

"I guess not." She smiled and rested her head on his shoulder.

He sensed a change in the atmosphere, as if the air had been sucked out of the hut. He couldn't breathe. Then the air rushed back in, pure and sweet, making him giddy. His heart raced. He wanted to lay his hand on her chest to check if her heart was beating as fast as his own. He pictured Bas cheering him on. He settled for stroking her wet hair and letting his fingers glide over the delicate bones of her neck. He turned her face toward his and bent forward.

She shoved him away and jumped up, her head swiveling from one side of the hut to the other. There was no escape unless she wanted to get drenched. She sank onto the bench and for a long time said nothing.

"Willem, I'm sorry if I gave you the wrong impression."

He waited for her to say she didn't find him sexy, or she was too old for him, or she thought of him like a little brother. But she didn't say any of those things. At least she spared him the humiliation of an explanation.

* * *

When the rain stopped, they headed back under patches of pewter-gray sky between cloud banks, Willem walking a yard ahead. The surf splashed, fizzled, and drummed on the shore, all but drowning out Katja's soft voice behind him, chatting about nothing important. In his mind, he kept replaying his clumsy attempt at a kiss and her rejection. He had ruined everything.

Overhead, seagulls wheeled and screeched. A half mile farther Willem spotted a seal resting on the sand. It lifted its head and began dragging its muscular body toward the sea in an inelegant rocking motion, like an injured animal carving a trail in the sand.

They followed the same path through the woods, but everything was different. A muggy stillness settled around them. There was no birdsong. No wind to rustle the tree tops. The only sound was the squish of their shoes on the soggy pine needles. A drop of water from a branch splashed on his eyelid. As they emerged from the path onto the lane, Katja grabbed his arm.

"It can't happen again, Willem. Louisa would kill me."

It took a second for her words to sink in. Then he tried to suppress the grin that wanted to spread across his face; inside, he was cartwheeling up the lane. Her rejection had nothing to do with his age or his physical attractiveness.

"Mom's going to be in Lake Como for four weeks," he pointed out.

Maybe the best four weeks of his life.

AUGUST 2004

CHAPTER

32

Jurriaan

"DIBS ON CARRYING the picnic basket," Jurriaan said as he dismounted from his bicycle. His foot caught on the crossbar, and he half tumbled off.

"No worries, twinnie. I've got it," Willem said.

Willem didn't trust him! Jurriaan felt a pang. He knew he was clumsy. He tripped over uneven pavement tiles, knocked over glasses of milk, and dropped small objects: coins, marbles, screws. But he wouldn't drop something as big as a picnic basket!

"You can be in charge of lunch," Katja said.

Jurriaan gave her a little salute.

They chained their bicycles to the rack behind the dune. Jurriaan pushed on his glasses, which had slid down his nose, and followed Katja. Her bright green bikini top showed through her white T-shirt. Ahead, Willem scampered effortlessly up the sand path, as if his backpack and the picnic basket weighed nothing. Jurriaan was panting when he crested the dune and the sea came into view—black and threatening. Sand stung his eyes. Then his feet slipped out from under him, and he plowed down the slope on his butt.

Willem pulled him to his feet. "Come on. It's too busy here. Let's find a spot farther away."

Jurriaan's thongs kept sticking in the sand, causing him to trip and lag behind. He wrestled them off and continued barefooted. The seashells half buried by the tide pricked the soles of his feet; at least he could keep up.

They had passed two beach markers when Katja stopped and twirled around like a dancer. "How about here, Willem?"

"Perfect."

Jurriaan glanced around. His mother liked the beach when it was deserted like this—not crowded like Scheveningen, which she called a circus. While he loved circuses, Louisa did not. She was coming in two days. Jurriaan had gone with Hendrik to the shop in Oerd to buy the wine she liked, but they didn't have it. The shopkeeper had phoned around. No one on the island carried it anymore. Louisa would be upset.

Katja spread out three towels and stripped off her T-shirt and shorts, revealing her green bikini and skin white as flour. She sat on a towel and smeared sunscreen on her arms and legs. The coconut scent of the lotion made Jurriaan's nose itch. She handed Willem the bottle, and he massaged the sunscreen into her shoulders until the creamy white lotion vanished. Jurriaan wondered how Katja's skin and muscles and bones felt under Willem's hands.

"Let's go for a swim before lunch," Willem said, setting down the bottle. "Last one in is a rotten egg." He sprinted across the sand, hit the water at full speed, and smashed headlong into the breaking waves.

Katja laughed, but she stayed seated. Jurriaan stretched out his legs and gazed at the sky. Clouds were building and darkening along the bottoms. Louisa would arrive just when the weather changed for the worse. His stomach pitched; Louisa hated being cooped up in the summerhouse on rainy days.

Katja pulled a small notebook and a pen from Willem's backpack and started writing.

"What are you writing?" Jurriaan asked.

"It's a diary. I write about my experiences and my feelings. It's private." She pressed a finger to her lips.

"Why do you write stuff that's private?"

"So I won't forget."

Then he understood. Memories, like dreams, faded with time, some faster than others.

"I don't want to remember the bad stuff," he said.

"Can you give me an example?"

"The bullies at my old school."

"I'm sorry." She thought for a moment. "You can learn from the bad stuff."

Jurriaan nodded. He had learned that some children hated him because he limped and had trouble learning. He wasn't smart like Willem, who earned high marks without even trying. When they were in elementary school, the playground had been a battlefield. Willem brawled with the boys who hurt Jurriaan or called him names. After Willem skipped a grade, they weren't on the playground together anymore, and the bullying got worse. Jurriaan had learned it was better to change schools—to a school for children with special needs.

A shower of cold drops startled him. Willem was standing a foot away, flicking water.

"Aren't you coming in?" Willem asked.

Jurriaan looked toward the sea. Close to shore the breaking waves were gray with muddy white foam. Farther out, the water darkened to oily black. He wasn't a strong swimmer like Willem and Katja. He couldn't coordinate the arm strokes and kicks. Each moment in the water became a terrifying struggle to keep from drowning. He imagined a rip current carrying him toward a far-off point on the horizon, where the sea seemed to end. What would he find? Water gushing over a dam?

"Later," he said.

Willem turned to Katja. She laid the diary on her towel and raced him to the water.

Jurriaan watched their heads bobbing, sometimes disappearing in a wave. He held his breath. What if they didn't reappear? Since there was no lifeguard, he would have to rescue them himself, and they would probably all drown. Each time their heads reappeared in the surf, he exhaled in relief.

His stomach rumbled. He reached into the picnic basket for the bag of cookies from the batch he had baked for Louisa. She expected the cookies like she expected the wine, but this time Hendrik hadn't been able to find her wine.

A man pushing a bicycle with bulging saddlebags appeared in the distance. As he drew closer, Jurriaan saw he had a red beard. His heart began to race.

He stuffed a cookie into his mouth and chewed. Maybe he could attract Willem's attention by waving his arms, but he was too frightened to move. Willem was too far from shore to help anyway. The beachcomber came closer. Jurriaan remembered Louisa's warnings: *"Don't speak to him. Don't accept his presents. Don't go with him."*

He recalled the inside of the beachcomber's cottage. Dust. Dim light. A fishy smell. Loose planks under his feet. Rust-covered treasures heaped on shelves and tables. Pitted old coins. Antique daggers, a pistol, and several iron cannonballs. Broken china with sharp, jagged edges.

Jurriaan curled himself into a ball and made himself small. He squeezed his eyes shut—remembering the police car, the blinding headlights, Louisa roaring like a bear protecting her cubs. He remembered the beachcomber, handcuffed and wrestled into the backseat, angrily protesting his innocence.

When Jurriaan opened his eyes, he saw the back of the beachcomber shrinking into the distance.

Willem and Katja emerged from the water, their bodies sleek as seals. Her hair looked black, plastered against her skull. She kicked sand at Willem with the side of her foot, and he kicked back. She poked him in the side with her finger, and when he lunged for her, she danced away, giggling. They grabbed their towels and dried themselves off.

Katja's forehead furrowed. "Jurriaan, I need to talk to Willem. Will you get lunch ready while we go on a walk? I promise we won't be long."

After a quick glance to make sure the beachcomber wasn't coming back, he nodded and watched them stroll away: Katja talking, Willem listening. Jurriaan got the same empty feeling he got when Willem and Bas whispered together, sharing secrets from their day at school.

He set out the lunch: sandwiches, a jumbo-sized bag of chips, water in plastic bottles, paper plates. The plates blew away, wheeling over the sand in different directions. He limped after them as fast as he could and collected all three. This time he weighted them down with the bottles of water, and his eyes fell on Katja's diary. He ran his fingers over the slick cover and wondered what secrets it held, but he reminded himself that what she wrote was private.

SEPTEMBER 2024

CHAPTER

33

Anneliese

"Good evening, Dr. Veldkamp," the waiter said.

Anneliese bit down on her lip. The waiter knew Willem's name. This must be his modus operandi: a walk along the river with his date, a pause on the bridge to watch the sunset, and dinner at the expensive French restaurant. Maybe even at the same table on the water's edge. Maybe always on the third date.

The evening seemed scripted, and the curtain had just risen on Act Two. He would want to make love to her tonight, in Act Three. The timing couldn't be more auspicious. It was what she wanted, but now she couldn't help wondering how she stacked up with the other women he had dated.

Dr. Jeanette Bruin, for instance, the woman at Antonio's. How could Anneliese, an unemployed office temp, compete with the accomplished psychologist from London? She told herself Dr. Bruin was a dumpy, middle-aged blonde with dark roots, an overripe peach left to rot on the tree. Anneliese had youth on her side.

"A penny for your thoughts," Willem said, laying aside his menu.

She reached across and lightly stroked the back of his hand with her finger.

"Do you bring all your girlfriends here?"

"You must be kidding. Have you seen the prices?"

"There aren't any prices on my menu."

"I rest my case."

She wasn't going to let him off the hook so easily. "Why does the waiter know your name?"

"Maybe he remembers a good tipper."

She frowned, unconvinced.

"I confess, I've been here a few times."

"I knew you weren't a monk," she said, raising an eyebrow.

He grinned.

They ordered dinner and sipped chilled white wine from crystal glasses. Willem was easy to talk to, unlike her old shrink, Dr. Hummel. He felt familiar; they had a connection. Did he feel it too?

Over their first course—chunks of rhubarb swimming in balsamic vinegar with something else unidentifiable—Willem said, "Tell me about your writing."

"My writing?"

"You said you were a writer."

Oops. Anneliese felt herself blush at the slip. The trouble with lies was they were enormously difficult to keep straight, to remember what she had said and to whom. She tried to keep variations to a minimum. Her rule was one version of a lie for all, but sometimes context was important, and a lie had to be tweaked. Then things got complicated. Now was the time to end the myth that she was an aspiring writer.

"I wrote a short story for Katja's workshop. It got crucified."

"May I read it?"

"Over my dead body."

He laughed.

"Was it weird for Katja to become your stepmother? She's your aunt, isn't she?"

He put down his spoon.

"I had to get used to the idea. Louisa helped raise Katja, and Hendrik must have been a father figure at some point, but she's not my aunt. We're not related by blood."

"I meant step-aunt," she said. A blood relationship would have made Anneliese and Willem first cousins, a complication she didn't need.

"To be honest, I didn't see it coming. I wasn't living at home."

"Katja is still beautiful. I bet she had tons of boyfriends when she was young. Was there anyone special before Hendrik?" Anneliese asked, her heart ticking like a Geiger counter.

"I don't know. She was away at boarding school."

"Didn't she come home on school holidays?"

"Sometimes she spent them with friends. You'll have to ask her about boyfriends." He dipped his spoon into the soup.

"Sorry, I'm so nosy."

"You aren't a celebrity stalker, are you?"

She tensed and forced a laugh, not sure if he was teasing.

After the waiter cleared their soup dishes away, Willem excused himself, and she watched him disappear into the restaurant. The river lapped at the fortified concrete bank. It was a six-foot drop to the water, now black except for the reflections of lights from buildings on the opposite bank. The horizon glowed an eerie orangey purple. Willem was taking his time. Had he run into someone he knew? Or seen through her lies? A sudden fear seized her, that he might slip out a side door and disappear down an alley.

A sigh of relief whooshed out of her when Willem reappeared, threading his way through the candlelit tables.

"Is something wrong?" he asked.

"No, I'm fine."

He laughed. "This is going to make me sound like an idiot . . . I was afraid you'd be gone when I got back."

"Why?"

"Because of my celebrity stalker remark."

"I was afraid *you* wouldn't come back."

They smiled at each, acknowledging their weird connection. Was this how it felt to find her soulmate? All the more reason to carry out her plan tonight.

Later, Willem put his hand over his glass when the waiter tried to refill it.

"No, thank you."

"Madam?" The waiter hovered with the bottle.

"I've had enough too."

She didn't want to spoil Act Three.

* * *

It was midnight by the time they drove home, and the weather had changed. Lightning lit up the sky with spidery bolts shooting from cloud to cloud. The air crackled with static. When Willem reached over the handbrake and squeezed her knee, sparks traveled up her thigh. They didn't talk or listen to music. She could hear Willem swallow.

They circled her neighborhood for ten minutes before finding a free space to park. She led him up the stairs to her apartment and switched on a small lamp, leaving the room in shadow. He had come inside once before for a drink, but this time was different, and the air thickened with tension. He stood only inches away, looking down at her, his eyelids heavy.

She cupped his face in her hands and felt the stubble on his cheeks lightly scratch her palms. He lifted her and she wrapped her limbs around him, molding herself to his body. He carried her through the short hall to the bedroom, where he set her on her feet, turned her around, and unzipped her dress; heat rippled down the backs of her legs. He undid her bra and kissed each breast. His lips trailed down to her stomach, and he slipped her panties to the floor. She felt his gaze glide over her naked body, the sensation as real as his touch. He undressed slowly, not taking his eyes off her. The hair on his arms and chest was a sandy blonde, and his skin glowed golden. His legs were muscular, and his thighs like bricks.

Taking his hand, she lay down on the bed and pulled him on top of her.

"Do you have a condom?" Willem asked.

"You didn't bring one?" she teased.

"I left them in the glove compartment."

"The drawer," she said, pointing to the nightstand.

Let him choose. The condoms were past their end date, making them unreliable, but she preferred leaving nothing to chance. It didn't matter which one he selected because she had used a needle to prick holes in all of them.

OCTOBER 2024

CHAPTER

34

Anneliese

ANNELIESE COULD BE the poster child for predictable cycles. She knew when she was ovulating. She knew when her period was due.

On the first day of her missed period, she woke early and headed for the toilet, too excited to stay in bed. She just knew she was pregnant, but Willem would want confirmation. After opening the pregnancy test kit, she peed in the cup and set the timer on her phone. Sitting on the toilet, she watched the seconds counting down. Three minutes crawled by like an hour. Then she peered at the test window. Blinked. She couldn't believe her eyes.

Negative.

She swore and shot the kit into the wastebasket.

Did her egg get stuck in a tube somewhere?

Was her womb a hostile environment?

Had she taken the test too early?

What if she couldn't get pregnant?

She had never had a desire to hold her girlfriends' babies or envied their ordinary lives with a terraced house, a garden the size of a cemetery plot, and a yappy little mutt. Baby talk didn't roll off her tongue. She couldn't picture herself changing a smelly diaper or offering her tit to an infant. Maybe she hadn't inherited a maternal instinct—Katja had obviously lacked one. Before meeting Willem, she had never given serious thought to having children.

But she had to be realistic. He was thirty-six and had never married or even lived with a girlfriend. There must be a reason for that. Her stomach lurched when she recalled his cool dismissal of the stuck-up psychologist at Antonio's. How long before he grew tired of her too? A child would cement their bond and guarantee her a place in the Veldkamp family—her family, after all.

He would think twice before dumping the mother of his child.

Her new—and very weird—craving for juicy, slightly sour white grapes returned. She had stocked up yesterday at the Albert Cuyp Market. Since she wasn't pregnant, she must have a shitty stomach virus. As if on cue, she felt an odd hollow feeling in her tummy, quickly blooming into nausea. Kneeling on the tiles, she dry-heaved into the toilet.

C H A P T E R

35

October 2024

Willem

WILLEM KEPT GOING over in his mind what to tell Bas. Every couple of minutes, he stopped obsessing, to check the clock on his computer screen. Why could Bas never be on time?

He arrived twenty minutes late.

"Sorry, Will. The bridge was up," Bas said, grinning.

Willem forced a smile at the old joke, and they went outside to feed the fish.

As they neared the pond, the koi swam to the edge, their bodies twisting and tails swishing—gleaming red, blue, gold, and black in the fading sun. Willem poured pellets from a container into his hand and dipped his palm into the water. The koi, measuring from a few inches to two feet, crowded around. Their mouths stretched open and sucked the pellets from his palm.

Bas laughed. "Sounds like kisses."

The fish scattered.

"Shh. You're scaring them."

"I wouldn't want to come between a man and his fish," Bas whispered, before giving a small bow and retreating several yards.

Taking care of the fish and monitoring the water quality was more bother than Willem had expected when he'd installed the pond—and more expensive. But he had grown fond of the koi: three in particular. Bashful, the smallest, floated away as soon as she took a few nibbles, and hid under a water lily. Grumpy swam to the opposite side whenever Willem approached, unless it was feeding time. Doc, the black koi, was his favorite, almost purring when Willem stroked him.

The fish usually took his mind off his worries.

But not today.

The fish soon reappeared, and after they had eaten their fill, they swam away, all except Doc. Willem stroked him from head to tail, and the fish wriggled, then dived.

He stuck his hand into the skimmer, pulled out green slime, and tossed the gunk onto the dirt under the maple tree. The leaves were turning yellow orange. Later in the autumn they would be flame red. He opened his water testing kit and examined the bottles and test tubes, but sensing Bas's impatience, he closed the kit.

"Want a beer?" Willem said.

"I thought you'd never ask."

They walked back to the terrace.

"Sit down. I'll be right back." Willem darted inside the apartment and returned with a crate, the glasses and bottle opener on top.

"You sounded serious on the phone. Is it about Jurriaan? About the boy he attacked?" Bas asked as Willem filled his glass.

"Finn is fine. They checked him over at the hospital and sent him home the same evening. The boy's father has political ambitions. He can't afford any adverse publicity, so he decided not to press charges. In return, Jurriaan isn't pressing charges against Finn for a hate crime."

"And the pensioner? The Prins boy knocked him down and kicked his dog."

"Mr. Verhoeven got a payoff from the father."

"So, everyone's happy," Bas said, and they clinked glasses.

After taking a gulp, Willem set his beer on the table. He opened and closed his mouth, but no words came out.

"Lighten up, Will. It can't be that bad," Bas said.

Bas was a lady's man, a Casanova, a womanizer—whatever. His charms and good looks attracted women, like the fish at feeding time. His face was all planes and angles, masculine and pretty at the same time. He had stunning blue eyes and a cleft chin. When it came to women, Bas had the most experience.

"Do you remember the girl I introduced you to at Katja's party?"

Bas ran a hand through his hair. "You mean Anneliese? I was pretty wasted, but I wouldn't forget a girl like her. Dark hair, great legs, red dress?"

Willem nodded. "I've been seeing her."

Bas's eyebrows shot up. "By *seeing* her, do you mean you've taken her out more than once?"

"Yes."

"This calls for a celebration." Bas raised his glass, but Willem drummed his fingers on the table. "Is there a problem?" Bas asked.

"Not exactly . . . Kind of . . . She's pregnant."

"How? I mean, didn't you use a condom?"

"They aren't a hundred percent reliable."

Bas stood up and started pacing, still clutching his glass.

"Was it your condom or hers?"

"Hers. Why do you ask?" Willem said, but he knew what Bas was insinuating, having briefly entertained the same suspicion himself, and immediately felt disloyal. They had made love on four separate occasions, using condoms from the pack in her nightstand. His supply, which he kept in his glove compartment, had gone missing.

"I always bring my own. Don't trust contraception to a woman of child-bearing age."

"Anneliese is too young to worry that her biological clock is ticking," Willem said.

Bas chugged his beer as he paced.

Willem knew his friend's worst nightmare was to be tricked into fatherhood, which would force him to take responsibility and get a job with a steady income. He opened two more bottles.

"How it happened isn't the point, Bas. The question is what to do."

Bas plopped into his chair again. "Does she want to keep the baby?"

"She said she would do whatever I wanted."

"Are you sure it's yours?"

"Yes."

"You said, and I quote, *'I'll never . . . ever . . . have children.'*"

"I know."

"There are options."

Not the advice Willem wanted to hear.

"Don't rush into something you'll regret later," Bas warned—it was the refrain from their childhood.

Willem had weighed the pros and cons and compiled a list, hoping on a different outcome, but each time the cons outnumbered the pros. But if he assigned a weight to each consideration based on its importance, the result seesawed.

"Willem, tell me what you're thinking."

"I asked Anneliese to marry me, and she said yes."

Bas fell back and squinted into the lowering sun. Shadows striped the garden, growing longer. "So, it's a done deal."

"Yes and no. We submitted our declaration of intent to marry. It's valid for a year. We can still change our minds."

"Have you set the date?"

"No, not yet."

Bas ran his hands through his hair, then refilled his glass. "You need a prenup agreement."

"I don't have any assets except for my car."

"But you'll inherit from your father. Didn't he and Katja sign a prenup?"

"Yes, but that was different."

"How?"

"Hendrik was a wealthy widow, and he had children. The prenup was actually Katja's idea." She had wanted Willem and Jurriaan to inherit the house and the bulk of Hendrik's estate. As his widow, she would be entitled to his pension, securing her a generous income. She didn't want more than that. Maybe she thought Willem would accept the marriage sooner if the issue of money was taken out of the equation. She had thought wrong. He was a long time accepting that his first love had become his stepmother.

"At least talk to an attorney," Bas said.

"I'll think about it. There's something else . . ."

"What's that?"

"Will you be my witness at the marriage ceremony?"

"Of course." Bas reached into the crate and removed two more bottles. "Congrats, Willem—for better, for worse, or until death do you part."

CHAPTER

36

October 2024

Anneliese

ANNELIESE'S GUT CHURNED. In the dreary mist, the mansion looked forbidding with its somber brick facade, small windows, and a paved-over front garden.

She kept telling herself that her meeting with Hendrik would be like a job interview. All she had to do was mold herself into the ideal daughter-in-law and plant a smile on her face. She wore a blouse buttoned up to her chin and a skirt with a hem hitting her knees.

She marched to the front door and smoothed her hair, which was windblown from the trip over on her bicycle. There were three bells: "H. & K. Veldkamp," "W. Veldkamp," and "Psychiatric Practice." Before she had time to choose, the door opened and Willem pulled her inside, kissing her deeply.

"Are you nervous?" he asked, releasing her.

"A little."

"Don't be. My father will love you."

"Is Katja here?"

"She sends her apologies. She'll catch up with you at the engagement dinner."

Hiding her disappointment, Anneliese gazed around at the wide entrance hall, the white stone floor gleaming in the light from a modern chandelier with light bars crossing at angles. At the end of the hall was a staircase enclosed in glass. The scent of Katja's jasmine perfume still hung in the air.

Willem kissed Anneliese again, a peck this time. "Hendrik is waiting in the living room. He wants to talk to you alone. I'll introduce you and leave."

She clutched at his sleeve.

"Do you have any tips?"

"Don't underestimate him. He's the smartest man I know."

"Anything else?"

"He has a habit of quoting proverbs."

"The Bible?"

"No. Old sayings."

She raised her eyebrows.

"Ready?" he asked.

She took a deep, calming breath and followed him down the hall. He pointed out the door to his office on the right and to his apartment on the left.

The glass door at the bottom of the staircase was locked—to keep out patients, she thought. He unlocked it and they climbed the steps to the landing, which doubled as a cloakroom. After taking her coat, Willem ushered her into an immense living room, bigger than her apartment, with pale hardwood floors, white furniture, and white walls. The room looked as if it had been bleached. An elderly man sat on the sofa, facing a white fireplace. His eyes were the first thing she noticed, black like pools of oil and enormous behind thick glasses. He wore a tan cardigan, brown trousers, and satiny slippers.

He stood up and offered Anneliese a thin hand that was dry and hot, as if a slow fire burned inside him.

"Won't you sit down," he said.

"Thank you, Mr. Veldkamp."

"Call me Hendrik.

She took the armchair and tried to send Willem a telepathic message begging him to stay.

"I'll leave you two to get acquainted," Willem said.

So much for telepathy. She forced a smile. What kind of daughter-in-law would Hendrik want? Sweet? Feisty? Shy? Outgoing?

He consulted a scrap of paper, then looked up.

"I understand you want to marry my son."

"Yes, I do."

"Do you love him?"

"With all my heart."

"Will you love him twenty years from now?"

She resisted the urge to roll her eyes. "Why wouldn't I?"

"Familiarity breeds contempt."

"I hope you're wrong."

He nodded. "Tell me about yourself."

She started with her childhood in Noorddorp, the childhood she wished she'd had. It was the same fairy tale she had told Willem, because she couldn't admit to anyone, especially to her prospective father-in-law, what her childhood had really been like. He might consider her damaged goods and oppose the marriage. Willem would marry her anyway, but she needed Hendrik's approval to live in the house. She described loving parents and a dear brother who died young. When she finished, she nearly said *"The end."*

"Your education?" he barked.

"I have a bachelor of arts."

"Any health problems?"

Enough was enough. She drew herself up, her chin high. "I'm sorry, but Willem isn't buying a horse."

"Never look a gift horse in the mouth."

"Pardon?"

"That's my grandchild in your belly. Of course, I'm concerned about your health."

"Aren't you shutting the barn door after the horse has bolted?" If Hendrik could speak in proverbs, so could she.

He laid the paper on the sofa and regarded her with a frown.

Had she blown it?

They stared at each other, taking each other's measure.

"May I ask *you* a question?" she asked.

"Yes, that's fair."

"How did you meet Willem's mother?"

His hand went to his throat and tugged absently at the loose folds of skin. "A mutual friend introduced us. Louisa could captivate everyone in the room. Men wanted to sleep with her. Women wanted her for a friend, for the status. I didn't think I had a chance."

"Why not?"

"I was an engineer. Not one of her usual crowd. Then she invited me to a concert. When I saw her perform on stage, I fell head over heels. But she pursued me. Louisa always got what she wanted."

Had Louisa married him for his money? She glanced at the huge abstract paintings—in neutral pastels—and the pristine furniture. It would be like living in the pages of an interior design magazine. It would take getting used to.

"Do you have any hobbies?" he asked.

"I used to play the piano."

His dark eyes gleamed with interest. "Will you play for me?"

There wasn't a piano in sight. "Do you mean now?"

"No time like the present."

"But I haven't played in years."

Hendrik insisted.

* * *

She followed him downstairs to the ground floor, where he opened a door off the hall and led her down a chilly concrete stairwell to the basement. There he unlocked a door and switched on the overhead light.

Goose bumps ran up her spine. It was like a mortuary. The room smelled of mold and chemicals. She stared at the baby grand piano, which reminded her of an ebony coffin with the lid raised. She imagined Daan's body, embalmed and dressed in his favorite black T-shirt, his hands crossed over his chest, his skin an unnatural white tinged with blue. She pressed the heel of her hand against her mouth.

"Do you feel all right?" Hendrik asked.

"Just a little morning sickness."

Cobwebs stretched across the ceiling, trawling for prey in the sealed-off room. Where did the dust come from? It blanketed the piano, the picture frames. She smelled the dust, a dead smell. Faded posters and photos of Louisa papered the walls. She moved around the studio to get a closer look.

In one photo, a pigtailed little girl was playing the piano, her plump legs dangling off the bench. The intensity in Louisa's young face was extraordinary.

She was pudgy as a teenager, pretty at twenty, striking at forty—tall and blonde with blue eyes and strong angular features. She had wide shoulders and muscular arms. The photos showed her performing on stage, taking a bow, receiving an award.

A cabinet with glass doors occupied most of the back wall. On the shelves were stacks of sheet music and music books.

"May I select a piece to play?" Anneliese asked.

Hendrik nodded.

She tried to open a glass door, and at first she thought it was locked, but she tugged harder, and the hinges reluctantly moved. She passed over the pieces composed by Louisa, judging them too difficult, and chose a sonatina by Mozart.

Hendrik sat down on the love seat facing the Steinway. The piano bench was too high, but the height wasn't adjustable, so she slid the bench forward and opened the fallboard. To think, she was about to touch the same keys

Louisa Veldkamp had touched. She practiced some scales to loosen her fingers, which felt as stiff as the hinges. The piano had a warm, rich tone.

She opened the sonatina. She could still read music, and her fingers knew which key went with which note, but her hand–eye coordination deserted her. After fits of stumbling and starting over, she stopped halfway through the first page.

"Sorry you had to listen to that," she said.

"Practice makes perfect."

She had murdered the piece, but excitement stirred inside her. What would it take to get back to her former skill level? Everything she needed was right there: the wonderful piano, the music books, privacy. A chill swept over her, and she hugged herself for warmth. Surely the temperature in the room was adjustable. She lifted her gaze and saw Willem standing in the doorway, glaring at something, maybe at her.

He said, "I hate to interrupt, but I'm expecting a patient. If you two are finished, I'll show Anneliese to the door." Her coat was folded over his arm.

"I think I'll sit awhile," Hendrik said.

* * *

At the front door, Willem helped Anneliese on with her coat.

"Did you mind me playing your mother's piano? It was Hendrik's idea."

"No. It took me by surprise. That's all. No one's played the Steinway since Louisa. No one except the piano tuner."

It was as if they were waiting for Louisa to return.

"Do you think I could play the piano after I move in?" She wasn't a literary talent like Katja Hart, or a pianist of the same caliber as Louisa Veldkamp. But she had a knack for piano; it was a means to impress the family.

Willem pulled her into an embrace. "Anything. I want to make you happy."

"Do you think Hendrik liked me?" she asked, resting her head against his chest.

"I do. He doesn't take just any girl to the crypt."

Crypt? Her skin prickled, recalling her first impression of the studio, creepy like a mortuary but coming alive when she played, even if her playing had been pathetic.

He stepped back and looked searchingly into her eyes. "Are you sure you don't mind living here? I can't move the practice after the fortune Hendrik spent on renovations, but we could find an apartment in the neighborhood."

"I know. You told me. But it's fine, Willem. I'm going to love being part of the family."

She climbed on her bicycle and waved goodbye.

Fallen leaves, broken branches, and paper trash collected by the wind carpeted the bicycle path. As she cycled home, the damp wind numbed her fingers, making her wish she had worn gloves. Her excitement at getting a thumbs-up from Hendrik ebbed. When she thought about the mansion, she pictured herself spilling coffee on Katja's pristine white sofa or—maybe worse—on the Steinway's keyboard. Her thoughts turned to Louisa's studio, to the pervasive chill, the dead smell, and the aging posters. Willem was right to call the room *the crypt*, and for a moment she wondered if it would have been better if Hendrik had *not* liked her.

CHAPTER

37

October 2024

Willem

DR. SIMON NAGEL's office was cool and dim like a homey cave. Willem felt safe in the shadows, hiding his warts and imperfections.

Bookshelves lined the walls, crammed with leather-bound tomes on psychiatry, well-used and grown shabby like Simon himself. His coarse gray mustache needed a trim, and his suit was shiny at the elbows—maybe the same suit he was wearing on the day Willem met him a decade before.

One peculiar fixture in the office that Simon used as a prop was a mahogany box on legs with a glass top, displaying figurines collected by the psychiatrist during his travels abroad.

They sat down on opposite sides of a small table. Simon was Willem's clinical supervisor, whom he paid to discuss his tough cases or anything else on his mind.

"What do you want to talk about today?" Simon asked.

The aborted therapy session with Mr. Ringnalda came to mind. Willem's heartbeat sped up. Under the table, his hands kneaded his thighs hard enough to leave red marks. He couldn't help but expect a punitive response. It didn't matter that his supervisor had always been supportive, treating his mistakes like learning opportunities rather than grudges against him.

"Did something happen, Willem?"

Willem had talked about Mr. Ringnalda before, referring to him as patient G233 to protect his privacy. He took a deep breath and launched into an account of the therapy session that Hendrik had interrupted.

"I've installed a lock on the door. My father won't be able to barge in again."

Simon nodded. "Has your patient been back since the incident?"

"No, but he's indecisive and nonconfrontational. I may still hear from him."

"Have you tried contacting him?"

"I texted him, but he didn't reply. I thought phoning would be too intrusive."

"Sounds like the right approach."

Willem's hands relaxed and his heart slowed to a normal pace. The conversation shifted to a depressed patient who wasn't responding to treatment with Prozac. Simon suggested increasing the dosage before switching to another drug.

"Why are you smiling?" Simon asked.

"I have some personal news. I'm engaged to be married. My fiancée doesn't have a high regard for shrinks, as she calls us. She says all we do is prescribe."

"Congratulations." Simon smiled, tilting his head to one side. "The last time we talked about marriage, you said it wasn't in the cards. What changed?"

"I found the right person."

A cloud must have drifted, because the room darkened a notch. Simon crossed to the window and adjusted the blinds.

"How long have you known her?" he asked, settling down at the table again.

Willem folded his arms across his chest, then, realizing his body language was defensive, he quickly *unfolded* them. *To hell with it!* He folded his arms again. It was counterproductive to hide his emotions from Simon—not that there weren't things he kept hidden.

"Not long," he said. "She's pregnant."

"Unplanned?"

Willem nodded.

"How do you feel about becoming a father?"

"At first, I was stunned. Then thrilled. I felt ridiculously proud, as if I had accomplished something unique. I was happy."

A silence fell.

"And now?"

"What do you mean?"

"I noticed you said 'at first' and used the past tense. Stunned. Thrilled. Did something change?"

It was a stupid slip.

The truth was his excitement had mutated to terror. He knew that some abused children became abusive parents themselves. Would he? Simon knew nothing about Louisa's abuse and nothing about her death that wasn't reported in the newspapers. Willem had kept him in the dark because when a psychiatrist said, "I'll keep anything you say confidential," it wasn't entirely true. If he suspected a patient was at risk to himself or to others, he had to act. And when a psychiatrist said, "Tell me anything. I won't judge you," that wasn't true either. Sometimes Willem couldn't help being judgmental about a patient's narrative.

Simon leaned back, his arms open on the arm rest. "Tell me about your fiancée."

"Her name's Anneliese." Willem pulled his phone from his pocket and showed him a photo.

"She's a pretty woman."

"There's something about her . . . I felt an instant connection." Willem shrugged. "I can't explain it."

"Why does Anneliese have a low opinion of psychiatrists?"

"Her adoptive brother killed himself while under a psychiatrist's care."

"Do you know anything about the brother's psychological history?"

"No. She hasn't opened up about him yet. I don't want to push her."

"Right. Right. But you want to know who you're marrying."

"I know enough." It was enough for now.

"We're out of time today," Simon said without a glance at a clock, fifty minutes having become part of his biological rhythm.

They both rose.

"One more thing before you go."

Willem swore to himself and trudged behind his supervisor to the display case of figurines. Simon used the figurines in a transparent attempt at delving into his patients' subconscious minds. The last thing Willem wanted was to reveal anything better left hidden.

Simon swung the glass lid back on its hinges.

"Willem, I'm going to ask you to choose a figurine. Don't think too much. Pick the first one that comes to mind when I instruct you. Do you understand?"

Willem's heart quickened. "Yes."

"Pick an object that makes you think of Anneliese."

His eyes scanned the objects spread out on a lining of black velvet: a bronze buddha, a hand-carved teak elephant, an apple made from brown glass, a pair of glazed ceramic doves, miniature animal figurines, dollhouse furniture. His eyes fell on a Russian nesting doll.

Perfect.

Willem picked up the doll and laid it in his supervisor's outstretched hand. The doll was actually a set of painted wooden dolls in decreasing sizes, placed one inside another. It was a safe choice. The symbolism was obvious: a woman's fertility and motherhood.

"Thank you, Willem."

A few minutes later, he joined the throng of tourists and locals inching along the sidewalk, while on the street a scooter zoomed by at a ferocious clip. Willem fought the urge to hail it, jump on the rear, and leave his past behind. Wipe the slate clean and start over. The bells in the Noorderkerk started clamoring, setting his nerves on edge. His session with Simon replayed in his mind, stuck in a continuous loop.

A therapist could help him become the nurturing parent he wanted to be. God knows he hadn't had suitable role models. But a therapist would expect him to talk about the past, and Willem would have to skate around patches of thin ice—to borrow a metaphor from Katja's famous novel. If he couldn't be honest, the success of the therapy was doomed.

Willem wondered what Simon would make of the Russian nesting dolls. He might assign a different meaning to the obvious one; he would seek a subconscious meaning. The outer doll was the powerful matriarch, and the hidden dolls might represent layers of secrets and lastly a baby wrapped in a quilt, the seed that had started everything. His head pounded. If only the damn church bells would stop ringing.

CHAPTER

38

October 27, 2024

Diary entry

WHAT AN AWFUL engagement dinner—intended to be a romantic evening on a canal boat.

Ray, Anneliese's father, reminded me of a toad. He was bald except for a tuft of hair sprouting behind each ear, and his belly hung over his belt. Her mother, Tineke, was a chain-smoker and chain-drinker. She had short spiky hair and wore a low-cut dress that revealed a flat chest.

"Don't judge a book by its cover," Hendrik said when we were getting ready for bed.

I knew I was being snobbish and unkind, and I tried in vain to find something to commend the Bakker family.

Anneliese purring. Willem, the tasty canary.

She moved in yesterday, and the house already smells different: a musky scent. My only consolation is the baby—Willem's baby.

Poor Jurriaan. Anneliese acted as if he was contagious. She actually flinched when he accidentally touched her arm. And Ray's jaw dropped open as he watched Jurriaan limp to the toilet, his left foot turned inward at an angle.

Once Jurriaan was out of earshot, Ray's sharp salesman's eyes homed in on Willem. "What's wrong with your brother?"

"Excuse me?"

"He walks funny. We're soon going to be family. Me? I'm an open book. Isn't that right, Anneliese?"

"Yes, but . . ."

Tineke coughed. "Is it genetic?"

Willem's smile slipped.

"I was born first, my brother thirty minutes later. Jurriaan didn't get enough oxygen and suffered brain damage. If the birth order had been reversed, it might have been me."

"It wasn't anyone's fault," Hendrik said, running his finger along the rim of his glass. "It was the luck of the draw."

A silence fell around the table. Forks hovered over plates.

"That's so tragic," Tineke said, dabbing at a dribble of red wine on her chin.

Ray said, "At least it's not a defect that can be passed on. We don't know much about Anneliese's family."

"What do you mean?" Willem glanced at his fiancée, whose eyes were fixed on Ray, telegraphing signals that went unread.

"It was a closed adoption," Ray said.

The boat glided silently through the water as the waiter refilled glasses. Cutlery tinkled.

Willem covered Anneliese's hand with his own. His face gave little away, but I realized that he hadn't known Anneliese was adopted, and I couldn't help wondering what else he didn't know.

NOVEMBER 2024

CHAPTER

39

Anneliese

EACH MORNING WILLEM'S alarm blared like an air-raid siren, making Anneliese's heart lurch, but by the third day she simply smiled and rolled over. Her days hustling menial office jobs as a temp were in the past. If she wanted, she could spend the entire day in bed.

When she woke up again, Willem was leaning over her, his blond hair damp from the shower, the stubble on his jaw trimmed. He was dressed for the office, which was a five-second commute across the hall.

"What are your plans today?" he asked, his face open and trusting.

She swallowed hard. How would he look at her when she told him Katja was her biological mother? Would he feel deceived? Used? She kept postponing the moment, and the longer she waited, the harder it got.

"Katja invited me for coffee," she said.

"I'm surprised."

"Why?"

"Because of her deadline."

"What deadline?"

"Ask Katja. See you at lunch," Willem said.

His goodbye kiss tasted of toothpaste; she hated to think what hers tasted like.

After he left, she gazed at her new surroundings. Willem's apartment wasn't any bigger than the one she had rented on the Vechtstraat. But it was open plan, and the rear wall was made of glass, adding to the goldfish bowl effect when the curtains were open. She missed her warren of cozy small rooms.

She pulled on leggings under her slacks and drank a cup of tea in front of the window. She gazed at the shivering bare trees and tried to visualize the garden in summer, with roses, clematis, and hibiscus in bloom, but it was beyond her imagination.

Bored, she went through Willem's suit pockets, finding nothing but lint. She took inventory in the kitchen and made a grocery list. She sat down with one of Willem's dull psychiatric journals. The morning dragged by, and at ten minutes before eleven, she was too impatient to wait any longer.

The house was fitted with locks like a prison, and Anneliese felt like a warden with a fat set of keys jangling in her pocket. Katja had instructed her to ring the bell by the front door, but it would be silly to wait outside in the cold when she had the key to the glass door at the foot of the stairs.

Upon reaching the landing, she faced another closed door. Knock? That would be silly too. This was her home. She was a member of the family, and Katja was expecting her. The door was unlocked, so she went through. The living room was empty, but she heard the scrape of furniture being dragged over a floor. She followed the sound, passed the longest table she had ever seen in a private home, and came to the kitchen.

Katja was standing on a chair, reaching for something on a top shelf. Anneliese smiled because she often had to do the same.

"Good morning," Anneliese said.

Katja visibly started and climbed down, a pack of sugar in her hands.

"How did you get in?"

"With a key."

Katja frowned. "I didn't know you had one."

"Willem gave it to me. Can I help you?"

"No, thank you. Take a seat." Katja waved toward a breakfast room at the other end of the kitchen, which gave onto what Willem called the roof terrace, though it was on top of the garage and not on top of the house. She sat down at the table and watched Katja fill a sugar bowl. Katja wore a smart cashmere sweater and tailored wool pants, making Anneliese feel shabby in her clothes from the clearance rack at H&M. Cold radiated through the sliding glass door and into her bones.

"How do you take your coffee?" Katja asked.

"With milk and sugar."

"Me too," Katja said. "That will be easy to remember."

Anneliese made a mental note to add Katja's coffee preference to the list she was compiling in her file called *Trees*.

"About the key," Katja said. "Willem should have told you. You should use it only in an emergency."

"I don't understand," Anneliese said, setting her cup on the table.

"Willem moved into the house on the condition his privacy—and ours—be guaranteed," she said, twisting her wedding ring. "To be clear, we treat the house as two separate residences."

"I thought the purpose of the locks was to keep out patients."

"That too."

"It seemed silly to ring the bell."

Katja chewed on her lower lip. "Think of it like an apartment building, if that helps, and Hendrik and I are your upstairs neighbors."

Anneliese forced a smile. "I've gotten off on the wrong foot."

"Don't give it another thought."

She felt Katja assessing her attributes and flaws, as if she were compiling a . . . What had Katja called it during the workshop? A character sketch. She flailed around for another subject.

"Where's Hendrik?"

"He's upstairs reading. His latest obsession is gas extraction in the Wadden Sea. Before that he kept bees."

"Where?"

"At the back of the garden. The hives are gone now. Before bees he collected antique pocket watches. He bought a microscope and tools and learned how to repair them." Katja glanced at her watch. "How are you feeling? Any morning sickness?"

"On and off. I've gained a pound or two. Willem says he likes my round tummy."

Katja's expression shifted slightly. "How sweet."

"Yes. And my sense of smell is insanely acute. You're wearing perfume, aren't you? Jasmine?"

"Yes, a dab behind one ear."

"You see? I could go on a game show where contestants are blindfolded and try to guess what they smell. I would win the prize." Anneliese knew she was rambling, and she caught Katja glancing at her watch again. She drew a deep breath. "Have you ever been pregnant, if you don't mind me asking?"

Katja didn't miss a beat. "Hendrik didn't want another child. More coffee?"

Anneliese admired the slippery reply. It was neither lie nor truth, and it didn't actually answer the question. "No, thanks. I'm cutting down on caffeine because of the baby."

Katja stood up and started gathering the empty cups, and Anneliese racked her brain for something to say before Katja dismissed her.

"Willem said to ask you about your deadline."

"I'm glad you brought that up. My editor wants a revised draft of my novel by Christmas. He said if I miss another deadline, the notion of a deadline goes out the window. I have to keep my nose to the grindstone. Of course, if you need anything, just ask."

Anneliese clenched her jaw. The message was clear: Don't be a nuisance, don't use your key, don't come unless invited.

"If I need something, should I WhatsApp you?" she said, keeping a straight face, and her sarcasm seemed to go unnoticed by Katja.

"I mute my phone while I'm working."

"Should I send smoke signals?"

Katja's face reddened. "You can leave a voicemail. I check my messages every three or four hours. Shall I show you out? I need to get to work."

Anneliese did something unprecedented, something that was totally out of character. She burst into tears, surprising herself as much as she must have surprised Katja. But maybe not so surprising. Her life had been turned upside down. She was pregnant and engaged. She lived in a claustrophobic goldfish bowl, though she knew that could be considered a contradiction in terms.

The locks. Her big secret. And now, Katja's rules—as if Anneliese were one of Willem's psycho patients. Her hopes for a cozy mother–daughter chat were dashed. She had no reason to think Katja even liked her, and it was on the tip of her tongue to blurt out that she was Mirella. If she did, maybe Katja would make time for her—or maybe not.

Katja lowered herself into the chair and handed Anneliese a tissue from her pocket. "I'm sorry I upset you, but I have to meet my deadline. I wish it were otherwise. Can I get you something? Tea or juice?"

Sniffing, Anneliese used the tissue to wipe one eye, then the other. "I'm not the weepy sort. Must be the estrogen." Or maybe progesterone? Or hCG? One thing she knew: acting snarky would not endear her to Katja. "I've taken enough of your time. I can find my way out, thank you."

CHAPTER

40

November 27, 2024

Diary entry

THIS MORNING ANNELIESE sat in my kitchen, trying very hard to win me over. But when she said that Willem liked her round tummy, I immediately pictured his lovely hands stroking her velvet skin. It felt like a blow to the solar plexus. For a moment, I wished I had a tasteless untraceable poison to slip into her coffee: a quick killer. There mustn't be the suffering of a lingering sickbed. Only a sudden slipping away, like falling into a bottomless sleep. I know death isn't like that because I've seen it up close.

When I stop and reread the lines above, I'm appalled at the turn my fantasy is taking. Maybe I should strike through the words, but they are only a jealous fantasy. So I let them stand.

Besides my murderous thoughts (momentary, I promise), I made her cry. Inexcusable!

It occurs to me Anneliese is the perfect model for Eveline, the sister of the protagonist in my novel in progress. Bright. Eager to please. Sly. (Anneliese trapped Willem into marrying her, didn't she?) She's beautiful in the way only the young can be. I couldn't take my eyes off her thick dark hair (much more suited to Eveline's character than blonde), her firm jawline, and smooth taut neck. I couldn't help but imagine her solid thighs parting for Willem—an image I blinked away before it fully formed.

I've aged badly: witness my thinning hair, the cellulite on my thighs, my sagging breasts. But if this is the punishment for my sins, I've gotten off lightly.

Hmm . . .

The changes I want to make to Eveline will mean reworking the scenes in which she appears—and a few in which she doesn't. I'll have to tweak the plot. I might even kill her at the end. The changes will set me back weeks, and my deadline is looming, but the novel will be better for it. I have to hunker down and make it work.

AUGUST 2004

CHAPTER

41

August 14, 2004

Willem

LIKE A CONDEMNED man, Willem had been counting down the days and the hours until Louisa's arrival. Now less than twenty-four to go.

He parked his bicycle next to the barbed wire fence that separated Doeksen's dairy farm from the dike road. The wooden gate gaped open. Jurriaan always refused to cross the cattle guard, afraid his lame foot might slip through the rails, but Willem crossed over with a skip and a jump. As he hiked up the gravel drive to the farmhouse, cows grazing in the pasture lifted their heads. The cows didn't bother him, but his heart fluttered when the bull lumbered his way, head bobbing, balls swaying, tail swishing. The bull could crash through the fence if he had a mind to, but he stopped, one brown eye trained on Willem.

An army-green Land Rover was parked in front of the house, but no one answered Willem's knock. Shading his eyes with his hand, he peered around the fields. There was no sign of Doeksen. He climbed over a stile and followed the well-beaten path to the barn.

The pungent smell of animals, manure, and hay nearly knocked him over. The farmer was pouring grain from a big burlap bag into the feed troughs.

"Mr. Doeksen," Willem yelled.

The farmer set the bag on the ground. He wore a work apron over a shirt with rolled-up sleeves and stained jeans. He was around Louisa's age, with a sunburned face and muscular forearms.

"Young Mr. Veldkamp?" Doeksen said in his heavy island accent. "How's your tae?"

Willem knew *tae* meant "father."

Hendrik and Doeksen enjoyed an unlikely friendship, the rich city slicker and the struggling dairy farmer. Both men were taciturn. Sometimes they met up at the pub in Oerd for a beer, and Willem imagined them drinking in silence.

"My dad is doing fine," Willem said. "Is it okay if I use the dinghy this afternoon?

"Is your tae going?"

"Yes," Willem lied.

Doeksen grunted something that sounded like, "You have to pay for the gasoline."

Willem crossed over to the farmer and handed him a tenner, hoping for change, but Doeksen shoved the money into his shirt pocket.

"Bring her back in one piece."

Willem froze. For a moment, he thought the farmer meant Katja.

Bring the dinghy back whole!

"Thank you, sir." He exited the barn and danced a little jig in the yard.

* * *

That afternoon, he and Katja chained their bicycles to the fence a half mile down the road from Doeksen's farm. She wore her usual attire: trainers, shorts, and a T-shirt with wide arm holes that revealed part of her bra. Her hair fell in waves on her shoulders. He tried to grin, but his face was too stiff. Did she suspect the reason for the picnic? Was she as nervous as he? Would being nervous affect his . . . performance? Jeetje.

They climbed over the dike path onto the rickety wooden pier that jutted out from the bank. Three weather-beaten boats were moored: an ancient fishing boat with peeling black paint, *Iron Lady* scrawled on the bow; a blue runabout called *Anne-Noor*, and Doeksen's once-white dinghy named *Glop*. A blue boat cover stretched over the little craft, keeping out the rain.

"Be careful. The boards are slippery," Willem said. But Katja was peering at the sky, not at her feet.

"Willem, don't the clouds look like sailboats scudding across a lake?"

"Yeah, sort of." The clouds were just clouds, and the blue was sky, not a lake. He guessed he didn't have a poetic bone in his body. Worse, his mind conjured up the image of Louisa drinking wine on a terrace, inventing ways to ruin his life while she watched real sailboats race around on Lake Como. With an effort, he pushed the image out of his head.

It was flood, the tide coming in. In the distance lay a sandbank that stayed dry even at high tide. It was Willem's favorite fishing spot, even if he caught only the occasional eel or flounder. The sandbank was a place Louisa didn't know existed; she preferred the white sand and the beach pavilions on the north side of the island.

He shrugged off his backpack.

"*Glop*?" Katja asked, reading the name on the bow.

"It's island dialect for 'narrow passage.'"

"Whose boat is it?"

"The dairy farmer's. We can use it as long as we pay for the gasoline. I paid him this morning."

"You've thought of everything."

Willem smiled, thinking of the package of condoms he had purchased in Oerd, now stashed in the inside pocket of the backpack.

"Dad taught me how to drive the dinghy. Sometimes, Jurriaan and I take it out to fish." What he didn't say was that he wasn't allowed to take the dinghy without Hendrik.

He unsnapped the boat cover, rolled it up, and threw it into the dinghy. He shoved his backpack under the rear bench. As he helped Katja into the front, she smiled in amusement. He felt his face flush, realizing she didn't need his help, but she didn't protest, and he liked touching her hand. Before casting off, Willem pulled two life preservers from the storage compartment and handed one to Katja.

The outboard motor wasn't all that powerful, only two horsepower, and it sounded a lot like the spin cycle of a washing machine. But Katja looked over her shoulder at him and grinned, her hair flying in a cloud of red gold. He wasn't old enough to drive her places in a car, but a boat ride was pretty impressive. He felt older. More confident. And he needed confidence for what he hoped was going to happen.

"Tell me where we're going," she yelled.

Until now, he had kept their destination a surprise. He pointed to a shadow on the water a half mile ahead.

"Is it an island?" she asked.

"No. It's officially a sandbank. It's not big enough to be an island." Lutine was a nature reserve and off limits to the public, but he and Jurriaan had never encountered a forest ranger or any human visitor—only seabirds, strutting around, and the occasional seal.

Fifteen minutes later, the dinghy was as close to the sandbank as Willem dared with the engine running. He cut the power and picked up the oars. After a few strokes, he stopped.

"We need to get out. Help me pull her the rest of the way." The water was up to his knees, higher on Katja, but the sand was solid under their trainers. Katja wasn't as strong as Jurriaan, but she was nimbler, and they soon pulled the dingy above the high tide line.

Katja turned a three sixty, pure delight on her face. Willem thought his chest would burst with pride, as if he had created the sandbank himself.

"I know the perfect spot for the picnic—this way." He hoisted the backpack and led her over a dune. They climbed over a second dune and found themselves in a dip protected from the wind and very private.

He pulled a tablecloth from his backpack and spread it in the little gully. They sat down on the sand, facing each other.

"I brought beer," he said, taking out the two bottles and leaving the sandwiches for later. *"Shit."*

"What's wrong?" Katja asked.

"I forgot the opener." He must have left it on the kitchen counter. *Idiot!*

She laughed, leaned forward, and kissed him on the ear and on the neck.

Willem heard Bas's voice in his head: *"Now or never."*

He kissed her deeply, and she kissed him back, but after a few moments, she jerked away, a spot of red blooming in each cheek. She stared wide-eyed at Willem. Her pupils were enormous. He slipped his hand inside her blouse and cupped a breast. He felt her nipple harden. Felt her heartbeat strong and fast. She was breathing hard. They undressed as though on silent command. The blue sky and the white dunes receded until there was only Katja, warm and soft in his arms.

He finished quickly—too quickly—and lay on top, panting, still throbbing, and cursing to himself. He hadn't satisfied her. A cardinal sin, according to Bas. An apology was in order.

"That was my first time," he said.

She shushed him with her finger on his lips. Stroked his hair, kissed his ear, and ran a fingernail along his spine. When she pushed her hips against his, he shuddered.

"Do it again," she said. "This time slower."

"Shit," Willem said afterward. "I think it leaked."

"Don't worry. I'm on the pill."

That made him pause. But of course he had figured she wasn't a virgin. She was twenty-three, and she'd had boyfriends. Maybe still had a boyfriend.

"Are you going to see the guy in Amsterdam again?"

"Who?"

"The one you dated this summer."

"We broke up."

He had more questions, but the closed expression on her face silenced him.

He brushed the sand off her breasts, off her rounded stomach, and off her soft thighs. While he dressed, he watched her pull on her panties and bra, then the rest of her clothes. She sat beside him on the ridge of the dune, and they ate the sandwiches. The sun was dim, the sky more gray than blue, a haze over the water. Soon, it would be ebb and the water would recede, exposing the mudflats teaming with crabs, worms, and cockles. The tide was predictable, unstoppable.

"Does the sandbank have a name?" Katja asked, tucking a lock of coppery hair behind her ear.

This was Willem's favorite story from Wexalia folk lore. "Lutine. It's named after the HMS *Lutine.* In 1799, the ship sank in the North Sea during a storm. It had a cargo of gold coins on board. All the crew was lost except one man."

"How tragic. What happened to the gold?"

"The ship broke apart, and the wreckage was silted over. The spot is famous for its dangerous currents. Once every fifty years or so, the silt shifts, exposing the remains for a short time. Salvagers have recovered only a small part of the gold.

"*Lutine* sounds French."

"The ship was a French frigate captured by the British. *Lutine* means 'a female elf.'"

"This is a magical place," she said, wriggling her toes in the warm sand.

He squeezed her hand. "I love you. I don't care who knows." He waited for her reply, his heart hammering.

Her posture stiffened. "Louisa can't find out."

"Why?"

"Because she's a jealous witch. Besides, we're family. She'll turn it into something ugly."

He slung his arm around her shoulders and tried to draw her closer, but she shook free.

"I'm serious, Willem. If Louisa finds out we're lovers, she'll be furious. I don't know what she would do." She clutched his arm, her nails digging into his flesh. "No touching. Don't come to my room. Don't even look at me. Not while she's here. You have to keep our secret. Do you swear?"

"Are you blowing me off?"

"Does it look like I'm blowing you off?"

He didn't know.

She unlatched her fingers from around his arm and stood up.

Willem stared at her freckled knees for several moments and slowly got to his feet. "Jurriaan asked me yesterday if you were my girlfriend."

"What did you tell him?" she asked, crossing her arms over her chest.

"I said you weren't." He hated lying to Jurriaan, and strictly speaking, he wasn't. You could hang out with a girlfriend. Go places with her. Hold her hand in public. You didn't have to hide a girlfriend.

"Does Hendrik suspect?"

"Are you kidding? Dad's in another world most of the time. How long do we have to keep our relationship a secret?"

She cast her eyes down and plucked a purple flower from a mound of flowering grass.

"How long?" he repeated.

"I don't know."

"A month? A year? Help me out here."

"Until it's safe."

"Until you don't need her money anymore?" He regretted the words as soon as they rolled off his tongue.

Her chin lifted. "There's that too."

She was right. It was a stupid idea to tell his mother. He was acting like a lovesick teenager. At least she hadn't pulled the *"I'm older and wiser"* routine.

He wadded up the tablecloth and tried to ram it into the backpack, but it didn't fit, so he yanked it out and started over, this time folding it first. Katja's anxious green eyes tracked his every move as he gathered up the unopened bottles of beer and their trash.

Shit. She hadn't said *"I love you"* back.

CHAPTER

42

August 15, 2004

Diary entry

I'M WRITING THIS at five AM because I can't sleep.

At midnight I had wondered what to do about Willem. It had been a mistake to let him make love to me. He's only sixteen (nearly seventeen, as he likes to remind me), he's infatuated, he's impulsive, and he's my stepsister's son. While we're not blood related, I've crossed a line. To make matters worse, I'm pining for a man I can't have. It's a recipe for disaster.

At three o'clock, I was still awake—and hungry. I went downstairs to get a bite to eat. A light shone under the kitchen door. Someone else couldn't sleep.

I smelled the whisky before I saw Hendrik sitting at the table. He was staring down at a half-full glass. A floorboard creaked under my foot, and he looked up. I was suddenly conscious that my thin nightgown clung to my breasts and hips.

"I couldn't sleep," I said.

"Me neither. Sit down. Please."

The curtains at the kitchen window billowed over the sink. My nightgown billowed between my legs, and I felt goose bumps rise on my flesh. The wind carried the dank smell of the sea.

I sat down and gazed at the small square of night that was visible. The moon and the stars were playing peekaboo behind thick churning clouds. My nerves were on edge: the change in the weather, Louisa's arrival tomorrow (actually today), the man sitting across the table.

"Would you like some whisky?" he asked, reaching for the bottle.

"No, thanks."

"A glass of wine?"

"A small one."

"Do you want something to eat?"

"Cheese. But I can get it myself."

"No. Don't move."

He rummaged in the refrigerator, opened cabinets, took a knife from a drawer, dropped it. He left it lying on the floor and selected another. A few minutes later, he set a bottle of wine, a glass, a plate of Saint Paulin, and baguettes on the table. He uncorked the bottle and poured, dribbling wine down the side of my glass, making me wonder how much whisky he had drunk.

I took a sip. "The wine is good, even if it's not Louisa's favorite," I said. Jurriaan had told me about the wine crisis looming on the horizon.

"She won't like it."

"She wouldn't admit it if she did."

He smiled at that. Most of the time Hendrik's thin face wore a hunted look, but when he smiled, his face was transformed, and he looked as handsome as he did in his wedding photos.

"It's been a joy having you with us again," he said, his words slurred. He reached out and caressed my face. "You're very beautiful."

I froze.

His eyes were black in the dim lamplight. I wished I hadn't come downstairs. I wished I had put on a robe.

"Katja, what do you think of me?

I pondered nervously. "You're brilliant. You're—"

"I mean what do you think of me as a man?"

My thoughts scattered in all directions, like a flock of birds startled by a sudden loud noise. Hendrik had always treated me like a favorite niece, if not like a daughter. What was this all about? It was obvious he had drunk too much. I wondered if he would remember our conversation tomorrow. I hoped that he wouldn't.

"I'm not the right person to ask," I said guardedly.

"Of course. Forgive me."

His shoulders slumped, and the hunted expression returned.

"Why are you getting drunk?" I asked.

"I just felt like it."

From the moment Louisa steps off the ferry, she'll take command, plot strategies, conduct inspections, mete out punishments. Was he bracing for her arrival?

He refilled our glasses and asked me if I was making progress on my novel. He's the only person in my life who takes a genuine interest. Louisa says I'm wasting my time.

By the time I had gone upstairs, the tension between us had eased and he had become Hendrik again—a lonely man married to a woman who took advantage of him in unforgivable ways—a woman whose abusive behavior he has always refused to acknowledge.

But I'm worse than her.

CHAPTER

43

August 15, 2004

Willem

LOUISA SEEMED TO float down the ferry ramp, her feet skimming the ground. She wore a wide-brimmed floppy hat, dark sunglasses, and a canary-yellow sundress. An aura shimmered around her like air over hot asphalt. A few heads in the crowd turned, but no one recognized her.

Willem glanced sideways at Katja standing beside him, her bare arm grazing his, so solid and real. She must have spotted Louisa too, because she shifted away, ensuring a no contact zone between them. Hendrik was twitchier than usual, and good old Jurriaan bounced on his toes, straining to get a glimpse of their mother.

A few moments later, Louisa greeted them with a wide smile and set her suitcase on the dock. She kissed Hendrik's cheek, leaving a thick, greasy coral lip print. "Hendrik, dear," she murmured.

She hugged Jurriaan and clapped him twice on the back, then held him at arm's length and looked him up and down, finally chucking him under the chin. In her eyes, Jurriaan could do no wrong. An old resentment flared inside Willem, but he was instantly ashamed. He touched Jurriaan's hand to show his solidarity.

"Willem," Louisa said, giving him a *"wait until later, young man"* kind of look.

His stomach pitched at the thought that she'd had an entire month to devise the most spiteful punishment possible for sneaking out in the car.

She beamed at Katja before branding them, one by one, with a coral kiss, each lipstick print fainter than the last.

"Phew. I'm sweating," Louisa said, and yanked up one of her shoulder straps.

They strode toward the parking lot, but after a few strides, she stopped and scowled at a man standing ten feet away. He had a tanned, leathery face, a deeply bracketed mouth, and dark squinting eyes. If not for the red beard, Willem wouldn't have recognized him wearing a clean shirt, trousers, and shiny leather shoes. It was Menso de Vries, the beachcomber. Menso scowled back at Louisa as the crowd split around them and moved on.

"Mrs. Veldkamp. It's been a long time," Menso sneered.

"Not long enough."

He tutted.

"I hope we can avoid each other," Louisa said, lifting her chin high, probably so she could look down her nose at him.

He shook his head in mock regret. "Won't be easy. It's a small island."

"Stay away from my sons."

Menso's face twisted with anger, and he opened his mouth. But before he had the chance to retort, a redheaded woman with a toddler in tow plunked down her suitcase on the wooden planks.

"Papa," the woman said, kissing Menso's cheek. He glowered at Louisa over the top of his daughter's head.

"What a nasty man," Louisa muttered, turning away.

"Where there's smoke, there's fire," Hendrik said.

Willem hung back a few moments, caught Menso's eye, and gave him a nod before hurrying after the others.

* * *

That evening Louisa insisted on having dinner on the terrace, even though storm clouds were gathering—as if she thought she could stop the rain by sheer willpower. She sat at the head of the table and filled their plates with steaming paella from a big iron wok. She raised her glass. "To family."

"To family," they chorused.

She took a sip of wine and pulled a face. "What's this?" she asked, lowering her glass.

"The shop doesn't carry the wine you like anymore," Hendrik said.

"Can't they place a special order?"

He shrugged. "You can try tomorrow."

You, not *I*? Willem eyed his father. Since when did Louisa have to order or shop for herself?

She gave Hendrik a searching look over her glass. "This one is a bit fruity, but it's not bad."

Willem sat up straighter. What was going on? Why didn't Louisa blow her stack? She still wore her big fake smile. A moment later her gaze landed on Willem. "How have you been spending your holiday?"

Willem forced himself not to glance at Katja. "Nothing special. Biking. Picnicking. Swimming."

"Not driving, I hope?"

"No."

"How is Bas?"

"I haven't heard from him."

"We'll talk after dinner," she said sweetly.

Willem's heart bonked against his ribs.

Jurriaan said, "We went fishing."

"Where?" she asked.

Willem cut off Jurriaan before he could get them in hot water. "On the pier at the dune lake."

"It's too dangerous for you to take the dinghy out by yourselves," Louisa said.

"We wouldn't," Willem said, avoiding Katja's sharp glance. He and Jurriaan had fished on the Wadden in Doeksen's dinghy since they were twelve, though not when Louisa was on the island.

Jurriaan said, "I caught an eel, but I threw it back."

"That must have been exciting," Louisa said.

A silence fell.

"How was summer school?" Katja asked.

"I had a fantastic group of students this year. Beautiful young people. Very talented. The six weeks flew by." Her smile was warm, maybe genuine.

Her good humor boded well for the week ahead, but her mood could swing in a flash.

"Katja, you're sunburned," Louisa said. "With your fair skin, you can't be too careful. I'll make a list of chores you can do indoors this week."

"Of course, Louisa," Katja said, and clenched her jaw.

"Hendrik, dear, one of the cabinet doors in the kitchen is sagging. Will you fix it?"

The cabinet door had been driving Jurriaan bananas, and he had fiddled with the hinges but succeeded only in making it worse. Hendrik could fix anything, but he didn't notice stuff like that.

When Hendrik didn't respond, Louisa shrugged and said, "Everyone, eat your dinner. Think of the starving children in Mozambique." She said that a lot, but Willem doubted she gave a hoot about starving children anywhere. "You too, Hendrik—clean your plate."

He fixed his eyes on Louisa and laid his knife and fork crosswise on his plate, his paella only half eaten. Willem watched in alarm.

"If you don't like the paella, dear," she said, an edge creeping into her voice, "Katja can get you something else."

A drop of rain pinged on Willem's plate.

"I'm not hungry," Hendrik said.

Louisa reached over with her own fork and speared one of the jumbo shrimps off his plate. "Take a bite. The least you can do is eat, after the trouble Katja went to."

Hendrik eyed the pale pink shrimp, which seemed to tremble on the fork, but Willem realized it was Louisa's hand trembling. Willem held his breath, fearing that his father was going to knock the fork from her hand. Several seconds dragged by. Hendrik opened his mouth and Louisa shoveled in the bite.

Relieved, Willem exhaled.

Katja scraped back her chair. "The dinner was no trouble, Louisa." She began stacking up the empty plates and set Hendrik's on top. "It's going to rain."

No sooner said than the heavens opened and rain poured down.

Louisa dashed inside while Hendrik and Jurriaan followed her with the dirty dishes and the half-full wok. Willem held the tablecloth over his and Katja's head, and they scurried into the mudroom, breaking apart as they entered the kitchen.

Louisa poured herself another glass of wine. "Willem, I want to have a word while the others clean up."

As he followed her through the hall to the sitting room, he played various scenarios in his head. She might ground him for the rest of the vacation and give him boring chores to do, such as weeding and mowing while she supervised from a lounge chair. She might renege on her promise to pay for his driving lessons when he turned eighteen. He was pretty sure she wouldn't hit him, because she must know he would fight back. But in that short hike down the hall, his nerve deserted him, and he decided to wait until after the vacation to tell her that he'd been expelled from the hockey club.

Still, there was no doubt about it. Now he was in for it.

DECEMBER 2024

CHAPTER

44

Anneliese

"I WASN'T SURE WHICH bell to ring," Carla said.

"You rang the right one." Anneliese pulled the door further open to let Carla squeeze her bulk through. The old piano teacher had visibly aged. Her red hair was dusted with gray, and her curls were thinner than eight years ago.

"It's good to see you, child." Her enormous arms hugged Anneliese. It was like being smothered in soft pillows.

"The house is fabulous," Carla said, her voice booming in the entrance hall.

Anneliese winced, having forgotten that Carla's normal speaking volume was a shout. She lowered her own voice to a whisper, hoping Carla would take the hint. "Willem's practice is through that door. We have the ground floor. His father and stepmother live upstairs."

She gave Carla a quick tour of the tiny apartment, taking all of two minutes, and served tea and sandwiches at the kitchen table. They sat facing the garden. A scattering of purple flowers poked through a blanket of dead leaves. The open space above the canal was visible, but the water was hidden by a box hedge.

"When is the baby due?" Carla asked between mouthfuls.

"June."

"How do you feel?"

"I've had some morning sickness. Par for the course."

"Did you hear that Renata had twins?"

Anneliese's mind wandered as Carla updated her on the marriages, babies, and divorces of her old schoolmates.

At noon Willem strode in. He looked especially handsome in his gray suit, lavender shirt, and navy tie, the colors turning his hazel eyes brown. He squeezed Anneliese's shoulder, kissed the top of her head, and took a seat. She introduced him proudly, as if he were a cake she had baked.

"Would you like a sandwich?" Anneliese asked him.

"No, I can only stay a minute. I'm expecting a patient, but I didn't want to miss meeting your piano teacher."

He smiled at Carla as he reached for Anneliese's hand. His touch sent a thrill of desire through her, reminding her of the things he had done to her in bed last night.

"I'm retired now." Carla patted her limp curls and simpered. "But I gave piano lessons to the children in the village for forty years. Anneliese was one of my most talented students. Such a pity she stopped playing. Have you been to Noorddorp?"

"Not yet."

"Have you met Tineke and Ray?"

"Yes, at the engagement dinner." He glanced at Anneliese, and she felt her face grow hot.

She was running out of excuses. She didn't want him to visit her provincial village, bereft of culture, taste, and sophistication. Or to visit the crappy little house in which she had grown up, with its nicotine-stained walls and sour memories. She didn't want him to become better acquainted with Tineke and Ray. They had been on their best behavior at the engagement dinner, a bit cowed by the fancy dinner party on a boat. Still, they had made everyone uncomfortable with their blunt questions about Jurriaan's disabilities, and they had managed to reveal that Anneliese had been adopted. In their own home, they would let down their guard. They wouldn't be able to hide who they were, or to know they should.

Carla said, "Ray Bakker is a big wheel in Noorddorp. He manages the local car dealership."

"He told me," Willem said.

Carla leaned forward. "Anneliese tells me Louisa Veldkamp was your mother. I once took a group of my students to Groningen to see her perform. That was in the early nineties."

"Louisa was in her heyday back then," Willem said.

"I used the Veldkamp lesson book series to teach."

Willem looked at his watch and stood up. "I'm sorry, I have to go. Have a safe trip home, Carla."

As soon as the door closed, Carla said, "You didn't tell me he was so yummy. Rich, nice, and sexy. It's obvious he adores you."

Anneliese smiled, happy that Carla was impressed. She was a gossip and knew everyone in the village. In no time at all, the village would know how well Anneliese was doing. Betsy Wetsy had landed on her feet.

She was saving the best for last. "Do you want to see Louisa's piano studio?"

* * *

Carla's chest was heaving when they reached the bottom of the basement stairs. Anneliese unlocked the door and stepped aside as Carla sailed straight to the baby grand.

"Hers?" Carla said in a hushed voice.

"Yes. Would you like to play?"

Carla pushed back the bench and sat down. There was a grace in her movements despite her bulk. Her long, thick legs reached the pedals easily. Anneliese stood next to her and listened to her play. The expression on her old teacher's face was nothing short of rapturous. A half hour later, Carla gently closed the fallboard and gave a deep, contented sigh.

Anneliese said, "Louisa's original manuscripts are in the cabinet. Come. I'll show you." She yanked on Carla's arm and helped pry her off the bench.

Together they sorted through the music books and sheet music, Carla gasping in delight at the treasure trove.

Anneliese said, "I want to give you something." On the bottom shelf was a stack of autographed lesson books. Anneliese lifted off the top one and handed it to Carla. "It's signed by Louisa. Look on the title page."

"I can't accept this. It must be valuable to a collector."

"No one will miss it."

Carla held the lesson book in one hand, as though weighing it, and pressed the other hand against her chest. She consulted her watch.

"I have to catch my train."

"There's still time. I want to ask you for a favor."

Carla glanced at the book and shifted her weight from one orthopedic shoe to the other.

Anneliese said, "I want to play piano again. I want to get back to my previous level. Will you give me lessons?"

"How long has it been, dear? Eight years? Playing the piano isn't like riding a bike. Your technical skills will have regressed. You'll have to practice consistently for months, maybe much longer."

"I'm willing to do that."

"Why?"

"Willem's a respected psychiatrist. His father is a brilliant inventor. Katja is a novelist. I'm nothing. The only talent I have is playing the piano."

"Honey, you're not nothing. Willem loves you. Anyone can see that. And you're expecting a baby. Look at this house. You've done well for yourself. I always said Anneliese Bakker had too much class for Noorddorp."

"Please, Carla."

A silence.

"Why didn't you return my calls?" Carla asked, sounding aggrieved.

"What are you talking about? What calls?"

Carla blew out her lower lip. "After Daan passed, you quit showing up for your lessons. I telephoned your house. Repeatedly. I left messages with Tineke. I wanted you to resume the lessons. Finally, I gave up."

"Tineke didn't tell me." Anneliese could guess why. Ray had complained about the cost of the lessons even as he showered Daan with gifts, including a new racing bicycle the week before his death. And later there were funeral expenses to pay.

"Water under the bridge," Carla said, looking at her watch again. "I'm retired, Anneliese. Besides, the commute is four hours round trip."

"I can pay you well."

"It's not the money. I don't have the energy, child. There must be dozens of excellent teachers in Amsterdam." Carla held out the autographed music book, and when Anneliese refused to take it, she laid it reverently on top of the baby grand.

Anneliese followed Carla's ponderous steps and jiggling hips up the basement stairs and through the hall to the front door. She saw her old piano teacher in a new light. Carla had become the embodiment of Noorddorp's failures.

"I'll call you a taxi," Anneliese said.

"The tram's cheaper."

"I'm paying. I insist."

Five minutes later, Carla stepped into the taxi, and Anneliese waved from the curb until the car turned the corner and disappeared from sight.

She could spend the duration of the pregnancy lounging in bed, eating bonbons if she wanted, but if she practiced the piano every day, she could get back to her previous level by the time the baby was born. The family would be impressed. All she had to do was follow the guidance in Louisa's lesson books.

CHAPTER

45

December 2024

Anneliese

ANNELIESE DITCHED HER plans to practice piano when she learned she had the house to herself for a few hours. Willem was attending a lecture, and Katja had taken Hendrik to the neuropsychologist.

She hesitated in front of the locked staircase, fingering the bundle of keys in a pocket of her cardigan—actually Willem's cardigan. Thick and warm, the sweater reached to her knees.

She turned the key.

She went up the stairs to the first landing, which led to the living room, and continued up the next flight, which was clad in a plush white carpet that absorbed the sound of her steps. The carpet was pristine, like freshly fallen snow.

The second landing gave on to a hall. The doors were closed. She opened the first: a spacious bedroom with a king-size bed. The walls were white, matching the carpet, and the furniture was white, with sleek, stark lines. No frills. Tidy and proper. She half expected to find a sign over the bed: "missionary position only." The ensuite bathroom was tiled in white, gray, and beige.

Next to it was a smaller bedroom, also white, and across the hall, what had to be Hendrik's study, his tan pullover draped over the back of the desk chair. This was where he spent most of his time. Her eyes were at once riveted to an enormous wall map pinned above the desk. She drew closer. It was a map of the North Sea and the bordering countries, filled with hundreds of curious pencil notations. She noticed the large, spidery letters in all caps: *DOGGERLAND*. She couldn't make sense of it.

In the hall, she passed a second bathroom before coming to the room at the front of the house.

She turned the handle.

The door opened.

Anneliese felt a wave of icy air that was thick with the scent of jasmine. She scanned Katja's study. The same plush white carpet, a bookcase crammed two-deep with books, an antique writing desk carved with curlicues, an ancient metal filing cabinet. The only window in the room overlooked the grassy median in the Apollolaan with its bronze statues. She buttoned up the cardigan and imagined herself in an igloo.

A clank from downstairs made her heart jump. She hastily retreated into the hall and listened, but the only sound she heard was a neighbor's dog barking. The clank she'd heard was possibly the boiler switching on. She returned to Katja's study.

Katja wanted to keep her child a secret, but if she had even one sentimental bone in her body, she might have kept something as a remembrance. If such a thing existed, where would she hide it? Katja could have slipped a letter or a photo between the pages of a book. Anneliese swore. She didn't have enough time to search in each book.

She started with the desk and found the usual desk crap: pens, paperclips, Katja's passport, a blood donor card, the device to access an online bank account—and a manuscript marked *Draft* on the front page. She lifted it out. The title was *The Lie*. Autobiographical, she wondered? A rubber band bound the five hundred double-spaced pages. She placed the manuscript in the drawer and turned to the filing cabinet. Locked.

When Anneliese was little, she'd sometimes wedged herself behind the living room sofa, a safe hiding place where Daan never thought to look. Once, she peeked over the back and saw Ray hide the key to the liquor cabinet on the top of the wall unit. He didn't know that Daan had learned how to pick locks from a library book.

She rolled the desk chair over to the bookcase and climbed up. The seat wobbled and the chair rolled whenever she shifted her weight. Carefully, she stretched up her arms and ran her hands over the gritty top. Nothing. She climbed down and rolled the chair a few feet to the next section. She didn't stop until she had run her hand over the length of the bookcase. No key.

Where else? She sat down on the chair and spun the seat, letting her eyes scan the room. The key might be behind a book or on Katja's key ring. She closed her eyes and spun again, thinking hard. If it was her own filing cabinet, she would hide the key someplace handy.

She hopped off the chair and crossed the white carpet. Kneeling, she squeezed her hand into the space between the filing cabinet and the wall, and felt along the floor. Her hand closed around a loose bit of metal and drew out a key.

The key fit. She slid open the top drawer, which was filled with bank statements, ledgers, and receipts. The middle drawer contained printouts of Katja's novels and short stories. Anneliese didn't know what she hoped to find—maybe her adoption papers or a love letter to Katja from Anneliese's father. Provided he had been more than either a random hookup or a violent encounter in a dark alley.

And then she had it.

Inside the bottom drawer were dozens of small spiral notebooks, each the size of a paperback and labeled with a year. She opened one at random and flipped through the pages. Her heartbeat raced with excitement when she realized what she had in her hand. The entries were written in a messy but legible hand. Here and there passages were crossed out with such pressure that the pen had torn the page. She shuffled through the notebooks until she found the one labeled "2000." Her fingers trembled as she turned to December. Her eyes skipped at random over the pages.

December 2, 2000

Sorry I've been neglecting you, dear diary . . .

December 21, 2000

The baby will be born any day now . . .

The slam of the front door didn't register. She kept reading.

December 28, 2000

The months of deception culminated in a visit today to an office of the Foundation for Aiding Unwed Mothers (FAM).

* * *

"What are you doing?" boomed a voice.

She startled and nearly dropped the diary. A folded sheet of paper slipped from between the pages and drifted to the floor. Hendrik stood in the doorway, his dark eyes fierce under heavy black eyebrows. Her face burned. The family would never trust her again. She might never learn who her father was. Worse, what would Willem think?

But it was only Hendrik. She could manage *him*. Surely.

She forced a bright smile. "I was looking for a book."

"In Katja's filing cabinet?"

The drawer gaped open behind her.

"Sorry. I confess. I'm terribly nosy. Will you forgive me?"

He stared at the diary in her hand.

She said, "Why are you back so soon? Did something happen?"

"The doctor was called away. I'm seeing him tomorrow instead."

"Where's Katja?"

"She went to the florist to buy flowers for Louisa."

Today was Louisa's birthday. After lunch, the family was going to visit her grave. It was an annual ritual, and Anneliese was invited, a sign they were on the road to accepting her as part of the family. Had she spoiled everything with her snooping?

She closed the diary, but every cell in her body rebelled at returning it to the drawer before she had read it properly.

"How does Katja stand the cold? I wonder if the radiator is closed. Would you check?" she said, trying to deflect his attention.

"Katja likes it cold," Hendrik said.

"But it's terribly damp. It can't be healthy."

When he turned toward the radiator, she stooped to retrieve the fallen sheet of paper, opening it for just a second to confirm what it was. She shoved the diary and the letter into a pocket of her cardigan and slammed the drawer of the filing cabinet. But she didn't have time to return the key to its hiding place, so she dropped it into her other pocket with the house keys.

Hendrik rotated the knob on the radiator and Anneliese heard water trickling in.

He turned. "Katja doesn't allow anyone in her study. She says it's her private place to write."

"I didn't know. I'm sorry."

"Now you do. Will you fix me a cup of tea?"

Was that it? No lecture? No righteous anger?

Her heart was knocking against her ribs as she followed him downstairs to the kitchen. Katja could be back at any moment. She switched on the electric kettle. After serving him a cup of tea, she fished the house keys out of her pocket, planning to make a quick, cowardly getaway.

"Join me, please, Anneliese. We need to talk."

Here it comes. Nervous sweat ran down her sides. She laid the keys on the table and tugged off Willem's cardigan. She hung it on the back of a chair and poured herself a cup of tea.

"I'm not going to tell Katja," he said.

"Why not?"

"It will be our little secret."

Not at all a satisfying answer, she thought. Did he plan to use their secret as leverage for something . . . someday? What was it he had said the first time they'd met: Never look a gift horse in the mouth? Maybe he was merely being kind. Maybe he liked her and wanted to help.

The front door slammed and their eyes met. Neither said anything. A few minutes later, Katja entered the kitchen, carrying a pot of crimson poinsettias. It was comical how her mouth formed a small *o* of surprise when she saw Anneliese.

"Hendrik invited me for tea. Do you want a cup?" Anneliese said.

"Sorry, I don't have time."

Anneliese pushed back her chair. "I was just leaving anyway. See you later."

She grabbed the keys and forced herself not to run out of the room.

C H A P T E R

46

December 2024

Anneliese

Anneliese squeezed Willem's hand as they followed Hendrik and Katja through the tall iron gates that flanked the entrance to Zorgvlied. She couldn't help but admire Katja's elegant figure in a camel coat and black ankle boots with high heels. Hendrik looked distinguished in a long wool trench coat. Jurriaan took up the rear, clutching the pot of poinsettias to his chest. He had been quiet in the car—resigned—the plant clamped between his knees.

The two-story white visitor center stood at the end of a short drive. The building had intersecting gable roofs with red roof tiles. Behind it, the driveway changed to a winding gravel path, straightening at the canal, the plots along the water close together, like cars in a parking lot. On the opposite bank, trees, bare of leaves, bordered the back lawns of villas. From her side, the trees reflected upside down in the water.

They followed the path, fairly straight for several minutes before curving sharply to the left. The plots in this sector were larger and not laid in a discernible pattern. Water dripped from the branches overhead.

"Is it much farther?" Anneliese asked, shivering.

"Five minutes. Her grave is in Paradiso. It's in the far eastern corner."

Paradiso was a newer part of the cemetery, set aside for large and unusual monuments—some of them bizarre. They passed graves adorned with statues: plump cherubs, a towering angel, an enormous gorilla holding a baby. Willem stopped at a grave under a sweetgum tree. The slab was covered by a mat of rotting black leaves.

"I pay them to keep the slab clean," Hendrik grumbled.

"Let me," Jurriaan said.

He knelt, set the flowerpot on the ground, and began brushing leaves aside with his gloved hands, the bottoms of his corduroy trousers soaking up the damp. The ends of his scarf kept getting in his way. Gradually, he uncovered the once-white stone slab, longer than six feet and nearly as wide.

Anneliese read the inscription.

Beloved wife, mother, and sister
Louisa Veldkamp
December 6, 1964–August 17, 2004

Sculpted in relief below the dates was a pair of hands poised over a piano keyboard. Each hand was three feet long from wrist to fingertips, and the fingers were disproportionately long. The details lent the hands a creepily lifelike appearance, with veins, knuckles, wrinkles, and short-clipped nails. She noticed Willem pushing his fists deep into his pockets.

Jurriaan scrambled to his feet, brushing off his cords. The family drew closer, pulling Anneliese with them, and formed a semicircle at the foot of the grave. They bowed their heads and closed their eyes. Anneliese peered from beneath her lashes at the somber faces. Was someone going to lead them in prayer? Make a speech? The seconds ticked by, and no one spoke. The icy drizzle coated Anneliese's face. Her lips went numb. A seagull wheeled overhead. All she could hear was the muffled roar of traffic from the highway that ringed the city. One minute. Two minutes.

An image popped into her head, and a little shudder rippled through her: Daan's body decomposing in a coffin in a cemetery on the edge of Noorddorp. She had attended his funeral solely to see for herself the coffin being lowered into the ground. But she swore never to visit his grave—never.

Heads lifted. Eyes opened.

Hendrik swayed.

"Are you all right, Dad?" Willem asked, reaching out to steady him.

"A little tired."

"Do you want to leave?"

"No," Hendrik said, staring at the grave. After a silence, he said, "Louisa shouldn't be alone. When the time comes, I want to be buried beside her."

Anneliese's eyes darted to Katja's face, which had flushed red.

"What about Katja?" Jurriaan asked.

"What about her?" Hendrik said.

"Don't you want to be buried next to her too?"

"No, son. I belong with your mother."

Jurriaan nodded.

Willem leaned toward Katja and whispered, "Hendrik doesn't mean it."

"I know," she said, her voice low. "But he's unpredictable. I never know what he'll do next. What happens when he has more bad days than good? We can't put him in a nursing home."

Why not? thought Anneliese, and she looked at Willem, but his gaze was fixed on Katja. A silent communication seemed to pass between them, suggesting intimacy and shared secrets, shutting Anneliese out. A burning sensation spread out from her chest.

It wasn't her place to comment, but her mouth had a will of its own. "Louisa isn't buried here, though, is she?"

Hendrik frowned at her but said nothing.

Jurriaan turned to Willem. "Where do you think Mom is?"

"Nobody knows. But when her remains are found, we'll give her a proper burial."

"I don't really remember her," Jurriaan said.

"That's okay. It was a long time ago, twinnie."

Jurriaan pondered a moment. "Once she brought me chocolates from Belgium and let me eat the whole box. I had a stomachache that night." Looking satisfied that he had recalled a memory, he dropped to the damp ground and began cleaning the rest of the rotting leaves off the slab.

Anneliese hugged herself. How long was she expected to stand in the freezing drizzle? She dug her phone out of her purse and checked the time. It was a few minutes early, but not too early.

"I have a surprise," she said. "I booked a table for drinks at the Amstel Boathouse. It's a two-minute walk from the cemetery. We can go now."

Four sets of eyes stared at her.

"That was thoughtful of you, but you shouldn't have." Katja said. "I brought a thermos of coffee. We always drink coffee at the grave."

"At the Boathouse, we can sit inside, where it's warm, and drink a glass of wine," Anneliese said.

"I made cookies, and anyway, should you be drinking wine in your condition?" Katja said.

"When did you have time to bake?"

Anneliese didn't expect a reply, and she didn't get one. But it felt important to go to the Boathouse, to get her way for once. Wine sounded especially appealing right then. "Willem?" she said.

"Cancel the reservation. Katja brought refreshments."

"But—"

He laid his finger on her lips.

Seething, Anneliese dug out her phone again and called the Boathouse.

Katja unzipped her oversized handbag and pulled out a thermos, a stack of Styrofoam cups, and a cookie tin. Jurriaan held the cups, one by one, while Katja poured.

The coffee smelled like boiled beans. Anneliese took a sip, and her stomach churned. The queasiness passed quickly, but she clutched her stomach anyway. "Willem, I think I'm going to be sick. Can we go home?"

He raised his eyebrows, and she saw the skepticism in his eyes, but he slung his arm around her. "Let's go home before we all catch pneumonia."

Jurriaan set the poinsettia on the slab and collected the used cups. Katja linked arms with Hendrik, who shuffled through the puddles like a kid. Jurriaan dumped the cups in a trash barrel at the visitor center.

In the car, Anneliese sat behind Hendrik and cracked the window, trying to stave off real nausea—brought on by Katja's perfume and Jurriaan's musty-smelling coat and damp trousers.

Rain hissed against the tires, and Willem switched on the wipers. Anneliese watched the scenery race by—murky patches of placid river between the dark, weeping trees. Unease stirred deep inside her.

CHAPTER

47

December 2024

Anneliese

THAT NIGHT ANNELIESE perched on the edge of the bed, listening to Willem get ready for bed in the bathroom.

As soon as she heard his electric toothbrush buzz, she jumped into action. She dragged his cardigan from under the bed, where she had stuffed it when they got home from Zorgvlied. It was unlikely Willem would hunt for his cardigan tonight, but she wasn't taking any chances. She had at least two minutes. She reached into the pocket, and her fingers curled around the small book inside, but even before she withdrew it, she knew something was wrong. It was the wrong size, wrong weight, wrong texture. She looked at the paperback novel in her hand.

She blinked several times and willed the paperback to transform into Katja's diary. She wondered if the diary had been a novel all along. Was it a case of her seeing what she wished to see? Was she delusional? She searched the other pocket. The letter and the key to the filing cabinet were also missing. She hung her head over the side of the bed and peered into the gloom underneath. Nothing apart from a dust bunny.

Willem's toothbrush fell silent.

Swearing, she shoved the paperback under her pillow, hung the cardigan in Willem's wardrobe, and flung herself down on the bed a moment before the bathroom door opened.

Her thoughts spun. She had left the cardigan in the kitchen when she had drunk tea with Hendrik. It had hung on a chair the entire afternoon, which was ample time for someone to substitute the paperback for the diary. How could she have been so careless? So stupid?

Hendrik must have waited for the chance to steal it back. But why hadn't he confronted her when he caught her red-handed in Katja's study? It made no sense. She supposed Katja or Willem could have taken the diary. Or Jurriaan, who had stayed for dinner. But why would one of them check the pockets? Did someone search her things regularly? The thought made her slightly sick.

Willem sat down on the bed and laid his hand on her knee. "Let's talk," he said.

His serious tone set off her alarm bells. The cardigan belonged to Willem. It was only logical that he was the one who had found the diary in the pocket.

"About what?" she asked guardedly, a confession on the tip of her tongue. She might have to admit she was Katja's daughter. Otherwise, he would think she was plain nosy and untrustworthy. She had to make him understand.

"I want to talk about your behavior at the cemetery today," he said.

Okay. Not the diary, then. "What behavior?" she asked as innocently as she could.

"Your competition with Katja."

"That's ridiculous."

"Is it?"

"I wanted us to have a pleasant drink together at the Boathouse."

"Anneliese, you're new to the family. You don't understand how we do things."

"You're right—I don't. Take the performance at the cemetery. That was pretty weird, if you ask me."

"How was it weird?" He cocked his head to one side.

She actually didn't know how people normally behaved when they visited a loved one's grave, never having visited one herself, but it was too late to take back her words.

"Okay, Dr. Willem. Why visit a grave, if not to reminisce about the person who's gone? To remember them properly?"

He studied her for several moments, and heat flooded her face. Her cheeks must be glowing. Was he thinking that she had never talked to him about Daan, her dead brother? As a shrink, he must be constructing theories for her silence. He might throw Daan in her face. She braced herself.

"We were devastated when Louisa died, especially Hendrik," Willem said, his condescending tone so like Dr. Hummel's that she wanted to puke. "He never worked again. He stopped talking. He didn't eat. Katja saved him, and the four of us made a pact. We promised not to dwell on what happened to Louisa. It seemed like the best way to move forward with our lives."

"Isn't talking supposed to be therapeutic? Isn't that what shrinks preach?"

Willem acknowledged her sarcasm with a faint smile. "I wasn't a psychiatrist back then. Besides, Hendrik refused to talk to a therapist."

"Did any of you have grief counseling?"

"No. In hindsight, I think counseling might have been beneficial."

Or maybe not, she thought, recalling her sessions with Dr. Hummel. The doctor, blindfolded, trying to pin the tail on Anneliese.

"Why do you visit her grave?"

"Hendrik says it's the least we can do to honor her memory."

Anneliese thought about Louisa's masterful compositions; her brilliant performances; her beauty; and her lonely, watery death.

"Suppose your mother didn't drown? What if someone killed her?"

She meant nothing by it—not really. But the effect on Willem was instantaneous. It was as if a mask fell over his face or lifted from it. He looked like a different person. He looked like someone dangerous. He gazed at her in the same way Daan used to do. She was nine years old again, back in her parents' shed, fumbling in the dark for a box of rat poison.

"Finding out what happened to Louisa was a job for the police. We accepted the coroner's verdict."

Anneliese's heart gave several irregular thumps. "Of course," she said, backtracking. "I'm sorry. What do you want from me?"

"Promise not to mention my mother to the others."

"The others?"

"Katja, Hendrik, and Jurriaan. Come to me with your questions. Go along with our weird ritual."

"But—"

"Then you'll be part of this family."

His words stopped her dead. Magic words. A frozen place buried deep inside her started melting. She didn't dare speak, afraid of breaking the spell. She said, "I want that, Willem."

"Good."

"Is there a ceremony? Do I swear on a Bible?" she asked lightly, trying to break the tension.

His eyes locked on hers. For a disorienting moment, she was looking into Daan's dark eyes. Eyes that were burning with a familiar intensity. Her mouth went dry.

"No Bible. Just a promise."

"I promise." Her voice was a croak.

He kissed her, his lips cold and hard.

"Thank you, Anneliese. It's been a long day. Let's get some sleep." He turned out the light. "I love you."

"I love you too," she said, but the words rang as hollow in her ears as she felt inside. She listened to his breathing slow down until she couldn't hear it, and she knew he was sleeping. *Willem, not Daan. Willem, not Daan. Willem, not Daan.*

Dr. Hummel had said the need to belong was one of the core human needs. He'd said it was her vulnerable spot. Willem was a shrink too. He knew which buttons to push. Had she been played?

She stared at the dark ceiling, laid her hands on her round belly, and tried to empty her head. Sleep was far away, and she felt heavy with foreboding.

CHAPTER 48

December 2024

Anneliese

Anneliese woke up with a start. Willem's side of the bed was cold, and the apartment was silent. It was the first time he had left without kissing her goodbye. Her insides churned with anxiety when she remembered their conversation last night. If she could do yesterday over, she would behave like a mature adult at the cemetery instead of like a spoiled child. She wouldn't snoop in Katja's study or steal the diary.

Last night she had let her imagination run away with her. Willem wasn't Daan. He was nothing like Daan. How could she have thought that even for an instant? But a chasm had opened between them.

Was it because of their secrets? Could they trust each other enough someday to share?

After a breakfast of tea and toast to settle her stomach, she went down the basement stairs and unlocked the crypt. She sat down at the Steinway, opened the *Veldkamp Lesson Book, Level Five,* and played a few exercises. She tried to concentrate, but her mind wandered. Who had the diary now?

She raised her eyes to the concert poster on the adjacent wall: Louisa's hands, large as a man's, but feminine, with long graceful fingers. A morbid image floated into her head. She saw Louisa's body, limbs askew, drifting wherever the currents took it. Marine predators devoured her flesh and scattered her bones over the seabed. Stray bones washed ashore on Wexalia and in Denmark and as far away as England. They couldn't put Louisa together again.

How did Louisa, while jogging on the beach, wind up in the water and drown? Anneliese wondered if there was more to the story than the family let on. Had she been depressed? Did she commit suicide? Was she murdered? But Anneliese had to respect Willem's wishes; the only past she had the right to dig into was her own.

When she'd had her fill of practicing scales and exercises, she sorted through Louisa's yellowed sheet music, looking for a piece that was challenging, but not too difficult. She found a prelude with chords that her small hands could reach.

* * *

Hours later Willem stuck his head inside the door.

"Anneliese, I've been looking everywhere for you. How long have you been down here?"

She stopped playing and shook her wrists.

"I don't know. What time is it?"

"Almost seven."

"Yikes. I didn't know it was so late."

"Shall we order takeaway?"

"Indian?"

"Fine with me." He waited, his broad shoulders filling the doorway, blocking her escape if she had needed one, which of course she didn't. Why had the thought of escape entered her mind?

"Are you coming?" he asked.

She followed him up the concrete steps.

That night in bed he pulled her close, and she felt herself stiffen. When his hand stroked her belly, she flinched. He withdrew his hand, and they lay side by side in the dark, her breathing ragged, his deep and steady.

"What's wrong?" he asked. She could hear the hurt in his voice.

"I'm nauseated," she said, though it wasn't the pregnancy making her sick, but the thought of his hands, so like Louisa's, amputated at the wrists and adorning a grave.

* * *

After a few days Anneliese decided Carla had been right. It would take months of practice before she could play at her old level. It meant endlessly playing scales, exercises, and arpeggios. To break up the tedium, she practiced the prelude.

Each day she practiced until her wrists ached and her eyes smarted. She skipped lunches, and Willem had to drag her away for dinner in the evenings. She ate little and lost the couple of pounds she had gained since becoming pregnant. Willem didn't try to make love to her again. They each seemed to be waiting for the other to make the first move.

After a week she was ready to play the prelude for Willem. At his usual lunchtime, she knocked on the office door, and when he called "Come in," she went inside.

He had visitors. Katja and Hendrik sat facing him across his neat glossy desk. The three faces turned toward her. She remained standing like a schoolgirl called to the head teacher's office.

Willem's eyes were guarded, Katja's frosty, and Hendrik's black as a tar pit. Her stomach twisted.

"Am I interrupting a group therapy session?" she joked.

Willem said. "Hendrik received a letter from his neuropsychologist with the results of his checkup."

Sheets of paper lay face down on his desk. She hadn't noticed which way the papers faced when she had entered.

She turned to Hendrik. "If you don't mind me asking, what did the letter say?"

"Of course, I don't mind. You're family now. To summarize, there's been no significant decline in my cognitive ability since the last checkup. The medicine is working."

"That's good news," Anneliese said, Hendrik's words echoing in her head: She was family now. Her hand went to her belly, where the new little Veldkamp was growing.

"It's wonderful news," Katja said.

Willem leaned back. "Did you want something, Anneliese?"

"I want to play one of Louisa's compositions for you." Inspiration struck her, and she turned to Katja and Hendrik. "Will you come too?"

The smiles faded.

"Sorry, I have to work," Katja said.

"It's time for my nap," Hendrik said.

Anneliese looked at Willem.

"Maybe later. I'm going to eat a sandwich at my desk and catch up on paperwork."

Lame excuses.

"Fine," Anneliese snapped. She turned her back to hide the tears of frustration clotting her eyelashes, and headed for the door. After a few steps, she stopped. They couldn't get away with blowing her off unless she let them. She wiped her eyes with her knuckles and slowly turned around.

"The piece takes less than five minutes to play," she said.

They agreed to attend her mini-concert at three o'clock.

* * *

At three, Katja and Hendrik came into the studio and sat down on the sofa.

"Better never than late," Hendrik said.

Willem carried in an extra chair from upstairs and set it next to Hendrik. The studio seemed crowded with four people in it, like standing chest to butt in a metro a second before it plunged into a dark tunnel.

Anneliese's hands went slippery with sweat. This was a bad idea. She was setting herself up for a huge humiliation.

She recalled her last recital a few months before Daan's death. Tineke, Ray, and Daan had arrived late and taken the only empty chairs, which happened to be in the front row. Daan had pulled faces at Anneliese. She'd stumbled halfway through the piece, and her mind had blanked. After an awful silence, she'd skipped to the last measure and played it with a flourish. The other parents had glanced at one another, but Tineke and Ray had clapped and cheered, unaware she'd played only half the piece.

Anneliese knew Louisa's prelude by heart, but she placed the sheet music on the rack, just in case. It was one of her early compositions, the manuscript handwritten, her drawing delicate and clear as the music itself.

She took a deep breath and began. The studio dissolved around her. Her fingertips connected to the keys, which raised the hammers, and the hammers struck the strings. It was as if the music flowed from deep inside her. She became the instrument. Her practicing paid off, and she came to the end without making a single mistake.

Beaming, she rose from the bench and imagined herself wearing a gorgeous red gown, bowing to applause in a packed concert hall, and Willem bounding across the stage with a bouquet of red roses in his arms. Her eyes rested on her audience's set faces, and she saw that their clapping was merely polite.

"Didn't you like it?" she asked, her smile fading.

Hendrik said, "There's more to a performance than playing the right notes. You have to take command. Feel the music."

"I felt it."

"The emotion doesn't come through in your playing. That was Louisa's gift. She could make her audience share her passion."

She bit down hard on her lip. "Anything else?"

"You move too much."

Katja said, "Don't pay any attention to Hendrik. No one expects you to play like a concert pianist."

"I'm impressed," Willem said, glancing at his watch.

Why were they still here? She wanted them to go—the sooner the better.

Willem cleared his throat and caught Hendrik's eye before speaking. "I have some news that may disappoint you, Anneliese."

"Oh?"

"Hendrik wants to convert the piano studio into a workshop. He wants to tinker with a new idea."

Anneliese blinked, taking a moment to let the words sink in. "What about Louisa's legacy? Her manuscripts, concert posters, and programs? The Steinway?"

"The National Library has been after Hendrik for years to donate her things. This time he said yes. They plan to create a permanent exhibition about her life. The centerpiece will be her piano."

Anneliese felt as if the Steinway had rolled over her. She looked at Hendrik. His face was unreadable, but she thought his dark eyes flickered. Why had he changed his mind after turning down the library's previous requests? Had her playing raked up painful memories? Was he punishing her for snooping?

Willem rose. "I'll buy you a digital piano for the apartment, and a first-rate set of headphones."

She tore her gaze away from Hendrik "There's no need, Willem. I'm done with the piano."

"But I thought you enjoyed playing."

"I won't have time after the baby is born, anyway."

Katja and Hendrik filed out and Willem carried the extra chair away, leaving Anneliese alone, her shoulders rigid with anger.

Her phone vibrated. She snatched it up and snapped open a text from a number not in her contacts.

I found Bep.

Her anger faded. Who had sent the message? Who was Bep? Then it came to her. The sender must be the old janitor at the hotel in Den Bosch, and Bep was the junkie housekeeper who had cleaned Katja's and Louisa's rooms.

CHAPTER

49

December 2024

Anneliese

ANNELIESE TOOK THE train to Veenendaal Central Station, and from there the bus.

The bus wound through a birch forest, the papery bark peeling off the tall, thin trunks that rose, straight as pins, from a cushion of dead leaves. It wasn't noon yet, but the sky grew darker by the hour.

She thought back on the text messages from Radboud—and his warnings. Bep wasn't reliable. She might lie. She might not know anything useful. But it was an opportunity too promising to pass up. Radboud had persuaded Bep to meet with Anneliese.

Blustery flurries of snow stung Anneliese's face as she got off the bus in Amerongen, and she wished she had worn something warmer than her parka. She used her phone to find Bep's house in a middle-class neighborhood of terraced brick houses. She double-checked the address. From the street, Bep's house looked more than okay—two stories with a steep roof.

Up close, neglect was evident, and the doorbell cover plate was missing. She knocked. A Labrador, barking his head off, appeared in the front window, but no one answered the door. Anneliese couldn't call Bep because the old junkie didn't have a phone. But she wasn't going to go all that way and not see her. She decided to kill some time and try again later.

She wandered through the village, looking for a coffee specialty shop. What kind of place didn't have a Starbucks or a De Koffiesalon? She backtracked to the bus stop and crossed the county road. That side of the village was a few centuries older, dominated by crumbling old houses with black shutters on the windows; and an old castle, complete with a moat. She walked the perimeter of the property. An icy wind shuttled over the polder and numbed her lips.

After an hour, she bought a bouquet at the supermarket and retraced her steps to Bep's house.

The door opened.

Bep was a pale, gaunt woman in faded blue jeans a size too large. Her white scalp showed through her thin gray hair. She looked seventy, but drug use might have aged her.

"I'm Anneliese. Radboud sent me."

"Are you the baby?" Bep said in a raspy voice.

"Yes. I brought you flowers."

"You could have gotten me cigarettes for what those cost." Bep shoved the flowers into the umbrella stand.

Anneliese hung her parka on a hook and followed Bep into the living room. It smelled like a kennel. The calico cat that was curled up in a chair lifted its head and regarded her with golden eyes. In the corner, a gray cat was hunched over, trying to cough up a hairball. The fat Labrador sniffed Anneliese's crotch and stretched out on the sagging sofa. On the coffee table was an enormous ashtray that overflowed with cigarette butts and ash.

Bep set the calico cat on the floor and motioned for Anneliese to sit in the chair. The cat hair would stick to her pants, but she didn't want to insult her hostess, so she sat.

"Tea?" Bep asked.

"No, thank you," Anneliese said, picturing the cats cavorting about on the kitchen counter.

Bep shrugged and wedged her skinny hips between the dog's head and the armrest. She stroked the dog's back, giving Anneliese a view of the underside of her forearm.

"What are you staring at?" Bep snapped.

"Your tracks."

"What's it to you?"

"Nothing. It's none of my business."

"Did you bring the money?"

"Tell me first what you know."

"That's not how this works. The money first."

Anneliese dug the wallet from her backpack, walked over to the sofa, and handed Bep two fifties.

"Where's the rest?"

"The rest?" Anneliese said, feigning innocence.

"I told Radboud I wanted five hundred."

"He told me a hundred." Anneliese couldn't ask Willem for five hundred without telling him what the money was for.

Bep swore. "A lousy hundred isn't enough."

"It's all I have. I had to use my overdraft facility to pick up this much. I'm in the red," she added in case Bep didn't know what an overdraft facility was.

The junkie muttered to herself, back and forth like an argument, and tucked the cash into the pocket of her jeans. "If a hundred's all you got."

Anneliese showed her the inside of her wallet and returned to the chair.

"Radboud said you were the housekeeper at the hotel when I was born. What can you tell me about my mother and her stepsister?"

"The older one was a snob. Miss Hoity-Toity I called her . . . not to her face, of course. She held her mouth funny when I came to clean her room. Like she tasted something foul. She wore a long coat and complained her room was too cold. The temperature seemed fine to me, but I wasn't sitting on my ass all day." Bep scratched at her forearm.

"And my mother?"

"She was a shy little thing." Bep bent over and nuzzled the Labrador's nose. "Most guests stayed for a couple of nights, but them two stayed for six weeks or so. They didn't hardly go out, not even for meals. They kept me running, bringing up trays of food and carrying away empty dishes. They didn't leave me a tip neither."

Anneliese said, "Radboud recalls you saying that something was odd. What did you mean?"

Bep screwed up her forehead. "I might've said that. It was a long time ago, mind you. The way they hid out in their rooms. And no visitors that I ever saw. It was odd, all right."

Anneliese tried to hide her impatience. She should have listened to Radboud. Bep couldn't tell her anything of importance that she didn't already know. The visit was a waste of time and money.

Bep turned the dog's head to the side, leaned forward, and rummaged in the ashtray until she found a cigarette butt long enough to relight. The gray cat coughed up the hairball, which was disgusting enough, but then it slunk over and rubbed itself against Anneliese's legs. Cats made her neck hair prickle. She kicked out her foot—not hard—but firm enough to let it know she meant business. It stalked away.

"Don't treat my Dora like that." Bep twitched all over.

"I didn't hurt her. I'm allergic to cats." Anneliese faked a sneeze.

Bep tutted. "I guess you can't help it if you're allergic."

"Can you remember anything else about my mother?"

Bep took a cautious drag on the cigarette butt, as if afraid she might suck it down her throat.

"One morning I went to clean her room. Before I could knock, I heard Miss Hoity-Toity shouting, then a loud crash."

Anneliese sat up straighter. "What did you do?"

"I should have come back later, but I was damn curious. I used my pass key. The duvet was in a heap on the floor. A lamp base lay nearby. I didn't see where the lampshade went. Your poor little mama was sitting on the floor crying, her arms covering her head. Her sister yelled at me to get out. I didn't have to be told twice."

"When was this?"

"A week before the baby came."

"Do you know what they were arguing about?"

"Nah. But I know what I heard: 'After all I've done for you. You can't back out now.' Something like that."

Anneliese felt something inside her shift, like twisting the focus of a microscope. She could guess why they had argued. Louisa must have missed playing the piano and missed the limelight. If Katja had changed her mind and decided to keep her baby, Louisa's sacrifices would have been for nothing. Louisa must have bullied Katja into going through with the adoption.

"You look a little peaked," Bep said.

The cloying stench. Cigarette smoke. Animal hair. Dirty clothes. Body odor. Stale grease. Anneliese's stomach heaved. After saying goodbye, she stumbled from the room and let herself out the front door.

CHAPTER

50

December 2024

Anneliese

ANNELIESE'S TRAIN PULLED into Central Station at a few minutes before four o'clock. She had left her bicycle in the fietsflat on the south side of the station. The three-story garage looked like a bicycle graveyard, filled with decomposing two-wheelers. A shiny new bicycle parked in an unguarded stall would be stolen in no time.

She unlocked her bicycle and exited the fietsflat, watching for ice on the pavement. She slowed as she approached the footbridge that spanned the canal separating the station from the city center. Bridges froze sooner than roads, sometimes before the salt trucks were called out.

After successfully navigating the icy bridge, she turned onto the Singel. Cars jammed the street, but bicycles moved at a steady clip on the cycling path. As she picked up speed, her front wheel wobbled slightly. She would ask Willem to look at it.

She fell into a trance, as she often did while cycling over a familiar route. She kept thinking about her visit with Bep. Louisa had thrown a lamp. She had yelled, "You can't back out now." It seemed plausible that Louisa had pressured Katja into giving up her baby. Why? And why go to such lengths to keep the pregnancy a secret? Other options would have been far less complicated.

A bicycle bell pinged. Hooded pedestrians scurried along the pavement. Umbrellas sprang up like mushrooms as a light rain fell. Anneliese's hands ached from the cold. She pedaled faster, eager to get home to central heating and hot coffee before the sky opened up in earnest.

Then things happened fast.

Anneliese's bicycle slipped sideways. She tried to catch herself by stretching out her left leg, but her bicycle disintegrated beneath her. One moment she was on the saddle, bent low over the handlebars. The next moment, the pavement flew up to meet her.

When she opened her eyes, she was sprawled on the wet gritty asphalt, cyclists rushing around her like a stream parting for a boulder. Until someone stopped. Then someone else. Soon a ring of concerned faces peered down at her, noses glowing red in the cold.

"Should I call an ambulance?"

"Stand back and give her some room."

"Can you hear me?"

"Did you hit your head?"

"Do you know where you are?"

"Can you move your toes?"

Too many questions. Too dazed. She sat up. Her left shoulder and arm throbbed with pain.

She could wriggle her toes.

Bicycles detoured into the street beyond the crowd. She glimpsed a familiar face—middle-aged, attractive, blonde. It disappeared before she could put a name to the face.

"Let's move you off the cycling path," said a man with a comforting bass voice.

The man helped her to her feet. A woman stopped the stream of cyclists while the man carried Anneliese to the sidewalk and lowered her to the ground, propping her up against the front of a shop. A teenage girl moved her bicycle to the sidewalk and went back for the front wheel. The bicycle traffic resumed. The three Samaritans—as Anneliese called them in her head—were bundled up in coats with hoods. Someone held a purple umbrella over her head.

Blood dripped steadily onto her lap.

"Hold this against your chin," the woman said, pressing a tissue into her hand.

"What happened?" Anneliese asked.

"Your front wheel came off," said the bass voice.

"Where am I?"

"On the Singel. What's your name?" he asked.

"Anneliese."

"Do you want me to call someone for you, Anneliese?"

Good idea. Call Willem. Willem will know what to do. "Where's my backpack?" she asked.

It was still strapped to her back. The man unzipped the outside pocket, found her phone, and handed it to her. She called Willem. Got voicemail. He must be with a patient. She selected Katja's number. Got voicemail again. Of course, Katja didn't take calls while she was working. She tried Hendrik, who answered on the first ring.

"Will you ask Willem to call me? Tell him it's an emergency."

"Can I help?"

"Just tell Willem." She hung up.

Willem called two minutes later. "What's wrong?"

Her words refused to come, so she handed the phone to the Samaritan with the bass voice. It was as if he were talking about someone else.

"Anneliese had an accident . . . No, I don't think so, but I'm not a doctor . . . Her arm and a bang on the head. Her chin might need stitches . . . Yes, she's responsive . . . The front wheel came off . . . I'll stay with her until you get here." The man gave Willem the address.

The Singel was only a couple of miles from the house, but distance in the city center was not a reliable indicator of travel time. Traffic snarls. One-way streets. Road construction. Moving vans blocking the way. The teenage girl and the woman Samaritan had left by the time a taxi pulled up. Willem jumped out, carrying a first aid kit, his handsome face creased with worry.

He examined the cut on her chin, which was still oozing blood, and covered it with a dressing. For a moment, his face transformed into Tineke's, a lighted cigarette dangling from her mouth while she bandaged six-year-old Anneliese's pinkie after Daan slammed a door on it.

Willem said, "Let's get you into the taxi."

The purple umbrella that had been sheltering her disappeared.

He helped her into the backseat while the last Samaritan loaded the remains of the bicycle into the trunk.

The taxi driver lowered his window. "Don't get blood on the seats."

"It's under control," Willem snapped. He shook the Samaritan's hand and climbed in next to Anneliese.

"Take us to the OLVG East," Willem told the driver.

"Address?"

"It's the hospital opposite Oosterpark."

"Sorry, sir, I need the street name and number."

Swearing, Willem consulted his phone and gave the address to the driver, who entered it into his satnav and eased the car into the traffic. The wipers swept the windshield.

"Why are we going to the hospital?" Anneliese asked.

"To make sure your arm isn't broken. And your chin needs stitches."

"Did my face get banged up?" she asked, touching her cheek.

He took her hand away. "It's just a scrape. It won't scar if it doesn't get infected."

Her chest tightened. The baby! She didn't feel any bleeding down there. Wasn't that a good sign? For the first time since the accident, tears brimmed. She started shivering and couldn't stop.

"Were you unconscious, even for a few seconds?" Willem asked.

"I don't remember. Maybe. Willem . . . the baby."

"I'm sure the baby's fine." He put his arm around her shoulders and pulled her closer. She leaned her head against him, his body warm and solid.

"Are you sure?"

"Do you have any cramping or bleeding?"

"No."

"A pregnancy can take a tumble."

Damn bicycle. "They said my front wheel came off."

"Yes, that's right."

"Were you with a patient when I called?"

"No, I popped out to the shops. I was at the checkout. Before I could call back, Hendrik rang. Did you have a nice lunch with your friend?"

"What?"

"You went to Utrecht to meet a friend."

He meant the imaginary friend who was studying at the university there. She nodded and gazed out the car window, which was drizzled with rain. "Where are we going?"

He gave her a searching look. "To the hospital. Do you know who I am?"

"Of course, Willem. Why do you ask?"

"You might have a concussion."

She closed her eyes. "Why did my wheel come off?"

"The nut that holds the wheel on the frame must have fallen out. Did you take off the wheel to fix a flat recently?"

Why was it so hard to think? Her head pounded with the effort. She couldn't remember ever having had a flat on the bicycle. "I don't think so."

"How old is the bike?"

"I bought it secondhand last summer. It was old then." She had a vague recollection of a man with stringy hair, bloodshot eyes, and dirty fingernails, on a side street, snatching a ten-euro bill from her in exchange for the bicycle.

"Maybe it was worn out," Willem said.

She tried to put together the pieces of the accident but drew a blank. The last thing she remembered was crossing the footbridge by Central Station. She wondered if her memory loss was permanent. The taxi was crawling in heavy traffic along the Prins Hendrikkade. On their left stretched the IJ, the water rippling in the rain. A few minutes later, the driver turned at the intersection before the tunnel; passed the fire station, which resembled an abandoned warehouse; and stopped at the red light by the old Catholic church.

A thought occurred to her.

"My bicycle was parked at the station. Do you think someone loosened the nut as a prank? Or maybe tried to steal the tire?"

"Was it a new tire?"

She shook her head no.

"The nut may have been loose for a long time. I'll buy you a new bicycle."

The taxi was warm. Willem's body was warm. She nodded sleepily, then recalled with a jolt the familiar face in the crowd, the one she couldn't place while she was sprawled on the bicycle path after her fall. The middle-aged blonde with dark roots. An overripe peach.

"After I fell, I saw the woman you introduced me to in the Italian restaurant—the psychologist."

"Jeanette Bruin? That's not possible. She's back in London."

"Are you sure?"

"Yes."

The longer Anneliese thought about it, the more positive she became. Either the woman on the bicycle was Jeanette Bruin, or she was her doppelgänger. Her head pounded. Willem was certain the psychologist was back in London.

Her thoughts flitted back to what she could remember in the immediate aftermath of her fall. Shock. Confusion. The three Samaritans. The purple umbrella. She didn't know anyone else whose wheel had come off while cycling. She racked her brain, trying to recall any recent bumps that might have jarred the nut loose, but nothing came to mind. Maybe the blame lay with the previous owner.

Willem was right. There was nothing sinister at hand.

Then she felt cramps like her period.

CHAPTER

51

December 2024

THE DIARY LAY on the desk, opened to the last entry.

The blue ink was faded, and the pages yellowed with age. Here and there, words were crossed out and other words inserted. On a few pages, entire paragraphs had been struck through and rewritten. Sometimes, more than once.

The entries recorded the progress of the pregnancy, tracking weight gained and vitamin supplements taken. Absent were doctor appointments and ultrasound scans. A debate raged on the pages about what to do with the baby. Emotions ran high.

The diary was damning. It had to be destroyed, but first the last entry had to be reread.

December 29, 2000

> *The months of deception culminated in a visit today to the Foundation for Aiding Unwed Mothers (FAM) in Den Bosch.*
>
> *The office was painted in the sunny colors of a kindergarten. Baby Mirella napped in the carry-cot on the floor. Only three days old, she was wrinkled and blotchy, and her fine black hair stood up in wisps. I had wetted it down in the hotel bathroom, but as soon as it dried, it sprang up again. Louisa sat next to me, her legs crossed, her foot swinging.*
>
> *Ms. Janssen, the young social worker from FAM, sat behind her desk, her bright blonde head bent as she consulted the form I had completed.*
>
> *"Your baby was born in a hotel?" she asked, her eyebrows raised in surprise.*

"That's right."

"Did a doctor or a midwife attend the birth?"

"No, only my stepsister," I said, without turning my head to look at Louisa. I didn't want to see the artfully arranged concern on her face. She was putting on an act for the social worker. When we were alone, she called Mirella "it" or "the baby." To Louisa, Mirella was a mistake to hide and forget. As if Mirella had no right to exist. I couldn't understand how she could be so heartless.

"Weren't you taking a risk?" Ms. Janssen said.

Louisa leaned forward, moving into my peripheral vision. "After her water broke, labor progressed quickly. We didn't have time to get to the hospital. Fortunately, there weren't any complications."

Labor had lasted six terrifying hours, and despite my pleas, Louisa had refused to call an ambulance.

"A precipitous labor is rare," the social worker mused, biting down on her pen. Then she looked at me. "Has a doctor examined you?"

"Yes," I lied. "And a doctor examined the baby." That part was true.

The social worker looked at the form. "Father unknown? Is that correct?"

"Yes." I wondered what she was thinking. Did she assume I was a rape victim? Or the father was married? Did she suspect I was lying? I gritted my teeth and endured.

Ms. Janssen nodded. "Why do you want to give up your daughter for adoption?"

"I explained in the form," I said. Louisa had dictated every word.

"I want to hear it from you," the social worker said gently.

"I can't give her what she needs . . . two loving parents and a stable home. I can't even support myself, and I want to go back to school. Adoption is best for both of us."

"Have you thought of alternatives? Can your stepsister help?

"No," Louisa said firmly. "I travel. I can't take care of a baby."

Louisa was keeping a low profile, I thought. For once, she didn't wish to be recognized. For once, her face was bare of makeup, and her hair pulled into a practical ponytail. She'd left her jewelry in the hotel safe. Her formless off-the-rack dress came from the local department store. Even her most avid fan wouldn't recognize her.

"I don't have any other family," I said.

"Have you considered foster care?" the social worker asked. "You can keep a tie with your daughter, and if your circumstances change—"

"I don't want a tie." I sounded like a cold-hearted bitch, even to my own ears.

"Adoption is final. You can't undo it."

Mirella woke up and started howling. Louisa dug into her bag and passed me a bottle filled with formula. I picked up the baby and pressed the nipple into her mouth. I tried to ignore her warm, soft body snuggled against my chest and her sweet smell. I wished there were a way I could keep her. I kept hoping Louisa would change her mind and say she had thought of a solution that worked for everyone. A solution that didn't mean giving up parental rights to Mirella.

"I understand. What happens next?" I asked.

"We'll notify the Child Protection Agency, and Mirella will be placed with a foster family for three months. During that time, we'll offer you counseling. You can visit her if you wish. If you change your mind within the three-month period, we'll reunite you with your daughter. Otherwise, she'll be placed for adoption."

"Katja doesn't need counseling," Louisa said.

The social worker tilted her head and studied Louisa briefly. "Do you mind stepping into the waiting room? I want to speak to Katja alone."

Louisa shot me a look, as if to say, "Can I trust you? You won't change your mind, will you? Not after all our trouble?"

I thought back on the bulky, shapeless clothes, the obsessive weight watching, the lies. It turned my stomach.

I nodded and Louisa left the room.

The nipple slipped out of Mirella's mouth. She was asleep.

"Well," said the social worker, fixing her eyes on mine.

I waited.

"I want to make sure adoption is your decision. Not your stepsister's."

I was sick of the charade . . . the claustrophobic six weeks hiding in the hotel, waiting for the birth. And the months before that, concealing the pregnancy. I should never have agreed to being Louisa's secretary. Never agreed to any of it. She was putting pressure on me, but not how the social worker meant. Maybe I should study to become an actress instead of a writer.

I bent over, shielding my face from the eyes of the social worker, and laid Mirella in the carry-cot.

"No, Ms. Janssen. This is my decision."

A fire blazed hot in the hearth. When the diary was thrown in, the flames flattened and sputtered. But a moment later, the flames raised their red-gold tongues and licked at the edges of the cover. Tasting. Testing. In a greedy gulp, the fire devoured the diary and sent clumps of soot swirling into the living room.

What to do about Anneliese?

The injuries she sustained in the bicycle accident looked worse than they were. Scrapes and bruises, a mild shoulder sprain, two stitches in her chin, a slight concussion. She had experienced cramping, but the ultrasound at the hospital showed the fetus was intact, an ugly new cycle beginning.

A more drastic measure was called for.

AUGUST 2004

CHAPTER

52

August 15, 2004

Louisa

LOUISA SNEEZED UPON entering the sitting room, the least used room in the summerhouse. Dust coated every surface. She would tell Katja tomorrow to dust and polish.

The sitting room might be cozy in the winter with a fire in the hearth, but she never visited in winter. They had bought the house fully furnished from the estate of the previous owner. She looked around. The furnishings were heavy and dark, with two armchairs in front of the window facing a plump upholstered sofa and a coffee table with ornately carved legs. The house exuded an old-world charm, but in the gloomy weather it was oppressive. Maybe her dark mood was because of the trouble brewing between her and Hendrik.

She sat down on the sofa because she didn't like turning her back to a window. She preferred seeing who or what was coming.

While sipping her wine, she studied her son. Willem's right knee jiggled, betraying his nervousness.

During her stay at Lake Como, she had given a great deal of thought about how to punish Willem. He was too big for corporal punishment, and she had already banned Bas from the holiday. She had decided a stern talking-to would be enough.

Until she checked the mail.

She'd flown back from Italy yesterday and spent the night at home. Letters and local newspapers were scattered on the floor in front of the mail slot. The hockey club logo on an envelope addressed to Willem jumped out at her.

She tore it open. Inside was a letter explaining the disciplinary committee's verdict. The letter confirmed what Willem had apparently been told on the telephone. They considered his violent behavior during the match so egregious that they had no choice but to expel him from the club. Willem had known since the middle of July, before she had left for Lake Como.

"What do you want to talk about?" Willem asked.

She shot him a look. She would decide when to start the conversation, but his expression was belligerent. If she wanted to keep the upper hand, she shouldn't wait too long. It was like performing at a concert. Walk slowly onto the stage, settle gracefully on the bench, wait for silence in the hall, and wait a few moments longer. Let the anticipation rise. Then play the first note. Wait too long and the crowd will start to stir and murmur.

She reached into the big pocket of her skirt and pulled out the folded-up letter. She held it out, expecting him to cross the room and take it, but he stayed seated. She shook it open with a flourish and read the contents out loud. Upon finishing, she glared at him, and to her satisfaction, he squirmed.

"What do you have to say for yourself?"

Willem jammed his hand on his knee and the jiggling stopped. "They called me the day before you left for Lake Como. I was going to tell you that night, but then you . . . accidentally . . . spilled wine on Katja's dress. You and Dad went out right afterward, and the next morning you left early."

Her hackles rose at his tone, making the word *accidentally* sound like *on purpose*. "Why didn't you call me at Lake Como?"

"You were looking forward to teaching summer school. I didn't want to spoil it."

He was lying, and they both knew it.

"I'm sorry, Mom."

She had been away for most of the past year, her career maybe at its pinnacle. During her absence, Willem had changed. He had gotten taller, his shoulders broader. The sun had lightened his hair and turned his skin golden brown. The shadow of a beard on his jaw surprised her. Most of all, he had acquired a new confidence. The comparison with sweet Jurriaan was sharp. They were identical twins, but Jurriaan was overweight, near-sighted, timid—and manageable.

"Does your father know they kicked you out of the club?"

Willem shook his head. "I wanted to tell you first."

"And when exactly did you plan to do that?"

"Tomorrow."

She tutted.

"Mom, I won't be able to play hockey any more. Don't you think that's punishment enough?"

"There's the matter of your little joyride in the car. You don't even have a driver's license."

"We learned our lesson."

She realized the plural pronoun encompassed Bas, but she wasn't through with either of them. Bas this. Bas that. Bas, Bas, Bas. She was sick of hearing Willem say his name.

She felt a clammy draft as the damp wind bored its way inside. The ditch would overflow, and the front garden would turn into a pond. Damn island weather. Predictably miserable.

"Are we done?" Willem asked, and stood up.

"No, we're not. Sit." She had thought of the perfect punishment, a way to strike his core.

He hesitated, then lowered himself onto the chair. "What?"

"You can't share an apartment with Bas in September. You'll live with us your freshman year."

Willem's face blanched, and he went still.

Louisa hid her delight with an effort.

"But, Mom. It was my idea to sneak out in the car. Bas didn't want to."

"He should have talked you out of it. Or refused to go with you."

"That's not fair," Willem said, punching his thigh.

She eyed his bunched-up fists and felt a twinge of fear. Although she never hit Willem with her bare hands, he had no such compunction to use his. He had proved that on the hockey field.

"Bas signed the lease on the apartment weeks ago," Willem said, his voice tight.

"Did you sign too?" she asked, eyeing the veins standing like blue cords on the back of his fists.

Willem hesitated.

"Don't lie. I can easily find out."

To her relief, she saw defeat settle in his eyes.

"No, the landlord wanted someone at least eighteen to sign."

She took a deep, calming breath. "Then I won't have to get my attorney involved. Bas can find someone else to share with."

She stood up.

"Mom, wait."

"There's no use arguing. I've made up my mind." She put her hands to her head and shut her eyes, trying to ward off a migraine. Colored lights zigzagged, danced, and exploded before her eyes.

Motherhood was not the rewarding experience it was touted to be, at least not for women destined for loftier things—like her.

CHAPTER

53

August 15, 2004

Willem

THE STORM WAS moving away, the thunder only a distant rumble, the rain diminished to a patter. Most nights, Willem conked out as soon as he crawled into bed. But not tonight.

In less than a day, Louisa had ruined the holiday and maybe ruined the rest of his life. If he reneged on the apartment, Bas might never speak to him again.

He wouldn't be able to sleep until he had talked it over with Katja. Maybe together they could devise a plan to change Louisa's mind. He had promised not to sneak into her room while Louisa was at the summerhouse, but everyone was asleep by now, and it was an emergency.

He groped under the bed for his flashlight and crossed the room barefooted, skirting the loose floorboard that creaked. He opened the door, peered into the dark, and listened.

The coast was clear. He crept along the hall to Katja's bedroom, slipped inside, and shut the door, his heart hammering as if he had sprinted the length of a hockey field.

"Katja," he called softly.

When she didn't reply, he switched on the flashlight. Although hers was the smallest bedroom, it was lavishly furnished with antiques and smelly old tapestries. She made a soft whistling noise each time she inhaled.

He aimed the beam at the little hollow in the front of her neck. In the reflected light, he could see the freckles on her eyelids. She hated her freckles, but he loved them; he loved everything about her—her coppery hair, her soft breasts, her scent.

Katja's eyelids fluttered open. "Willem?"

The bedsprings whined, and the lamp on the night table blinked on, casting a yellow glow. He snapped off the flashlight.

Scowling, she sat up. "What are you doing here? You promised."

"I'm sorry."

An angry flush spread over her face. "What if Louisa catches you? What good will sorry be then?" Her eyes darted toward the door. A huge hint, which he ignored.

"Don't worry. Mom's zonked out on her pills. I have to tell you what happened."

Her eyes widened in alarm. "What?

He sat on the edge of the mattress and told her Louisa had decreed he was to live at home his freshman year. "Bas will hate me. He's already signed the lease."

"He'll be angry, but he'll get over it."

She brushed his cheek with her fingers, and despite the circumstances, desire made his gut somersault.

"Now you have to go. We'll talk tomorrow." Sadness flitted across her face.

"What's wrong?" he asked.

"Nothing. Just go." She waited until he reached the door, to turn off the lamp.

He stepped into the hall, conscious of each sound he made: the click of the doorknob, the soft pad of his feet, his heartbeat thudding in his ears.

Straight ahead was the landing and a window overlooking the trees behind the house—dark now. Rain smeared down the glass. He heard footsteps coming up the stairs. Before he could decide whether to duck back into Katja's room or dash to his, the overhead light flicked on, blinding him. Was this how a fox felt when it was caught in headlights? Trapped. Frozen in place. An adrenalin rush. *Let it be Dad.* But it was Louisa who materialized on the landing, in a long white nightgown and carrying a glass, her blonde hair snaking around her shoulders.

"Willem, you startled me."

He thanked his lucky stars she wasn't a half minute earlier.

She glided toward him. "Why do you need a flashlight?"

"I didn't want to turn on the hall light."

"Where are you going?"

"Bathroom."

She regarded him with a suspicion that was uncalled for, since a nocturnal visit to the toilet was perfectly plausible. He felt her eyes on his back as he staggered to the bathroom, imitating to the best of his ability someone half asleep. He locked the door, leaned against it, heart pounding. After counting to sixty, he flushed the toilet, and when he emerged, she had vanished. The hall was dark except for the glow in the transom window above Katja's door. Maybe she had turned on the lamp to read. As he passed her room, the rumble of angry voices stopped him in his tracks. He detected Katja's soft voice and his mother's deeper one. Had Louisa seen through his lie? He should have stayed in bed. Jeetje, this was his fault. He needed to fix it, and he reached for the doorknob.

On second thought, he might make matters worse if he butted in. They weren't necessarily arguing about him. He wasn't actually the center of the universe. Whatever the subject of the argument was, Katja wouldn't appreciate his interference. She would want to handle it herself.

So he slunk to his room, his legs heavy with dread.

CHAPTER

54

August 16, 2004

The beachcomber

MENSO SPEWED OUT a string or curses. That crazy wiif Louisa Veldkamp was on the island. She had accused him of being a pedophile in front of his daughter. *Stay away from my sons.*

He jerked his bike along the beach, angrily swinging his shaggy head from side to side as he scanned the damp sand for objects of value that had washed up in the storm. He worked on autopilot while his thoughts swam in a gulf of hatred.

The wiif didn't belong on Wexalia. This was his home. He was a third-generation islander, a beachcomber same as his father and grandfather before him. At least her visits were brief, but they were long enough to start tongues wagging. Memories stirred. People whispered, nudged one another, pulled their kiddies closer. Her visits to the island were something he had learned to endure, like the chemotherapy for his kidney cancer two years ago.

Shitty luck the wiif was here the same week as his daughter Hilka and her meiske Famke. Shitty luck they took the same ferry—the past vomited at his feet. Hilka was forced to relive the humiliating accusations and sidelong glances that cost her parents their marriage: her father accused of being a pedophile. Menso's stomach roiled. Though Hilka tried to hide it, he saw doubt lurking in her eyes, and she always made an excuse not to leave Famke alone with him.

There had been times when he had wanted to strangle Louisa Veldkamp with his bare hands. For instance, when he was charged with assault for slugging Kees Doeksen at the Fair Weather Pub. It wasn't Doeksen's first disgusting crack about Menso and the Veldkamp twins. Or his last.

Menso had made it his business to learn her habits when she visited the island, and he knew when she was at her most vulnerable. He toyed with various scenarios. It had become a hobby or a favorite fantasy, but not a fantasy that he planned to act on. The satisfaction lay in knowing he could. She ran on the beach at seven in the morning, usually alone, sometimes with her son, Willem. It was seven now. He parked his bicycle and turned, surveying the beach in every direction.

DECEMBER 2024

CHAPTER

55

Mertens

THE SHIP DROPPED anchor in a deep channel as close as it could get to Lutine without running aground. The crew launched the rigid inflatable boat down the slipway ramp, Mertens and his partner, Lubbers, onboard, the only two men going ashore. Polypropylene bags were stacked in the bottom.

They picked up the paddles and rowed toward the sandbank, stopping when the boat scraped bottom. Mertens glanced over his shoulder at the ship sailing toward Wexalia. The major cleanup effort was focused on the beaches on the North Sea side of the island.

Mertens didn't know whether he was lucky or unlucky to be assigned to the cleanup operation on the desolate sandbank, especially with only Lubbers for company, a taciturn man twenty years his senior. Even if Lubbers had been inclined to talk, the raw wind made conversation impossible. The ship would return an hour before sundown, giving them until half past three to fill the bags. At least his asshole boss wouldn't be around to breathe down his neck.

"We'll have to wade the rest of the way," Mertens shouted, and laid his paddle on top of the polypropylene bags.

Lubbers nodded, indicating he understood.

Their feet sank in the thick mud to the top edge of their boots. Lubbers cursed—expletives seemed to be the only words in his vocabulary. When they reached Lutine, they hauled the boat onto solid sand.

Mertens' lips were numb. He scanned the sandbank. Although it was a nature reserve, there were no trees or buildings to break the wind. The cold stung his face, snatched his breath away. The captain had mentioned a bird-watchers stand, but it must have been felled by the wind and washed away. During the storm, the sandbank had been underwater for the first time in recorded memory.

Two days before, a cargo ship underway to Germany had hit rough water to the north of Wexalia. Some two hundred containers plunged overboard, their contents littering the island's beach and the neighboring sandbanks. Sports shoes, lightbulbs, pink plastic toys, Styrofoam packing material. Valuable cargo had become junk. Each high tide washed up more junk.

Lubbers's bulbous nose glowed red.

"There's one way to keep warm." Mertens had to shout in order to hear his own voice.

"Collect wood and build a campfire?"

"Ha ha," Mertens said, surprised Lubbers could talk, let alone say something remotely witty. He turned a three sixty. He couldn't distinguish the point where the gray sky ended and the muddy sea began. It was disorienting as hell.

"Let's get to work. We'll be sweating in no time."

Mertens scooped up debris and filled the bags.

Gulls swooped down, the first sign of life if he didn't count Lubbers. The flock pecked at the Styrofoam packing material that was littering the sand.

Stupid birds. They'll make themselves sick. Maybe die.

He ran at them, waved his arms, tried to shoo them away. Squawking, they scattered but regrouped as soon as he stopped.

Hopeless.

Mertens went back to work. He picked up a sports shoe and checked to see if it was his size. Too small. He stuffed it into the bag.

Once the bag was full, he threw it on top of the growing pile next to the boat. His back ached, and he glanced at his watch. They had been working nonstop for longer than two hours. No wonder he was hungry.

"Lubbers! Lunch!" He waved his arms to attract the other man's attention.

Lubbers dropped the bag he was filling and made his way toward Mertens, leaning into the wind, his hair blowing straight back, revealing a deep receding hairline. There was no escaping the wind.

Mertens said, "Let's eat on top of that slope. At least we'll have a view."

Retrieving their lunch boxes from the boat, they climbed to the highest point on the sandbank, which was only slightly higher than the lowest point, and sat with their asses in the sand. Mertens made out Wexalia to the northwest and the mainland to the south. Both land masses were light gray shadows on the darker sea.

Several yards away, two gulls pecked at something in a depression. Probably loot left behind by the tide. Mertens poured coffee into the cup of his thermos. The coffee was strong and hot. It tasted heavenly, and the heat warmed him. He started to offer the rest to Lubbers, changed his mind, and decided to save it for later. Mertens closed his lunch box and pushed himself up, his legs gone stiff, reminding him of his old man fetching a beer from the fridge. Lubbers chomped on an apple and stared into space. He hadn't said a word during their break.

Mertens strolled over to the spot where the gulls were congregated. They took wing, then settled a few yards away and watched Mertens stoop down.

At first glance, he saw a scattering of twigs and sticks. Peering closer, he thought they might be bones. Old. Stained brownish black. Not polished white. They were too large to be from a bird. Maybe a dead seal? He pulled on his gloves, squatted, and dug his fingers into the sand, uncovering a swatch of rotting fabric. What the hell? He kept digging until he uncovered a bone that was dome-shaped. The top of a skull? He should stop, leave things be, call his boss, and alert the coast guard, but he didn't want to make a fool of himself or get fired for wasting everyone's time. The remains might belong to an animal. He carved a small trench around the skull, exposing it on all sides, and lifted it carefully with both hands. At the sight of a matted lock of long hair, his stomach heaved. The skull slipped from his hands back into the hole. The hair was worse than the bones.

"Lubbers," he yelled. "You need to see this."

CHAPTER

56

December 2024

Hendrik

HENDRIK HAD WAITED twenty years for the telephone call. After hanging up, he leaned closer to the map covering much of the wall behind his desk, and stared at the handwritten scrawls and sketches. The notations told the story of the rising sea level and weakening currents—tracked by tidal gauges, buoys, and the radar altimeter in Jason satellites orbiting eight hundred miles above the earth.

The call came on a day when his head was clear, when he could focus and plan. Too much was at stake to panic. He told himself there wouldn't be proof of anything after all these years. But that wasn't quite true, and time was running out to do something about it.

The earth had been warming since the waning of the ice age, and in recent years at a terrifying pace. Glaciers melted. Rivers swelled with melted snow from mountains and gushed into the open mouth of the ocean. More water evaporated in higher than normal temperatures. More moisture in the atmosphere caused more rain. More flooding. Powerful storms whipped the sea into foam, breeched dikes, flooded low-lying areas. The sea level kept rising.

The coastline was at risk of suffering the same fate as the lost world of Doggerland—now the North Sea—but once marshes, hills, and forests. Doggerland had been home to hunters and gatherers until rising water forced them to higher ground six thousand years ago.

Climate change wasn't the only danger threatening the mudflats.

Gas production underneath the Wadden caused the sea bottom to sink. If too much subsidence was detected, production would be restricted or halted. They called it the "hand on the tap" principle. But whose hand? Environmentalists claimed a conflict of interest because the institutions hired to advise the Ministry also worked for the energy companies. As gas was extracted, the area of mudflats that stayed dry during low tide shrank.

Now the most powerful storm in a hundred years was ravaging the country. Hendrik had followed the weather reports and studied the satellite pictures. In Amsterdam, rain filled basements like bathtubs.

He brushed his teeth and combed his hair in front of the bathroom mirror. He had watched his reflection change over the years, seen it sag, thin, wrinkle, until the promising young man he had once been vanished. Until he barely felt like a man anymore. Human, but impotent. Invisible. And yet, deep inside him, a flame burned. He had a wrong to right before it was too late. After pulling on his clothes, he went downstairs to deliver the news to the family.

CHAPTER 57

December 2024

Brigadier Terpstra

BRIGADIER TOMAS TERPSTRA planned to question the prime suspect before the family's arrival on the island. His partner, Karel, like most young people, liked to sleep late, a habit he needed to break during a murder investigation—even when it was a cold case.

Yesterday they had spent a wet, blustery day on Lutine, observing the crime scene investigators process the scene. A sense of urgency prevailed as the weather deteriorated. The team pitched a tent over the grave, but wind shook the canvas and threatened to pull out the stakes. Rain formed gullies that streamed in from all sides. The bones were hastily collected. The sandbank was photographed and videoed. Soil samples taken. Debris from the container spill sent away for forensic analysis. Tomas knew that the likelihood of finding evidence beyond the immediate gravesite was nearly nil after twenty years of exposure to wind, rain, and animal activity.

He didn't know if the victim was murdered on Lutine or killed elsewhere and dumped. His department didn't have the budget or the resources to waste. When the weather made further investigation untenable, the crime scene coordinator released the scene, and her team returned to the mainland by police boat. A couple of men would come back to tidy up as soon as the weather lifted. Tomas and Karel spent the night on Wexalia, at a B&B with thin walls, grubby bathrooms, and special low winter rates.

While Karel drove, Tomas took in the scenery. *Gray* was the operative word. They passed dreary villages and a stunted pine forest. Past the midpoint of the island, the landscape changed to polder. Karel parked the car in front of the beachcomber's house, an old fisherman's cottage.

The cottage had low brick walls and a high pan-tile roof. A lean-to was built onto one side, and the main roof brought down over it at a less steep pitch. The lean-to housed the Castaways Museum.

They walked up the shell driveway. A small, fiberglass boat, repurposed as a planter, dominated the tiny front yard. The planter was half full of muddy water, the plants submerged, a few leaves floating on the surface.

The museum had its own entrance. Tomas pushed on the door, and a bell jingled. The ceiling sloped with the roof. He could stand up without ducking if he kept to the left. Karel, who was shorter, had less of a problem. The wood interior was dry and brittle as kindling.

An eclectic assortment of objects filled the shelves. Chipped pottery. Old coins. A cannonball. A life preserver. Empty Russian vodka bottles. Tomas read the nearest label: SS *Surrey*, cargo steamer lost in December 1884.

"A ticket costs three euros each," said a gravelly voice.

Tomas hadn't noticed the old man sitting in a rocking chair behind the counter, knitting something with blue yarn. His shaggy white hair and reddish-gray beard framed a lined face. He was wearing what looked like a hand-knit turtleneck sweater, possibly one of his own creations.

"I'm Brigadier Tomas Terpstra, and this is Detective Karel Rijkaard. We're with the Noord-Nederland police." Tomas showed the man his identification card. "Are you Menso De Vries?"

"I am. Are you going to buy a ticket or not?"

Tomas didn't have a search warrant, so he nodded at Karel, who pulled out his wallet and laid a bill on the counter.

Menso put down his knitting needles and made change. "What can I do for you?"

"We have some questions about Louisa Veldkamp's disappearance twenty years ago."

"There's talk her body's been found on Lutine. Was it her?"

"The remains match her description."

Her identity still needed to be confirmed, but Tomas felt confident enough to reopen the case. The remains were those of a female Caucasian, age between thirty-five and fifty. Based on the length of her femur, she was tall, an inch or two under six feet. At least ten years had elapsed since the time of death. Everything fit.

"It was because of the storm, wasn't it?" Menso said. "The Wad gave up her bones."

"Can we sit down somewhere?" Tomas asked.

The beachcomber ushered Tomas and Karel through an interior door to the main house. The scarred plank floor groaned under Tomas's feet.

Tomas guessed that walls had been knocked out to create a spacious room. In the rear was a basic kitchen with a wood-burning stove, and in the center of the room was a table made from old wood nailed together, four mismatched chairs pulled up around it. A sagging sofa lined the wall on the museum side. The steep wooden staircase in the corner probably led to a bedroom.

"Tea?" Menso asked, and motioned for them to sit at the table.

The cottage was even colder than the museum. Tomas left on his coat. Karel took off his; his belly fat gave him natural insulation. While Menso fed a log into the stove and put the kettle on, Karel turned on his iPad, and Tomas gazed at a few family photos that were arranged haphazardly on the walls. One photo showed a younger Menso fishing in a boat, but Tomas couldn't make out the name on the hull.

"Is it the same boat—?" Tomas asked, waving his arm toward the front garden.

"That's her. The Dogger," Menso said as he placed steaming mugs on the table. "I bought her in the eighties. Kept her washed and waxed. Patched up cracks in the fiberglass. A couple of years ago, the hull failed. The old girl deserved better than to end her days in a wrecking yard. The planter was Famke's idea. That's my granddaughter. She has a master's in marine biology. Funny, her mim couldn't wait to leave the island, but Famke can't keep away."

Tomas struggled to follow Menso's West Frisian accent and occasional lapse into dialect. He set down his mug. "I appreciate you taking the time to talk to us. This isn't an interview. We're here for background."

Menso nodded. "I got nothing to hide."

"When was the last time you saw Louisa Veldkamp?"

"It was the day the Veldkamp wiif arrived on the island. I was at the harbor, picking up my daughter and granddaughter. They came over on the same ferry. We had words on the dock. I won't lie to you. There was bad blood between us. But we went our separate ways."

"I know about the incident with her sons when they were ten years old. What's your side of the story?"

Menso's face flushed magenta. "The wiif didn't like me being friendly with her boys. Jealous, if you ask me. Willem and Jurriaan used to bring me objects they found on the beach. Most of it worthless, but I pretended they were treasures. I once gave them lemonade and cookies when my wife was on the mainland. The boys were late getting home. When their mim found out where they'd been, she raised hell. Called me a pedophile." He took a sip of tea, the mug shaking in his hand.

Tomas nodded. "Go on."

"The police locked me in a cell overnight. Willem swore I hadn't touched them. So that was that. But the islanders started looking at me sideways. Just when the talk died down, the Veldkamp wiif disappeared. It's harder to prove you didn't do something than to prove you did."

"How did her necklace wind up under the floorboard of your cottage?" Tomas said.

Menso's face darkened. "She drowned. Right?

"Please answer the question.

"Not until you tell me the real reason you're here."

"The manner of death hasn't been determined, yet," Tomas said.

"I have nothing to add to what I told the police twenty years ago," Menso said, his eyes shifting between Tomas and Karel. "I found a pair of shoes on the beach. I picked up one and the necklace fell out. It looked valuable, so I dropped it in my pocket. I knew I was doing wrong, but I took it anyway. They sentenced me to community service."

"Describe the necklace."

"Gold chain and a piano pendant."

"The pendant is unusual. Possibly unique. Did you know the necklace belonged to Louisa Veldkamp?"

"How would I?"

"She was wearing it when she got off the ferry."

"I had other things on my mind."

Menso's eyes must be sharp as a gull's, finding objects in the sand that other people missed, especially shiny objects. But Tomas let the matter drop for now.

Tomas said, "You were arrested for drunken and disorderly conduct in 2000. Would you tell me about that?"

Menso jumped to his feet, the cords in his neck standing out. "Do I need a lawyer?"

"You're not under arrest. You don't have to talk to us, but I'd like to hear your side of the story."

The only sounds were the crackling of the fire and the tapping of Karel's fingers on the iPad.

Menso leaned his fists on the table, his face wrestling with indecision. "I was drinking a pint in the Fair Weather Pub. Old Doeksen implied I liked little boys. I slugged him. I wouldn't have done that if I'd been sober. I swore off alcohol and haven't touched it since."

"Where were you at the time Mrs. Veldkamp went on her run?"

The beachcomber sneered. "Like I said in my statement. I was combing the beach as usual. If Mrs. Veldkamp went on a run that morning, I didn't see her. Now, get out of my house."

* * *

Tomas sank into thought as he and his partner passed the boat planter on their way to the car. He considered whether to ask the crime scene investigators to examine the boat. Although it was nearly impossible to remove blood residue from every crevice, the biological elements in blood degraded fast. He decided not to waste his limited budget.

He climbed into the car and checked his phone for messages. There was one from Hendrik Veldkamp, informing him the family had arrived on the island.

"What do you think of our prime suspect?" Tomas asked as Karel started the car.

"Menso is the only person with a motive."

"It's the only motive that was uncovered in the original investigation," Tomas said. "But remember, it wasn't a murder inquiry then. She was presumed drowned. We'll need to dig."

"He has a history of violence," Karel said.

"A man once provoked him when he was drunk. That's not much of a history."

"He has a temper."

"And he knits," Tomas said.

Karel grinned.

The Wadden wasn't visible from the cottage, but even with the car windows raised, Tomas could smell the rotten-egg stench of the mudflats.

A few minutes later, Karel drove onto the dike road. On their left, a mist had settled over the Wad, thin close to the shore, thicker in the distance. The sky stretched dark and low over the island like a moth-eaten blanket, silvery light glowing through the holes.

At last, Karel broke the silence. "I was thinking. Menso has only been arrested once for theft. What if he knew the necklace belonged to Louisa? Maybe he found it in her shoe—just like he said—and stole it to spite her."

"Does this mean you don't believe he's guilty?" Tomas said.

"If he killed her, he wouldn't take a piece of jewelry off her body knowing it could incriminate him."

Tomas thought for a moment before replying.

"Criminals do foolish things all the time. They take trophies. Make mistakes. That's how they get caught. Let's pay the Veldkamps a visit."

"Can we grab a sandwich first? I'm starving."

Tomas looked at his watch. Karel had eaten a huge greasy breakfast at the B&B only a few hours ago.

"Lunch can wait until after we talk to the family."

CHAPTER

58

December 2024

Brigadier Terpstra

After hanging their coats in the entrance hall, Tomas and Karel followed Hendrik Veldkamp into the sitting room. The room was oppressive, with heavy dark furniture, Tiffany-style table lamps, and an oriental rug that must be the source of the musty odor.

The detectives remained standing as the family filed into the room. Tomas introduced himself and Karel.

Hendrik said, "This is my wife, Katja Hart. Louisa was her stepsister."

The attractive, well-dressed woman was the picture of a law-abiding citizen, but Tomas knew from experience that looks could be deceiving. She had married her stepsister's widower, which was an interesting development. There was no mention of a love triangle in the case notes, but if Katja and Hendrik had been having an affair, it was a possible motive.

On the other hand, Tomas's best friend had married his wife's cousin only months after the wife's passing. His friend had rhapsodized to Tomas for years about the cousin's great legs. That didn't mean he killed the wife. Liver cancer killed her.

Hendrik introduced his sons Jurriaan and Willem, and Willem's fiancée, a girl with black hair and splendid dark eyes, whose name Tomas didn't catch, having been distracted by those eyes. Everyone sat down.

The girl shifted under his gaze and adjusted the sling on her left arm. Since she was irrelevant to the case, he turned his attention to the sons.

Jurriaan twitched like a rabbit, whereas Willem didn't move a muscle, though tension seeped from his pores. According to the case notes, Jurriaan and Willem were twins and had been sixteen at the time their mother disappeared. The surge of hormones in a boy during puberty could unleash powerful emotions. Although rare, it wasn't unheard of for a teenager to kill a parent.

The radiator ticked, but a stubborn chill hung over the house. Tomas's wife was always saying he needed meat on his bones to keep warm.

"Before we start with the interviews, do any of you have questions? I'll answer them as far as I can."

"You aren't the same detectives," Hendrik said.

"That's right. My team specializes in unsolved cases involving a serious crime."

"What crime?" Willem asked.

Terpstra considered how much to tell.

"Louisa's remains were found in a shallow grave on Lutine. We're treating her death as suspicious."

"In a grave? We thought she drowned," Willem said.

"We don't know yet the cause of death."

"Are you positive it's her?" Hendrik said quietly.

"We won't be sure of the victim's identity until the mitochondrial DNA analysis is complete. It's a time-consuming process. It could be months before we have the results, but the remains match the victim's profile."

"What is mitochondrial DNA?" Katja asked.

"It's a form of DNA that can be extracted from very old bones. It's inherited solely from the mother."

"Can't you use dental records for identification?" Willem asked.

"There weren't enough teeth left." Tomas tried to keep his tone matter-of-fact. "I'm sorry. This must be hard to hear. Any more questions?"

"Can I see her?" Jurriaan asked.

"That's not possible, I'm afraid," Tomas said. A skull, bones, a scrap of fabric. "As I told Hendrik on the phone, the roof of the local police station leaked like a sieve during the storm. They're still mopping up. We'll ask you to come in and update your original statements once the station reopens. Meanwhile, we would appreciate your cooperation in clarifying a few points. Bear with us, please, if we ask you questions that you answered in the original investigation. The case is new to us."

Tomas took their silence as consent.

"We want to speak to each of you alone."

The girl's face had paled. He looked closer—at her dark eyes, her delicate nose, the bow-shaped lips, now colorless—and gave a start. Tomas was terrible with names but he was good with faces. He was certain he had met the girl before, maybe years before.

"Are you all right?" Tomas asked her.

"Headache," she murmured, avoiding eye contact.

"Feel free to leave if you wish. We don't have any questions for you."

She looked at the floor as she left the sitting room.

Tomas mused over the girl, confident he would remember who she was in due course, and turned to Hendrik. "I want to start with you, Mr. Veldkamp—Hendrik, that is."

The others stood up.

"We'll wait in the kitchen," Willem said.

CHAPTER

59

December 2024

Anneliese

ANNELIESE RAN UPSTAIRS and flung herself on the bed, her breathing quick and shallow, her heart racing. Rain rapped against the windowpane, and wind ferreted its way through cracks and crannies, carrying with it the moan of the sea. Her head pounded. She pulled up a thin, rough blanket.

Downstairs in the stuffy parlor, she had almost fainted in shock when she saw Lurch, her nickname for the former hoofdagent, now brigadier. She calmed herself with the thought that he must have worked hundreds of cases since they last met, and she was older. She had grown up. She didn't think he had recognized her.

Hers was the perfect excuse to stay upstairs. The doctor at the hospital who had examined her after the bicycle accident had ordered bedrest. By rights, she should have stayed at home. But she couldn't bear to be left behind in the mansion, especially while a nightmare unfolded around the family. Quite unexpectedly, Hendrik had taken her side.

Even if Lurch had recognized her, it didn't have to be a total disaster. She would owe Willem an explanation—that was all. But the mere thought of dredging it all up again made her slightly sick.

She clung to the fact that she had been a child in Noorddorp when Louisa disappeared or was murdered. She was the only member of the family above suspicion. The brigadier had no reason to interview her; what had happened when Anneliese was sixteen had no connection to the cold case whatsoever.

A half hour later, someone knocked on the door.

CHAPTER

60

December 2024

Hendrik

HENDRIK TURNED TO the cold case detectives. In their rumpled suits and muddy shoes, the policemen looked as if they had spent the morning tramping around Wexalia. *Get on with it, Brigadier Terpstra,* he thought. *I have things to do . . . important things.*

"I'm sorry for your loss," Terpstra said, enunciating his words clearly, as if speaking to a child or a foreigner.

"Thank you. It was a long time ago."

"I'm sorry to rake up painful memories."

"Isn't that what a cold case team does?"

"We try to get justice for the victims and closure for the families."

"But you can't bring Louisa back."

"No."

A silence fell.

Terpstra said, "I understand you're an inventor. Is that correct?"

"Yes, I'm an engineer by profession. But I never worked after Louisa . . ." He didn't know how best to finish the sentence. Disappeared? Died? Was killed? In his mind's eye, he saw her standing on a stage and wearing a long beaded gown in a delicate shade of oyster, her golden hair curling around her broad shoulders.

"Will you walk me through the day your wife disappeared? I mean your *first* wife."

Hendrik flinched. He didn't need to be reminded which wife disappeared. "It's in my statement."

"You might tell me something new. A small thing could help. Give me as many details as possible, even if they seem irrelevant. It's okay if you don't remember everything, or if you get it wrong. That would be understandable after twenty years."

Hendrik shut his eyes. He felt every minute of his sixty-six years, and he saw himself as he must appear to the detectives: a wealthy old man married to a much younger woman. He had married his first wife's stepsister. The detectives must think he had murdered Louisa so he could marry Katja.

"Take your time," the detective said.

Hendrik opened his eyes and repeated the well-worn story. "Louisa rose at seven to get ready for a run. She liked to run in the morning before it got hot. I went downstairs to make coffee. We drank a cup together. She left. Sometimes she stayed gone for hours, but this time she never came back."

After a respectful silence, Terpstra said, "Was it raining? Sunny?"

"It wasn't raining when she left."

"Did she take her phone?"

Hendrik tensed. "No, she didn't always."

"Did Louisa run the same route every morning?"

"I don't know.

"Were you a jogger too?"

"No."

"What did you do when Louisa didn't return?"

"We didn't worry until lunchtime. We went out looking for her. I reported her missing that evening."

"Why did you wait?"

"She was a grown woman. Not a missing child."

Terpstra waited for his partner to catch up with note taking before continuing. "Tell me about the days leading up to her disappearance."

"She taught piano at a summer school program in Lake Como. When the program ended, she joined us at the summerhouse. That was a couple of days before she disappeared."

"Did she seem upset or worried?" Terpstra asked.

"No, she felt the summer school had been a success. She was in good spirits."

Terpstra nodded. "How would you describe your marriage? Strong? Troubled?"

"I loved her."

"She traveled a lot for her work. Do you think she was faithful?"

"I have no reason to suspect she wasn't."

"And you? Were there other women in your life?"

"Absence makes the heart grow fonder," Hendrik said with a burst of emotion, half anger, half despair, which he immediately regretted.

"Answer the question, please."

"No, there wasn't anyone else." He had been like a faithful old dog, waiting by a cold hearth for its master to return and lay a fire.

"Did you inherit money or property from Louisa? Or benefit from her life insurance policy?"

Hendrik bristled. "I made my own fortune, and I'm sure you know she didn't have a life insurance policy."

He wished that the interview would end. There was so little time, and yet its weight was crushing. Terpstra's questions seemed endless and sometimes irrelevant. Hendrik felt like a fish hooked on a line. Each time he started swimming away under the mistaken belief he was free, Terpstra reeled him back in.

"Did you have a boat?"

"No." It was a logical question. Whoever had buried Louisa on Lutine would have needed a boat. He wondered if the detectives planned to interview the dairy farmer.

"Thank you, Mr. Veldkamp. That's all for now. Would you send Willem in, please?"

Hendrik found Willem waiting with Katja and Jurriaan in the kitchen, probably getting their stories straight.

"Willem, you're next."

AUGUST 2004

CHAPTER

61

August 16, 2004

Willem

A HALF HOUR AFTER his cringe-worthy trip to the toilet, Willem heard Louisa leave Katja's room, and then another door shut. After that the only sounds were the creaks and groans of the old house and rain gushing from a downspout. It took all his willpower to stay put, like Katja wanted.

He woke up to pearly morning light seeping through the curtains. A moment later, his worries rolled over him like a stack of logs. There was no point in tossing and turning in bed. Besides, it was eight thirty. He threw back the covers, pulled on his clothes, and went downstairs.

Katja sat at the kitchen table, staring at an untouched cup of coffee, her suitcase parked next to the chair. Jurriaan was spooning porridge into his mouth like a robot. Hendrik was gazing out the window, with the telephone receiver pressed to his ear and the cord stretched taut. His tool chest was open on the counter beneath the sagging cabinet door that he had promised to fix.

Willem looked again at the suitcase, and his heart took off at a gallop. "Are you going somewhere?"

"Louisa knows," Katja said.

That could mean only one thing. "How?"

"She saw you leave my room last night."

"But she didn't, Katja. She was bluffing."

Katja sighed. "That's not what she said. Anyway, you know how she is. Sometimes I think she can read minds."

"I know . . . but shit."

Jurriaan pushed back his chair, carried his bowl to the stove, and turned the burner on under the pan of porridge. Willem saw by the set of his shoulders he was listening to their every word.

Willem said, "I'll talk to her."

Katja placed her hand on his wrist. Despite the fact that his world was falling apart, her touch sent a thrill through him.

"No, Willem. You'll make things worse. I'm going back to Amsterdam today and pack my things. I'm moving out."

"Where will you go?" He glanced at Hendrik for help, but he should have known better. Hendrik looked away, as always. "C'mon, let's go somewhere private to talk."

"Sorry, but if I don't leave now, I'll miss the bus to the harbor."

He gripped the back of a chair and squeezed until his knuckles turned white. His head buzzed, his ears buzzed, even his skin buzzed. It was all he could do to keep from hurling the chair across the linoleum.

"We'll give you a lift," he said, a desperate note in his voice.

Footsteps came up from behind him. "No, she can take the bus."

Louisa stood in the doorway with her hands on her hips, dressed in running gear: a blue tank top, matching blue shorts, and white trainers. Her blonde hair was pulled back tight in a high ponytail.

Hendrik put down the phone. "The ferry this morning is fully booked," he said, his voice flat.

Louisa's gaze burned into Katja for a moment before shifting to Hendrik. She ignored Willem.

"What time is the next one?"

"Three o'clock."

"So, buy a ticket on the three o'clock," she snapped.

"But Mom—"

"I don't want to hear it, Willem. Katja tells me you two are having a fling. How could you do that to me? She's my stepsister."

It didn't surprise him that she wanted to make this about herself, but the word *fling* hurt. Wasn't a fling something casual, temporary, meaningless? Just sex. Katja wouldn't say that.

"We love each other," he said, and shot a glance at Katja, whose face had flushed tomato red.

Louisa snorted. "Katja doesn't love you. I offered her money to leave, and she took it."

"You're lying."

"I never said I loved you," Katja said softly.

The words felt like a kick in the gut. "Did you take money?"

She nodded, her eyes cast down.

Louisa smirked. "Katja's always been a slut. I put her on the pill when she was fourteen—"

"Shut up!" he shouted.

She smiled the stupid triumphant smile he had seen a million times before, confident she had the upper hand, but he wasn't a kid anymore. Blood pounded in his ears. Katja tugged on his T-shirt—a warning that he ignored.

"What did I do to make you hate me?" Willem said. "Nothing is ever good enough. My grades, my music, my friends."

"If you mean Bas Debose, find yourself a better class of friends. I bet his parents have never set foot in the Concert Hall."

"Jeetje, Mom. Who cares?" She was so close, he could see red flecks in her eyes, the pores in her nose, the ugly necklace with the piano pendant she never took off. "You can't stand the fact I have a friend. That's why you won't let me share an apartment with Bas."

"It's your own fault," she said. "You sneaked out in Hendrik's car. You got yourself kicked off the hockey team."

"And the broken arm when I was eight? Was that my fault? The concussion? The bruises?" His list of grievances was a mile long, and he could have gone on, but he stopped, maybe because Katja was listening. It occurred to him for the first time that perhaps his pride—or his shame—had made him complicit. He could have gotten help, but hadn't. "Why don't you hit Jurriaan when he screws up?" he threw back at her.

Hendrik intervened. "That's enough, Willem.

Willem glanced guiltily at Jurriaan, who had quit stirring the porridge and was staring down at the pan, his shoulders hunched in misery. Willem whirled around to confront Hendrik, who had never taken his side, had never believed him—or had always pretended not to.

"She treats you like shit too. Why do you take it?"

"Calm down, Willem. You're upset," Hendrik said.

"Why do you stay married to her? You're gutless."

Hendrik flinched.

"Gutless—the both of you," Louisa said, repeating the word as though savoring the taste.

The pounding in Willem's ears intensified: flood water against a dam.

He pushed her.

She stumbled back. Her arm flew up as if to strike him, but she let it fall. She wouldn't hit him with her bare hands, the hands that were insured for a million dollars. How many times had she said that? She shoved Jurriaan aside, grabbed the pan of porridge by the handle, spun back, and flung the contents at Willem. It was so absurd, so unexpected, that he froze in place. Clumps of scalding porridge spattered his face, his right ear, his bare feet. The pain seemed far away.

His vision dimmed. As he reached into Hendrik's toolbox, he caught a flicker of movement at the corner of his eye.

His hand closed around the hammer.

And the dam broke.

CHAPTER

62

August 16, 2004

Willem

LOUISA LAY ON the gritty linoleum floor in front of the stove. Hendrik, who was kneeling beside her, blocked Willem's view of her upper body. One pale leg was bent slightly at the knee, resting on its side, the other stretched out straight. He picked up her hand and pressed his thumb against her wrist for several moments, then bent down and laid his ear against her chest.

"Louisa. Can you hear me?"

Jurriaan stood nearby, visibly shaking, the bloody hammer dangling in his hand, a wet stain down his pajama bottoms. Willem blinked, unable to process what he saw, and tried to remember who had done what.

"Louisa," Hendrik repeated.

Willem held his breath.

One of her trainers twitched.

He exhaled in relief. He had hated her for years—and sometimes had fantasized about her death in random accidents. A plane crash or a car accident or a fall down the stairs. But she was his mother, after all.

He tried to recall what had happened after he grabbed the hammer, but the next thing he could remember was bending over the sink while Katja rinsed the porridge off his face with shockingly cold water.

He crossed the kitchen, slipped the bloody hammer from Jurriaan's hand, squatted, and laid it on the floor.

"Mom," Jurriaan wailed.

Willem pinned his arms, held him back, kept him from throwing himself onto their mother.

"Take Jurriaan upstairs," Hendrik said. "Give him one of Louisa's sleeping pills."

Jurriaan struggled against Willem's hold.

"We'll take care of her, Jurriaan," Katja said, her voice quavering. "Go upstairs with Willem."

Jurriaan twisted his neck around, peering over his shoulder as Willem hustled him through the kitchen door and up the stairs.

* * *

Jurriaan sat down, robot-like, on his bed while Willem fetched the sleeping pills and a glass of water from the bathroom.

"Here. Take these." Willem gave him two.

"Is Mom dead?"

"No, she's just tired."

Jurriaan nodded. "I wet my pants," he said, looking miserable.

"Doesn't matter. I'll get you clean ones."

"Another T-shirt too," Jurriaan said. His was spattered with blood, like flecks of red paint.

Willem peered down at his own shirt, which was dark blue, making the spatters difficult to see. The blood was already dry. Stiff. He balled up their shirts and stuffed them into the wastebasket. He found a clean pair of shorts for Jurriaan and T-shirts for them both.

The pills didn't work instantly. Willem perched on the edge of the bed, reassuring his brother that their mother was going to be all right. It took a good ten minutes for Jurriaan to fall asleep.

Hendrik must have called the emergency number, and Willem wondered if an ambulance would arrive with its siren wailing. Once Louisa regained consciousness, she could tell the doctor—or the police—who had struck her with the hammer, unless she had amnesia or didn't want to admit to the world what went on in her perfect family. Someone would be in big trouble, maybe Willem, but it would be much worse if she didn't keep breathing. He clung to the thought that her foot had twitched.

* * *

Downstairs, the kitchen was transformed. The blue tarp from the shed was spread flat on the floor. It was caked here and there with clumps of dried mud, some of which had disintegrated into little piles of dirt on the linoleum. Louisa's face was turned, and he could see the wound an inch above her ear.

Blood matted the hair at her temple and smeared her cheek, but the bleeding had stopped, which must be a good sign. And the hammer had vanished. But why the tarp?

"Jurriaan's asleep," he said.

"Good," Katja said.

"Is an ambulance on the way?" he asked.

She looked at Hendrik.

Hendrik said, "Okay, Katja. On the count of three. One, two, three."

Willem watched as they rolled Louisa's limp body onto the tarp. Her face flopped toward Willem, making him jump. Her lips were parted as if in surprise, and her eyelids slitted, the whites visible between her eyelashes. Panic thrashed in his chest. Why didn't they answer him about the ambulance?

"Take off her shoes and socks," Hendrik said to Katja.

She loosened the laces and slipped off the trainers, and Hendrik dropped something shiny into one of them. Katja pulled off Louisa's ankle socks and stuffed them into the shoes.

They were making her more comfortable, Willem thought, and his panic eased.

But when Hendrik covered the bloodied face with the tarp, Willem's stomach heaved. That's what you did to dead people. He lurched down the shadowy hall to the toilet and fell to his knees. He retched, stomach acids burning his throat. The tile floor felt like broken glass. When he was finished, he sat back, heart pounding. The room was claustrophobic. Spinning. Rain pelted the small window that was set high in the wall. He pushed himself to his feet, leaned against the sink, and rinsed out his mouth. He trudged toward the light spilling in from the kitchen.

Hendrik and Katja were drinking whisky at the table. In the center of the floor lay an elongated bundle bound with rope. Katja raised her eyes, and in that moment, Willem knew he had become just a lump of living flesh to her, nothing more. There was only one reason she would look at him like that. His gaze shifted to the bundle.

Hendrik cleared his throat. "Now listen carefully, son. This is what we're going to do. We'll report her missing tomorrow."

Missing? Confused, Willem looked at the tarp and back at Hendrik. He started to interrupt, but Hendrik spoke with such authority that he kept silent, listened, tried to take it in.

"Nothing's going to bring back your mother, but I won't have a son of mine branded a murderer or sent to prison. Your mother wouldn't want that either. I'll make her body disappear—permanently. Tonight. After dark."

"What are you going to do?" Willem said, and glanced at Katja, whose eyes were fixed on Hendrik.

"It's better you don't know." Hendrik stood up and began to pace, his hands clutched together behind his back. He was wound up tight, the same way he got when perfecting an invention. "Everything's going to be all right, Willem."

Katja nodded her head like a bobbling dashboard ornament.

Willem knew if anyone could cover up a murder, it was Hendrik. He wasn't much of a dad, but he was a brilliant inventor, happiest when solving a difficult problem. And for the first time, Hendrik wasn't looking away.

CHAPTER

63

August 16, 2004

Willem

HENDRIK STOPPED PACING. "I'm going to move her to the sitting room."

Touching the tarp was the last thing Willem wanted to do. He didn't want to go anywhere near it.

"Do you need help?" Katja asked, her thin shoulders pulled halfway to her ears.

"No, I have to do this alone . . . tonight . . ." Hendrik's voice trailed off.

"Wouldn't it be better to put her in the car now?" Katja's voice trembled. "The trunk will be like an oven by noon."

Willem stared incredulously at the two of them, discussing Louisa's dead body as if it were meat that might spoil in a hot car on the way home from the butcher's.

While Hendrik dragged the bundle out of the kitchen, Katja filled a bucket with soapy water. On hands and knees, she started scrubbing the blood from the floor, scrubbing in wider and wider circles, not just the one spot. She didn't speak to Willem or make eye contact. She was finished with him, and he couldn't blame her. He had dug himself a shithole. Even if Hendrik's plan succeeded, how could he live with what he had done—or might have done?

"Katja? Are we doing the right thing?"

She kept scrubbing, trying to remove an invisible stain. Without looking up, she said, "I don't know, Willem. I hope so."

"We should call the police and tell them what happened."

That got her full attention. She hurled down the sponge and looked at him for the first time in what seemed like forever. "For God's sake, Willem. Don't think only about yourself."

"Jeetje," he sputtered. "Is that what I'm doing? Really? Dad's going to make Mom's body disappear. Whatever that means. Sometimes I hated her, but she was my mother."

"Willem, I know it's hard, but—"

"Tell you what. I'll confess. I'll take the blame."

"Don't be ridiculous. Think about your future. And Jurriaan's. Listen to Hendrik for once."

The girl who had taken his side on everything had become a stranger.

He had to get out of the house. As he passed the sitting room, he saw Hendrik kneeling next to the tarp. He looked as if he were praying. Tears blurred Willem's vision. *Shit, shit, shit.* He wrenched open the front door and slammed it behind him, remembering too late that Jurriaan was asleep. He heard Katja call his name as he clambered over the gate, but he didn't look back, and he sprinted toward the woods.

Mud splattered his bare calves as he raced through rain puddles on the hiking trail. It didn't matter if his trainers got muddy, because Louisa was dead. She would never yell or find fault with him again. But he had proved her instincts regarding him were right, hadn't he? A waste of space. Worse, he should never have been born. He ran on, trying to put as much distance—as fast as possible—between himself and Louisa's corpse.

Deep in the woods, he slowed to a stop and leaned forward with his hands on his thighs. After catching his breath, he picked up a soggy pine cone and hurled it into the vines under the trees. It didn't matter who had hit her: him or Jurriaan. What had happened was his fault, and he should take the consequences. He picked up another pine cone. And another. He hurled them faster and faster until his shoulder ached.

He knew the trails; his feet took him west. Could Hendrik make her body disappear? Louisa was famous. The police would search for her. The islanders would help. They wouldn't stop until they had found her.

He wished he could ask Bas what to do. But his best friend wasn't there—Willem's fault too.

The woods were airless: hot and thick with humidity. He felt a sting on his cheek and batted a mosquito away. An itchy red welt rose instantly. He and Jurriaan were both allergic.

Katja would check on Jurriaan. She would prevent him from going into the sitting room if he felt so inclined. The room was dark and formal, not somewhere to hang out to snack on chips and drink Coke. On an ordinary day, it wouldn't occur to Jurriaan to open the door and go inside, but this wasn't an ordinary day.

The woods thinned and the hiking trail ended. Willem emerged into a tree-lined lane in the village of Westerend. He felt faint, and he realized he hadn't eaten. His mind was fuzzy just when he needed a clear head.

He soon came to a sidewalk café. Only two other customers sat outside, both with umbrellas leaning against their chairs. Thunder growled in the distance. Willem sat down at a table, gulped down a glass of water, and studied the menu. It was like looking at letters floating in a bowl of alphabet soup.

As the waitress approached, he remembered he hadn't any money. He fled into the lane, passed cottages with small fenced-in gardens and shops selling souvenirs, cranberries, and cheese. The few people he passed—on bikes, on foot, or sitting behind windows—seemed to stare at him accusingly. He kept his head lowered and plowed on.

At the intersection, he stopped and stared at the building on the corner. On the bricks below the flat roof were big blue letters: *P-O-L-I-T-I-E*. Memories stirred. He had gone inside only once, years ago, to swear that the beachcomber hadn't touched him, that Louisa was wrong. He had possessed more guts at ten than he did now.

Willem turned right, toward the harbor. A huge ferry that was moored at the dock dwarfed the small fishing boats, which were rocking in the foaming water. Hot wind slapped his face and whipped his hair. The rotten-fish smell of the Wadden was everywhere.

He turned around and trudged back to the corner, sensing that the police station had been his destination all along. He wavered at the edge of the empty parking lot. What was the right thing to do? His gut told him one thing, his head another. His feet started across the asphalt, toward the entrance, but halted just short of the glass door.

If he confessed to killing Louisa, the police would find her body trussed up in the sitting room. They might arrest the entire family as accessories. Jurriaan would have to testify at the trial—and lie. But he couldn't lie any better than he could swim or play ball. It wasn't likely that he and Jurriaan would share a cell or be sent to the same prison. Jurriaan wouldn't be able to defend himself against the other inmates, and Willem wouldn't be there to protect him. He tried to banish the thought.

He yanked on the door handle, but the door didn't budge. He tried pushing, throwing his weight against the heavy glass, but the door didn't give. Then he noticed the sign with the opening hours and a telephone number for emergencies. The crappy police station closed at noon!

An off-duty policeman might respond to a break-in, so he glanced around for a rock or a brick to smash the glass and set off the alarm. But there was nothing suitable. Lightheaded and sick, he sank to the ground and leaned his back against the door. After a while, he realized he was being stupid, and his face flushed. Katja was right. He had been thinking only about himself. Jurriaan needed him. He had no choice but to go along with Hendrik's plan. Either that or dump everyone in the shit.

He felt a sudden prickly sensation and glanced furtively around. Across the street, two little kids stood in a patch of garden, staring curiously at him. The oldest, a towheaded girl of around five, held a green watering can nearly as big as she was. The younger one, a toddler, pointed a pudgy arm in Willem's direction. The front door opened, and a woman appeared in the doorway.

Jeetje. Sitting on his ass in front of the police station wasn't a brilliant idea, especially now that he had decided against confessing. Jurriaan would need him when the sleeping pills wore off, so he started back toward Oerd, taking the path along the dike because it was shorter than through the woods. Still, it took two hours to reach the summerhouse.

Katja must have been watching, because she met him halfway up the driveway.

"Where have you been? I was worried."

"Worried about what?"

"We were afraid you might do something foolish."

We meant her and Hendrik.

"Like what?" he asked, his heart a fluttering, achy thing.

"Like ruin everything," she snapped.

She had been worried about the plan, not about him, and she'd been right to worry. He *had* come close to ruining everything.

"Where's Jurriaan?" he asked.

"He's in the kitchen. We told him Louisa was in bed with a migraine."

As Willem shoved past her, he glanced at the closed door to the sitting room, and his stomach twisted.

It was hours before dark.

DECEMBER 2024

CHAPTER 64

Willem

WILLEM SAT DOWN on the sofa, facing the detectives. His thoughts turned to that afternoon twenty years ago at the Wexalia Police Station. He should have set off the alarm and alerted the police. *No . . . rewind.* He should have called the police from the summerhouse before things had gone so far. He had been old enough to know right from wrong, though not old enough to foresee all the consequences. Now it was within his power to put things right. But at what cost? Everyone he held dear would suffer.

Terpstra got straight down to business.

"Walk us through the events of the day Louisa went missing."

Willem had gone over his original statement so many times in his head that it was engraved in his memory. He related his story again.

Terpstra nodded. "Your recall is excellent."

It didn't feel like a compliment. Who remembers so much minutiae after twenty years? He should have stumbled in the retelling, left something out, pretended to forget the color of Louisa's T-shirt.

"Describe your relationship with your mother," the brigadier said.

"You sound like a therapist," Willem said, forcing a smile.

Terpstra smiled back, like an oily politician. "Did you get along with her?"

"Most of the time."

"Were you rebellious?"

"Not particularly. I wasn't a big drinker, and I didn't touch drugs. I earned good grades."

"Were you and your mother close?"

"She was away a lot. She gave concerts all over the world."

"How were things when she was home?"

"She kept us on our toes."

"Which of your parents was the disciplinarian?"

"I told you, my mother wasn't home much."

"The fact is, you haven't told me much of anything."

"I've answered your questions," Willem said, but the detective was right. He knew how to engage while revealing nothing of importance.

Terpstra grunted. "I understand Louisa disappeared two days after she arrived on the island. Did you and she argue during that time?"

"Not about anything important."

"About what, then?"

"Tracking sand into the house. Playing my Walkman too loud."

"How did she punish you? Did she hit you?"

"Grounding me was as violent as she got."

"Did *you* ever hit *her*?"

Willem's mouth dried up. "Of course not. Why do you ask?"

"I understand you were expelled from the hockey club that summer for fighting. It was in a letter found among her things."

Willem tried to make light of it, though the incident still rankled. "The fight was a one-off, and I didn't start it. The club's decision was unfair."

"Did the other player get expelled too?"

"No."

Terpstra nodded, as if he had scored a point. "Go back to the day Louisa disappeared. What did you think had happened to her when she didn't return from her run?"

"We thought she might have twisted an ankle. We looked for her."

"How did you know where to look?"

"I jogged with her sometimes. She kept to the same route."

"A visitor to the island found her shoes and socks in the sand dunes. What did you make of that?"

Willem took in the brigadier's long, wrinkled face and his intelligent, deep-set brown eyes, and wondered when he would mention Louisa's necklace. "My mother suffered from hot, sweaty feet. It wasn't unusual for her to cool them off in the water. We were afraid she had drowned."

"Would she have gone for a swim in her running clothes?"

"No. But you don't have to wade far to get into trouble. The currents are dangerous in that part of the beach. Especially after a storm."

"Is that so?"

"Ask anyone."

"In that case, didn't Louisa know?"

"Not necessarily. She didn't spend much time on Wexalia."

"But she can read warning signs."

"My mother didn't think rules applied to her."

Terpstra glanced over at the younger detective, whose head was bent over his iPad. After a pause, he said, "Why is your fiancée's arm in a sling?"

For Christ's sake. Did the brigadier think he had hurt Anneliese?

"What does that have to do with the investigation?" Willem asked.

"Just answer the question, please."

"She had an accident on her bicycle." He started to add that there had been half a dozen witnesses, but that would make him sound defensive.

Terpstra stood up, perhaps needing to stretch his long legs, and turned toward the window, clasping his hands behind his back. The rain had stopped, but the wind tossed the bare trees back and forth.

This was Willem's first trip to Wexalia in winter; he didn't know it could be so bleak, so bone-chillingly cold. What was the detective thinking? Did he know something he wasn't telling? The uncertainty was unnerving. Willem felt pressure building inside him, but he couldn't afford the relief of letting go. He had to hold himself together for a while longer.

Terpstra took his seat again.

"Can you think of anyone who might have wanted to hurt your mother?"

"No."

"What about Menso de Vries, the beachcomber? She accused him of molesting you and your brother."

Willem shook his head. "He didn't molest us."

"I read Jurriaan's statement. That's not what he said. Was he lying?"

"He was confused. Jurriaan is highly suggestible. My mother hammered home the story he told the police. But in the end, he recanted. Didn't you read his amended statement?"

"Being falsely accused of molesting a child is a powerful motive. During the previous investigation, the police found her necklace hidden under the floorboards of his cottage. Terpstra looked at his notes. "A gold chain with a pendant in the form of a piano. What did you think when you heard that?"

"Menso lived off the objects he found on the beach. He may be a thief, but he's not a murderer."

"He stated he found the necklace tucked in her trainers. Why would she take it off to go wading?"

"If it came off, she would never find it in the water," Willem said. The real reason was obvious to him. Leaving the necklace in her shoes had been a clumsy way of linking the shoes to Louisa and supporting the supposition that she had drowned.

After a silence, Terpstra said, "What did you and Jurriaan do for fun?"

Willem raised his eyebrows at the turn the questions had taken. "On the island? We built a fort in one of the old Nazi bunkers. We cycled. I learned to surf. Some nights, we camped out behind the house. And we fished."

"Where did you fish?"

It was a loaded question. "On the dune lake. At the west end of the island."

"Did you have a boat?"

"No." Willem thought back on their secret fishing expeditions to Lutine in Doeksen's dinghy, and the picnic with Katja. He knew not to mention the dinghy because it was now obvious to Willem that Hendrik had used it to transport Louisa's body to the sandbank. He prayed Terpstra wouldn't ask Jurriaan about the boat, at least not before he had time to warn him.

"Did you drive a car that summer?" Terpstra asked.

"I was only sixteen."

"That's not what I asked. Let me rephrase. Did you know how to drive?"

"No. I didn't take lessons until I was eighteen."

Terpstra's jowly face was inscrutable. "That's all for now, Willem. Would you send Jurriaan in?"

"Are you aware of his cognitive disability?"

"Yes. I've been apprised. This isn't a formal interview, and nothing he says can be used as evidence.

"Nevertheless, I should be present. Jurriaan is vulnerable. He gets flustered. He'll be more at ease if I'm there." Jurriaan might fall apart. He might tell Terpstra about the assault on Louisa with the hammer. But Jurriaan believed that Louisa had disappeared on the day after.

"Of course, but please interfere as little as possible."

CHAPTER

65

December 2024

Jurriaan

JURRIAAN SQUIRMED UNDER the steady gaze of Brigadier Terpstra. The detective looked nothing like nice Surveillant Meyer in Amsterdam. For one thing, he had a long creased face and droopy eyelids that made him look like a bloodhound. For another thing, he didn't wear a uniform. Jurriaan knew from TV that detectives dressed in plain clothes. His clothes were plain all right: a baggy brown suit, a brown knitted tie, and brown lace-up shoes.

Jurriaan could remember little about his mother's disappearance. Willem had said that Jurriaan's subconscious had suppressed the memories. He might never get them back. It was the mind's way of protecting itself from pain.

He scratched his ankle, pulled up his socks, crossed and uncrossed his legs. He sat on the end of the sofa by the hearth, and Willem sat on the other end. He could hear the wind moaning in the chimney.

Terpstra said, "There's no need to be nervous, Jurriaan. It's all right if you don't know an answer or have forgotten. Do you have any questions?"

Jurriaan pointed at the other detective, whose face was round and smooth. "What's he doing?"

"Detective Rijkaard will take notes on his iPad."

"Why?"

"Because my memory is terrible. I hope yours is better than mine," Terpstra said. "When did you see your mother for the last time?"

"I don't remember."

"No problem, Jurriaan. Now, think carefully. Did you see her the morning she disappeared?"

Willem had told him what to say.

"I think she was gone when I came downstairs."

"You're not sure?"

"I forget." Jurriaan adjusted his glasses.

"What *do* you remember about that day?"

"We looked for her."

"Where did you look?"

"Outside. In the woods, I guess."

Terpstra raised an eyebrow and exchanged frustrated glances with his partner. Jurriaan relaxed a bit. He was used to getting those kinds of looks from people. From a *lot* of people. The detectives thought he was dumb, but for once it didn't bother him, because maybe they would stop asking questions.

"Describe your relationship with your mother."

Jurriaan scrunched his forehead. Now who was dumb? "I'm her son."

A smile flashed on Rijkaard's face, fast as lightening. Terpstra raised his eyebrows. "I meant, did you get along with your mother?"

"Oh yes. I was her favorite," he blurted out before remembering that Willem had told him not to volunteer information. Was Willem angry? He peered first at Terpstra's serious face and then at Rijkaard's amused one. He didn't glance at Willem because he was supposed to pretend he wasn't in the room, but of course he knew he was there, and that knowledge gave him courage.

"Why do you think you were her favorite?" Terpstra asked.

"Because she told me. Can I go now?"

"Soon. I have a few more questions. Then you can go."

Jurriaan eyed the detective with the sad bloodhound face and the detective with the moon face. "Okay."

He worried that they might ask him if he had gone fishing in a boat while visiting Wexalia. Willem had said that it was important to say no if the detectives asked, although he hadn't explained why. But the detectives didn't mention a boat. Jurriaan was relieved because he wasn't very good at telling lies.

CHAPTER

66

December 14, 2024

Diary entry

TOMAS TERPSTRA, THE older detective, surprised me with his first question.

"I've read all your books. When will your new novel come out?"

I didn't expect a cold-case detective to have a literary bent, and especially not this detective with his sallow, sagging face and baggy suit.

"Not until next year," I said. The book was guaranteed to be a bestseller now that Louisa's remains had been found, but I was getting cold feet. The parallels between real life and fiction were too close for comfort. Maybe if I paid back the advance from my publisher, I could wriggle out from under the contract. It had been a mistake to write something semi-autobiographical, no matter how much I disguised identities and events, but the story practically wrote itself, and in my defense, I thought the past had been buried.

The new novel isn't a mystery, but it contains a mystery, that of a beautiful actress who goes missing. The woman is talented, rich, adored by her fans. She has a husband who worships her and three beautiful young daughters. But her career comes first. She neglects her family, and she's abusive as well. She's kidnapped by a psychopathic stalker and held captive on an uninhabited island. After twenty years, she escapes, but she has lost everything. Her public has forgotten her. Her talent and her looks are gone. Her husband has remarried, and her children are strangers. She has nothing left to live for. But with the help of a psychotherapist, she learns the restorative power of love.

It didn't happen that way in real life, but by definition a novel is fiction.

The detective asked me to tell him everything I remembered about the day Louisa disappeared, no matter how irrelevant it might seem. He said if there were gaps in my memory, not to worry.

I stuck to the script.

When I finished, he said, "How would you describe your relationship with your stepsister?"

"Louisa was seventeen years older. My mother died in childbirth, and my father married Louisa's mother, a divorcée, a year later. They were killed in a car crash when I was in middle school. Louisa had her hands full with her career and her young family, so she sent me to a boarding school for children whose parents worked abroad. I stayed with her and Hendrik sometimes during the school holidays. She paid my school fees after my inheritance ran out. I'll always be grateful to Louisa."

Terpstra's last question was one I was expecting because finding a motive must be a priority. Find the motive, find the killer.

"Were you and Hendrik lovers before Louisa died?" Although his tone was matter-of-fact, the young detective stopped typing and leaned forward, awaiting my answer.

"No, not until several years later. He encouraged my writing. He was my first reader. I wouldn't have enjoyed the career I've had if not for Hendrik. He is . . . was . . . brilliant. No, Brigadier Terpstra. He was devoted to Louisa while she lived."

It was true almost to the end.

CHAPTER

67

December 2024

Anneliese

THE KNOCK CAME again. Anneliese rose from the bed and padded to the door in her socks, the blanket draped around her shoulders. She opened. Hendrik stood in the hallway, his face in shadow.

"Come with me." He held out her coat.

"Where to?" she asked, taking the coat with her good arm.

"To meet someone."

"Who?"

He swelled with impatience, towering over her.

"Are you coming or not?"

She bristled. "I had a serious bicycle accident. I'm supposed to rest."

"Don't you want to meet your biological father? It's the reason I wanted you to come with us to Wexalia."

She froze. "I don't understand. What do you know about my father?"

"I'll wait on the landing."

"Hendrik, we can't just leave. The police are investigating a murder."

"The detective said he didn't have questions for you. And we'll be back before they know we're gone."

"All right. Give me a minute."

She dropped the blanket onto the bed and pulled the coat over the sling. She reached around her back to put her good arm in the other sleeve. Pulling on her boots was easy, thanks to the zippers. She went into the hall.

Hendrik pressed his finger against his lips. She rolled her eyes at the theatrics and followed him down the stairs.

The runner in the hall muffled their footsteps, and they slipped out the front door, meeting no one. They passed the sitting-room window, their boots squelching on wet leaves. The overcast sky made the afternoon look like dusk. The two cold case detectives, with their backs to the window, were visible in the lighted interior, like actors on a stage. Willem sat on the sofa, facing the police officers, his face ironed of expression.

She wanted to believe Hendrik. It was possible Katja had hooked up with a local boy and gotten pregnant while vacationing at the summerhouse. It was possible her lover might still live on the island. But even if Hendrik was wrong or lying or delusional, she had nothing to lose by playing along. A wild goose chase was better than sitting around waiting for Brigadier Terpstra to recognize her. She climbed into the car and buckled up.

The detectives had left the gate open, and Hendrik drove into the lane. As the Mercedes sped up, Hendrik's white-knuckle grip on the wheel relaxed slightly, and he glanced at Anneliese.

"Do we really need this cloak-and-dagger stuff?" she asked.

"I promised your father I'd let him explain."

He turned onto the dike road in the opposite direction from the harbor. They passed squat old houses, a tiny grocery with no front window, and a pub with a parking lot full of bicycles. A church steeple rose in the mist from a side street. Soon they left the village behind, and the pine forest gave way to a flat grassy polder. The road curved in closer to the dike. Black boulders lined the slope to the water.

She was looking at the Wadden Sea. They had crossed it on the ferry, following the buoys that marked the shipping route along the deep channels. Except for the wind dimpling the surface, the water looked stagnant.

"Is the tide coming in or going out?" she asked.

"Neither. It's dead tide."

"What does that mean?"

"It's when the water has reached its highest or lowest point, and the tide halts before it turns. It will be ebb soon."

They passed a farmhouse on the left, with a long, sloping roof, and behind it a low-slung metallic barn, but no sign of farm animals. A barbed wire fence sagged between the road and the pasture. The two lanes merged into one, following the coastline, and at a point ahead, vanished into the mist. Hendrik slowed the car and parked next to the fence.

There were no houses or villages, only windswept polder. A flock of gulls pecked in the shivering grass. Hendrik was staring toward the sea, which had darkened in the last few minutes, turning the water black.

"Follow me," Hendrik said, and climbed out of the car.

Anneliese stayed seated. "I'm not going anywhere until you tell me what we're doing here."

"Your father is waiting. He'll explain everything."

"You said that already, but waiting where?"

Hendrik turned and disappeared over the dike.

She tried to shake off the ridiculous unease stealing over her. She opened the car door and stepped onto the road. The damp wind whipped her hair, and the mist clogged her eyelashes. She belonged in bed, not freezing her butt off with a man who was not in full possession of his faculties. But Hendrik was harmless.

They climbed over the boulders and onto a wooden pier, which extended forty or fifty feet across the water. They walked past several fishing boats and stopped at a dinghy.

Hendrik unsnapped the canvas cover and shook off the rain.

"I didn't know you had a boat."

"It belongs to the dairy farmer. He lets me use it whenever I want."

He jumped in first, then took her right arm and helped her onto the bench at the front of the dinghy. He was careful not to knock against her sling.

"Do you have a life preserver for me?" she asked.

"Don't worry—we'll stay near shore." After untying the mooring line, he opened a storage compartment under the rear seat and took out an orange lanyard. He attached one end to the motor and looped the other end around his leg.

"What's that?"

"A kill switch. It cuts the motor if I'm thrown overboard. The propeller blades can maim or kill."

"Where are we going?"

He pointed toward the water, and in the distance Anneliese saw a dark shape that wasn't moving. Hendrik turned on the ignition.

"Is it an island?" she yelled over the thrum of the motor.

"Lutine is officially a sandbank."

"Isn't that where Louisa's remains were found?"

Hendrik said nothing.

She recalled the map in his study, the North Sea and the surrounding countries covered with hundreds of notations scribbled in pencil. Had

Hendrik been tracking the storm? The rising sea levels? The currents? The eroding coastline? Was he monitoring Lutine?

She hadn't worked everything out yet, but a chill spread through her.

"Turn the boat around. I want to go back."

The lines of his face hardened.

The dinghy plowed ahead through the black water, the icy spray stinging her face. Jump? Swim back to shore? She couldn't survive for long in the freezing water, even if she stayed afloat with the useless shoulder. What kind of mother put her unborn child in danger so carelessly? She scrabbled in her pocket for her phone. It wasn't there. In her haste, she had forgotten to bring it. She tried not to panic. *Think!* Hendrik was eccentric, and he had memory issues, but he wasn't dangerous, and he had no reason to harm her. But fear had its claws in her.

Lutine—any solid ground—looked very attractive, but Hendrik changed course away from the sandbank. The boat sped up, bucking wildly over the swells. She could barely hang on with her one good arm. The ferry hadn't sailed a straight line either, zigzagging to avoid running aground on submerged sandbanks. She expected Hendrik to change direction and make for Lutine. But he held course. They were rounding the tip of Wexalia, headed for the channel that led to the open sea—to the stormy North Sea with its treacherous currents and crashing waves. Waters that sank ships far more seaworthy than the little dinghy.

Hendrik reduced power and cut the engine. The dinghy swung around and swirled helplessly in a circle for several seconds, then straightened and drifted sideways.

The tide had turned.

CHAPTER

68

December 2024

Willem

WHILE THE DETECTIVES were interviewing Katja, Jurriaan made tea. Willem watched him bump his head on the cabinet; drop a spoon on the floor; and, when he set the cups on the table, slosh scalding tea on the saucers.

"Sorry," Jurriaan said.

"No worries, twinnie. Are you okay?"

"I guess." He sat down and stirred in sugar. "I shouldn't have said I was Mom's favorite."

"Forget it."

"Do you think they'll want to talk to me again?"

"If they do, don't volunteer information. Answer their questions and stick to the story. Promise?"

"Promise."

Willem was more worried about what Hendrik might say, his illness making him unpredictable. He looked at his watch and wondered if the detectives would call everyone back to the sitting room after concluding their interview of Katja.

A half hour later, she came into the kitchen, with Terpstra and Rijkaard in tow. She raised her eyebrows at Willem in a gesture of helplessness as she walked past and turned on the teakettle.

Terpstra said, "Dr. Veldkamp, we request your permission to look around the property. We can get a search warrant, if necessary."

Willem's heart raced as he imagined the detectives poking around in their things, lifting rugs, opening closets. He remembered Katja's manic cleaning twenty years ago, scrubbing real and imaginary blood spatter from the kitchen floor, cabinet doors, and walls. He remembered Hendrik going through Louisa's suitcase and the boxes in the attic. And Hendrik burning photos and letters—to protect her privacy, he'd said. But he had missed the damn letter from the hockey club, which made Willem wonder what else he had missed.

"You'll have to ask my father for permission, but I'm afraid he's taking a nap."

"Do you mind if we wait here until he wakes up?" Terpstra asked.

Willem's impulse was to order the detectives out of the house, but they would come back with a search warrant. Perhaps it was better to keep up the appearance that they were cooperating with the investigation.

* * *

Willem knocked on Hendrik's bedroom door. Getting no reply, he went inside. Two folded sheets of paper lay in the center of the bed, one with Willem's name on it, the other with Katja's. He unfolded the one addressed to him. As he read, his hands started shaking, and he sat down on the bed, turned the letter over, and read the back. The handwriting was small and cramped—illegible in places, Hendrik's cognitive decline evident. There was a rambling account of how Louisa had died, and an incoherent passage about someone named Mirella, whom Hendrik seemed to confuse with Anneliese—something to sort out later.

He buried his head in his hands, a low groan escaping his lips. His hands curled into fists, and he pounded the bed until his anger seeped away, leaving bitter relief—he finally knew what had happened to his mother. He unfolded the other letter, this one brief.

After reading it, he jumped up and ran from the room, with the letters in his hand. He flung open the door to his old bedroom, hoping to find Anneliese curled up under a blanket. Although the bed covers were in disarray, there was no sign of her. Nor was she in the bathroom. A chill ran down his spine. He folded the letters into quarters, and slipped the one addressed to him into his trouser pocket and the one addressed to Katja into his shirt pocket. He bolted down the stairs, two steps at a time. Without stopping to put on his coat, he ducked out the front door and raced toward the carport. Slush from the overhanging trees splattered his face. The carport was empty.

He tried to harness his thoughts, which were scattering in all directions, as he hurried back to the house, his heart hammering against his ribs. The detectives were sitting at the table with Katja and Jurriaan, cups of steaming tea in front of them.

Willem pulled the letter to Katja from his shirt pocket and slapped it on the table in front of Terpstra. "Read this."

Terpstra picked it up.

"What's going on, Willem?" Katja asked.

Terpstra read the letter to himself, then out loud.

Dear Katja,

The truth will out. I killed Louisa because she deceived me with another man. I'm taking Mirella. I know you'll understand. This is goodbye.

Love always,

Hendrik

"Who is Mirella?" the detective asked Katja.

She bit down on her lip. "She's the baby I gave up for adoption. Oh my God. Hendrik thinks Anneliese is Mirella."

"Is she?" Terpstra asked.

"It never . . . I don't know."

Questions shot through Willem's head. Was Anneliese Katja's daughter? Did Anneliese know? Was it more than a coincidence that she had come into his life? But he pushed his questions aside for the time being and turned to the detectives. "My father's not well. I think he took Anneliese. The car's gone. She may be in danger. We have to go after them."

Terpstra jumped to his feet, his keys jangling in his hand. "We'll take my car. Where to?"

Good question. Fear crushed Willem's chest. Hendrik could head for anywhere on the island. The dunes, a bunker, the harbor, the dune lake. But then it came to him. It was a guess, but it made sense from a psychological point of view.

"He's taking Anneliese to Lutine."

"Are you sure?" Terpstra asked.

"I know my father."

"Won't he need a boat?"

"There are boats moored at the old pier."

"Let's go," Terpstra said.

"Me too." Jurriaan jumped up, nearly toppling his chair.

"We'll all go," Katja said.

The detectives' car was parked in the lane. Terpstra and Rijkaard climbed into the front seat; Willem, Jurriaan, and Katja into the back.

Willem leaned forward, giving directions to the detectives. The wipers swept hypnotically over the windshield in time with Willem's heartbeat and whispered *hurry, hurry.*

He did the math. Anneliese celebrated her birthday on her adoption day, March 28, 2001. Her birthday was probably a few months before. Louisa had been on tour in the summer of 2000. She had engaged Katja to be their housekeeper. Katja had been taking a hiatus from university. Louisa's secretary quit without notice, and Katja replaced her. She didn't look pregnant when she left Amsterdam, but he might not have noticed: he had been only twelve. He couldn't recall when he saw her next, months later, possibly not until spring. She'd had a baby and never told him. He glanced at her, sitting on the other side of Jurriaan, her lips clamped together, her face drained of color. He couldn't help wondering what other secrets she was keeping. It hurt more than it should have.

Jurriaan stifled a groan.

"What's wrong?" Willem whispered.

"I remember . . . I remember everything."

Willem shot him a hard look, and Jurriaan fell silent.

Katja took Jurriaan's hand and squeezed. "It will be all right. I promise."

Willem wondered if it was a promise she could keep.

CHAPTER

69

December 2024

Anneliese

As soon as Hendrik cut the motor, the silence was filled by the roar of the wind and the gurgle and the spitting of the sea. With each passing second, the tide carried the dinghy farther from shore. Anneliese knew little about boats or the sea, but surely conditions were too rough to be out in the dinghy.

"Turn the boat around," she repeated.

Hendrik was looking in her direction, but past her.

"Where are we going?"

He made no reply.

"Hendrik, answer me," she said, her voice rising in pitch.

His eyes slid toward her. "Louisa is dead because of you."

For a moment she stared. He wasn't well. He was confusing her with someone else. She pushed back panic.

"Look at me, Hendrik. I'm Anneliese, Willem's fiancée. I was a child when Louisa died."

"We argued about you the night before. If not for you . . ." His voice trailed.

She glanced across the water at Wexalia, shrinking into the mist. Willem was at the summerhouse, possibly already missing her and worried. She had to get back to him.

"Start the motor," she yelled.

"You're Mirella."

"What?"

"Your laptop," Hendrik said. "Don't you know better than to use your birthday as a password?"

Not even Willem knew her actual birthdate. "You looked at my laptop?"

"Everything's in your folders and your search history. Your deceitful little plan. Katja didn't want to meet you, did she? You should have respected her wishes."

Hendrik must have read the social worker's letter, which Katja had kept inside the pages of the diary. Hendrik was the one who had removed the diary, the letter, and the key from Willem's cardigan. But why was he threatening her? It didn't make sense.

She glanced around for another boat—for rescue, for safety. But they were alone on the water. What to do? Jump? Talk? Push him overboard?

"You got pregnant on purpose, so Willem would marry you. Don't bother denying it. You left a trail. The site you visited: *Five sneaky ways to get pregnant.*"

No, no. She couldn't let Willem find out.

She would delete her search history.

Willem would believe her over crazy old Hendrik.

The hair on her arms rose as the pieces of the puzzle slotted together. She wondered why the possibility hadn't occurred to her before. Hendrik was tall, but like her, his build was slight, his eyes dark, his gray hair still streaked with black.

"Are you my father?"

"Stupid girl."

"Who is?"

"It's the wrong question."

The swells grew larger, the peaks and valleys more pronounced. The dinghy swung wildly and tipped, taking in water before righting itself. Anneliese thought she might start praying.

"What in hell is the right question?"

"You should ask who your mother is."

"Katja is my mother."

"She can't have children."

"You're lying."

"It's the truth."

Her brain shifted into gear. There had been two women hiding at the hotel in Den Bosch. She wished she'd had the chance to study the diary. What if Katja had only pretended to be pregnant? What if it was Louisa who had been pregnant, and they were hiding from Hendrik?

Anneliese felt no connection to Katja. Oh my God! She had felt an instant connection to Willem. If Louisa was her mother, he was her half brother, and he was the father and the uncle of the child growing in her belly.

She howled and jerked off the sling. She grabbed the paddle from the bottom of the boat and swung it at Hendrik. He blocked the blow with his arm. The paddle made a sodden thud when it struck flesh and bone.

A broken arm would help level the playing field, but he ripped the paddle from her hands and raised it. He froze in that position. His eyes gleamed, as if he were rekindling a long-forgotten memory. She took advantage of his indecision, if indecision it was, and scrambled up, rocking the dinghy with her feet. Hendrik grabbed the sides to keep his balance, and Anneliese jumped over the side.

The cold water took her breath away. Her coat billowed, and for a moment she floated. But she couldn't move her limbs to stay afloat. Murky water closed over her head as she sank to the bottom, only two meters at most, but it might as well have been twenty. Darkness surrounded her except for a ghostly glow above. It took her full concentration to keep from inhaling water. Seconds ticked by. A half minute. The shock of the cold abated. She could move her limbs again. She pushed off the bottom with her feet and shot upward, toward the light. Broke surface. Mouth open and gasping.

The paddle slammed into the water, missing her head by inches, and she dove again. She stayed under until her lungs screamed for air. When she surfaced, she saw that the dinghy had drifted away. Hendrik started the engine. She pulled another deep breath into her lungs and ducked, hoping he hadn't caught sight of her, but she had gotten her bearings. Lutine was closer than Wexalia, and she swam toward the sandbank. She moved her good arm and kicked, but she couldn't make headway, the tide carrying her farther out to sea.

Her life depended on making her left arm pull its share. Each stroke hurt more than the last, until she couldn't bear the pain. From behind her, the rumble of the engine increased to a roar. She dove and a dark shadow passed overhead, the water churning in its wake. She came up gasping and sputtering, swallowing water and breathing it into her lungs. The dinghy was coming back.

First her hands and then her knees scraped something solid beneath the surface. Lutine. She crawled onto the sand and staggered to her feet, her teeth chattering nearly hard enough to break. She saw Hendrik jerk the steering wheel, but he was too late, and the side of the dinghy slammed into the sandbank. The impact threw him overboard. The engine cut and the little craft spun away. Seconds went by. A minute. Maybe two. Still no sign of him. Her relief was immense, and she collapsed on the ground.

She heard splashing.

Hendrik crawled dripping onto the sand like a prehistoric sea monster. She looked around for a weapon. Strange objects littered the sand, strange because they didn't belong on a sandbank in the middle of the sea. Sports shoes. Lightbulbs. Pink plastic toys. Flashlights. Her eyes darted back to Hendrik, his face screwed up in hate.

She grabbed a flashlight, lunged, and landed a one-handed blow on the top of his head. Before she could hit him again, he grabbed her ankle and she toppled backward. Pain like an electric shock shot through her tailbone. Jerking her ankle free, she kicked him in the face, felt the crunch of cartilage or teeth. She scooted backward and scrambled up, wielding the flashlight. She aimed for his head again and swung.

His face exploded into red pulp. He turned and dragged himself on hands and knees toward the water, guttural strangling sounds escaping from his ruined mouth. She tightened her grip on the flashlight, ready to have another go at him if necessary, but he slid into the water and dog-paddled toward the dinghy, which was drifting away in the outgoing tide.

She dropped the flashlight and leaned forward with her hands on her thighs, breathing hard, watching Hendrik's head bobbing in the water until it vanished beneath the waves. She watched for a couple of minutes longer, to be sure. She felt as if her insides had been sucked out, leaving behind an empty shell. Wearily, she straightened and turned toward Wexalia. It seemed impossibly far away; she could never make it. But if she waited on the sandbank for rescue, she might die of exposure. Her best option was to attempt the long slog over the mudflats.

First, there was something she had to do.

She followed the footprints left by the police—just messy indentations in the sand. The individual steps had merged and been filled in with rain. The storm had all but leveled the dunes. Her shoulder throbbed. She missed the sling. Her face stung from the raw wind, and her ears ached. She trudged over a slight rise and found what she sought: a stretch of canvas flat on the ground that was held down by pegs. The police hadn't filled in the grave, which meant they intended to return and finish the job. She knelt and, one by one, worked the pegs out of the sand. She peeled back the canvas and peered into the hole. She thought about Louisa's decomposing remains alone on the sandbank, her location and fate unknown to the outside world, the people who were supposed to love and cherish her silent except for their lies. What kind of person deserved such an ignominious passing?

She spat into the grave.

CHAPTER

70

December 2024

Hendrik

HENDRIK TRIED TO keep his mouth above the swells. The distance between him and the dinghy was twenty yards and increasing with each passing second. The saltwater burned his raw wounds. His smashed nose throbbed. He ran his tongue over the jagged edges of broken teeth. Anneliese was Louisa's daughter, all right.

He thought his life might flash before his eyes as he drowned, like in Katja's novel *Through the Ice.* The protagonist, Wouter Dekker, fell through the ice while skating on a frozen canal, the ice trapping him in the dank water beneath. Near death, Wouter's mind replayed the most wonderful moments of his life, prompting him to make one last effort to save himself.

Hendrik's head went under. He inhaled saltwater and reared back, spluttering, snorting, and gasping, his arms flailing, his eyes darting wildly.

It was too late to change his mind; he had to finish what he'd started. His only wish was for peace at the end, but the memories engulfing him weren't wonderful Wouter Dekker–type memories. Nothing inspiring in any sense of the word. Just the opposite.

* * *

That August night twenty years ago, he hadn't dared turn on the car's headlights. Hunched over the steering wheel, he had concentrated on the feel of the old coastal road beneath his tires. When the car veered too far left, the tires sank into soft, spongy grass. Too far the other way, and the tires scraped the basalt boulders lining the dike.

Once past the gate to Doeksen's dairy farm, he slowed the car and parked alongside the barbed wire fence. He groped for the trunk release switch below the radio, pressed it, and heard a muted thud. Then he stepped into the weeds and for a moment let the damp wind whip across his face. He tasted salt on his lips.

His eyes shifted around warily.

The nearest village was miles away, on the other side of the polder. Behind the fence was pasture, dotted with dark mounds that he took to be sleeping cows. The windows in the farmhouse were dark. The barn was dark except for a security light over the door. In the other direction, beyond the dike, a motley collection of fishing boats was moored to the pier.

He started around to the back of the car. Suddenly his insides turned wobbly, and his legs gave way. He grabbed the fender to keep from collapsing into a quivering heap, a moan swelling up inside him. He squeezed his eyes shut. Gave himself a moment. He was all right; he could do this—he could do whatever it took.

He opened his eyes, heaved a deep sigh, steadied himself. He raised the trunk lid, stupidly hoping that the body had magically vanished, that he would wake up and find today hadn't happened yet. But she was still there. Wrapped in a tarp and bound with rope. He lifted the head end of the bundle and pulled, his back straining. The feet flopped to the ground, and he lugged her by the shoulders, picking his way backward over the dike.

Doeksen's dinghy was tied up halfway along the pier. He nearly lost the bundle overboard before finally wrestling it into the boat, sweat running down his back. He returned to the car for the flashlight and shovel, tossed them into the dinghy, and sat down on the rear seat. His hands shook violently, and he lost precious minutes untying the dock lines.

He had to get the job done before the first gray light of morning, before the early risers—fishermen, farmers, runners. All potential witnesses. He didn't turn on the motor, afraid of attracting attention and being remembered. The tide was coming in. Perfect. Safer to row against the current than to risk being caught in the outgoing tide, which might sweep the dinghy through the channel and into the raw North Sea. He wiped his sweaty palms on his trousers and gripped the oars.

As he rowed, the dinghy bounced on the swells, and the dark sandbank grew larger.

There was little light pollution over the Wadden Islands, and if not for the clouds, the sky would have been ablaze with stars. In the early days of their marriage, they had sometimes slept outdoors behind the summerhouse and picked out the constellations or watched for falling stars. Tonight, the stars weren't visible, but the moon was huge and low on the horizon, casting a ghostly path on the sea.

Twenty minutes later, the bow scraped sand. He laid down the oars and stepped into the muck, which rose to the top of his boots. Cold water sloshed inside, soaking his socks. Glancing back at Wexalia, he made out the black silhouette of the island, shaped like the whale carcass he had once seen floating in the sea. A once magnificent animal, rendered grotesque by death.

Shoving the dinghy up the slope was like budging a piano up a ramp. He heaved and got it out of the water, but no further, so he tipped it on its side and dumped the bundle onto the sand. The little craft was still heavy, but light enough to push past the tidemark. He went back, seized the rope that bound the tarp, and tugged, burning his palms. He should have worn gloves. What else had he forgotten?

He dropped the bundle next to the dinghy, picked up the shovel, and trudged across the sandbank. He leaned into the wind, the roar all but drowning out the hiss and gurgle of the tide. The flashlight illuminated ghostly clumps of marram grass and flowering searockets, colorless in the night. His foot struck something solid: a small sign warning that trespassers would be prosecuted. Trespassing! He gave a short, hysterical snort.

Halfway across, he stopped. It was the highest point and escaped flooding at high tide or even during a severe storm—the reason the sandbank was a resting place for birds and seals.

He had worried that the sand would be packed too hard to shovel, but the top layer was loose, mixed with broken seashells. He set about digging a trench six feet long and two feet wide. The deeper he dug, the firmer the sand, until it was impossible to dig further. Three feet down would have to do.

He followed his footprints back to the dinghy and pulled the bundle up the rise. The tarp kept catching on clumps of grass and he had to yank it along. He stopped at the edge of the trench.

As he stooped to untie the rope, an urge came over him to see her face one more time. He peeled back the tarp and, with shaking hands, aimed the beam.

The pale blue eyes staring back at him blinked.

He was so startled he dropped the flashlight, and the light blinked out. He tapped it, beat it. Nothing. Cursing, he knelt and reached out his hand. Her cheek was cold and rubbery. His fingers traveled upward, tracing over her eyelids. A faint flicker. Recoiling, he fell back on his heels, fighting back nausea for a long minute.

The old Hendrik would have rushed her back to the island and called an ambulance. But Louisa would make him pay, make them all pay. She had deceived him for years. She had had her lover's child in secret. Unforgivable! She might never have told him if he hadn't confronted her about her new lover. She'd had the gall to ask him for a divorce. Her *asking* him. *He was the injured spouse. When was that? Last night? The night before? He had lost track of time, lost track of himself.*

He realized with a jolt that he wasn't the old Hendrik.

What to do?

Press his hand over her nose and mouth? He imagined her body wriggling like a worm on a hook. Asphyxiation would take a couple of minutes or longer. That was too long for him.

He gripped the shovel with both hands and raised it. She whimpered, but he didn't hesitate, afraid of losing his nerve. The shovel plunged. The sharp edge sliced through her neck—softer, more vulnerable than the skull. Blood sprayed his face, forced itself into his mouth, a salty, metallic taste. He turned and spat into the sand. Death filled his nostrils. Or was it the rotten smell of the mudflats?

Bracing himself, he turned back and peered at the blood-soaked bundle. Her head was all but severed from her shoulders. He made his mind a blank as he rolled her out of the tarp. He shuddered at the dull thud when her body hit the bottom of the grave.

The shovel had become impossibly heavy. He had to stop, his arms tingling with exhaustion. He leaned on the shovel and stared at the dark hole, wondering where he would find the energy to finish what he had started. But it would be stupid to be caught with a mutilated corpse and an open grave because he had run out of steam. He had no choice except to carry on. Cold drops of rain pelted his face. A cloud drifted in front of the moon, leaving him in utter darkness except for the light buoy in the water behind him. Tears stung his eyes. Whether for her or for himself, he couldn't say. He banished thoughts about what she had once meant to him.

Scooping the sand back into the hole proved to be easier than shoveling it out. The rain fell harder. Rain would obliterate the signs of digging, but he would be stuck until the downpour passed. By daybreak, his chance of being seen by a fisherman increased to nearly a hundred percent.

The rain faded into mist. He drained the water from the dinghy and rinsed off the tarp. Sunrise was still an hour away, but the horizon was growing lighter. Grasping the stern with both hands, he waded into the cold water, chin high after only a few yards. He dunked his head and scrubbed the blood from his face and hair. As he tried to haul himself into the dinghy, he heard barking and fell back into the water, his heart pounding, his eyes wide. A fisherman with a dog aboard? The wind made it difficult to pin down from which direction the sound came. There was no sign of another boat. When he looked toward the sandbank, he made out a harbor seal undulating over the ground.

His arms trembled wildly as he hauled himself into the dinghy and collapsed on the floor, tears he could no longer hold back trickling down his cheeks. After a few minutes, he climbed onto the seat and picked up the oars.

* * *

Two decades had passed. Hendrik braced himself for the inevitable. Summoning his last reserves of energy, he lifted his head above the water and glimpsed the dinghy grow smaller, dancing and twirling in the waves, teasing him as the tide carried them both out to sea.

CHAPTER

71

December 2024

Anneliese

EBB.

The sea receded, exposing dozens of sandbanks separated by snakes of muddy water. Anneliese shivered so violently that her spine rattled. She couldn't count on the crime scene investigators returning to Lutine today. Willem didn't know her whereabouts. He didn't know she was in danger. They wouldn't find her until it was too late—when she was dead from exposure.

Her sodden coat protected her from the wind, but its weight slowed her down. She wrestled herself out of it and at once felt lighter. She forced one foot in front of the other, the mud sucking at her boots, holding her back in its greedy clutches. She was too tired, the island too far. A tear tracked down her cheek. She couldn't make it.

But a baby was growing inside her. No longer an embryo, officially a fetus, a person to her. She was conscious of its presence by the roundness of her belly, by the nausea, and by the spells of weepiness. Her job was to protect the baby, so she kept going.

Her quadriceps cramped, worse than any charley horse in a calf. She had to stop. The cramp passed, leaving her thigh muscles sore but mobile. Only then did she notice the cold, smelly mud oozing into her left boot.

She had lost the sole without being aware of it. Hopping on one foot, then the other, she yanked off both boots and flung them away. She watched the mud suck them under. Swallowing hard, she blinked back tears. She took her bearings. The next sandbank lay fifty yards ahead, and like a mirage in the desert, it seemed distant and unattainable.

She trudged onward, sinking to her knees in the mud. The cold crushed her chest, left her lightheaded. Pain exploded in her shoulder with each jolt of her unsteady slog.

Time crept by, drawn out and stretched to the breaking point. When she stumbled onto the next sandbank, she longed to throw herself down and rest, but she might lack the strength to get up. She might lie there for hours until the tide came back to claim her.

A patchy mist had descended over Wexalia. In the gaps, she made out the pier jutting into the water and a dark object behind the dike—Hendrik's Mercedes. Her eyes burned, and tears blurred her vision. Squinting, she made out a second car, parked closer to the tip of the island where she was headed, and a group of figures, no larger than ants, gathered in front of it. One figure broke apart from the others, and as she watched, it started slogging through the mud toward her. The mist closed.

Arms encircled her, lifted her.

"Hold on to my neck."

Willem's voice.

She laid her head against his chest, solid and real, and held on to his neck with her good arm. Her eyelids kept falling shut like broken shades.

"Stay awake, Anneliese. Will you do that for me?"

She nodded.

Their journey across the mudflats took forever. Willem slipped and stumbled, but she wasn't afraid of falling. She had left fear behind in the outgoing tide. Willem would keep her and the baby safe.

Later his boots thudded on firm ground. She turned her head and gazed around her. This was the eastern tip of Wexalia and cluttered with spoils from the shipping container disaster. The hundreds of bright-pink plastic toys looked bizarre against the packed brown mud and dull white seashells. Faint voices carried on the wind, dispersing and blowing away like plumes of sand.

"Call an ambulance!" Willem shouted.

"One is on the way," a familiar voice said, and Lurch appeared in Anneliese's field of vision. He stared at her as if she were a mermaid or some other mythical sea creature.

She heard the wail of a siren, though muted, as if she wore earplugs.

Katja and Jurriaan hovered nearby, their arms around each other. Katja's face was red and pinched with worry, Jurriaan's white and terrified.

The younger detective tore off his jacket and tucked it around Anneliese.

She felt like a bystander, as if the drama were happening to someone else.

"Where is the nearest hospital?" Willem asked.

"On the mainland," Terpstra said. "An ambulance helicopter has been dispatched to Wexalia. We'll meet it at the heliport."

"Where's that?"

"At the harbor."

"How are you, Anneliese?" Terpstra asked, his bloodhound face inches from hers.

"Tired," she mumbled.

She was no longer cold, and she had stopped shivering. Her eyelids drooped. She was so sleepy, it was torture to stay awake.

The siren reached a crescendo, cutting through the roar of the wind and the Wad, then abruptly fell silent. The ambulance parked a short distance away, and two men in turquoise uniforms piled out, flung open the rear doors, and rolled a stretcher across the sand.

Gentle hands lifted her onto the stretcher and covered her with a blanket.

She looked into Willem's face. Worry had taken its toll. His eyes were glassy and sunken, his complexion pallid. His shoulders sagged under the weight of the last few hours.

"The baby," she whispered.

"Sorry. What did you say?" the nurse asked.

She tried again, but her words came out slurred.

"Don't talk. Save your strength," the nurse said.

"Baby," she spat out, but the nurse's face remained a blank.

"My girlfriend is three months pregnant," Willem said.

Anneliese relaxed and closed her eyes.

"What's your girlfriend's name?"

"Anneliese."

"Let's get Anneliese inside," the nurse said.

She peeped through her eyelashes at the nurse's troubled face. Her heart hammered. Could the tiny, fragile life floating in her womb survive the stress and the ice cold? Was her baby dead?

The stretcher rose on its undercarriage and was slotted into the ambulance. Scissors snipped up the side of her pants leg. Her wet clothes were peeled off. Calloused hands probed. Smooth, cold metal pressed against her naked flesh. She felt a pad being wrapped around her good arm; the pad tightened for a few moments before being released. The nurse shouted at the driver, and the engine rumbled to life.

"What's her temperature?" Willem asked in a low voice.

She didn't hear the answer, only his soft curse.

A warm hand enclosed hers.

"Willem?" she mumbled.

"I'm here," he whispered into her ear and squeezed her hand.

"How long before the helicopter arrives?" Willem asked.

It took her a moment to realize he was addressing someone else.

"We'll be at the helipad in less than fifteen minutes," the nurse said. "The helicopter should arrive shortly after that. We'll take care of her until it does."

The voices faded as darkness engulfed her.

CHAPTER

72

December 2024

Jurriaan

"JURRIAAN," KATJA SAID softly.

He opened his eyes. He knew it was morning because the sliver of light framing the curtains was gray instead of black. For a moment, he didn't recognize the bedroom. But even with the window shut, the salty stink of the Wad was everywhere. Dread squeezed his heart. Bad things happened on Wexalia.

Katja stood next to his bed. She was wearing the same navy sweater and mud-spattered green skirt from yesterday. "How do you feel?"

"Funny." He felt impossibly heavy, as if he might sink straight through the mattress. He wasn't sure he could raise his head, let alone get out of bed. To demonstrate, he lifted his right arm and let it fall limply on the bed. "What's wrong with me?"

"The doctor gave you a sedative to help you sleep."

The events of yesterday trickled into his brain, like the incoming tide. He sat up.

"Is Dad dead?"

"I'm afraid he is."

"Can I see him?"

"His body hasn't been found."

He started hyperventilating.

"Focus on your breathing, like Willem taught you," Katja said.

He pursed his lips and forced himself to inhale slowly through his nose and exhale through his mouth. He repeated this until he finally felt normal.

But he couldn't bear to look at Katja's sad face. He might start hyperventilating all over again. Instead, he let his eyes travel around the small brown bedroom. Brown curtains and matching brown bedspread. Brown lampshade. Brown rug. The only thing *not* brown was the silvery sheen of dust on the bedside table. He closed his eyes and wished for his clean, purple apartment in Amsterdam, but when he opened them again, he was still in the brown bedroom.

"I need to talk to Willem," he said. It was important—urgent even—to talk to his brother.

"He's taking a shower." She sat down on the chair. "What do you want to talk to him about?"

"Is Anneliese going to die?"

"She got very tired and very cold, but she's young and strong."

"How about the baby?"

"We don't know." She looked worried.

Jurriaan took a deep breath and asked the question that had been preying on his brain since yesterday.

"Why did Dad write in his note that he killed Mom?"

Katja nervously pushed a lock of hair behind her ear. "Because that's what happened."

"Then why do I remember doing it? I hit her with a hammer. You were there."

Her brow creased in the middle, as it always did when she was thinking hard. "You didn't kill her. Willem told me what you said yesterday on the mudflats. That it was you, not Hendrik. Why didn't you say something before? We could have set you straight long ago."

"I didn't remember before," he said, which was true enough. Only bits and pieces bobbing around in the darkness. The flash of an image. A distant word. Nothing whole until yesterday.

"Willem calls it a false memory. You think you remember something that didn't really happen. Your mind is playing tricks on you."

Once again, Jurriaan felt the solid weight of the hammer in his hand, heard the sickening smack when it hit Louisa's head, but the reason he'd picked up the hammer eluded him. Like breath evaporating on a mirror.

Katja leaned toward him, her hands twisting in her lap. "You mustn't tell anyone else you remember hitting her. It didn't happen like that. You would only muddle up the police investigation. We would have to stay longer on Wexalia. Promise?"

He nodded. The hard gleam in her eyes reminded him of Louisa, reminded him of other promises not to tell. Promises made and kept. He wanted to go home in the worst way.

"Why did Dad kill her?"

"They were arguing, and he got angry. He didn't mean to."

Dad must have snapped, like when Jurriaan hit Finn to protect Mr. Verhoeven and Tricksy. Now, Mr. Verhoeven called Jurriaan his buddy. Each time he did, a warm glow filled his chest.

"When can I go home?"

Her forehead creased again. "We want you to stay with us for a while."

"Can't I go home to my apartment?"

"Not yet. Not until things blow over. You can have the attic room. We'll fix it up nice. Hang your cat pictures."

No, no, no. Visitors didn't drill holes in the wall to hang their own pictures. His mouth quivered.

"Willem and I think it's for the best," she said. "Get dressed. The crime scene investigators are on the way. After they arrive, Willem will take you home—to the house on the Apollolaan."

She left, closing the door softly behind her.

A scene flashed in his head, as if lit by a bolt of lightning. Willem reaching for the hammer, putting it down, Jurriaan picking it up . . . then only black.

Louisa's spirit had never left Dad's house, and now Jurriaan knew why. She had been waiting for the return of the son who had killed her. She wanted to watch over him. At least he didn't have to go to a real prison. He wiped away tears with the back of his hand.

"I love you too, Dad. Thank you," he whispered, and headed for the bathroom to brush his teeth.

CHAPTER

73

December 2024

Brigadier Terpstra

"CAN WE CLOSE the case and go home today?" Karel asked, stifling a yawn.

"Ask me again after we interview Katja Hart."

A handwriting analyst had confirmed that Hendrik Veldkamp had written the note. But Tomas's instincts told him the case wasn't over, even if the loose ends tied up neatly.

They had commandeered the interview/storage room at the small police station on Wexalia, where two police officers with the rank hoofdagent were assigned. One was a part-timer who lived on the mainland and commuted by ferry. The other, a full-timer, lived on the island. They investigated burglaries and vandalism but referred any serious crimes to the police department in Leeuwarden.

There came a knock at the door, and the hoofdagent ushered in Katja and withdrew, closing the door behind him.

She looked lovely, though haggard. Tomas sat up straighter and contracted his stomach muscles. He had shaved carefully and washed his hair, prepared to interview the new widow. Correction. She was only *presumed* to be a widow until Hendrik Veldkamp's body had been recovered. The locals said the sea eventually gave back those it took. How long depended on the weather, the depth of the water, and the tides.

Katja regarded him with her striking green eyes under neatly arched eyebrows, but her eyelids were swollen with grief.

"I'm sorry for your loss."

"Thank you."

"I hope that Anneliese and the baby will pull through."

"I'm going straight from here to the hospital."

Karel was giving him an impatient look that said, *"Let's get on with it, shall we, sir?*

Tomas turned on the recorder and cleared his throat. "Today is December fifteenth, 2024. The time is nine AM. The interviewee is Katherine Hart . . ."

After dispensing with the preliminaries, he asked his first question. "Did you know Anneliese was your daughter?"

She tucked a lock of copper hair behind her ear before replying. "Not until yesterday. I didn't suspect until I read Hendrik's note."

"How did *he* know?"

"The diary I kept in 2000 recently went missing. That was the year Anneliese was born. He must have read it and made the connection."

"Why didn't you make the connection?"

"I'm afraid I've been focused on meeting my publisher's deadline."

"Why do you think Hendrik tried to kill Anneliese?"

"I can only speculate."

"Go ahead."

"Hendrik wanted a child by me, and when I couldn't conceive, he was bitterly disappointed." She paused to collect herself. "When he found out about Anneliese, he must have blamed her for our fertility problems. He was a quiet man who tolerated poor treatment and didn't complain. But injustices, both real and imagined, build up, don't they Brigadier Terpstra?"

"Are you referring to his relationship with his first wife?"

"Yes. He loved Louisa. He truly did, but she took advantage of his gentle nature. She saw it as a weakness, and she knew how to leverage a weakness to get what she wanted. Until she went too far, and he broke."

Tomas couldn't help wondering if Louisa had spotted a weakness in Katja. She was brittle, like an exquisite vase that had been broken and then glued back together. If he were to tap at a vulnerable spot, she might shatter. Her hand kept returning to the same lock of hair. Most people were nervous when interviewed in a police station, sometimes the innocent more so than the guilty. When it came down to it, everyone was guilty of something.

"How did he kill her?" he asked.

"You're the detective."

Tomas had spent a sleepless night mulling over the case.

"This is my take," he said. "Hendrik probably killed her in the summerhouse. There may have been a witness. I think one of you—or perhaps all of you—helped conceal the murder."

Her head tilted. "Shall I tell you what I think happened?"

"You're the writer."

"Louisa rose early to run. Hendrik made coffee while she got ready. When she came downstairs, they argued. He may have pushed her, and she fell and hit her head. But I can't believe he meant to kill her."

"In your scenario, what did they argue about?"

"The affair he referred to in his note."

He caught Karel's eye for a moment.

"Did *you* know?" Tomas asked.

"Louisa confided in me. Before you ask, I don't know her lover's name."

"Why didn't you tell the police about the affair when she went missing?"

"I believed she had drowned, making her infidelity irrelevant. If the media had gotten wind of it, they would have had a field day. So I said nothing."

"Why didn't you mention it yesterday when I interviewed you at the summerhouse?"

"I forgot."

"That seems unlikely."

She shrugged. He sensed her uncrossing and then crossing her legs under the table. What else could he say except call her a liar? "Go on."

"Hendrik panicked and hid her body in the trunk of his car. When Louisa didn't return for lunch, we looked for her. We called the police around six that evening. They organized a search, disbanded at nightfall, and promised to continue the next day. We were too worried and upset to sleep. We each took one of Louisa's sleeping pills, though in hindsight not Hendrik. While we slept, he transported her body to Lutine and buried her. None of us was the wiser."

"How did he transport her to Lutine?"

"The same way he took Anneliese—in the dairy farmer's dinghy. Hendrik and Mr. Doeksen were old friends. Hendrik could use the dinghy whenever he wanted."

Another thing the family had forgotten to mention.

A silence fell, and Karel looked up from his iPad, silently entreating Tomas to get on with it. He knew Karel wanted to go home to his own bed, and Tomas didn't want to spend another night in the grubby B&B, listening to the surf pound against the shore, the repetition irritating him profoundly, like a dog barking all night.

"Wasn't that risky? Everyone on the island was looking for Louisa. The police might have discovered her body in the trunk. Or a fisherman might have spotted Hendrik in the dinghy."

Karel quit typing and straightened up. Tomas saw by the pink glow in his cheeks he was on to something.

"Yes, it was a risk," Katja agreed. "But what was his alternative?"

"So, there's no connection between Louisa's murder and the attempt on Anneliese's life?"

"I don't see how there could be."

Karel looked as if he could barely contain himself, so Tomas nodded at him to go ahead.

Karel leaned forward. "Suppose the family reported her disappearance the day *after* Hendrik killed her. He could have transported her body to Lutine during the night before anyone was on the lookout."

Possibly, Tomas thought.

She considered. "That scenario would work, but it would be fiction."

Karel started typing again.

"May I go now? I need to catch the ferry," Katja said.

Tomas ended the interview and turned off the recorder. "Thank you for your cooperation."

After she left, Karel said, "What do you think, sir? Case closed? Twenty-one instead of twenty-two cold cases left on our plate?"

"You might be right about the timing of Louisa's murder. No one apart from the family saw her after she got off the ferry. She could have died on the day before Hendrik reported her missing. If so, the entire family is complicit. But there's no evidence."

His mobile rang.

The call was brief. When he put down the phone, he turned to Karel. "CSI just arrived on the island. They have a warrant to search the summerhouse. Let's hope they find something."

"Do you think they will? It's been twenty years."

"Honestly? No, I don't."

It was clear to Tomas he would never know beyond doubt who had murdered Louisa Veldkamp.

CHAPTER

74

December 2024

Willem

WILLEM AND JURRIAAN crossed by ferry to the mainland, rented a car, and drove to Amsterdam. Jurriaan carried his suitcase upstairs to the mansion's small attic room, and Willem withdrew to his office. He read and reread Hendrik's letter until he understood everything.

Katja phoned from the train on her way home from the hospital and updated him on Anneliese's condition. He climbed into the rental and headed for the hospital in Leeuwarden, a two-hour drive if he was lucky.

He found Anneliese asleep and sedated. The nurse said that she had only picked at her dinner. She had asked for him several times. He sat down in the visitor's chair next to her bed and held her hand. He watched her chest rise and fall. Hendrik's letter burned in his coat pocket. They were half siblings; they had each inherited half their genes from the same mother. He sought resemblances in their physical appearance, but found none. He was blond, tall, and powerfully built. She was a petite brunette, dark and exotic looking. He thought about the baby that she carried in her womb. He had never felt so exhausted in all his life.

Around nine PM he asked the nurse to recommend a nearby hotel where he could spend the night. "If she wakes up, would you tell her I was here?"

"I will, Dr. Veldkamp."

When he returned the next morning, Anneliese was climbing into a freshly made bed. She was clearly stiff and sore. She'd had two narrow escapes in less than a week.

A housekeeper was bundling together soiled sheets. She acknowledged Willem with a nod, and as she strode past with the bundle, he caught the whiff of urine.

Anneliese looked wan and fragile, with one arm in a sling and the other attached to an IV. Her dark eyes were clouded, and her usually lustrous hair was dull. When she saw him, her smile transformed her face, and for a moment she looked like herself.

He gave her a sisterly kiss on the cheek, and her smile faded.

"You look better than yesterday," he said, and waited to see what tack she would take.

"I was on death's door." After a pause, she said, "Did Katja tell you? The baby's heartbeat is strong."

"Yes," he said, his tone neutral. He glanced toward the door. "Katja said you agreed to go along with our story."

"Yes. It's perfect. It solves everything, doesn't it?"

The new lie was a patch, not a repair. He braced himself for a tough conversation. "Not everything," he said.

She motioned toward the visitor's chair as if she were mistress of the manor, dressed in elegant attire instead of a white hospital gown.

He sat down and gazed at her for a long time.

"Katja told me about Hendrik's note," Anneliese said.

She meant the letter addressed to Katja. The police were holding it as evidence. They knew nothing about the other letter, the one folded up in his coat pocket. He hadn't killed his mother, but he was the one who'd picked up the hammer, an action that had led to her death. The fact that Jurriaan had snatched the hammer out of his hands and struck Louisa was irrelevant. Willem had always defended Jurriaan, and his twin had been returning the favor.

Neither of them had killed her: Hendrik had killed her on Lutine. They weren't blameless, and Willem had taken part in the cover-up. He told himself that they had been abused children, though he knew that didn't justify what they had done or absolve them of wrongdoing. If only Hendrik had told them the truth years ago. The past might have been easier. Why did their own father let them suffer? But Hendrik's silence shouldn't have surprised him—all the years of looking away, of tolerating, of making excuses for his wife's abusive behavior.

"Willem?"

He blinked and focused on Anneliese.

She said, "Hendrik might have been wrong about me being Mirella. He could have been delusional."

"But he wasn't wrong, was he?"

"No."

Willem hesitated about how to frame his next question, the answer to which would determine the tone of their future relationship.

"How long have you known Louisa was your mother?" He studied her, watching for signs of prevarication. He was trained to detect lies, but it wasn't an exact science.

She didn't miss a beat. "I didn't know until Hendrik told me in the dinghy."

"Did you think Katja was your mother?"

"I didn't know who my mother was. It was a closed adoption."

"Do you expect me to believe it was just a coincidence you signed up for Katja's workshop?"

"It was a total coincidence."

Her gaze held steady. It was as if she had read somewhere that a liar looked away. He recalled her quizzing him about Katja, which he had attributed to the curiosity of an ardent fan. He thought back on what Bas had said: *"Never trust contraception to a woman of childbearing age."* Now he wondered if Anneliese had gotten pregnant on purpose.

"What are we going to do?" she said, her dark eyes imploring. "I didn't know you were my half brother. I swear."

He wanted to believe that she was telling the truth because he had fallen in love with her, and, damn it, he still was. He wanted to believe her because the alternative sickened him. His eyes traveled from her face to her abdomen, slightly rounded under her nightgown.

He said, "We can't legally marry."

"But Willem, nobody has to know."

"I'm sorry, Anneliese. I can't."

"I'm keeping the baby, no matter what you decide."

Her tone was so protective, he loved her even more.

"You won't have to worry about money. I'll buy you a house in the country. Limburg is nice. I'll support you and the baby." He rose to his feet. If he didn't leave now, he never would.

"Wait. Give me two more minutes," she said reaching for him, her small hand closing on his wrist, her warm touch giving rise to unbrotherly yearnings. He loved her because she was the mother of his child and because she was his own blood. He loved her in a way that had become impossible, and longed for her in a way that he shouldn't. The least he could do was listen to what she had to say.

"What is it?"

"All I ask is that you postpone your decision. You need time to mourn your father—"

"He killed my mother. He tried to kill you. I won't mourn him."

Anneliese shuddered and pulled the bedcovers up to her chin, like a child afraid of the dark. "He was sick in the head, Willem. I think he was the one who sabotaged my bicycle."

Willem knew she was right. Hendrik had been aware of Anneliese's secret identity. He wanted her dead, and he possessed the technical skills to make a bicycle wheel break off and cause a serious accident. Hendrik's hold on reality had been slipping for years.

Anneliese closed her eyes and lay back, the color drained from her face.

Panic rose inside him. "Are you all right? Should I call for the nurse?"

Her eyelids fluttered open. "No . . . let me finish."

"Go ahead."

"Wait and decide what to do after the baby is born. I won't move out of the house, but we'll sleep in separate bedrooms. I won't put any pressure on you to marry me. I'll accept your decision, whichever it is. Deal?"

He wouldn't change his mind in six months or six lifetimes, but he hoped to change hers.

"Deal," he said.

"The doctor said I can go home tomorrow. Will you pick me up?"

"Of course."

She smiled, looking pleased with herself.

Willem took the stairs to the basement level and crossed through the tunnel to the parking garage. In the low light the rows of cars looked like identical black sedans, and it took him several minutes to find the rental car. The police had impounded Hendrik's Mercedes for forensic examination, a futile exercise since the car was only two years old and unlikely to yield any evidence relevant to the murder.

Maybe Terpstra wasn't satisfied with Hendrik's confession, but he knew when to cut his losses. The brigadier could never know for sure who had done what—or why. It was all too long ago. Time had destroyed any evidence not willfully destroyed by the perpetrators. Witnesses silent. The only satisfaction that the detective was likely to get was a twisted pleasure from impounding the car and inconveniencing Willem.

CHAPTER 75

December 2024

Anneliese

After the nurse carted away her breakfast tray, Anneliese used the remote control to turn on the television. It was tuned to a twenty-four-hour news channel, but she wasn't watching.

Willem's visit yesterday had left her shaken. He had practically accused her of lying, which, of course, she totally deserved. He wanted to buy her off and banish her and their child to Limburg! She might succeed in changing his mind, but not if he found out she had deceived him from the start . . . getting pregnant on purpose . . . believing Katja was her mother. Katja had promised not to tell him about the letter from Ms. Jansen, the social worker. The letter proved only that Anneliese was searching for her mother. It didn't prove that she had discovered her identity, but it would be enough to sow doubt in Willem's mind.

There were secrets she could never share and lies she had to defend as if they were truth. Rain pattered against the pane in sympathy with her distress.

Then she had a visitor.

Anneliese shut off the TV with the remote control when Lurch entered her hospital room—a private room, thanks to the Veldkamp's money and influence. Her blood family.

Dark grooves were carved under Brigadier Terpstra's eyes. His long wool coat was dark with rain. He hung the dripping garment on a hook by the door. She had known he would come. The question was, about which case?

"How are you feeling?" Terpstra asked.

"I'm going home this afternoon."

He sat down in the chair next to the bed, his long legs extended across the linoleum, his wet shoes disappearing under the bed.

"Did the crime scene investigators find anything?" she asked.

"They're still busy. We don't know that he killed her in the house."

"I was only four years old. Am I a suspect?" It was a weak joke, but the best she could muster under the circumstances.

"I'm not here about that."

Had he remembered her? She had been sixteen. Skinny, with black hair down to her waist, parted in the middle and falling over her eyes most of the time. Daan used to call her Cousin Itt, from the character in the *Addams Family* film.

"Why are you here?"

"You're Liese Bakker."

She shifted on the hard bed. Her hips ached, her back ached. Whoever said a hard mattress was best was an idiot.

Terpstra said, "And you're in the middle of another drama."

"Bad luck."

"It's funny how bad luck seems to dog certain people."

"What do you mean?"

He dragged his feet toward the chair and sat up straighter. "I'm checking a few details. Can you tell me again what happened in the dinghy?"

She tried to blink back her surprise. She was expecting a question about Daan's death.

"I gave the police a statement already."

"You might remember something new."

"Hendrik drowned."

"We can't know the cause of death until we recover his body."

"Do you think I killed him and buried his body on Lutine?"

"Did you?"

She shook her head in disgust.

Terpstra leaned back. "Tell me again how Hendrik ended up in the water."

Once his body was recovered, an autopsy would show Hendrik had suffered blows to his arms, head, and face before his death. Whereas she was unscathed, apart from minor cuts and bruises.

"Do I need a lawyer?"

"You're not under arrest."

She had practiced her story enough times with Katja to be confident of not making a mistake.

"We were in the dinghy—" she began.

"Why did you go with him?"

"Why wouldn't I? Hendrik wanted to show me around the island. He said he needed to take his mind off the investigation." She didn't plan on telling anyone about Hendrik's promise to take her to meet her biological father. If Willem were to find out, he might suspect she had always believed Katja was her mother. She had to protect the lie, or risk losing him.

Terpstra nodded. "Go on."

"When I realized he wanted to kill me, we struggled. I hit him with the paddle. He wrestled it away from me, and I jumped overboard." She stopped talking, reliving the terrifying moments underwater, the paralyzing cold. The dinghy bearing down on her, the sharp propeller blades chopping the water. "I swam to the sandbank. The dinghy slammed into it and tipped. When Hendrik came after me, I grabbed something and hit him. Stunned him, not killed him. He got caught in the current. I hit him in self-defense."

"Why did he want to kill you?"

"It's in my statement."

"Tell me again."

She stuck to the story that the family had thrown together. As far as the outside world was concerned, she was Katja's daughter, not Louisa's secret child, not Willem's half sister.

"He and Katja couldn't have children, and he blamed me for that."

"Why?"

"Katja told Hendrik an infection after an abortion left her infertile. He read her diary and guessed that I was her daughter. Possibly because my birthday and Mirella's were the same. Complications after my birth left her unable to conceive. Not an abortion."

Terpstra didn't look convinced.

"He wasn't thinking straight because of his illness," she said

"Thank you, Miss Bakker."

She waved a hand at the door. "If you don't need any more clarifications, I need to rest."

For several moments, he didn't move or even blink. It was unnerving.

"I never believed Daan committed suicide," he said.

Her heart jumped into her throat.

"Do you want to know why?" he asked.

"Not really, but I think you're going to tell me."

"Hanging is one of the most common methods of suicide. But drop hanging is rare. Most suicides suspend themselves from something low. A doorknob, for instance. Or from a hook like the one I hung my coat on. They slip the noose over their head and lean forward, the noose tightens—"

"Daan was always a drama queen," Anneliese said, feeling sick.

"His psychiatrist didn't consider him to be a suicide risk."

"So? He was a crappy shrink."

"Daan was accused of certain crimes committed in the village. Cats maimed. Excrement smeared on doorsteps."

"There was no proof against him."

"It stopped after Daan died."

Anneliese said nothing.

"He wouldn't have spared his little sister. She would have been his favorite target. Did he violate you? Or was he content to terrorize you?"

She looked at her lap, afraid he could read her face. Tineke and Ray hadn't listened or cared. Daan was their son, their own blood, and Anneliese never doubted where their loyalties lay. His death was their fault. Not hers. She took a moment to collect herself.

"Daan hanged himself," she said, meeting his gaze.

Terpstra shrugged. "I understand if you pushed him. I wouldn't blame you, but it's still a crime."

"I'm tired. Please go," Anneliese said.

"Goodbye, Miss Bakker."

After he left, she collapsed onto the hard hospital pillow, her heart trying to knock a hole in her chest. She began to hum. Loud at first, then softer. The detective had no choice but to accept the family's version of what had happened to Louisa twenty years ago. No choice but to accept her version of events in the dinghy. And no choice but to accept her story of how she found Daan hanging by his neck from the balustrade. They had all gotten away with their crimes, if you could call them crimes. Was it a crime for the victim of abuse to kill their abuser when it wasn't clearly self-defense? Whatever . . . Terpstra couldn't prove anything.

CHAPTER

76

2016

Anneliese

ANNELIESE SCURRIED ALONG the lane bordering the forest, head down, long dark hair hiding her face. The evening was darkening, the birds returning to their roosts, and the night creatures stirring, poking their heads out of their lairs and hiding places. The air smelled different in the dying daylight. Like damp earth and moldering leaves.

The streetlamps were blinking on when she turned into her own street. On the front porch, she fumbled the key in the lock, pushed open the door, and slipped inside. To her surprise, the entrance hall wasn't empty. Daan sat on the second from the bottom step of the stairs. Her gaze fell on a rope that was coiled in his lap. What was it for? The house was silent, no kitchen noises, no blare of the television.

She swallowed hard.

"Where are Mama and Papa?" she asked.

"They went out to dinner. They gave me money for the snack bar."

"Why didn't they tell me?" Anger rose inside her, but fear was stronger. If she had known, she would have stayed for dinner at her piano teacher's house, as she had done on several occasions.

Daan shrugged.

She looked at the rope. Was he going to tie her up? Once, he had bound her to a tree deep in the woods and left her for hours. At twilight, hundreds of bats darkened the sky, filling the air with their eerie cries. She had squeezed her eyes shut and whimpered in terror while she'd waited for the bats to bite and drain her blood. But she had suffered nothing worse than mosquito bites.

He uncoiled the rope.

She stepped back and reached behind her for the doorknob.

"Liese," he sobbed.

He only wept when he was off his meds, but it could be a trick. *Stay one step ahead,* she reminded herself, and her hand tightened around the doorknob.

He held up the rope, and now she saw he had tied a noose. Her mouth was so dry her tongue stuck to the roof of her mouth.

He rose and trudged up the stairs to the landing. She watched him fasten one end of the rope to the top rail of the balustrade. He ignored her, as if he had forgotten her presence. She started up the stairs but stopped three treads from the top. A safe distance. He slipped the noose over his head and climbed onto the balustrade.

"Daan, no."

He swung over a leg.

"Are you off your meds?" she asked.

"What if I am?"

"Take the pills. They'll make you feel better."

"Is that what you want?"

She said nothing, her thoughts conflicted. What did she want, if she were honest? He watched the emotions playing on her face and hooted with laughter. She shut her eyes, thinking he would climb down, but when she opened them, he was still perched on the balustrade, his hands clutching the top rail and his legs hanging over the side.

"Gotcha, didn't I?"

It was another one of his stupid jokes! She climbed the last treads, turning over options in her mind.

"Let me help you down," she said softly.

She stepped onto the landing, and as he turned his head in her direction, still laughing, he lost his balance. He managed to grab a baluster with his left hand as he fell. His legs dangled in space. The noose still loose around his neck.

"Liese."

She stared at his pleading eyes. He couldn't hold on much longer.

"Shit," he said.

His fingers were slipping.

Her mind reeled. She had been ten years old when Daan crawled into her bed for the first time, before she learned to barricade the door. She remembered her doll sliding off the bed and landing with a soft plop on the carpet when he climbed on top of her. She had felt Daan's heart hammering in his thin chest as he pushed against her, hurting her private parts.

She imagined his heart thrashing wildly now.

"Don't. Please, don't," she whispered, just as she had whispered then.

His fingers let go.

He gave a terrified grunt. The rope tautened, and his body flopped, the legs flying upward for a moment. He started spinning, his legs kicking in every direction. He grabbed at the rope, tried to haul himself up, hand over hand, feet pedaling. The noose cut into the flesh under his chin, cut off his air, prevented him from crying out. Deprived his brain of blood. But the rope hummed. The railing creaked. His clothes rustled. She crouched against the banister, eyes wide open, stomach somersaulting. The spinning gradually slowed. He swayed like a bell. His urine splattered onto the floor.

She stayed crouched at the top of the stairs, unable to move or tear her eyes away. Time lost its meaning. It could have been seconds, minutes, or hours. She didn't know what she had done or failed to do. Or what she should do next.

* * *

The next thing Anneliese remembered, she was drinking hot, sweet tea on the neighbors' sofa and nibbling on a stroopwafel cookie. Their house had the same layout as hers but smelled of a lemon-scented cleaner instead of stale cigarettes. Mrs. Grootheest had yelled up the stairs to her son and ordered him to stay in his room. The boings, chords, and chimes of a computer game were audible downstairs, making what had happened next door seem unreal.

Through the big window, Anneliese saw a real ambulance, police car, van, and motorcycle arrive, headlights glaring. Mr. Grootheest waited for the police on the driveway, waving his arms to attract their attention. Mrs. Grootheest untied her apron and jerked the curtain shut.

A few minutes later, Mr. Grootheest ushered in the tall, morose hoofdagent, whom Anneliese dubbed *Lurch*. He sat down in a chair facing her, long legs slightly apart, feet flat on the floor. He asked questions in a deep, dispassionate voice: *"Were you present when Daan hanged himself? What did he say? Did you touch anything? Start at the beginning and tell me everything that happened."* He paused often to write notes in a pocket notebook.

She answered with only half her attention, her mind lost in a fog, but she had enough presence of mind not to mention she had mounted the stairs. What would they do if she told the whole truth? She saw herself again at the top of the stairs. Daan's fingers clutching the rail. Slipping. They would ask why she hadn't tried to save him, but she was the only one who knew how Daan had violated her and hurt her in a thousand ways; she could pretend none of it had ever happened.

Her thoughts drifted. She imagined officers in white suits cutting down Daan's body—the rope suddenly slack. Did they catch him when he fell? Maybe it didn't matter since he was dead. It was all taking too long. Where were Tineke and Ray? Finally, the policeman's questions ended, and he stood up.

"I'll show you out, Officer Terpstra," Mr. Grootheest said. His wife followed the men into the entrance hall.

Anneliese tiptoed across the living room and pressed her ear against the door, straining to hear what the grown-ups were saying. After the front door thudded shut, she heard Mr. Grootheest tell his wife if the rope had been longer or made from hemp instead of stretchy nylon, Daan would have been decapitated. His words chilled her blood. Her hands began to shake, her legs wobbled, and she slid down the door to the floor.

That was the night her problems with urination began.

DECEMBER 2024

CHAPTER

77

December 18, 2024

Diary entry

ANNELIESE BEHAVES LIKE a queen, tended to by her lady-in-waiting (me). I'm sorry to say I've fallen into old habits, waiting on the daughter as I once waited on the mother . . . at least, for now.

This morning she felt well enough to eat breakfast in the kitchen. She sat with her elbows propped on the table, her chin cupped in her hands, and stared at the sliding glass door. I wondered what she saw in the icy drizzle, which streamed down the pane and blurred the view of the garden.

"Are you ready to eat?" I asked, refilling her cup of tea.

She looked up. "Yes, Mom."

"Don't call me that," I said, wincing.

She grinned. "Sorry, Katja."

As far as the outside world is concerned, I'm her biological mother.

"I've been wondering. How did you get your name on my birth certificate? Did you bribe a midwife?" she asked.

She meant on her original birth certificate. After she was adopted, my name was replaced by that of the Bakkers.

I said, "It was Louisa's idea. She'd read about a couple charged with fraud for collecting child benefit payments for nonexistent twins. The only document required to register a birth is the mother's ID. All I had to do was show the registrar my driving license and sign the forms."

I set the dishes in front of Anneliese: brown bread spread with butter, thin slices of salty cheese, smoked mackerel, melon, and freshly squeezed orange juice. A big breakfast for a petite woman, but she's eating for two.

I looked after Louisa when she was pregnant with Mirella. The déjà vu is disorienting. Only this time, I don't have to wear a pillow strapped to my waist, dress in ugly maternity clothes, and stay confined to a hotel room.

"Don't go," Anneliese said, patting the chair next to her.

I took a seat.

"Are you settled into the apartment?" she asked.

While Anneliese was recovering, Willem and I moved their things upstairs and mine downstairs. My books, my papers, my clothes. The police boxed up Hendrik's personal possessions and carted them off, labeling them as evidence. Terpstra was clearly disappointed that the diaries for 2000 and 2004 could not be found. The presumption was that Hendrik had destroyed them.

Willem is sleeping in the guest room until he decides whether he wants Anneliese as a wife or a sister.

"Yes, I've unpacked."

Anneliese insists I stay and help create her imaginary, ideal family. The arrangement works for me while I finish my novel. (I let Willem read the draft, and he convinced me there would be no harm in publishing it.) Curiously, I'm reluctant to leave Willem—guilty secrets and lies binding us—even as they once drove us apart.

Anneliese said, "I don't like Jurriaan living here. I can hear him walking around in his room at night and coming down the stairs to use the bathroom. It's creepy."

This complaint is becoming a familiar refrain, but Willem's mind is set, and Jurriaan gave notice to his landlord. His neighbor, Mr. Verhoeven, is planning a surprise leaving party. I'll warn Jurriaan because surprises upset him.

"I'll buy him some slippers with soft soles. Then you won't hear him."

She looked unconvinced.

"He's family, Anneliese."

Magic words.

"Are you going to tell Willem about the letter you got from FAM?" she asked.

"I promised I wouldn't." If Willem knew Anneliese had been searching for her mother last spring, he might not believe her enrollment in my workshop was a coincidence. It would destroy the fragile trust between them.

"Thank you."

"The baby needs a father," I said.

A silence fell.

Anneliese speared a chunk of melon with her fork. "Do you think Willem will marry me?"

"I don't know."

She put down the fork. "I don't think the police believed the story you two told. I know I didn't." She gazed at me, her eyes questioning. Finally, she said, "It doesn't matter."

She squeezed my hand, and I saw it truly didn't matter to her what part Willem and I had played in Louisa's death. She didn't care who had killed Louisa or what their motivation had been. She was content for now. And why not? She got what she wanted: a family of her own blood, a child in her womb, two half brothers, and a mother—albeit a pretend mother.

But I'll never reveal who her father is, and for a moment, the Italian orchestra conductor's handsome face flares in my memory like a guttering candle.

I'm good at keeping secrets.

SEVEN MONTHS LATER

CHAPTER

78

Willem

WILLEM WAS CURLED up in bed with Anneliese. Sweat puddled between their naked bodies. She was fast asleep.

They had postponed their honeymoon and were spending their wedding night at home after a small civil ceremony with Bas and Jurriaan as witnesses. Max was only a month old, and in Willem's book, too young to travel or to entrust to a nanny's care.

From the moment he first held the splotchy newborn in his arms, he knew he would lay down his life for his son. At the same time, he had felt scarily incompetent despite having read several baby books. He had never actually changed a diaper, prepared a bottle, or even held a baby. A month later—those skills mastered—he could laugh at himself for worrying about the wrong things.

Max slept across the hall in the nursery, formerly Katja's study. Willem and Anneliese had decorated it together—pale blue wallpaper with fluffy white clouds, and glossy white furniture.

On impulse, Willem had bought a crib mobile with cloth birds in bright colors. Before he could unpack the box, Anneliese insisted he exchange the mobile for one with airplanes. He should have realized that her phobia of small creatures—from frogs to birds, to cats—extended to images. They exchanged Bas's gift—a cuddly stuffed rabbit—for a Raggedy Ann with embroidered eyes. Willem had cut off the yarn hair and the red ribbon bows so Max couldn't choke on them.

He rolled over onto his back, his front sticky with sweat, and peered into the dark bedroom: the furniture, black lumps darker than the rest—little islands in a murky sea. He was still navigating around them, but Anneliese had quit wetting the bed, a sign she had put the past behind her.

If not for climate change and underwater mining conspiring together, Louisa's remains would still molder on Lutine, guarded by black-headed gulls, sandwich terns, and gray seals. Only the moon, the stars, and a light buoy to ease the darkness. The people at Zorgvlied had raised her coffin and deposited her bones inside it.

Hendrik's body had washed up on Wexalia two weeks to the day after he drowned. Katja declined to honor his wish to be buried next to Louisa. Instead, she laid him to rest in a plot on the opposite side of the cemetery.

Through the open window came the distant rumble of a night train. Then the whine of a motorcycle speeding on the Beethovenstraat. Backfiring twice. Like the crack of gunshots. A dog started barking frantically. The city was never silent. The Wadden was never silent either, where the wind roared, the tide hissed, and foghorns wailed.

Willem swore, remembering his heavy schedule the next day, his first Zoom call at eight o'clock. He tried to keep his mind a blank, forcing back the dark memories that crept forward like floodwaters. After a while, his eyelids grew heavy, and he felt himself sinking, when a howl jolted him. The frantic squall of a newborn, like a catfight in surround sound.

Max.

Christ. What did the child want now? He counted off the possibilities. It wasn't time for a bottle. He had changed his diaper only an hour ago. Was he frightened? Sick? Anxiety washed over Willem.

Why didn't Anneliese wake up? It was her turn.

He would have to go, but as soon as he sat up, nerve endings jangling, the crying ceased. A faint light seeped under the door.

Who?

He glanced toward the baby monitor on Anneliese's side of the bed. It was blocked from view, so he peeled back the sheet, pulled on his pajama bottoms, and tiptoed into the hall.

A shadowy figure emerged from the guest bathroom.

"Twinnie," Willem whispered.

Jurriaan turned. It was too dark to see the purple half-moons under his eyes or register the weight loss. Signs he hated living in the mansion. Jurriaan denied it, but Willem knew. Finding Jurriaan another place to live was high on his to-do list. A place where Jurriaan could be independent, but also protected and watched.

Jurriaan waved an arm and limped up the attic stairs.

Willem pushed open the door to the nursery.

A small lamp on the changing table cast a circle of soft light, the rest of the room in shadow. Katja sat in the nursing chair, her head bowed over Max. She wore a bed jacket over a thin nightgown, and her feet were bare.

"I'm sorry the baby woke you," he said, glimpsing Max's sweet face in the crook of her arm, his fringe of thick eyelashes, his rosebud mouth. He was a fine baby boy, with Willem's blond hair and Anneliese's dark, almond-shaped eyes.

"I wasn't asleep," Katja said.

"Anneliese was out like a light."

"She looked exhausted at city hall."

"Max keeps her busy."

"How are *you*?" Katja raised her chin, looking at him for the first time.

"Tired."

"You should have taken a few days off from work."

"Too late now."

"At least let me do the night feedings. Give you and Anneliese a break."

"I'll talk to her." Katja had offered before, but Anneliese was adamant. She said Max was their child. He was their responsibility. It was as if she feared the infant might disappear on Katja's watch. It was nonsense, but understandable after what she had been through.

It wasn't only the baby keeping him awake at night. He had married his half sister, for God's sake. Not just illegal, but to many people repugnant. Never mind that royalty had married close relatives for centuries.

He was putting his career at risk, but Max's birth had caused a shift in his priorities. A child deserved to be acknowledged by his father. Max deserved two parents. How could that be wrong? Willem had started therapy, committed for the long haul, determined to be the best dad he could be.

Christ, how easy it was for a human being to justify his most flagrant offenses.

As if reading his mind, Katja said, "You did what you thought was best."

"You always know what I'm thinking."

The wistful ache in his chest surprised him. He moved closer and laid his hand on her thin shoulder, felt her body tremble.

She tucked a lock of copper hair behind her ear.

The familiar gesture sent him spiraling from a precipice. He was sixteen again, and Lutine was a scenic spot filled with seabirds and flowering dune grass—not a makeshift grave for a murder victim. Lost days. Lost innocence. Stripped away in the most brutal way.

Willem swallowed hard. "Do you remember the picnic on Lutine? Do you ever wonder, what if? You and me—"

"No." Katja cut him off in mid-sentence.

It was a jab in the heart.

A faint rustling made Willem turn.

Anneliese stood in the doorway.

His face burned. What had she seen on the baby monitor? Heard? How long had she been standing there?

She marched into the room, her expression rigid.

"I'll take Max," she said.

Katja kissed the baby's head, rose from the chair, and transferred him to Anneliese's arms. He woke and started howling.

"I'll go now. Good night," Katja said.

"Thank you," Willem called after her.

After a few moments, Max settled down, and Anneliese laid him in the crib. She gave Willem a crooked smile. "Let's celebrate our wedding night again."

She was staking her claim.

She locked him in her arms and mumbled, "I'll never let you go."

"I like the sound of that." He loved her in all the ways he should and in the ways he shouldn't.

He rested his chin on her head, inhaled the musty scent of her hair, and listened to the sound of Katja's footsteps fading down the stairs. Above, the floorboards of the attic room creaked. Step, drag. Step, drag. Jurriaan pacing.

Everyone he loved, accounted for and safe.

He couldn't help wondering how Louisa would have reacted to him marrying her secret love child. But his heart was light. It really didn't matter what she might have said or thought or done. She was gone, and they were here. They were creating a new family. A new narrative.

He gently extricated himself from Anneliese's embrace, looped his fingers through hers, and guided her back to their bed.

* * *

ACKNOWLEDGMENTS

MANY THANKS TO my editor, Tara Gavin, for believing in my novel and to the entire team at Crooked Lane Books, who helped make this book possible, especially Thaisheemarie Peréz and Rebecca Nelson. Thanks also to Jill Pellarin for the meticulous copyedit.

I owe a great deal of appreciation to Lisa Friedman from the Amsterdam Writing Workshops for her support and guidance. Special thanks to Shelley Anderson, David Escorial, and Annie De Benedictis from the workshops for their helpful feedback and encouragement.

I'm grateful to Dea Parkin, editor-in-chief at Fiction Feedback in the UK, for her assistance in shaping the novel at the early stages.

My writing groups provided invaluable critique and motivation. I am especially indebted to Tori Egherman, Anna Heldring, Mark Bruinkreeft, Karen Kao, Maali Jamil, and Emanda Percival. You made the novel so much better! Thanks also to Carolyn Chang, Danny Glasser, Michèle Bartlett, Lisa Holden, Emma Lee, and Leslie Lee for their insights and support.

A debt of gratitude goes to Dipika Mukherjee, who invited me to join her critique group way back at the beginning; I have learned so much.

And to my wonderful friends for their unwavering support, including Sharon Davis, Nella Stern, Linda Cleary, and David Lee. To Joe McNamee: for setting deadlines and holding me to them.

To Deborah, my very own twin, who inspired me to write about twins, though she's nothing like the characters in the novel!

To my daughter Evelyn, for the honest critique and the brilliant brainstorming sessions. And for taking care of our dog when deadlines loomed. To my son Bob, whose conversations sparked some great ideas and who reminded me to stop and eat while writing *What You Made Me Do.*